FOREWORD

Writing *Sam Hain* has been an adventure. A most unexpected one, at that.

It all began late one night, at the usual hour of 3am, when reality ceases to be real and insomnia has a habit for inspiration. "Samhain," I thought, the oft-mispronounced Pagan festival from which Hallowe'en was born, "Sam Hain… Sounds like the name of a noir occult detective." I chuckled to myself, fell asleep, and didn't think much more about it. I returned to life working as a freelance journalist and a would-be actor, who spent more time throwing his headshots at film studios than he did actually working in said film studios. But the idea never quite left me. Sam Hain rattled around in the back of my mind, just waiting for his time.

It wasn't until one day in late September of 2013, while I was in a taxi heading back from a costume fitting (for a film which was so Eighties that I was clothed in a sequinned vest, flared jeans, and a pair of very large, very vibrant, very red platform shoes), that the idea finally came together. The pieces fell into place. I would write a short story. It was only a month before All Hallows' Read (the celebration of gifting spooky, scary and supernatural books around Hallowe'en), and I decided I would write the story for it. It was to be a short, one-off, thing; a quick read for the season of spookiness.

And so, *Sam Hain: All Hallows' Eve* was conceived. I was especially proud of the title; a story about Sam Hain on samhain, to be released on All Hallows' Eve. Looking back, I think I was more excited by this pun than I was the idea of actually writing a story to go with it. I got to work with writing what would become the first draft of *All Hallows' Eve*, feeling my way through the story as I wrote,

i

figuring out who this Sam Hain was, and how he fit (or, as the case may be, did not fit) into the world.

I released the first short story as a free download on Hallowe'en night, and I was surprised by the reception. Not only did people download it, but they actually *read* it and, beyond that, even *enjoyed* it. And I did as well. I enjoyed writing Sam as a character, how Alice accidentally caught a glimpse of a world beyond, playing with the concept that maybe things are not as normal as they may seem, and what strange, metaphysical mysteries might be hiding just behind the veil of the real. And, more than that, I was thrilled by the fact that other people enjoyed my story too.

But, as you can tell by the fact that this is a book with over four-hundred pages instead of a print-out on ten sheets of A4 paper, that was only the beginning. More ideas formed in my mind; more stories stirred themselves up. What happened next to Alice Carroll, after she had her eyes opened to the weird and wonderful? What was Sam Hain up to outside of that case on Hallowe'en? How much work, precisely, does an occult detective get, and how could he possibly afford to live in London's ever increasingly expensive accommodation? I took a pen and a notebook, secreted myself away in a café off of Carnaby Street, and began to draft out more story ideas.

There were some good ideas, some bad ideas, and some ideas which didn't really get any further than having a witty or amusing title. Out of this, six ideas stood out the most; six stories which would form the first series of *Sam Hain* novellas. So I returned to that same café, with an old laptop which would overheat if I tried to do anything more taxing than open a word document, and began writing.

From there, it developed exponentially. *All Hallows' Eve* came in the top ten of Inkitt's user-rated *Shiver* competition for paranormal stories in 2015. In 2016, I found myself sitting behind a table at one of London's

SAM HAIN
OCCULT DETECTIVE

VOLUME I

BRON JAMES

For Sarah,
Who left this world too soon.

CONTENTS

comic cons, with the first three *Sam Hain* novellas spread out before me as actual, real, physical paperbacks. They had ISBNs and barcodes and a copyright page and everything. Somewhere along the line, I had accidentally become an author, which caught me quite by surprise.

The reception I received from readers was beyond anything I could have hoped for. People would return to me over the comic con weekend, expressing their enjoyment of the stories, and, in a couple of cases, cursing me for making them miss their tube station the previous day because they had been too engrossed with reading. Which I feel is the best possible way to inconvenience someone. Knowing that people appreciate my stories, and want to read more, is a driving force for me to keep on writing more. Not just for my own enjoyment, but also to share with others who enjoy it too.

So, as I see the word count on this foreword edging over its limit while I ramble, here we are. From a one-off short story to a collection of adventures, which has grown into something beyond my expectations, with even more in the works. It's not been an easy path, often sheltering away from distractions/people/the sun to focus on writing, revising and editing the drafts ad nauseam, but it's one I would not change for anything. The adventure and the joy of writing these stories, and the excitement and immodest pride of seeing my words coalesced into this volume is beyond description.

Thank you, dear reader, for picking up this tome, for reading its pages, and for encouraging and indulging my addled imagination. The feedback I've received from people reading my tales, the response each new instalment has been met with, has helped spur these strange stories on. Without the people who enjoy his adventures, and share a slice of my Imaginarium, Sam Hain would not exist. These books, this compendium for Volume I in the series, would not have been made possible without your enjoyment and your support.

And a thank you to Camilla Winquist, who provided the cover for this book and created the illustrations contained within. She came into my life quite by chance (although, of course, there is no such thing as coincidence; the Universe is rarely so lazy), inspired me with her artwork in ways I hadn't expected, and has been a great support to me, even when she may not have realised it. Camilla's art has captured the essence of the world inside my head, without which this compendium would not be half as exciting as I believe it to be.

The stories contained within these pages are, in a roundabout sort of way, inspired by myriad events in my life. Some elements are true, some are exaggerated to make them more interesting, and others are pure fabrication. As for which parts are which, I shall leave that to you to decide. I hope you enjoy reading these as much as I have enjoyed writing them.

Be aware of the things which lurk in the shadows, shine light onto the darkness which may try to cloud our lives, and believe in the magic and wonder of the world. There's more to it than meets the eye.

-Bron, by the river in Richmond upon Thames

April 2018

The Veil between Worlds thins this Night,
Giving rise to things both Dark and Light.

Sam Hain
Occult Detective

All Hallows' Eve

Chapter I

That Halloween had started out just like any other.

The annual after-work costume party had kicked off early in the evening, rapidly descending into an alcohol fuelled frenzy. Inebriated skeletons and zombies danced the night away, while the vampires tried desperately to get off with the scantily clad nurses. The other drunken denizens of the night – those who had come dressed as something other than the undead, like the inside-joke-costumes and the mock-costume of Geoff from Admin – sat in the corner, explaining to one another the inspiration for their outfits and exactly why they were supposed to be funny.

Unlike previous Halloweens, Alice Carroll had decided to leave the party early. The turning point for her had come somewhere between King Kong throwing up on her shoes, and the party-goers spontaneously deciding to go tipsy trick-or-treating. At one o'clock in the morning. In the east end of London. As far as brilliant ideas were concerned, this was not one of them. Alice could only see a group of drunk Halloween caricatures knocking on people's doors in the small hours of the morning turning out particularly poorly.

Having rinsed the last of King Kong's vomit from her formerly bright yellow shoes in the kitchen sink, Alice brushed back her blonde hair and put the comically springy antennae of her sexy bee costume back on her head. Throwing her denim jacket around her shoulders, she took her leave.

She managed to leave the party with very little hassle. Alice had let her flatmate, Rachel, know she was going to start heading home, to which Rachel had responded with an 'aw, no, you should stay' before drunkenly dancing off

1

in the direction of Frankenstein's Monster. Other than that, everyone else seemed too wrapped up in their night to notice the girl in the yellow-and-black striped corset leaving.

Alice walked through the crowded hallway, pushing through groups of chattering ghosts and werewolves, squeezing past the wholly unsettling sight of Marilyn Monroe making out with the Creature from the Black Lagoon. She slipped out of the front door, sidling through the team of off-duty Ghostbusters who were congregated, chain-smoking, on the doorstep, and began to make her way down the road. She was thankful she didn't have to keep explaining she was leaving to everyone she passed; there was nothing more frustrating than repeatedly having to answer that yes, she was leaving, and no, she couldn't stay a little bit longer, when all she wanted to do was get home. It did feel surreal, though, going straight from the loud, crowded house party onto the quiet, empty streets, alone and without really saying goodbye to anyone.

The walk home was an old and familiar one. Alice had moved to Islington a little under a year ago, but she had already found the roads which made her feel most at home. Her favourite part of the walk home was up through an old street just off of the main road. It was the kind of old, side-alley street which would host a farmers market on Wednesdays and an antiques fair over the weekend. There was a distinctly quaint, Old London air to it. It felt like a small bubble in the city, separated from the rest of metropolis, and seemed perpetually stuck in the past.

For Alice, it was a homely street. It was where she frequently bought her fresh vegetables mid-week and where one weekend she had bought an old mantel clock for a fiver, only to discover upon getting it home that it did not work. However, this night, on Halloween, in the cold of winter, when no other person was about – save for the small groups patrolling the main road an alley or two away

– there was something eerie about this old cobbled street. Alice's every footstep echoed off of the aged, soot-covered brickwork. In the distance, she could faintly hear the noise of parties finishing their pub crawls out on the main road. The distant sound of the crowd made her feel almost safe, not entirely alone in the night, but somewhat vulnerable too. Getting home, she thought, could not come soon enough.

She walked through the empty streets back to her flat, the boggle-eyed springy antennae bouncing annoyingly as she went. The sexy bee costume had been a dare, a forfeit for having to work a slightly longer shift and turn up late to the party. It had never really occurred to Alice exactly why the sexy bee costume existed; it wasn't the most intuitive of sexy costumes. Most bee drones lived out their entire lives as virgins, and queen bees were hardly renowned for being gentle lovers. Honey bees, despite being associated with the sweet, sticky food, had a particularly bad time of things, as they ripped out most of their internal organs in the process of stinging their victims, leaving them to die a slow and painful death. In fact, Alice thought, there was very little that was traditionally sexy about bees. It also wasn't the best choice of costume for walking home on a cold winter's night, but here she was in the stripy corset and black lace tutu, walking the cold, dark streets of Islington.

Maybe it was the in-depth thoughts she was having about bee costumes, or the mild detachment from reality caused by more jellied-vodka eyeballs than she would care to count, but Alice had failed to notice that she was being followed.

A short distance behind her walked a man. He was hunched over, his neck craning forward and his head angled almost entirely parallel to the ground, with a hood pulled low over his face. He shambled along the cobbled street, stumbling on the uneven road, and stopped in his tracks when Alice eventually turned to look at him. The man stood eerily still. Although she couldn't see his eyes, Alice could feel him watching her. The noise from the nearby main road had fallen silent, as if everyone had suddenly decided to call it a night, and a haunting quietness hung heavily in the air. It was as if the world had abruptly ground to a halt. There wasn't even the faintest whisper of a breeze. The night was perfectly still.

Alice carried on, quickening her pace. She was a good five minutes walk from home, but she really didn't fancy being in the street with this man for any longer than needed. One of the street lamps ahead of her flickered uncertainly. She could hear his footsteps behind her, uneven and clumsy, but gradually speeding up. His footsteps matched hers. She didn't want to provoke anything by breaking into a run, but she quickened her pace further, gradually picking up speed. She continued to walk faster and faster, almost approaching a light jog. The man sped up also, and Alice could feel her heart pumping rapidly in her throat.

Suddenly, something slammed into her. She was pushed to the wall of the street in one whirlwind motion, knocking her jacket from around her shoulders and winding her as she hit the hard brick surface. The force that had pushed her moved away, and she turned around, staggering and dazed from the impact. As she struggled to regain her balance, she saw the man who had been walking behind her charge past at full pelt and come to an abrupt stop. He turned slowly, unnaturally, and out of the corner of her eye she caught a glimpse of another person standing over her. A tall figure silhouetted against the orange glow of the street lamps, dressed from head to toe in black, a greatcoat flowing down to his ankles, and a fedora-style hat perched on his head.

'Run!' the silhouetted figure shouted, gesturing towards one of the nearby side-streets. Alice stood for a moment, dumb-founded, and watched as this other man squared up to her initial pursuer. The hooded man moved towards them, slowly, purposefully, and his head juddered unnaturally. For a brief second, the street lamps went out, leaving the alleyway in darkness. With a buzzing sound, the lights struggled back on, albeit dimmer than before. The man in the coat and hat turned to her again and waved his arm frantically in the direction of the street. 'Go!'

She didn't think to question the man's orders. She ran. The bee antennae bobbed up and down irritatingly in front of her face, swinging back and forth and bouncing off of her forehead as she sprinted away. She didn't stop to catch her breath as she ran, and even sacrificed one of her shoes to the night as she continued to sprint as fast as she could through the winding alleyways.

Behind her, Alice heard a loud zapping sound, and something not unlike the crackling of electricity. She turned to see the street behind her illuminated by a bright blue flickering light. She squinted at the light for a second, before carrying on running in the opposite direction. Away from whatever that was, and, unwittingly, away from home.

She had not been down these roads before and, in her panic and confusion, she had lost all sense of direction.

Rounding a corner, Alice allowed herself to slow her pace, from a sprint to a jog to an exhausted but hurried walk. Eventually, she came to a stop. She leaned against a wall, struggling to catch her breath as a mix of panic and exhaustion overwhelmed her. Looking around, Alice tried to get her bearings. She was in a back-alley, the narrow street lined with old, scorched brick walls, and every few feet sat small piles of black bags. The way was lit by only a few dimly glowing street lamps, giving everything a gentle orange hue.

An icy wind blew through the alleyway, chilling Alice to the bone. She shuddered, wrapping her arms tightly around herself to brace against the cold. In her panic, she hadn't stopped to pick her jacket back up before running

from... She paused, thinking, trying to make sense of what had just happened. She vigorously rubbed her arms, which were starting to pimple in the cold of the night, to keep at least a little warm. Whatever had happened back there didn't matter, she concluded; what did matter was getting back home, back into the warmth, and as far away from strange men in hoods and overcoats as possible.

Reaching into the breast of her corset, Alice pulled out her phone. Thankfully, she didn't like leaving her valuables in her jacket pockets. She fumbled with the screen-lock as she tried to calm her sudden rush of nerves. She flicked her way through the pages of apps and tapped at the Maps icon impatiently, desperately hoping it would tell her what road she was on now, and the best route home.

Location settings disabled. Insufficient data.

'Shit,' Alice muttered under her breath. She tried calling Rachel, but it didn't matter where she stood, there was no signal. She sighed in frustration, and squeezed her phone back into the corset's breast.

As she stood there, perplexed and alone and more than a little bit frightened, a tall figure loomed out of one of the pitch black alleyways. It stepped into the dim, orangey-yellow glow of the street lamps. Alice let out a slight whimper when she caught sight of the ominous silhouette. The figure stood for a moment, eerie and unmoving. The recognisable shape of the coat and hat did nothing to calm Alice's already frayed nerves.

'Sorry about that,' the figure spoke in a calm and friendly voice, the greatcoat billowing out behind him as he made his way forward. As he came closer, Alice knew for certain it was the man from a few moments before, and although it seemed like it would be a good idea, she didn't feel compelled to start running again. The man leaned against the wall next to her. 'Are you okay?'

'Really? Do *you* think I'm okay?!' Alice immediately exclaimed, staring almost accusingly at the man. 'I've been followed home by some creepy guy, been pushed into a wall, run from a fight, I've had King Kong throw up on my shoes – one of which is now missing – I'm cold, I'm tired, I'm dressed like a slutty bee, and I don't know where I am any more. Am I okay?! You bloody tell me!' Most of Alice's fear and panic had converted itself into anger. She just wanted to get home and be done with the night.

The man simply looked deep into her eyes, and smiled kindly at her. 'I'm sorry you had to experience all that,' he said, far too calmly for Alice's liking, 'these kind of things, they shouldn't happen. Difficult to keep on top of it all at this time of year, of course.'

She glared at him, and got the first proper look at the man since he'd rather abruptly slammed her into the wall. He must have been in his mid-to-late-twenties, possibly early thirties, and a little over six foot tall. His scruffy, mid-length dark brown hair flowed out from under his hat and rested on the upturned collars of his overcoat. A silver talisman, a five-pointed star contained within a circle, hung from a cord around his neck. It looked as if he'd decided to dress as a contemporary Van Helsing for Halloween.

'What? What are you talking about? What was all that back there, and who the hell are you?' Alice asked, still on the offensive. 'And what about the other guy?!'

'One question at a time,' the man said wearily. 'First of all, that was something which crossed the threshold from another world and into this one. I came to send it back.' Alice simply stood staring at him, incredulous. He continued. 'This is one of those strange supernatural stories people read about online or in Esoteric Express. Most people dismiss these stories as myths, rumours or hoaxes,' he chuckled, 'if only they knew.'

He was incredibly matter-of-fact about the whole affair, and Alice couldn't help but wonder if this was all some kind of elaborate Halloween prank.

'It's gone now, though. Back to the Void space where it

belongs. At this time of year, the veil between worlds is incredibly thin; easier for them to cross the threshold, but easier for me to send them back too.' He straightened his lapels with the air of a man congratulating himself on a job well done.

Alice was silent for a while, just staring at this man, taking in everything he was saying, but refusing to believe a word of it. She shook her head, and with a sarcastic 'yeah, right' she began to hobble away. She took off her remaining shoe to even herself out. She'd had more than enough of this evening, and wasn't going to put up with much more of this nonsense. She just wanted to go home.

'No, you're quite right. It's all rather hard to believe. Too far-fetched,' he retorted, and tipped his hat in her direction. 'Have a good evening.'

Alice turned to give him a snarky response – her evening had been far from good by anyone's standards – but he had vanished. It was as if he had evaporated into thin air. *I've definitely had enough of this evening*, she concluded, and scurried back the way she had come, hoping to find her way back to somewhere she recognised. It didn't take long for her to find somewhere vaguely familiar, and once she had got her bearings, she headed straight for home.

Almost falling through the door to her flat, Alice stumbled in, overcome with stress and fatigue and alcohol, and she unceremoniously flopped herself onto the sofa. She had barely taken the ridiculous bee antennae off of her head before she fell asleep, and drifted off into a strange and uneasy night's dreaming.

That night, her dreams were haunted by strange visions. Of tall men in overcoats fighting demons in hooded jackets, of a giant gorilla climbing the Empire State building with a yellow high-heel shoe, and of bees with weirdly cartoon-y eyes on springs, dancing seductively. It was not the best night's sleep she had ever had by any means.

CHAPTER II

Alice woke up the following morning with the hangover from hell. It was the kind of hangover that felt like goblins had crept in during the night and had decided that her head would make the perfect addition to their percussive band. She groaned as she shifted about on the sofa, trying to heave the dead weight of her reluctant body around. Every muscle ached as she lazily tried to move them, and the tight yellow-and-black striped corset did nothing to help her sit up. She flopped herself back into the cushions of the sofa, refusing to move any more than was strictly necessary.

She blinked dazedly into the room, slowly adjusting to the beams of cold morning light which poured in through the window. Her eyelids seemed to make a scratching sound as she blinked, her eyes dry and feeling like they were held in place by clamps. Screwing her eyes tightly shut and giving them a firm rub, Alice squinted out into the world. Through blurred and bleary vision, something caught her attention and startled her into feeling much more alive.

It was the clock on the mantelpiece. There was nothing particularly startling about the clock in and of itself – it was just an old mantel clock – but the angle at which its hands were positioned. *Two o'clock.* Alice's brain felt as if it had been given a kick-start. *Two o-bloody-clock?! How did I sleep so long? I'm late!*

Moving quicker than she believed she was capable of, Alice swung herself around and leapt up from the comfort of the sofa. The world continued to swing ever so slightly after she herself had stopped moving. She swayed a little while she tried to keep her balance, and staggered forwards like a fawn learning to walk.

Earlier in the week, Alice had rearranged today's shift for the afternoon, anticipating precisely this kind of day after the party. She hadn't accounted for sleeping in for quite so long, though. Reaching for her phone, which lay unceremoniously on the floor a few feet from the sofa, she thought she had better call in and make her excuses for why she was coming in so late. Or, better yet, try to get away with taking a sick day. She swiped her finger across the phone's screen, and saw the time displayed in big, friendly-looking digits.

Nine forty-seven. Nine forty-seven?

Alice glanced back to the clock on the mantelpiece. Its hands remained adamant that it was two o'clock. It took a little while for her to realise the reason for this discrepancy. As she was now forcibly feeling more awake, she remembered. *Bastard clock doesn't even work.* She shot an accusing glare in its direction for daring to deceive her, and breathed an exaggerated sigh of relief.

It was just as well, she thought, that she didn't need to rush to get into work on time. The world was a terrifyingly spinny and throbby place that morning, and rushing would certainly do her no favours. Alice resolved – as she so often did after a night out – never to drink again. She balanced herself as the world took another sickening spin, placing her hand on the back of the sofa to stay upright, and she hobbled into the kitchen.

At first, there was very little she could piece together of the night before. Fragments of events hazily drifted through her mind like long-forgotten memories, and what felt like the weird fever-dreams that only a certain amount of vodka could produce. *Geoff had been there... Or was it Tim, dressed as Geoff? Dracula was doing a little more than sucking the blood from the neck of Nurse Naughty... Someone had come dressed as King Kong, too...* She had lost a shoe at some point, that was certain. Her feet felt cold and blistered. There was only one bright yellow high-heel in the middle of the living room floor, looking quite worn and sorry for itself. And she couldn't quite remember what she had done with her jacket.

Pouring more than a generous amount of coffee granules into a mug, Alice put the kettle on and gazed vacantly into the fridge. *Something fried will do*, she thought, *like fried eggs in a sandwich. With bacon. Dripping with oil and ketchup.* She set about preparing her decadent cure, poured herself a coffee strong enough to raise the dead, and leaned on the kitchen counter while she waited for the bacon and eggs to fry.

Van Helsing was also there last night, she seemed to recall. Although that seemed more distant than other parts of the evening. Maybe an odd dream. She thought she could remember Van Helsing beating up a hoody, but that seemed more like it would fit in with her strange night's sleep rather than the Halloween party. She pushed all thoughts of the night before aside. She'd have breakfast, wake up properly, boot the hangover and clear her head, go to work and get on with her day.

The breakfast she had prescribed herself did just the job. The strong, bitter coffee scared off the fuzziness in her brain, and the sandwich, dripping in grease and ketchup and packed so full with eggs and bacon she had to open her mouth as wide as she could just to take a bite, helped her feel a bit stronger and more steady. Even if it did rest heavily in her stomach. She still felt a little fuzzy, her vision slightly blurring around the edges like an artful vignette, but at least the pounding headache was starting to ease off and she didn't feel half as nauseated as she did before.

Alice made her way into the bathroom, turning on the tap with a deafening whoosh of water, and splashed her face with a handful of cold water. It was a refreshing sensation, and one she hoped would wake her up properly. She rubbed her eyes to clear the tiredness, gently massaging and patting her cheeks. Leaning against the sink, she let out a quiet groan. It was going to take more than coffee, fried sandwiches, and cold water to completely shift this hangover.

As she looked up into the mirror, Alice saw something which shook her to the core. She froze. What little colour she had left in her hungover, pale face was suddenly drained. There, stood immediately behind her and staring back from the reflection, was the hooded man from the night before. She wheeled around to face him, wide eyed and much more alert than she thought she was capable of being, but suddenly he was nowhere to be seen. The bathroom was empty. She turned back to the mirror, and all she could see was herself reflected in its surface, the bath and toiletry cabinet being the only things behind her.

Adrenaline pumped through her body, and she let out a deep, shaking, panicked breath. Steeling herself, Alice walked slowly, cautiously, towards the bath. The shower curtain was drawn half-way across, and with a tentative, trembling hand she reached out to pull it away. With a swift flick of her wrist, Alice whipped the curtain across, pulling it open in a flash

A single sad droplet of water dripped from the end of the tap.

She breathed a sigh of relief, and returned to the living room. Settling back down on the sofa, she checked the time on her phone, and told herself she would nap for a little bit to digest breakfast and finish off the hangover. She tried to push all thoughts of last night's misadventures and nightmares aside, thinking that once she'd had a bit more sleep she would forget all about it.

Of course, she did not forget.

As she tried to relax, her mind was flooded with strange visions from the night before. It was not quite like a dream, but definitely not reality. She could see the old cobbled street and the hooded man. The scene was vivid, almost tangible, as if she was really there, yet somehow it all felt so distant and hollow. She knew she was still just sprawled out on her sofa, but there was something inescapably present about this strange, waking dream.

She was running down the street, her legs pounding and lungs tight as she tried to breathe. She knew that if she stopped, even for a second, he would catch up with her. The street stretched out before her, growing longer and longer as she ran, until eventually it seemed as if it carried on for eternity. No matter how fast she ran, she could not get away. The hidden face of the man emerged behind her, leering in close to her.

'*Tenebris venit*,' he breathed down the back of her neck. His breath was icy and cloying, and she felt shivers run down her spine and her blood run cold.

BANG! Alice woke from the dream with a start, sitting bolt upright and breathing heavily. It took a while for her to compose herself and gather her bearings, snapping back to reality from the dark and the cold of the nightmarish alleyway. She was home, she was safe. The noise of the flat's letterbox slamming shut had startled her awake, and for a change she welcomed the unexpected wake-up call. She turned to see the letterbox still flapping slightly, creaking on its hinges as it slowly swung back and forth, but no post had been delivered.

The nightmare felt like it had lasted forever, but when she checked her phone, Alice saw she had only been asleep for half an hour. Reaching for her mug, she drank the last gulp of the grainy, now particularly cold, coffee and grimaced. Today was going to be a difficult day.

Alice tried to push the strange thoughts to the side while she focussed on getting ready for work. She showered, put on something a bit more suitable for work than the corset and tutu of the bee costume, and started to do her make-up. She had half considered talking to Rachel about her nightmare, just for reassurance, but when her flatmate came staggering through the door shortly after noon, clutching a bottle of schnapps shouting 'woo, hair of the dog!' she thought better of it. Rachel slammed the door behind her, making Alice's brain shake.

'Please, don't,' Alice said, clutching one hand to her still-hungover head, 'not so loud.' Rachel bounced over to the sofa and sat down next to Alice.

'You need some of this in you, then,' Rachel said, holding the bottle of schnapps out to her. Alice took a quick swig and made a "nope" face.

'Ew, no, bad plan. I feel crap enough as it is.'

'How? You didn't have that much last night, and you walked home. I don't feel that bad.'

'Maybe because you carried on drinking.'

'True,' Rachel said, and she took another swig from the bottle, 'how'd you get home last night, anyway?'

Flashes of the street, of the man in the hood and then of the man in the coat and hat, ran through Alice's mind. She thought about the ache in her legs as she ran, the panic tight in her chest, and losing a shoe and her jacket somewhere along the line. Then she remembered the bright blue flash, and the strange things the man had said to her.

'There was a fight down the alley on my way back, and I think someone was following me for a while. I don't know, I was very drunk, it's all a bit of a mess.'

'Are you okay?' Rachel asked, putting a hand on Alice's knee sympathetically.

'Yeah. Yeah! I'm fine. Just a bit of a bad night really.'

'Not still going to work, are you? I've called in sick, me.'

'Yeah, I am,' Alice said dejectedly as she reached for her hairbrush and quickly ran it through her hair. She stood up and glanced around, looking for her shoes.

'No, stay home! We can watch films and order takeaway and wallow in drunken self-pity.'

'As fun as that sounds, I really can't afford to take the day off, Rachel. My manager was bad enough when I asked to move my hours to the afternoon, let alone if I don't go in at all.'

'Oh, you're no fun,' Rachel said teasingly. 'Tonight, though. Pizza, cider, chick-flicks, the works.'

'Fine! You've twisted my arm,' Alice said with a smile, 'Friday night in. Sounds good. Just what I need.'

Rachel nodded in sagely agreement. 'You're overworked and spend your time worrying about silly things-'

'Like the rent?' Alice interrupted.

'You know what I mean. You're always stressing about something or another. You need to take some time to chill, babe.'

This time it was Alice's turn to nod sagely. 'Yeah, you're right,' she said, 'I've not been taking much time for myself. Maybe I am just overstressed.' She had been running herself into the ground with work just to try and keep a roof over her head, but it hardly gave her a sense of self. She was simply Server #0, working on the shop floor for eight hours a day, and receiving more abuse from customers and staff alike than she really believed was possible.

'Perfect! It's what we both need to relax,' Rachel said. 'And whatever's on your mind, I'll try to help take it off of you.'

'Thank you. But first, work,' Alice declared. She threw her coat around her shoulders, wrapped her scarf tightly around her neck, and pulled her bobble hat on. 'I'll see you tonight,' she said with a wave, and left the flat.

The weather outside was bitterly cold that afternoon. It was the kind of weather that was equal parts refreshing and misery-inducing, and Alice was more inclined to feel the latter. She sat huddled on the crowded tube carriage on the way to work, nestled under her thick, woollen coat and wearing more layers than she could count. Her scarf was tightly wrapped up around her neck, and pulled up to cover her nose from the cold. She much preferred the summer. At least it was warmer on the underground than it had been outside, even if the air was a little dusty.

The journey to work always made Alice feel miserable, always dreading stepping off of the tube and walking around the corner to the store where she worked. Day in, day out, she would fall into the same old routine, sat on a claustrophobic and increasingly packed train on the way to work, where all she did was stand behind the tills, serving customers and packing their bags, likely getting shouted at because she wasn't folding their shirts quite right, or receiving disgruntled remarks whenever she had to direct someone to customer services. Then she would likely make fewer sales than her co-workers and be told to "up her game if she wanted to make it in retail", which, of course, she did not. Same old, same old.

The tube had been stopping and starting from the minute they pulled out of Highbury and Islington station. Something to do with signal failures on the Victoria line, although Alice wasn't really listening; for the second time that day, she was worrying that she would be late for work. She may not have wanted to go in, but nor did she want to announce her lateness after management had already picked her up for clocking in ten minutes late because of a tube delay in the past. She glanced at the time on her phone. *Not too late yet*, she thought, *I should have five minutes to get there from the station*. As if to mock her optimistic outlook on time, the train came to a grinding halt again. Sparks flew up outside of the window, briefly illuminating the normally unseen passages of the London Underground. A number of men in suits tutted with world-weary irritation as the tube came to a full stop.

'We apologise for the delay,' a voice came crackling

through the tannoy, 'but due to a signalling issue at Warren Street Station, we will have to wait here for approximately five minutes.'

Alice rolled her eyes. *Just typical.*

The glare of the fluorescent lights above the passengers' heads began to flicker, and the carriage started to grow dimmer and dimmer. Then, with a unified buzzing noise, the lights went out, plunging the carriage into darkness. Alice looked around nervously, she was uncomfortable on the underground at the best of times, let alone when sat in pitch blackness, stuck in a tunnel with no way out. She could just about make out the outlines of her fellow passengers, some of whom were still trying to read the Metro in spite of the absence of light. It was then that she noticed the person sat opposite her. He was hunched over, his head facing the floor, and his features covered by his hood. She felt a shiver as she recognised the unearthly air about the figure, but it couldn't possibly be... *Could it?*, she wondered, staring at the all too familiar clothing.

As she stared at the man, trying to convince herself it was not her nightmarish apparition, his head slowly began to rise. The lights flickered back on for only a moment, and she saw him staring back at her with haunting, unblinking eyes. But they were not really eyes. Where eyes would normally be, there were two, almond-shaped black holes. They didn't look so much like holes into the head, but holes torn in the fabric of reality, and it wasn't really a blackness as much as it was... Nothingness. Alice froze in fear, unable to break her eye-contact with this thing that seemed to have manifested itself from her nightmares. She was too afraid to blink, and she could feel the man staring into her soul with his unseeing, non-existent eyes.

The man stood up and leaned forward, putting his face directly in front of Alice's. 'Darkness is coming,' he intoned, his voice hollow and haunting like a strong wind echoing through a deep cavern. Alice tried to scream, but she made no noise. She was completely paralysed. The rest of the carriage seemed utterly oblivious to the man now leering so ominously close to her. With another silent scream, Alice tried to kick the man away from her.

The train jolted back into motion and the lights snapped back into life, just as Alice's legs kicked out. The man was no longer leering over her. Her head was throbbing with a pain worse than before, and she looked around the carriage nervously. It was perfectly well-lit, still filled with men in suits reading newspapers, but there was no sign of her nightmarish vision. The man sat opposite her was just an elderly gentleman reading the newspaper through his bifocals, and he most certainly had proper, human eyes. She gazed out of the window, trying to calm herself, as the tube stopped at the platform for Warren Street.

'The next station is Oxford Circus,' announced the automated service. Alice briefly toyed with the idea of just staying on the underground until the end of the line, but she couldn't really afford to take the day off, especially not on a whim. She had already been given a written warning for taking two sick days, and management had told her that a third would result in a non-specific "disciplinary action". Begrudgingly, Alice stood up and made her way to the carriage doors, off to face another tedious day.

CHAPTER III

'And what time do you call this?' A particularly stern-faced woman in an ill-fitting polyester shirt accosted Alice the moment she stepped through the door and onto the shop floor. She tapped her watch admonishingly, eyes fixed on Alice with an unwavering glare.

'One o'clock,' Alice said, looking back at Jan, her manager, with utter confusion. Something about Jan had always put Alice in mind of a rather disgruntled parrot. Maybe it was the way her long, beak-like nose curved over her perpetually downturned mouth, or the way her exaggeratedly large and bulging eyes stared, unblinking and ever so slightly off-centre as if she was never quite looking at you, or the way her hair sprouted like feathers from atop her head. The way her arms flapped and her nasally voice squawked whenever she was stressed – which was almost constantly – certainly did not do her any favours.

'It's actually a minute past one. And what time does your shift start?' Jan asked flatly. She wore the face of a middle school teacher about to administer detention. Her mouth narrowed and lips crinkled inward as if she had just bitten into a grapefruit.

'One o'clock?'

'Then you should have been on the shop floor ready to start your shift at least five minutes ago. Try to be on time for your shift, Alice. That's a minute we're paying you for that you haven't worked.' She stared at Alice with eyes that seemed to bore into her soul, as if waiting for an apology. Alice said nothing.

What do you want me to do, pay you back the 10p of overpay I'll "earn" from that minute? Alice thought to herself, bitterly and thoroughly not in the mood for this today, while she tried to maintain the simpering smile she had forced onto her face.

'Right, well,' Jan said conclusively, as if she had got all she had wanted from this interaction, 'I need to meet with the Regents Marketing Group about this month's figures. You're on the till.' With that, she walked off in the direction of the staff room.

Alice watched as she left, before turning to the till. A rather impatient looking man was already stood in front of the desk, tapping his foot and glancing over his shoulders as if he was expecting someone to creep up on him at any moment. He locked eyes with Alice, and maintained his expectant stare. She smiled sweetly in his direction and, with a resigning sigh, she bottled up her thoughts and made her way over towards him.

'Good afternoon, sir,' she greeted him cordially as she tapped her login details into the till, 'how are you?'

'Hi,' said the man, but he offered no further conversation. Instead, he presented her with a pack of socks, placing them indelicately on the desk. The till, presumably eager to serve, beeped enthusiastically as the barcode rested on the peripheries of the scanner.

'Will that be everything this afternoon, sir? Is there anything else I can help you with at all?'

'Yup,' replied the man, and Alice awaited further details to clarify whether that was a "yup, that will be everything" or a "yup, there is something else you can help me with". No clarification was given, however, and the man simply stood, waiting. She tapped at the till screen, and gestured to the card reader in front of him.

'Do you need a bag for that?'

'Yup.'

'Okay,' Alice said, unfurling a small carrier bag and shoving the socks in. The till whirred as it dispensed the receipt, which she tore of and slid into the bag alongside the socks. 'I've popped the receipt in the bag for you, as well,' she added through a forced smile as she handed the bag to the man. 'Would you be interested in signing up for our-'

'Nope,' he said, and promptly walked away.

'Have a good afternoon,' she called after him, and hoped she did not sound quite as sarcastic as she thought she did. Leaning forward across the desk, propping herself up on her elbows and resting her chin on her hands, Alice settled in for the monotonous wait for the day to eventually come to an end. *Only seven hours and forty-five minutes to go.* She stared out at the shop floor.

People milled around the store, drifting lazily from rail to rail. They glanced over the items on display, casually shifting the clothes hangers along the rails as they rifled through the sizes. Occasionally, they would rub the material of the clothes as if inspecting the quality, but would take no further interest in the items. They meandered in a vacant, almost dream-like state, until something caught their interest and they would make a bee-line for it. This was often followed by them either taking several items from a rail and not putting them back on their hangers, or rummaging through a neatly organised stack of clothes and transforming it into a sprawling mess of a mound.

Alice tried to offer her assistance to the customers, but they very rarely acknowledged her existence unless they wanted to complain about something. She soon found herself following the trail of destruction left behind in the wake of the browsing shoppers, tidying up after them, only to find a few minutes later someone else had come along and undone her work. Normally, she would make small-talk with her colleagues, but she wasn't much in the mood for talking so mainly kept herself to herself. Until, of course, she was presented with inexplicably long queues of customers or subjected to intense questioning about what sizes may or may not be in stock.

Typically, during the store's busiest hour that day (possibly even that month), Alice managed to hold up a long and increasingly agitated queue. In her haste to serve everyone as quickly as possible, she had forgotten to take one customer's change out of the cash drawer before closing it. This, in itself, was not much of an issue; the issue was, the till adamantly refused to open the cash drawer again until it had received the authorisation number from her manager. Neither Alice or her colleagues could authorise it, and she and her indignant customer had to wait while they tried to get Jan back from her tea break. The customer took it as a personal insult that she had forgotten to give them their change. Jan took it as a personal insult that she'd had to interrupt her tea break for this. Neither party was particularly shy about letting Alice know precisely how put out they were from this whole ordeal.

When the change had been given, and Jan disappeared to finish her tea break, the till happily started to print reels of receipts on a whim. After spewing out twenty different gift receipts, the printer jammed itself, once again putting Alice, the till, and the queue in a deadlock.

Today, she thought while smiling through gritted teeth, was most certainly not her day.

By the time her break came around, Alice was quite ready to call it a day. She tried to tell herself it wasn't that much longer – only a few more hours before she could clock off – but it didn't help. She was tired, she could feel her face turning paler by the second, her feet ached from standing, and if she had to smile politely again while a customer seemed to blame her, quite personally, for something beyond her control, she might go mad. The minute it was five o'clock, she removed her name badge from the breast of her shirt and marched hurriedly off of the shop floor. She did not want to stay there a single second longer than was necessary.

Pushing the door to the staff café open, Alice slowly walked in. She was relieved to discover that the place was entirely empty; the only noise was coming from the television, as the news was broadcast to an otherwise quiet and deserted room. She felt exhausted, drained of all life, and it was a blessing she could enjoy her break, taking time to herself, without having to hold polite conversation with anyone. She pushed the large button which read "coffee" on the drinks machine, placing a polystyrene cup beneath the nozzle. The machine spluttered a murky brown liquid, the whole unit convulsing as if it were choking on its dying breath. Alice stood patiently, watching the machine as it struggled through its death-throes, coughing up the last of its life fluids before falling into silence.

She took the steaming cup of not-quite-coffee and tentatively took a sip, instantly regretting it. She scolded the roof of her mouth on the boiling soapy water which barely passed as a drink, and for legal reasons really shouldn't have been labelled "coffee". At least it was better than the dishwater they called "tea". She thought she heard someone come through the door and stand behind her, presumably waiting for the machine, but when she turned around to smile politely there was no-one else there. She took another sip of the unpleasant brown liquid, grimaced, and tipped the remainder of the drink down the drain, opting for a bottle of mineral water instead.

She fell back into an armchair facing the TV, letting herself sink into the cushioned seat (despite the crumbs and anonymous stains covering it), and took a gulp of water. It was icy cold and hurt her teeth, but it was refreshing after working on the dry shop floor for so long. She watched the news for a little while with only a fleeting interest. Politicians talked an awful lot but managed to say nothing, there was heavy traffic on the M25, and someone had been found dead in their home in Brentford. Then the news cut away to a man standing in front of a map of the UK while he droned on about winter being cold, cloudy and wet.

'And we have a large mass of clouds coming in from the south-west this evening, bringing heavy rain and storms through Saturday and Sunday. With shorter daylight hours and heavy cloud cover, it looks like darkness is coming this weekend,' said Tom the Weatherman, his hands gesticulating like a marionette. Alice's head snapped up as she heard this, and stared, transfixed, at the screen. The image flickered unsettlingly, distortions running up and down the TV screen, the signal cutting in and out. She stood up to fiddle with the aerial, but she discovered it was plugged in securely. Her head began to ache, and she told herself it was just from her fatigue and watching the screen flash and go in and out of focus.

'Have a good evening,' said Tom the Weatherman, and Alice jabbed at the power button. The image faded to black.

With a final gulp of the water, she chucked the bottle into the recycling bin, and steeled herself for the remaining few hours of work.

'Are you feeling okay?' one of the visual merchandisers, Daryl, asked when he caught sight of Alice emerging from the staff area. She seemed paler than before, her eyes looking more tired and slightly bloodshot, framed by darkened bags underneath.

'Yeah,' she said somewhat distantly, 'yeah, no, I'm good. Just a bit tired, that's all.' She blinked at him. 'Do you have any paracetamol I can borrow?'

'You wouldn't exactly be borrowing it, now, would ya? I don't fancy you giving it back to me after you've used it!' He shot her a cheeky grin, and held out a packet of painkillers. 'Ibuprofen alright?'

'Yeah, anything that'll take the edge off this bastard

headache, thank you.' She quickly popped one of the pills into her mouth and swallowed, regretting not saving a mouthful of water for it.

The shift carried on in much the same way it had started, and the ibuprofen did not do much to alleviate the headache. By the time the end of her shift came, Alice couldn't have clocked out any quicker if she had tried. Her head was now pounding, like someone was hammering nails into her skull, and she figured she was just getting too stressed out, especially since she'd been deprived of a decent cup of tea or coffee for a good many hours. Tired, stressed, and wondering if she was experiencing the onset of an aneurysm, Alice brushed her staff card against the door lock, beeped, and headed straight for home. She couldn't wait to get in, chill out and settle down for a lazy night in with Rachel.

By the time she'd alighted at Highbury and Islington, Alice was clearly fatigued. Her eyes had started to play tricks on her. In the twilight of the evening, even the most mundane of things seemed to hide some dark secret. Her walk home was plagued by these evil illusions, as shadows cast by piled up bins seemed to hide hideous, hulking monstrosities, and unearthly nightmares appeared to lurk in every corner and alleyway. However, whenever Alice turned to see what these things were, they would promptly vanish or shape-shift into an innocent shadow, and she would console herself that it was likely just an illusion caused by her impending migraine. It reminded her of when she was eight or nine, and come bedtime she would see nothing but monsters; lurking in her cupboard, hiding under her bed, waiting at the end of the hallway... She didn't have her imaginary friend to chase away the shadows tonight, though.

She opened the door to her building – a row of old town-houses that had been knocked through and converted to accommodate a number of basic studios and apartments – and she headed up the stairs towards their flat on the second floor. The place was dimly lit at the best of times, but evidently a fuse had blown again and taken out all of the lighting on her floor. Not that it really mattered, as a glimmer of street-light shone through the window at the far end of the corridor, faintly illuminating the way. They would just have to light a couple of candles or use the lights on their phones for tonight, she thought, and wait for the landlord to fix the fuse in the untimely fashion for which landlords are so famous. She was fumbling around in the dim light of the corridor, looking for her keys, when from behind her she heard a low, guttural rumble. Icy breath caressed the back of her neck, and she felt her hairs stand on end.

She whirled around, and was greeted by a tall, dark figure. Again, she recognised the hooded figure with its sinister leer, those dark soulless eyes seemingly draining the light from the world. She froze in terror, trapped and helpless against this thing that seemed to constantly haunt her, and tried to convince herself it was only a stress-induced hallucination. This explanation did nothing to dispel the demon, or quell her anxiety. She tried to scream, but found herself paralysed. Out of the corner of her eye she saw something moving at the end of the corridor. She tried to look towards it, and stood in the faint orange glow from the street outside she could see the silhouette of another familiar shape: the man in the coat and hat. His long coat swayed from side to side as he made his way towards her, and in that instance Alice realised with horror that her nightmare from Halloween had not been a nightmare at all.

She crumpled to the floor, tightly squeezing her eyes shut and willing this all to be some horrible dream, begging to wake up and find out it was Friday morning again. It meant she would have to drag herself through that shift again, but it seemed like a worthwhile compromise to be rid of this terror. The man/creature/thing continued to bear down on her. She remembered the thoughts of the monsters she had imagined as a child, trying to convince herself that none of this was real, but as she tried to push it away, more and more images were conjured up in her imagination. She found herself back on that street, where this had all began the night before. She could hear shouting, a familiar voice which sounded as if it was from some distant memory or half-remembered dream, but she couldn't hear what it was saying. There was a hiss, a growl, and the inexplicable crackling of electricity, and she suddenly felt two hands clasp either side of her head.

Panic truly overcame Alice, and she was certain that this was either the end or that she would need to be committed to a psychiatric ward. She tried to open her eyes, but all she could see was darkness. Oily shadows swam in front of her mind's eye, swirling around like a swarm of eels. She could faintly hear whispers coming from the liquid shadows. The darkness enveloped her, surrounding Alice's entire being, caressing her body like the ebb and flow of the ocean.

She was adrift in an endless black sea, and she could feel herself being taken away by the current.

CHAPTER IV

The next thing Alice knew, she was waking up in the flat. Her head throbbed with an agonising headache which extended from her forehead, down through her teeth and into her neck. Her vision was blurred and blotchy, as if she'd been staring at the sun for too long. She was sprawled out, unceremoniously, on the sofa, one of the throw cushions propping her head up. The lights were back on. Swinging her legs around, she tried to stand up, but paused mid-motion to stop her head spinning. *Bloody hell, what a dream*, she thought as she regained her balance. She felt like she had an horrendous hangover, but at least it had all been just a dr-

'Hey, hey, hey! Not so fast. Take it easy,' a voice said from somewhere behind her. She craned her neck, which made a disconcerting noise not unlike the crackling of crushing a plastic bottle, to see who was speaking to her. She felt a sinking feeling in the pit of her stomach as reality started to dawn on her again.

'What the hell do you think you're doing?' Alice screamed, leaping to her feet with fury, and immediately regretting it as her head threatened to explode.

The kitchen looked as if a bomb had gone off. The cupboards had been emptied, their contents scattered across the counter tops. The bins had been upended, rubbish strewn across the floor. The fridge stood with it's door lazily hanging open. At the heart of the debris, and presumably the catalyst of this chaos, was the man in the coat and hat. He was knelt down amongst the contents of the bin, but stood up when Alice shouted at him. He dropped a torn-up page of the Guardian. *Oh god, it wasn't all a damn dream.*

'Have you received anything unusual lately? Strange gift,

unexpected letter, something out of the ordinary? Weird arcane artefacts which give you a lingering sense of dread?' The man questioned, completely ignoring the visible rage, fear, confusion and myriad other emotions etched on his unwitting host's face, and clearly oblivious that breaking and entering – and rummaging through someone's bin – is generally considered impolite and unacceptable behaviour in a civilised society.

'What?! No! Who are you and what are you doing in my kitchen?' Alice asked furiously, mixed with the panic of having a complete stranger pillaging her kitchen, and she felt as if her eyeballs were about to pop out of their sockets. 'What are you doing *to* my kitchen?'

The man took a few steps forward, kicking aside empty bottles and packets as he went. 'Sorry, I don't believe I've formally introduced myself yet. Terrible manners. I'm Sam. Sam Hain.' He extended a hand towards her, but Alice refused to shake it.

'Like the Pagan festival?' she asked indignantly.

'As a matter of fact, I do, although that's pronounced "sah-win",' Sam replied helpfully.

Alice didn't care. She simply stood the other side of the sofa from her unwelcome guest, uncertain as to what to do. She eyed the house phone, off of its base unit and laying on one of the kitchen counters. Her mobile wasn't in her pockets. If she wanted to call for help, she would just have to make a run for it. She span on her heels, and made a dash for the door.

It was locked.

In her panic, she fumbled with the lock, trying desperately to open the door, but she wasn't able to release the catch on the handle fast enough. The man who called himself Sam Hain was stood immediately behind her. He lifted his hands to hold her by the shoulders, but he left them hovering.

'Please, don't panic. I'm not an intruder – well, I suppose

I sort of am – but I certainly don't mean you any harm,' Sam spoke softly, trying to calm her down. She didn't trust his calmness, and turned around as she pushed herself back against the door.

'So what, precisely, do you think you're doing in my home?' Alice spat through gritted teeth.

'You've been having piercing headaches, sometimes with disturbing visions. Like a nightmare you can't quite wake up from. Am I right?' He slowly took a step back, allowing her some space.

Nervously, she nodded.

'That's why I'm here, Alice. I know about these sorts of things. I know about them in ways a lot of people don't.'

'How do you know my name?' Alice asked, her voice quivering more with worry than with anger now.

'You really shouldn't throw out your old bank statements, you know. Don't you keep account of your finances? Bit of a risk for identity fraud, too.' Sam sat down on the sofa, and gestured for Alice to take a seat. 'That's not why I'm here, though. I'm here because of what happened last night, and what's been happening since. Oh, before I forget,' he added, reaching over the arm of the sofa and picking something up from the floor, 'this is your jacket, isn't it?' He held up Alice's denim jacket, the one she had lost to the alleyway when she and Sam had first indelicately met.

'Yes, thank you,' she replied uncertainly, 'you didn't find a bright yellow shoe as well, did you?'

'Afraid not, sorry.'

She was still wary. Nothing about this situation put her at ease. She could feel herself shaking as she tentatively walked towards the man who was holding her jacket out to her. Gratefully, she took it from him. He smiled warmly at her. Despite everything, Alice had a feeling that this man really did not mean her any harm, even if he had completely trashed her kitchen. Cautiously, she stepped back and took a seat in the armchair nearest the door. She just wished Rachel would get back home soon. *Where the hell is she?*

'So, you *know* about "these sorts of things"?' Alice asked.

'Yes. More than you'd probably think,' Sam answered, and he removed his hat, ruffling his flattened hair. 'I deal with the... extraordinary. Last night, Halloween, I was on a case. There was something here that shouldn't have been, and I had to do something about it.'

'That man that you started fighting?' Alice asked.

'Well, he wasn't so much a man as a thing shaped like a man. He was an entity from another dimension, causing trouble where he really shouldn't be.'

Alice eyed him incredulously. 'Of course. So you're a demon hunter? Right? Am I supposed to believe that?'

'Well, not really a demon-hunter, although that is part of the job description. I'm an occult detective. I deal with cases involving the esoteric and the supernatural.' The man who called himself Sam Hain spoke with such conviction that Alice was almost willing to believe him.

'All right then. Supernatural sleuth. Gotcha. Forgot to take your pills this morning?' she retorted. Again she considered making a move for the phone, but rather than calling the police she was now thinking about getting in touch with Bedlam to let them know they were missing a patient.

'"Darkness is coming". Am I right?' Sam asked casually, watching Alice closely for any kind of reaction.

Time felt as if it had come to a standstill. Alice stared back at him, and she could see a knowing glint behind the strange man's eyes. His words had suddenly made this whole nightmare all the more terrifyingly real. Her voice lowered to almost a whisper. 'Yeah. Something like that.'

Sam stood up and made his way over to the window. He gazed out, overlooking a terrace of houses, beyond which the tiny pin-pricks of light from the rest of the city could be seen. He clasped his hands behind his back pensively. 'I've been following the signs for some time now. "Darkness is coming", they warned. Forces beyond our reckoning are stirring in the Void, trying to breach the walls between our world and their own. I'm trying to get to the bottom of what's going on, and – for whatever reason – on All Hallows' Eve, things have been converging on you, Alice.'

Alice sat in silence for a while, her mind elsewhere. She thought of the man in the hood, of running in fear and of the ever-present niggling sensation at the back of her mind that something sinister was going on. 'Why me?' she eventually asked, her voice quiet and uncertain.

'May I?' Sam asked, returning to sit opposite Alice. He raised his hands towards her head, and she jerked backwards, eyeing him suspiciously.

'What are you doing?'

'I'm going to take a peek inside your mind,' he said, and he saw the look of concern written across Alice's face. 'Don't worry,' he added, 'I won't see anything you don't want me to see, only the things I need. But I need your consent, if you'll allow me?'

Alice nodded silently as she allowed Sam's hands to gently hold either side of her head. She felt his forefingers against her temples, the tips of his fingers resting by the sides of her eyes, and she felt the pain in her head begin to fade. It ebbed and flowed like the coming and going of the tide, the headache gradually waning. First, the pain receded from her teeth. Then her forehead stopped throbbing, and she could feel the ache shrink towards the back of her head.

'Very clever... They must really like you,' Sam muttered, 'unfortunately for them, I'm clever-er.'

Like water draining down a plug hole, Alice felt the pounding headache swirl out of the back of her head. It was as if a great weight had been lifted from her. She opened her eyes, and the world appeared like she was seeing it all for the first time. Sam merely grinned at her and said, 'how's your headache now?'

Alice blinked in confusion. Her headache had gone entirely. No remnant of the migraine remained, not even a vague tingling in her teeth. She didn't even feel anxious or panicked. Apparently her look of confusion and realisation was fairly evident, as Sam gave a knowing chuckle.

'How did you do that?' she eventually asked.

'Quite simply,' Sam stated matter-of-factly.

'It's gone completely.'

'When I first bumped into you, I was tracking a rift, a rip in the barrier between our world and another,' Sam began to explain. 'Around Halloween, the veil between worlds is at its thinnest, allowing for easier interactions between different dimensions, even to cross from one plane of existence to another. That entity seized the opportunity to come into our world, taking on the form of a man. Why? I don't know. Maybe the foothold for the coming Darkness... Some of its essence imprinted on you. Something drew it to you, and when I tried to banish it back to the Void, a part of it was left behind. Like a metaphysical bee sting,' Sam paused, and with a sideways smile he added, 'nice costume, by the way.'

'You mean a part of that thing was in me?' Alice exclaimed. 'That's what was causing the headaches. The nightmares?'

'In a manner of speaking, yes. That's why it seemed to still haunt you. But I've removed its essence from your mind, you should sleep soundly tonight.'

Alice nodded, a little dumbstruck by what she was hearing. 'You know this sounds like a very flimsy plot for a fantasy horror story, don't you?' She mocked, but from the little time she had spent with Sam Hain, and the things she had experienced, it was all strangely starting to sound plausible. A few days ago, she was a perfectly normal girl in her twenties, going about a perfectly normal life. Now, she had somehow found herself in a world of demons and monsters and strange men who didn't seem to think twice about breaking and entering. 'Again, why me?'

'I wish I could say that you just happened to be in the wrong place at the wrong time. I really do. And to be honest, that is a large part of what's brought me here. But there's something special about you, Alice. You have a gift not many people have. I saw it in you last night, and I see it in you now,' he said, and he sounded almost sorry for her. 'Let me ask you something, when you were growing up, did you ever believe in monsters under your bed? Hiding in your wardrobe?'

Alice nodded. 'I used to think I could see monsters lurking in the shadows of my bedroom, when I was about nine. Sometimes they appeared to be so real... My mum kept trying to tell me that it was just my imagination, and it was nothing to be scared of.'

'Well, it's not your mother's fault for not knowing. Not a lot of people do, not really,' he said. 'There are things which exist in the places beyond this world. Things from other realms, other dimensions, other realities. They weren't just in your head, Alice, you didn't imagine them... The monsters beneath your bed were real. As were your imaginary friends. You've been given the soul-sight, the ability to see things which others don't, and to distinguish the light and the dark. Whether this is a blessing or a curse is up to you.' He spoke in a tone not unlike an adult telling a child about the dangers of playing with fire. A shiver ran up Alice's spine.

'You're serious, aren't you?' she asked and, on some level, she knew she did not need him to answer. She could sense that what Sam was saying was the truth. 'You're really, properly serious...'

'I don't joke around with things like this,' he replied, his face like stone.

'So, that thing... It doesn't feel like it's in my head any more, and I can't see it. It's finally gone?'

'Oh no, quite the contrary. It's still here, somewhere,' Sam said with a dismissive wave of his hand, 'I just removed its hold on your mind. But now that its link to you is severed, I doubt it's going to be very happy...'

As if on cue, there was a sudden, ear-piercing scream from outside. 'That'll be for us then,' Sam said with a grin, and in one swift motion he jumped up, threw on his hat, unlocked the door and sprinted off down the corridor.

Alice started after him, running along the corridor and down the stairs only a few steps behind, being careful not to step on Sam's coat as it billowed out and trailed on the staircase behind him. They heard another terrified scream coming from the street, and Sam leapt down the last few steps and barged through the front door. As Alice followed, she could see the light from the streetlights flickering on the pavement just outside of the door.

In the middle of the street stood Rachel, two pizza boxes balanced in her arms with a plastic bag slung around her wrist, and a man, a hood pulled low, partially concealing his face, walking slowly towards her. He moved in an eerie, inhuman manner, his body twitching erratically, and his hollow eyes were as black as the night. Alice's heart dropped. The unearthly being staggered towards Rachel with its uneven gait. Occasionally it would appear to crack, like old plaster peeling away from a wall. The streetlights flickered on and off as the creature approached, and each light it passed would fade to darkness. The road behind it was completely shrouded in the shadow of the night, the light of almost every home and lamppost now dead.

'That's-'

'The thing from your nightmares? Yes, I know.

Persistent bugger,' Sam whispered, and reached into his pocket, withdrawing something which looked like a wand. Except it wasn't quite a wand. It was a narrow metallic tube, its chrome-like sheen glistening in the dark, with a clear, pointed crystal attached to one end, and a rounded, shiny black stone at the other. From the way he was holding it, Alice presumed the pointed crystal was the front. Putting on a pair of circular sunglasses, Sam raised the metal wand and aimed it towards the hooded entity. 'Someone's clearly not very happy I broke its hold on you.'

Rachel remained in the middle of the road, standing entirely still, staring directly at the man in the hood, her mouth hanging silently agape, frozen in fear as the thing approached her. The inexplicable shadow emanating from the man stretched out, causing the remaining streetlights to go out, and an unnatural darkness descended upon them all. Wordlessly, Rachel dropped the pizza boxes to the floor.

'Hey, you! Person!' Sam shouted towards the inanimate woman in the road.

'Rachel,' Alice said helpfully.

'Rachel! I'd step away from the being of unimaginable darkness if I was you,' he said, but she didn't seem to hear him.

Taking a couple of steps forward, Sam addressed the creature. 'You know you don't belong here,' he declared, and the being in the hood stopped. It remained stock still in the middle of the road, a few paces from Rachel. Its body convulsed and juddered, and from somewhere in the shadows beneath its hood, the creature hissed viciously at Sam. 'I sent you back to the Void, and you just came crawling back. But your power is fading, and try as you might you can feel your grip on this plane weakening. Now, you can either do the sensible thing and go grovelling back to your Dark Masters, or you can try your luck with me.'

The creature leered forwards. It began to stagger towards Rachel again, and wisps of shadow reached out to her.

'Oh, suit your-bloody-self,' Sam said, almost wearily, and he raised his wand, pointing it at the creature. 'Being of Darkness, Devourer of Light, I banish thee back to the Void from whence thee came!'

The creature writhed uncomfortably as Sam spoke, hissing and spitting in defiance. But nothing happened. The darkness continued to spread, unabated by Sam's magick, and tentacle-like shadows lapped at Rachel's feet, coiling around and around, until one latched onto her ankle. The creature seemed to have her completely paralysed. Sam spun on his heel and faced Alice.

'Alice, this thing has a foothold on this world and, like it or not, it used you as an anchor. When it left a part of itself in your mind, it was like a foot in the interdimensional doorway. I need you to be one-hundred percent focused.'

Alice felt fear grip her once again and she tried to look him in the eyes, but she couldn't see through the dark lenses of the circular glasses. She nodded uncertainly to him.

'Good. Now, I need you to cast this demon to Hell.'

'What? How do I-? What?' Alice stammered. She glanced over towards the entity, the body of the hooded man now swathed in darkness, a shadowy form of something far more sinister and foreboding looming large behind him.

'My will alone can't banish this thing. It used your mind to bring itself into this world, and your mind can send it back.'

Alice steeled herself for the worst. Twenty-four hours ago, she had been at a Halloween costume party, forgetting about the day-to-day reality and having a good time. Upon reflection, her life had taken a very decided nose-dive from the moment King Kong threw up on her shoes. Now, everything which had once been the day-to-day seemed

like a distant memory. She would've been afraid, but fear no longer seemed like a strong enough emotion to describe what she was feeling. It was like being called up in front of the class to do a presentation in primary school, but a thousand times worse and involved shadow demons from another dimension. She glanced back at Sam, her eyes watering. He simply nodded to her.

'I banish thee to the void from whence thee came,' Alice said, her voice wavering uncertainly. She was about ready to crumble and collapse to the floor. The creature in the man in the hood snapped its head at an unnatural angle to face her, and she froze in place. *I can't do this*, she thought, *why the hell am I even in this mess? I don't- I can't-*

'Believe in the words you're saying, Alice,' Sam said, 'believe you have the power to send this thing back to the Void. Nine-tenths of magick is intent. A spell is nothing but empty words if you don't believe in it.' Sam held his hand out to her, and smiled gently. 'Take my hand, we'll do this together.'

Something about the man called Sam Hain was peculiarly calming. Maybe it was something about the way he spoke, she didn't know, but Alice felt her nerves slowly begin to settle. Hesitantly, she took hold of Sam's hand, and felt his grip tighten.

'Now let's send this bugger back to the shadows, hey? Let's show them not to mess with Sam and Alice!'

'We banish thee to the Void from whence thee came!' They shouted in unison, and Alice felt an energy course through her veins. It tingled and surged throughout her body like electricity, resonating in every fibre of her being. It felt as if she was being enveloped in some kind of etheric energy. For a brief moment, her essence seemed to meld into Sam's too. The crystal at the tip of the wand began to glow.

A bolt of violet energy burst from the wand and struck

the man squarely in the chest. The thing that looked like a man began to convulse, its body shook violently, and a brilliant light erupted from its eyes and mouth, ablaze in violet fire, as it screamed an unearthly scream. Its limbs wobbled uselessly at its sides. There was a sudden flash of dazzling light which forced Alice and Rachel to cover their eyes. When they were able to look again, the figure of a man had disappeared, and where it had once stood only a pair of shoes remained. One by one, all of the lights along the street fizzled back on.

'What just happened?' Rachel asked, her voice wavering and a look of fear mixed with confusion washing across her face.

'Halloween trick,' Sam said nonchalantly without missing a beat. He removed the sunglasses and put them back inside his coat's pocket, along with the thing which resembled a wand. 'Good, isn't it?'

'B-but, the smouldering shoes? The, the-'

'Amateur theatrics. Not as good as some of the stuff they can do on the West End, but this has been our best trick yet. Wouldn't you say, Alice?' He nudged her with his elbow and tilted his head towards her, waggling his eyebrows.

'Oh, yeah. Yes. Definitely,' Alice stammered. Everything she had experienced had finally caught up with her, and she was feeling more than a little overwhelmed by it all.

Despite everything which had just taken place in front of her, this seemed to be a good enough explanation for Rachel. She knelt down to pick up the pizza boxes and made her way towards the door to the townhouse. 'If these pizzas are ruined because of your little trick, you're paying for them, mister,' she shouted, and hurriedly disappeared through the front door.

'You know, I really didn't think she'd buy that,' Alice said, looking up at Sam.

'Nor did I...'

They both stood in silence for a while, staring at the pair of shoes which now sat in the middle of the road in Islington, a few faint wisps of smoke still drifting from them and dissipating in the cold night breeze. It was still and serenely quiet on the street, and for the first time in what felt like forever, Alice didn't have a sense of dread hanging over her.

'The Earth plane is shifting again. In a few hours, the divide between this world and the next won't be quite as thin,' Sam said, standing with his head towards the sky, as if he could feel the change in the wind. 'You can feel it too, can't you?'

'This is all so... insane,' Alice said to him. Sam simply nodded.

'I understand. It's a bit much to take in all at once. When you've had some time to process this, or if you ever need anything, here's my card.' He handed her a business card. It was black with golden text, and a pentagram in its centre.

Sam Hain
Occult Detective
Divination – Evocation
Astral Projection – Magickal Protection

'If you do decide to venture down this particular rabbit hole, please get in touch. I could use someone with your skills. After all, the walls between worlds may be building back up, but things are never as normal as they appear.' He secured his hat firmly on his head, and with a final nod he bid her farewell. 'I have a feeling this won't be the last I'll be seeing of you, Alice Carroll. Until our paths cross again. Take care.'

Alice watched as the strange man walked down the road, his coat billowing in the cold night air. For the briefest of moments, she was sure she could see the glimmer of an aura around his figure, but in the blink of an eye it was gone. Although she could not quite explain everything, she felt as if something important had happened to her. She turned and made her way back towards the door of the townhouse, and she cast one last glance over her shoulder towards Sam, but he was already gone, vanished into the night.

She stood for quite some time, staring down the street and out into the night, lost in her thoughts.

'Do you want your pizza or what?' She could hear Rachel calling out to her from the second-floor window.

'Just coming,' Alice shouted back, looking up at the window with a wave. She skipped over the doorstep, closed the door, and walked back up the stairs towards the flat.

It was perfectly, reassuringly normal inside. The lights cast a warm glow over the room, where Rachel was sat on the sofa flicking through the channels on the TV. The smell of fresh takeaway pizza and chips filled the air.

'Fancy a drink?' Alice asked as she flung her coat over the back of the sofa.

'Yeah, please. Cider's in the fridge,' Rachel said. She must have bought the whole Halloween trick thing, because she didn't seem to have a care in the world. 'What do you want to watch?'

'I don't know, what's on?'

Rachel began to reel off the exhaustive list on the TV guide, but Alice didn't hear a word of what she was saying. She stood in the entrance to the kitchen, dumbstruck, faced with the horror which awaited her. The contents of the bins, strewn across the room from Sam's haphazard investigation, still in the state of chaos he had left them in.

That bastard.

Sam Hain

Occult Detective

A Night in
Knightsbridge

Prologue

It had been a long, tedious, and stressful day for Elena Turner.

She and her family had recently moved into their new home in Knightsbridge. It was a large, three-storey, Regency era townhouse overlooking a private residential garden. Only residents of Cadmus Square had the keys to enter the garden and experience this quiet, gentrified slice of the city, tucked away from the bustling crowds of Brompton Road and Hyde Park. It was like it was in its own ostentatious little bubble, each of the houses boasting traditional Georgian front facades and expensive-looking saloon cars parked against the curb; it was every bit as posh and pretentious as it sounds.

However, for Elena, behind the facade it told a very different story.

It is no coincidence that the words "moving house" and "fun" are very rarely uttered in the same sentence, and when they are it's often with a healthy dose of sarcasm. A week after moving in, 32 Cadmus Square looked less like a family home and more of a particularly stately storage space. Most of the furniture was now placed precisely as Elena and her husband, Lloyd, had imagined it when they first viewed the property, but each room was piled high with unpacked boxes from floor to ceiling. And the ceilings were quite high, as the estate agent had been very keen to point out.

Conveniently, Lloyd was occupied with meetings and drawing up contracts for a high profile business deal (the details of which he could not divulge), so he spent most of his time in the office while Elena took on the seemingly Sisyphean task of turning this house into a home. She wondered, wearily, as she tried to move a rather large oakwood bookcase by herself, whether Lloyd was only doing so much work at the office to get out of the work at home. She wouldn't put it past him. With an involuntary grunt, she heaved the bookcase by an inch, and concluded that that was as good of a place as any.

Her day had been spent, almost exclusively and terribly dully, sorting out the study. She had unpacked boxes, stacked books and placed ornaments on shelves, shifted furniture around, and set up the computer. When the computer refused to connect to anything beyond her email account, Elena spent a good hour trying to call up their provider, only to have *Greensleeves* play on a seemingly endless loop down the phone at her. She gave up twice before having any success getting through to the call centre. Then she discovered, upon moving one of the bookcases to put it nearer the desk, that a large portion of one of the walls was growing patches of black mould. It was one of the risks of purchasing a Grade II listed house, she thought, but it was a problem nonetheless. The rising damp had managed to spread onto the back of the bookcase, too, and damaged a number of the as-yet-unpacked boxes. Moving house was rarely a relaxing experience at the best of times, without having to contend with rising damp damaging one's property.

Between cleaning mould off of the walls and shelves and anything else that had been damaged, Elena also had to look after Charlie, their seven-year-old son. It wasn't easy, keeping an eye on the young boy and making sure he was entertained, while not wanting him to get anywhere near the mould growth. By the time she had finished cleaning everything off, moved the bookcases back to where they were, and Charlie was happily playing with his dinosaur toys in the living room, everything looked exactly the way it had done before she had even started. Lloyd had not been happy when he came home only to find that nothing had been done in *his* study (despite the fact that they had agreed it was a shared work room). Quite why he couldn't do it himself, especially if it really was as easy as he kept saying it was, was beyond her.

Another wasted day, she thought to herself as she took off her bathrobe and stepped into the shower. She turned the taps as far as they would turn, and a powerful stream of steaming hot water shot out of the shower-head. Closing her eyes, Elena tipped her head back and let the water spray onto her face and trickle down her body. She was quite ready to call it a day, just relax in the shower for quarter of an hour and then get into bed. Not that she was getting much sleep at the moment, anyway. She rolled her head around, feeling the aching tension that had been built up in her shoulders, and sighed.

She had only been in the shower five minutes when she suddenly heard something crashing. Opening her eyes, she paused and listened out for anything else, but heard nothing. Turning off the shower, she stepped out into the steam-filled bathroom, wrapping her bathrobe around herself. In the corner of the room, she could see that the contents of the cabinet had emptied out onto the floor, its door hanging wide open. Shampoo and conditioner bottles were strewn about the room, and numerous other cosmetics lay in a pile beneath the cabinet. Elena picked up the scattered toiletries and started to put them carefully back in the cabinet, shutting it firmly, and stepped back in surprise. Across the steamed-up surface of the cabinet's mirrored door, in big, capital letters, were the words: "THE VOID AWAKENS. DARKNESS IS COMING".

'Very funny!' Elena said sarcastically, walking into the living room with her bathrobe wrapped around her and her hair hidden up inside the large beehive-like towel on her head. Lloyd was sat in the armchair by the fireplace, reading a book.

'What've I done now?'

'The writing in the mirror. You know how spooked I've

been about all this ghost stuff recently. I don't like you taking the piss out of me like this!'

Ever since moving in, Elena had been convinced that she had seen a ghost wandering around the house, and on one occasion thought she had seen it knocking crockery off of the kitchen counters. Sometimes she even thought she could hear someone whispering to her in the dead of night (although she couldn't quite hear what they were saying), or walking up the stairs and opening and closing doors. There was never anybody there, though.

'What writing in the mirror?' Lloyd had a look of genuine confusion on his face. Elena felt her heart sink. If it had been him, he would have had that irritating smug smirk of his plastered across his face.

'That wasn't you?'

'I haven't done anything. Wasn't Charlie?'

'Darling, I don't mean to sound sarky, but do you really think a seven-year-old would write a message of foreboding like "the void awakens, darkness is coming" on a mirror he can't even reach?'

Lloyd sat in a vacant silence. He briefly glanced down at his book, and then back up to Elena. He cleared his throat uncomfortably. 'No, I suppose not.'

Fiddling nervously with one of the rings on her fingers, Elena sat down in the chair opposite her husband. She gazed distantly into the fireplace, lost in thought. 'We need a psychic, a medium or an exorcist or something,' she said conclusively.

Lloyd looked up at her sceptically, and returned to reading his book.

CHAPTER I

It had been a slow week for Sam Hain.

The life of an occult detective was a strange and unpredictable one, one which was often spent dealing with the weird and the fantastical. However, much like most other walks of life, the supernatural sleuth would hit the occasional slump. There was the odd mysterious occurrence, inexplicable bursts of light in the sky or things that went bump in the night, but Sam was starting to feel bored. The transmundane had begun to seem more and more mundane. The most interesting case that had been presented to him that week, which had promised to be an exciting hunt for a particularly destructive poltergeist, turned out to be little more than a mischievous and clumsy cat.

It was only while idly browsing online late one evening, perusing paranormal forums for a good mystery or extraordinary event to sink his teeth into, that Sam finally found something that sparked his interest. It was exactly the kind of thing he had been looking for and, he thought, a good introductory case for his new associate, Alice Carroll.

It had been over a month since Alice had last seen Sam. Their first and last meeting – when Alice had been haunted by visions of a being from another realm on Halloween – had left her feeling like she'd tumbled down the rabbit hole into a world far stranger than she could ever have imagined. She had checked out the occult detective's website shortly after their first encounter, to try to find out more about this strange man. His blog hadn't really given her much more of an insight into the life of Sam Hain; he didn't update it very regularly, and when he did it was either to write brief overviews of former cases or vague, mysterious posts.

Since then, Alice had been feeding her curiosity, trying to learn more about the supernatural world and researching the paranormal (when she wasn't busy with work), and she'd tried to keep in touch with Sam as and when she could. He wasn't the easiest person to keep in contact with, and at one point she didn't hear from him for over a week, but he always got back to her in the end.

She'd been asking him about his line of work, enquiring about the supernatural and learning more about the wondrous and fantastical things which exist just outside of the boundaries of reality. In between being cryptically vague about his own experiences, Sam had suggested a number of resources for Alice to read through, but warned her that in amongst the mystery, intrigue and magick, darker forces often lurk in the shadows. As much as Alice's own experience had left her feeling shaken, and Sam's sinister and foreboding warnings had further added to her fear, she felt far too intrigued to simply turn away from all of this now. A part of her still remained dubious, but her own curiosity drove her to find out more.

In her spare time, she'd browsed the websites Sam had recommended, with a mix of fascination and cynicism. Some of the "eye-witness" testimonies and rumoured happenings sounded like works of fiction, and others were clearly written by people who were desperate to find something extraordinary in the ordinary (her favourite of these was the idea that all clouds were secretly alien spaceships, simply disguised as clouds so they didn't startle anyone), but amongst them all there were a few cases which Alice thought seemed credible. Some even bore similarities to her own experiences, and reading them was all too hauntingly familiar.

Sam had also sent her what he called his official manual, or as she had now dubbed it: Demonology for Dummies.

It wasn't so much a manual as it was a large, well-worn notebook with Sam's handwriting scrawled across its pages in an almost entirely illegible manner. Amongst the pages of scribbled sentences and bullet-pointed notes from former cases were a handful of poorly drawn illustrations of things Alice couldn't even begin to recognise. Somewhere towards the middle of the book, between a page about metaphysical parasites and something about interdimensional portals, was a surprisingly normal shopping list.

Alice had only briefly skimmed over the pages of the notebook, but amongst the scrawlings and indecipherable text, some of it had caught her interest. Before meeting Sam, she had never really given the supernatural much thought – not since childhood, anyway – and had it not been for him then she probably would have ended up seeing a therapist about her hallucinations. But everything Sam had introduced her to since Halloween had reignited her imagination and opened her eyes to a new world. She wanted to discover and experience these things first hand and, after much deliberation, she decided to take Sam up on his offer. She was ready to join him on one of his cases.

One evening, after amusing herself with reading the latest blog post on a website titled "Clouds: What are they really?", she sent Sam a message asking about joining him on one of his adventures, and waited. It was almost three days before he replied to her, and when he did it was ambiguous and brief.

Would be my pleasure, the message read, *have just the thing in mind. Meet in Knightsbridge, outside the tube station, tonight, 6pm. -SH*

The evening was cold and windy, as many a winter's night tended to be in London. The stars were blotted out by a sickeningly beige mass of clouds hanging low over the city, and the occasional cold spattering of rain added an extra chill to the air. Christmas decorations adorned every shop and street, and the roads of Knightsbridge were alive with shoppers, rushing about in the bright lights of the street and the warm glow of the shop windows.

Standing outside of the London Underground station, Alice pulled her coat tightly around herself and folded her arms. She had been waiting in the cold for a quarter of an hour now, and was staring longingly at the people who were settling down to large mugs of coffee in warm, cosy-looking cafés. Sam had only told her to meet him there at that time, nothing of what they were going to be doing and, despite her intrigue, Alice was starting to feel nervous. She habitually checked the time on her phone. Sam was now ten minutes late. Glancing around, she noticed a familiar silhouette striding towards her, overcoat billowing out behind it and hat slightly slanting to the right.

Sam Hain walked up to her, and tipped the rim of his hat in greeting.

'You're late!' Alice mockingly accosted him.

'I'm never late! I may not always be on time, but I turn up exactly when I'm meant to,' he retorted, a wry grin on his face. 'Hope you weren't waiting too long.'

'Only twenty minutes or so. Could do with warming up a bit.' She looked longingly at one of the inviting cafés. It looked warm and comfortable in there; its rosy-cheeked customers reclined luxuriously on cushiony sofas, their winter coats draped over the backs of their seats, as they sipped from large mugs piled high with whipped cream and marshmallows, with decadent slices of cake on the tables next to them. Decorated fir trees glittered festively, standing several feet taller than the customers, filling the place with Christmas cheer.

'Let's find somewhere to go and warm up then,' Sam said, and he started to head down the road towards the parade of shops.

The chip shop they soon found themselves in was fairly standard as far as chip shops were concerned. The white tiled floor was by no means shiny, slightly grimy from the occasional dropped and trampled food and splatterings of vinegar and ketchup, but still the floor glared under the fluorescent lights.

As they entered, Sam and Alice were greeted by the sight of the Happy Fish (for that is what the shop was called), a large cartoonish cod standing proudly by the counter, a broad smile across its face and giving a reassuring thumbs up in the direction of the door. This was not nearly as reassuring as it was probably meant to be, because – as Sam rightly pointed out – fish do not have thumbs with which to give a thumbs up, nor are they able to smile broadly. Secondly, the overly cheery mascot was completely at odds with the man behind the counter, who glared at nothing in particular while he miserably shovelled chips into small polystyrene boxes.

The man grunted as he thrust two polystyrene boxes over the counter, and scattered the change for the chips vaguely in Sam's direction. Not all of the coins managed to stay on the countertop. Holding the boxes in one hand and scooping up his change, as well as some unidentifiable crumbs, with the other, Sam walked over to the table where Alice was sitting. He placed one of the portions in front of her, taking a seat in the uncomfortable plastic chair opposite her. Producing two tiny chip-forks from his coat pocket, he handed one to her. She looked at him and raised a sarcastic eyebrow.

'You really know how to treat a lady...'

'Well, I'm sorry I couldn't see any empty seats in the other cafés. Anyway, it's sort of all right here, isn't it?'

The man who had gruntingly served them came to the table carrying their two cups of coffee. He indelicately placed the polystyrene cups down on the table, spilling coffee on Sam's chips in the process, grunted again, and walked away. Sam looked dejectedly at his now coffee-soaked chips, and picked one up to inspect it. The chip flopped loosely between his fingers, dripping with murky brown liquid. With a tentative nibble, he gave a surprised 'hmm!' and a strangely approving nod. Alice sampled one of her chips (without a coffee dressing), and discovered that it was actually quite good. The coffee, she learned, was disappointing at best.

'So, how've you been?' Sam eventually asked, through a mouthful of chips.

'Fine, I suppose. No demons have tried to set up camp in my head, so all things considered I'd say I'm doing pretty well,' Alice said. She treated the situation with more levity now than she had at the time, but the memory of what happened that night still made her feel uneasy.

'Always a good thing,' he nodded, taking a gulp of his coffee and grimacing.

'And how have things been with you? Any exciting adventures?' she asked.

'Bored, mostly. Things have been quite quiet, no paranormal phenomena really worth investigating,' he paused momentarily, as he thought about everything he had done since they'd last met. 'Most of my cases recently have turned out to be nothing more than faulty plumbing, clumsy cats and some easily spooked clients. Actually, you were my last interesting case,' he added. It sounded almost as if Sam had complimented Alice, but it was difficult to tell.

'So, I'm curious... What are we doing here?' She looked at Sam and noticed a glint in his eyes. 'And before you say anything, I know we're eating chips.' The glint disappeared, and he looked down, disappointed, as if she'd just spoiled the punchline.

'Well,' he began, and leaned in, taking care to not plant his elbow in any of the spilt coffee, 'you recall that around the time I met you, there was something about "darkness is coming"?'

Alice nodded and a cold frisson ran down her spine. She shivered involuntarily as the demon's ominous words resonated in the back of her mind.

'I've been doing some searching,' Sam continued, 'trying to find any other references to it. I've seen signs, heard whispers, but nothing substantial. For a while, it seemed like yours was an isolated case, the only direct incident, but then I found this...' He trailed off as he reached into his coat pocket and pulled out a small notebook. He removed some poorly folded sheets of paper from between its pages and pushed them across the table to her. Intrigued, Alice unfolded the pages and examined them.

'There's a house just around the corner that's apparently being haunted by a poltergeist,' he said, as Alice looked over the information he had printed out.

On the first page, in a large, bold typeface, was the title: "Help! I think my house is haunted." It was a post on a forum for would-be ghost hunters, written by a woman named Elena Turner. She had recently moved into a new house in the Knightsbridge area with her husband and seven-year-old son, and after just one viewing they had put an offer in immediately. The estate agent had been delighted to sell the property so soon. Although the Turners had fallen in love with their new home almost instantly, ever since moving in Elena had felt a lingering sense of uneasiness. She initially put this down to the stress everyone suffered when moving house, and she didn't think much of it at first and simply carried on as usual. That was until last week, when things had taken a turn for the inexplicable.

The next page showed photographs, taken on Elena's phone, of broken crockery and smashed glass tumblers – allegedly targeted by the ghost – and a picture of the staircase in which "the shadow of a person can clearly be seen." It was more of a vaguely humanoid-shaped patch in the image that was a slightly darker shade than the rest of it, and Alice was starting to feel sceptical. It wasn't until she turned to the next page that something caught her attention.

'Darkness is coming,' Sam said as Alice read the words. Another photograph showed the three words written on the steamed-up surface of a bathroom mirror, along with the equally ominous "the void awakens." Although this kind of evidence for ghostly activity could easily be faked, the fact that it echoed Alice's own experience with the supernatural could not be ignored.

'This can't be coincidence,' Alice said, and Sam nodded in agreement.

'No such thing as a coincidence. The Universe is rarely so lazy.'

The post continued to describe how things would move seemingly without cause, and sometimes things would mysteriously disappear. Nothing quite as simple as a pair of glasses or a set of keys, these things had a habit of vanishing by themselves, but at one point the butter dish went missing from the fridge for an hour, before reappearing again on one of the arm chairs in the living room with less butter than it had left with. On other occasions, cups and plates would smash, as if they were pushed off of the kitchen counters by an invisible hand. Disembodied noises could be heard throughout the house, like someone moving furniture or knocking on the door, and Elena sometimes thought she could hear someone whispering to her. Her son also suffered from recurring nightmares of being chased by monsters, which Elena was now sure was connected to the haunting.

'I got in touch with the woman who wrote this earlier this week, and I've offered to investigate their situation. She and her husband are expecting me there this evening. I was wondering, if you're interested, whether you'd like to join me on the case?' Sam grinned at Alice. He already knew her answer.

'Absolutely!' she exclaimed, and the man behind the counter looked up and grunted in admonishment. With a final gulp of the drink that wasn't quite coffee, Sam stood up and threw his coat on.

'Let's get going, then.'

CHAPTER II

The night was even colder than before, and a light fog was starting to settle on the city. Alice and Sam walked along the darkened road towards a terrace of tall and slender Georgian houses which overlooked the private garden in the middle of Cadmus Square. As they approached the Turners' home, Sam strode purposefully along the pavement, bounded up the steps towards the front door and knocked. A light came on in the hallway, dimly lighting the doorstep from a small window above the door frame. They could hear the sound of jangling keys, the repeated clunking of the lock, and a man angrily muttering 'bloody thing...' from the other side. Eventually, the door swung open to reveal a ginger haired man in a comfortable looking green jumper. He wore a haggard look on his face.

'Good evening. I'm Sam Hain – occult detective and expert in all things supernatural – and this is my friend and colleague, Alice Carroll. We're here about your ghost.' Sam stood proudly, straightening his coat lapels with an air of self-importance, and extended his hand in greeting.

'Ah, yes, Elena said we'd be expecting you. Lloyd, Lloyd Turner,' the man replied. Traditionally, this would be the point when one would shake the other person's hand, but Lloyd simply turned to head back inside. 'Come in, then,' he said, gesturing for them to follow him, 'you'll have to excuse the mess, we moved in last month and we've only just got the place looking like home.'

The house was not in a mess. For a house that had only been moved into a month previously, it was astoundingly neat. There were no traces of boxes or of furniture that had yet to find its place in the home, and the house itself seemed spotless. Lloyd led Sam and Alice through to the living room, where the lights were on low and an open fireplace burned and crackled contently, bathing the room in a warm glow.

'Take a seat, I'll be back in a moment,' Lloyd said, indicating an arrangement of green velvet armchairs by the fireside. Alice and Sam sat down as their host left the room, and the head of Elena Turner peered around the door.

'I'll be with you in a sec, just making some tea,' she said, and her head disappeared back behind the door again.

Sam peered around the room with curiosity. The four armchairs were seated a comfortable distance from the fire, which seemed to be the heart of the room. A spotless coffee table sat in the middle of the armchairs. Two bookcases stood in the corner by the front window, their shelves lined with a vast array of books from the complete collection of Shakespeare's plays to the numerous works by Plato. Various ornaments and pictures decorated the rest of the room. The place was incredibly well-kept, which, for a house that had only recently been moved into and was allegedly being terrorised by a ghost, was nothing short of incredible. Sam had stood up to look at the picture hanging above the fireplace (a piece reminiscent of van Gogh) when Elena and Lloyd returned. Elena placed a tea tray – laden with cups and saucers, a large, steaming teapot, and a selection of biscuits – down on the coffee table. Sam sat back down, and poured himself a cup.

Lloyd reclined in the seat opposite the two of them. His ginger hair and beard seemed to be ablaze in the fire-light, and his eyes were a very prominent shade of green. He took a sip of his tea, and placed it back on its saucer. His wife sat down next to him. Elena Turner was a mousey-haired woman, and she appeared to be several years younger than her husband, but signs of ageing were beginning to show around her brown eyes.

Both of them looked like they had not had a decent

night's sleep in several weeks.

'So, Mister Hain. Your message said you might be able to help with our, uhm, problem,' Elena said.

'Indeed, I believe I can,' Sam said, and he leaned forward towards the pair of them. 'I'll need your utmost trust in this matter, though. Both of you.'

Elena nodded. 'Of course.'

Lloyd simply replied with a non-commital 'hrrmm.'

'Excellent!' Sam clapped his hands together, and leaned back into the armchair. 'Well then, could you please describe exactly what's been going on here.'

'Well, we moved in about a month ago, and everything was fine,' Elena started to explain. 'We began unpacking, getting the house together and decorating, and that's when the trouble started. I wrote about most of it on the forum. You know, things like cups breaking, as if someone was pushing them off of the sides, and strange noises in the night. I've even seen these, uh, apparitions. Of a person, like a ghost, upstairs on the landing.'

Sam nodded as he listened to Elena's account, although he already knew most of these details. Lloyd hadn't said a word about any of it and had simply sat there, sipping his tea and watching Sam with a sceptical eye from over the rim of his teacup.

'And what about you, Mister Turner?' Sam enquired. 'Have you experienced any of this supernatural activity?'

Lloyd Turner was a stoic looking man; he was the kind of person who could break his leg, wince for a second, and almost instantly return to stone-faced neutrality as if nothing had happened. His face remained unchanging as he answered. 'I'm not going to lie to you, Mister Hain. I'm not a believer in ghosts. There are often perfectly reasonable, rational explanations to what others may attribute to the supernatural.'

'And what of the writing in the bathroom mirror?' Sam

asked, removing the crumpled paper from his pocket and pointing at the picture of the steamed-up mirror. 'When did this happen?'

'This was taken about a week ago,' Elena said, taking the paper from Sam and looking at the image. 'We can't think of any explanation for it. What do you make of it, Mister Hain?'

'Please, call me Sam. And that's what I'm here to find out. It takes a fair amount of effort for something ethereal to influence the real, so whoever and whatever did this is determined to get your attention,' he said, consulting one of the other pieces of paper he had printed off. 'You also mentioned your son has been having recurring nightmares?'

Elena nodded. 'Yes, ever since we moved in Charlie's had dreams that he's being chased by monsters. He often wakes up in tears...'

'Do these dreams coincide with any of the other activity you've noticed? For example, Charlie waking up from a nightmare around the same time you spotted the apparition.'

'Sometimes, yes. I think so.'

'Okay. Well, I already have my suspicions about what we're dealing with here. Would it be all right with you both if my colleague and I stayed a while to figure things out?'

'Of course,' Elena said with a faint smile.

'Thank you.' Sam stood up and made his way towards the living room door. 'Just one more thing, Misses Turner-'

'Just call me Elena.'

'Okay then. Just one more thing, Elena, do you know if you have any electrical issues in this house?'

'It's an old build. Fuses can be a bit of a bugger sometimes. Why'd you ask?' Lloyd interjected.

'Oh, it's just that your lights appear to be flickering.'

The lights were indeed flickering, and despite the fireplace lighting up most of the room, the fluctuating brightening and dimming of the light-bulbs was slowly becoming more and more noticeable.

'I don't know if you've noticed this before, but in cases like this, paranormal activity is often preceded by disruptions to electrics,' Sam said, and as if on cue the lights went out completely, leaving the room lit only by the warm light of the fire.

'See. This is exactly the kind of thing I mean,' Elena said.

'Damn fuse must have gone again...' Lloyd said as he stood up and made his way out of the room to find the fusebox.

Alice walked over and stood by Sam's side, looking around the room nervously. 'What's going on?'

He brashly shushed her and stood silently, surveying the room, searching for the faintest hint of activity. Nothing happened. He turned to Elena. 'Does this happen a lot?'

'It's happened four times now. Twice in the past week alone,' she replied, looking nervously around the darkened room.

Alice moved slowly into the centre of the living room. She felt something unusual, something almost like the prelude to a thunderstorm but with decidedly less rain. The air had become stale, unmoving, and the atmosphere seemed to be inexplicably heavy. It was as if the pressure in the room was slowly building up. There was a sudden, loud bang as something hit the floor, causing Alice and Elena to jump. It startled Sam, too, but he tried not to show it.

A book had fallen off of one of the shelves, landing at the foot of the bookcase, as if someone had simply pushed it off. There was no slant in the shelves or the floor to suggest it was merely an act of gravity. Tentatively making his way over to it, Sam knelt down to examine the book.

'Hmm, Edgar Allan Poe,' he said with a tone of approval, and was struck in the back of the head by another book. 'Christ almighty,' he muttered, rubbing where it had hit.

Another book flew off of the shelf, striking Sam again, and another propelled itself towards Alice. She ducked just in time, narrowly dodging *War and Peace*, and it struck the wall behind her with a papery thud. *A Remembrance of Things Past* flew over Sam's head and soared straight into the door. Elena had scurried over to take cover behind the door, holding it open and using it like a shield. Sam and Alice quickly followed her example. They strategically retreated to the door, ducking and weaving as the bookcase continued to take pot-shots at them, until they took shelter out of the bookcase's clear line of sight.

There were two more thuds of books striking wood, and then silence. The minute all three of them were safely behind the door, things stopped flying off of the shelves. The lights suddenly flickered back into life. Alice felt the pressure in the room lift and return to normal, as if someone had just opened a window and a gust of fresh air had blown through the place. Sam moved back into the middle of the room, and looked around. Several books now lay strewn across the room, but there were no other signs of disturbance. Elena began to pick up the books and return them to their shelves, and Alice started to help her while Sam stood obliviously looking around the room.

'Had to turn the bloody fusebox off and on again,' Lloyd announced, returning to the now perfectly lit room. It took him a few moments to notice that things were not quite how he had left them. 'Why're my books on the floor?'

'Had a bit of an incident. Your ghost started throwing things at us,' Sam said. 'If it's all right with you, we'll stay to investigate this room a bit further.'

Elena nodded in agreement. 'Will you need us to stay in

here too?'

'No, no,' Sam replied, 'just go about your evening as usual and we'll see what happens. I'll let you know as soon as I have something.'

'Thank you,' Elena said, and Lloyd nodded in resigning agreement, 'we'll leave you to it then.' The two of them left the room to go about their evening, leaving Sam and Alice to get to work. As the sound of footsteps slowly making their way up the stairs grew fainter and fainter, Alice was sure she could hear Lloyd's voice grumbling 'bloody ghost nonsense.'

When the Turners were finally upstairs, Sam took the last sip of tea from his cup, and walked over to the offending bookcase. Reaching into the breast pocket of his jacket, he withdrew a strange, rod-like device. Alice faintly recalled the item from the night after Halloween, but she hadn't had a good look at it before. It was a short metallic thing, gleaming and chrome-like, probably no more than ten inches long and about an inch in diameter. It seemed to have symbols faintly inscribed onto its surface. At its tip was a pointed quartz crystal, and at the opposite end a round, polished black stone. To Alice, it resembled a sort of technological wand, as if an electronics store had opened a new department for the modern mage.

Sam started to move the device slowly around the outside of the bookcase, waving it along the shelves. The crystal at the wand's tip seemed to glow with a soft light, brightening and dimming at intervals, and Alice thought she could hear a faint humming sound coming from it. Every now and again, Sam would nod and 'hmm' knowledgeably, briefly examining the device or giving it a tap, and carried on with waving it around.

'What are you doing?' Alice asked, somewhat perplexed as Sam continued to waft the thing about as if he was performing some kind of interpretative dance.

'I'm checking the energy disturbance around the

bookcase,' Sam said, and with a final flourishing wave of the wand, he put it back in his coat pocket. 'There's still some residual energy traces from whatever it was throwing books at us.'

He knelt down next to the bookcase and, producing a small piece of chalk from his back pocket, he quickly drew a five-pointed star, muttering something which sounded like an incantation under his breath.

'What are you doing now?' Alice asked, looking over to the occult detective knelt on the floor, quite happily defacing a stranger's carpet. 'Stop drawing Satanic symbols on the Turners' carpet!'

'It's not Satanic,' he said wearily, 'it's a pentagram, a symbol of magickal power. Its five points represent the four elements: Earth, Air, Fire and Water, plus the fifth element; Magick, Arcana, Spirit, call it what you will. With the fifth point directed upwards, it represents the mind and the spirit binding the elements in magick. A symbol of spiritual shielding, banishing negative energies. It'll keep us safe from more incidents, in this room at least.' He drew a circle around the star, encasing the pentagram, and he turned to face Alice. He saw her dubious expression. 'Don't worry, the chalk will lift right out with a good hoover.'

'So what do you think it was then? A ghost?'

'Almost certainly,' Sam said. He fell back into one of the chairs, bouncing slightly as he landed. 'It's not just a passive apparition either, it's interacting with the physical world. And it seemed quite intent on letting us know we're not welcome. And the message that darkness is coming...' He held his chin between his forefinger and thumb, running them back and forth over his stubble as he thought.

'Just before all of that happened, I felt something. Like pressure was increasing. It was like the room was building up to what was about to happen,' Alice said. She almost didn't mention it, thinking it wasn't worth bringing up or that it would sound strange, but Sam had said several outlandish things in the past few minutes alone. She hoped he might be able to shed some light on what she had sensed.

'That would've been the increase of localised energy in the Akashic Field. It takes a fair amount of effort for something incorporeal to interact with things on our plane of existence, there's bound to be a build up of etheric energy.'

'The whatty field?' Alice looked confused.

'*Akashic* Field. Didn't you read the manual?' He sounded almost accusatory.

'Some of it!' she retorted. 'Just, y'know, not actually the part you're talking about.'

'The Akashic Field is a zero-point subspace nexus that permeates the entirety of existence,' Sam said plainly, as if he was explaining that water is wet. Alice simply stared at him vacantly.

'Could you talk like a normal human being for a change, please?'

'It's kind of like an underlying energy field that connects everything in the Universe. Everything's interconnected, everything bound by the Field to some extent. With the right knowledge, one can feel its energy, learn to tap into it, and even come to use it to interact with the world around them.'

Alice nodded with a vague sense of understanding. 'Like the Force in *Star Wars*?'

'Like the Force in *Star Wars*,' Sam said with a smile.

'So the ghost was Obi-Wan Kenobi-ing those books at us?'

'In a sense... Because the Akashic Field links me to, say, that book there, with the right mental discipline and concentration, I could pick it up and flick to a particular page, read it, and put it back on the shelf, all without lifting a finger.'

'And can you?' Alice asked eagerly.

'No,' he said. He wished he could. 'Anyway, whenever something or someone uses the Akashic Field to interact with the physical world, it causes a temporary increase in the amount of Akasha energy in the area.'

'And that's the weird feeling I had just before things started flying off the shelves? The build-up of Akasha energy?'

Sam nodded. 'Yes.'

'How do you know all this stuff?' Alice asked. What sounded like nonsense to most people seemed to make absolute perfect sense to Sam. The reverse was probably also true.

Sam simply waved dismissively at her. 'I had a Guide,' he said, standing up and starting to pace around the room. He wandered back and forth, occasionally stopping and looking around before carrying on. His face was a mixture of unbreakable focus and yet complete confusion, like a performance artist who'd forgotten their next act. He suddenly whirled around and pointed at Alice.

'I tell you what,' he started, and Alice suddenly had a sinking sensation, knowing what he was about to say next, 'you give it a go.'

She sighed, resigning herself to her new duty as room-pacer, and stood up. 'Okay, what am I doing?'

'Just walk around the room,' Sam said. That was somewhat apparent. 'Tell me where you feel the energy change. We're looking for particular spots in the Akashic Field where the flow of energy shifts, like little energetic eddies in the room.'

'Right, looking for energetic Eddie... And how do I know when I've found him, exactly?'

'No, *eddies*, sort of like whirlpools. Just in this case, it's not a whirlpool in water, but in a living room. You'll know when you've found one,' he said, unhelpfully, throwing himself back into the armchair with a grin, watching Alice intently. She marched from one side of the room to the other and back again, and shrugged.

'Nope, I'm not getting anything,' she said.

'You're doing it too fast, not paying attention. Try to move more slowly and follow your intuition. Close your eyes if that helps,' he said. He suddenly almost sounded like a mentor.

Alice began to move around the room again, not as fast this time, and she shut her eyes. She seemed to slowly glide, as if she was being carried by the flow of an invisible current. She hovered over a spot for a second. There was something different about it, something she could not quite place her finger on. It wasn't real, but somehow it was. A faint tingling in her mind. Sam noticed the hesitation in her step as she swayed back and forth over the spot.

'Trust yourself,' he prompted her, and she found his words to be reassuring. Alice continued to hover over the spot for a second or two more before she opened her eyes and pointed at the floor.

'Okay then, here,' she announced, and there was a glimmer of triumph in her eyes.

Sam stood up and made his way over to where Alice was stood, and removed the chalk from his pocket. 'Here?' he asked as he knelt down by the spot she was pointing to.

'Yes,' Alice said.

'You sure?' he asked, teasingly.

'Relatively sure,' she nodded.

'Certain?'

'Just do whatever the hell it is you have to do, will you!'

Sam chuckled to himself as he drew a small twisting

symbol on the floor. He then scurried over to another part of the room and drew another one. Putting the chalk back in his pocket, Sam dusted off his hands and headed over to the pentagram. He stood in the centre of the symbol, facing in towards the room, and pulled out a dried white leaf and a lighter from one of his pockets.

'Salvia apiana, sacred sage,' he said, holding the leaf up, 'it'll help cleanse the room, and bring the energy back to a more neutral state.' He lit the sacred sage, almost burning his fingers in the process, and a plume of thick white smoke rose from the burning leaf. It smelled herbal and musty, yet oddly refreshing. Still holding the slowly burning leaf, Sam stretched his arms out and waggled his fingers in front of him, closing his eyes.

'I call on elements of Earth and Water, of Air and Fire. Invoke thy energies, weave them higher. Guard this space both day and night; push back the dark, bring in the light. So mote it be.' Sam then clasped his hands together in a single clap, scattering ash and what remained of the charred leaf. Bowing his head, he opened his eyes, and stepped out of the pentagram as if he was stepping over a rope with the sign "please do not walk on the grass."

'There,' he said with a sense of finality, 'that should stop any unwanted guests from entering this room. Now then...' He rifled through the printed pages from Elena's blog. 'I think it's about time we have a look around the rest of the house.'

CHAPTER III

Standing in the hallway at the foot of the staircase, Sam and Alice looked up to the floor above. The landing was dark, faintly illuminated by only a few beams of light which escaped through an open doorway somewhere upstairs. The elongated shadow of Lloyd Turner swept across the landing as he carried a box from one room to another, muttering irritably.

'All right, I think it's best if we split up. I'll take upstairs, you take the downstairs,' Sam said.

'Wait, what? Why?' Alice asked. *I've had books thrown at me from across the room by whatever's in this house*, she thought, *you're not bloody leaving me now!*

'We'll cover more ground. The sooner we finish here, the sooner the Turners can get back to their lives.' He saw her look of concern. 'Don't worry, you'll be fine. Listen, take this,' he said, and produced a small silver pendant from his pocket. It was a five-pointed star within a circle. 'The pentacle will keep you safe.'

'Won't you need it for... something?'

'No, no, don't worry about me. I've got this.' He brandished his wand-like device with a knowing smile. He spun on his heels and began to head up the stairs, taking two steps at a time.

'Wait! What am I looking for?' Alice asked after him as he bounded up the stairs. She wanted to make a good impression on him, but to say that she felt like a fish out of water would have been an understatement.

'Just keep a third-eye out for anything unusual,' he replied before disappearing around the corner and into the dark of the landing above.

Yeah, fine, really useful, Alice thought as she watched him leap away. *No idea what I'm even looking for... Why did I think this was a good idea?* She glanced at the pentacle pendant, its silver chain resting gently across her hand. She unfastened the catch on the chain, and hung the pentacle around her neck.

Pushing open one of the doors which led off from the hallway, Alice peered into the pitch black room beyond. She couldn't see much, only vague shapes illuminated by the small amount of light which was now coming into the room from the hallway. Fumbling around on the inside wall, she felt for the light switch, flicking it when she felt the raised switch beneath her fingers. There was a sudden twanging sound from above. The lights immediately flickered on with a dazzling white light, and Alice found herself in the Turners' kitchen.

The kitchen was a reasonably small room. The walls were lined with cabinets and counters, and a small breakfast bar jutted out into the middle of the room. By the side of the sink, Alice noticed a small pile of cups and saucers, either chipped or smashed into several pieces. She took a closer look, and recognised some of them from Elena's message. She picked up a fragment of a china teacup, and examined it. *I'm guessing these fell victim to the ghost...*

She considered what Sam had said about keeping a "third-eye out" for things, and she tried to focus on what her intuition was telling her. She had never really paid much attention to her intuition, especially not in the way Sam was expecting her to. She often got what she called "vibes" about things, but whenever she did get a vibe it was mostly as an abstract feeling, an indefinable sensation which more often than not made very little sense, and the more she would try to work it out the less sense it would make. Now she thought about it, when she felt vibes about a person or a place, they were not all too dissimilar to the sensations she had experienced in the living room. She felt vaguely confident about trusting her instincts; Sam would've told her if she was wrong earlier on. She just had to trust that she was right.

She tried to feel whether there was another presence in the room with her. Closing her eyes, Alice stood still in the middle of the room. Her arms stretched out instinctively, and she took a deep breath.

Nothing.

Turning to leave the kitchen, concluding there was nothing there, she suddenly felt a strange sensation run through her. It was faint, almost imperceptible, but she had the distinct impression she was being watched by something. Or someone. She froze. She was sure she could hear something, a soft and subtle rustling of movement from somewhere behind her. And it was drawing closer. The hairs on the back of her neck prickled. Slowly, tentatively, Alice began to turn around, craning her neck to look over her shoulders and tried to peer out of the corner of her eye. She warily gazed in the direction of the noise, her breathing shallow and her nerves on edge. There was nothing there.

Something quickly brushed past her leg, and Alice leaped backwards with a stifled shriek. Her mind raced and her heart pounded, but in a fraction of a second she saw what it was. A black, fluffy cat sat at her feet, gazing up at her. She breathed a sigh of relief, kneeling down to stroke the cat and feeling more than a little bit silly.

'I've never been so pleased to see a cat,' she said to the purring creature in front of her. She gently ruffled the fur on its head before standing up. Other than being spooked by a cat – which rolled luxuriously onto its back, begging for more attention – Alice didn't get a ghostly vibe in the kitchen at all. Much to her relief. She turned the light off and pulled the door to behind her, and made her way up the hall into the next room.

The door slowly creaked open as she pushed it. There was a small light towards the far end of the room, a red glow shining through the dark. Feeling around for a light switch, Alice struggled to reach behind the bookcase which was positioned immediately next to the door. She couldn't find the switch. Reaching for her phone, she turned on the torch and shone the light ahead of her and into the room.

It was a fairly narrow room, but seemed to run the full length of the house. The walls were lined entirely with bookcases, adorned with books, ornaments and unopened boxes. At the far end of the room was a large desk, facing out of the window and onto Cadmus Square. A wide-screen monitor sat towards one of the back corners of the desk, its red stand-by light blinking. There was a subtle musty smell about the room, but other than that there was nothing immediately noticeable. Alice idly glanced at the bookcases as she slowly walked through the Turner's study. The place was more cluttered than the rest of what Alice had seen of the house, and she assumed it was being used as extra storage until the Turners had settled in properly.

The light from her phone cast weird and elongated shadows across the room, as jagged and unearthly shapes stretched out and across the walls. Through the corner of her eye, Alice thought she saw something moving in the shadows, but the second she turned to face it there was nothing there and the shadows shrank away from the torch light. Something seemed to dart away from the light, moving through the shadows and over the desk at the other end of the room. Again she shone her torch into the black, and again there was nothing there. Only the patient blinking light of the computer screen and some very official looking clutter. Then she noticed something. A drawer in the desk, left slightly open. She felt inexplicably compelled to look inside, and against her better judgement to not go snooping through other people's stuff, she approached the desk.

Cautiously, Alice pulled the drawer out. Inside, she found a mess of stationery. Jumbled up paper-clips were irrevocably bound together by the mysterious forces which seem to uniquely afflict paper-clips. Scrunched up pieces of paper rustled noisily, and pens rolled about from the front to the back of the drawer and back again. However, something amongst all of this caught her eye. Underneath the clutter was a folder, and she reached in to retrieve it.

Placing the folder on the desk, Alice removed the papers and shone her light over them. It was a document, several pages long, the first page displaying the heading "Property Deed Contract". Alice read on.

Lloyd Turner ("Buyer") and Robert Haversham ("Seller") hereby agree as follows: This agreement concerns the following real estate property, commonly known as: 32 Cadmus Square, Knightsbridge, London SW7 1DY

She skipped ahead, skimming over the terms and conditions as most people are wont to do, looking for something less boring and, ideally, more relevant. She wasn't entirely sure what she was looking for; maybe reference to any encumbrances mentioning that the house was built on top of a burial site, or a requirement to leave the loft untouched lest it unsettle the spirit beings which dwell within. To her disappointment, she found nothing of the sort. However, she did find something which she thought seemed to stand out. Towards the end of the document, just before the signature boxes, was a single clause.

The sale of this property has been conducted in accordance with the will of the late Louise Haversham, former occupant and home-owner. Outstanding mortgage payments and tax accountability are hereby the responsibility of Robert Haversham, son of the deceased.

She heard the stairs creaking as if someone was coming down, and she quickly put the paper back in the folder, hurriedly stashing it away in the drawer. *I better show Sam this,* she thought, and turned to leave the room. She immediately halted, and stood completely still as she felt her heart leap up into her throat, dive back into her chest, and promptly stop.

Standing in front of her was a woman. At first glance, she seemed to be in her seventies and did not look quite like what one would describe as "real". She stood, huddled in an old-looking cardigan, and her skin was eerily pale. Her eyes were sunken and tired-looking. She was also almost entirely transparent. Alice reached out with a nervous hand.

'Hello?' she said uncertainly, as her hand slowly made its way closer to the apparition. She could feel her hand shaking. Just as she was about to touch the almost-woman, the figure faded away, completely vanishing from Alice's sight. 'No, no, no… Come back?' Alice said to nothing in particular, hoping the apparition would return. It did not. *Now THIS is something I must tell Sam!*

Upstairs, Sam had been investigating a couple of the rooms. He hadn't set foot in either Charlie's or the Turners' bedrooms; he didn't want to disturb them too much while he was looking around. From what Sam had overheard while upstairs, damp had damaged some of the boxes in the master bedroom, and from the other side of a closed door he could hear the sound of someone vigorously washing down a wall. He thought it best not to intrude, and instead turned his attention to the unoccupied rooms.

The spare bedroom had proven to be an uneventful search, revealing nothing more than the fact that the Turners had hidden most of their unpacked boxes and general clutter in there. The bathroom was the only place left for him to look in to, so he made his way towards the end of the landing.

Pulling on the light cord just inside of the door, the bathroom light flickered into life. It hummed a persistent and irritating hum. He peered around the room in curiosity. It was sparsely decorated, all of the cosmetics and amenities stored away in the small cupboards which were dotted around the room. Above the sink was a large mirror, and next to it a smaller mirror on the front of a cabinet, which appeared to have been freshly cleaned. Sam held up one of the printed sheets of paper in front of it, and looked at the photograph. A steamed-up mirror on the front of a cabinet, the words "darkness is coming" written across it. He folded the paper back up. *This would be the same mirror, then.*

Sam waved his wand-like probe around the room, pointing it towards the cabinet and the mirror in particular. It glowed a strange shade of purple, flickering and pulsating unusually. He whacked it against the palm of his hand, and it glowed steadily for a few seconds before fading into inactivity. It started flickering again a few moments later. *Bloody thing...*

It was then that something caught Sam's eye. There was a weird shape forming in the mirror, as wisps and patterns danced in the reflection, coming together to form... Something. It was a something vaguely humanoid in form, slowly coalescing and taking shape behind Sam as he stared at it in the reflection. He turned to look behind him, but there was nothing there. Yet the image in the mirror remained. It wasn't quite like a normal human shape, it looked more like a three dimensional shadow, face-less and only partially visible. Its form seemed to shift slightly, and it appeared to be writhing on the surface. As Sam stared at it in fascination, the shadow-person leaned forward and from its faceless head a large, menacing mouth opened wide, revealing sharp, shadowy teeth. It looked like it was screaming at him, but no scream came. Only a long, echoing, hissing noise.

Almost as suddenly as it had appeared, the shadow-person disappeared, its form dispersing into a number of smoke-like tendrils before spiralling away into nothingness.

'Fascinating,' Sam muttered, and he quickly checked the probe. Its crystalline tip flickered as it had done before. *Maybe it hasn't been malfunctioning... I best tell Alice.*

As Sam was running down the stairs, he saw Alice emerge from one of the rooms and start running up the stairs towards him. Meeting in the middle of the staircase, they grabbed each other by the arms.

'I've just seen the ghost!' They both announced in unison.

'What, really?' Sam asked, looking a little stunned.

'Yeah, she appeared to me just now in the Turners' office.'

'It just appeared to me in the bathroom mirror.'

'Is that normal? Can a ghost be in two places at once?' Alice asked.

'I don't know. Then again, nothing's normal in th- Wait, *she*?'

'Yeah, and I think I know who she is, too. I'll show you,' she said, leading him back down the stairs.

'Mine was just shapeless and shadowy...' Sam muttered.

Back in the Turners' study, Alice made her way towards the end of the room. The folder was sat on the desk, open, ready and waiting for her. *Didn't I put it back in the drawer?* She was relatively sure she had, although documents aren't really known for moving about of their own accord.

'Here we go. Have a look-see,' she said, handing Sam the contract. His eyes quickly scanned over the document.

'Could Louise Haversham still... You know, still *be* here?' Alice asked as she watched Sam reading over the contract.

'Not a bad theory. I wouldn't say it's conclusive, but it's certainly something,' he said, putting the contract back in its folder. 'So tell me, this apparition you saw, you said she was a she?'

'Yeah, like a ghostly old woman,' Alice replied matter-of-factly.

'So she actually had some kind of form? What did she look like?'

'She was sort of...' Alice paused, trying to think how to describe the ghost she thought was Louise Haversham. She had only seen her for a moment, and quite frankly she had been too taken aback by the vision to really note down the details. 'She was old. Pale and wrinkly, with silver hair. And wearing a cardi. She wasn't quite "real", though, sort of like she was half here and half not. Kind of see-through.'

Sam nodded and made an intrigued 'hmm' sound. 'She manifested a lot more vividly for you... Interesting.' He turned and began to make his way for the door. 'Oh, and good find, by the way.' He shot Alice a sideways smile, waving his hand in the direction of the contract, before disappearing back out into the hallway.

Alice grinned, and quickly followed after him.

The probe started to flicker again. Holding it out in front of him, Sam started to slowly spin, tracing a circle around himself with the wand, slowing himself whenever the crystal glowed brighter, in much the same way someone divining water may use dowsing rods. The purplish glow began to grow in intensity. It shone brightly for a second before flickering and dimming again, fading to nothingness. Sam pivoted on his heel, spinning back the way he had just come, until the glow intensified again. Fixing the probe on the door ahead, its crystalline tip glowed and flickered erratically. He gestured towards the door and strode across the hallway, pushing it open and flicking the lights on as he walked in.

'Are you there, Louise?' he asked, raising his voice as he addressed the air. He paced around the large oakwood dining table at the heart of the room. Alice watched him from the doorway with baited breath. Nothing happened. 'I call upon the spirit of the house, and I summon thee. Louise Haversham, I know you can hear me. Give me a sign that you're there,' he continued talking at the nothingness.

'How do you know she's going to be here?' Alice asked. 'How do you even know it's her we're dealing with, for that matter? You just said it wasn't conclusive.'

'I don't, and it isn't,' Sam said, 'but it's all we've got at the moment. A ghostly old woman and a contract involving a recently deceased old woman, it connects.' The crystal at the tip of the probe glowed and pulsated. 'Something's here. Just keep an eye out.'

'What are we looking for?'

'Something. Anything. I don't know yet,' he said as he continued to pace around the room.

Sam held the probe up high above his head as he marched around the perimeter of the room. The crystal continued to pulsate, stronger and faster than before, and it started to emit a high-pitched noise which made Alice's ears twinge. She thought she could hear something else, like a distant voice calling from somewhere remote, but she couldn't hear what it was saying. She suddenly felt the sensation she had experienced in the living room. Pressure began to rise in the room, and her ears started to feel muffled, as if she was underwater. Just out of the corner of her eye, Alice thought she saw something move, and without a moment's hesitation she shouted.

'Duck!'

With that, one of the chairs took flight and launched itself towards Sam. He immediately crouched down and felt the chair soar over his head. It hit the wall behind him, snapping off one of the legs. The probe carried on emitting its high-pitched whine. A cabinet filled with china began to shudder, and the crockery rattled uneasily. Sam stood up again and pointed the probe directly at the cabinet.

'Louise! If that's you, I command you stop this.' His words apparently fell on metaphysical deaf ears, as the cabinet doors flung themselves open and launched an expensive looking teacup in his direction, followed by a projectile fork and a spinning plate. He narrowly dodged the airborne crockery, and avoided being stabbed by the flying fork, throwing himself to the floor and crawling beneath the table for cover.

'Stop that thing from making that noise!' Alice shouted at him as a series of knives hurled themselves in Sam's direction, embedding themselves in the tabletop with a succession of *thunk*s. She retreated back to hide behind the door, using it to shield herself from any more wayward cutlery in much the same way they had taken cover from the ballistic books.

Sam hit the probe with the palm of his hand in frustration as it continued to screech its piercing screech. Suddenly, it fell silent. Crockery ceased to take flight, and cutlery stopped throwing itself at him. Things felt a lot calmer, and Alice could sense the pressure lifting from the room. Slowly crawling out from beneath the table, Sam cautiously looked around the dining room. Fragments of broken china littered the floor, and cutlery marred the surface of the table like a dart board. He breathed a long sigh of relief.

'What the *hell* happened in here?!' An angry voice bellowed, shaking the entire room. A solitary teacup fell pathetically from the cabinet, smashing on the floor. Sam nervously looked up and into the furious face of Lloyd Turner. His ginger beard seemed to be a deeper shade of red than before, and Sam entertained the idea that perhaps his facial hair changed colour to match his mood. He stood up and dusted himself off, and Alice slowly backed away from the doorway.

'Ghost happened. It's fine, it's gone now. Sorry about the china,' he said, nervously trying to lighten the mood. He hoped, in vain, that an upbeat demeanour would help diffuse the situation. Lloyd did not seem amused.

'Listen. I allowed you into my home simply to humour my wife's superstitions. I don't believe in ghosts, and I certainly don't believe you're a detective of any variety,' Lloyd spoke with a sinisterly calm and collected voice. He was no longer shouting, but he still spat his words out with just as much anger. 'I was willing to tolerate you for so long, but when I come down here to find you trashing *my house* just to reinforce your nonsense ghost stories...' He paused, and breathed a furious and exasperated sigh. 'You're no longer welcome here.'

'Mister Turner, I can understand your frustration, but this thing is real whether you believe it or not,' Sam said, making his way over to the terrifying man in the comfortable looking jumper. 'I am so close to having this whole situation sorted. Just give me another hour, and I promise we'll be out of your hair.'

'Let him finish his work, dear,' said the voice of Elena, who now came and stood by the side of her still fuming husband.

'But j-just look at this place!' Lloyd exclaimed, waving his hands wildly, gesturing to the state of the room.

'I know, I know... But how many things have broken on their own *without* anyone here? Just give Sam another hour, and if nothing's changed by then he'll have to leave.'

Lloyd's face visibly contorted into an image of pained

irritation before spitting through gritted teeth, 'fine.'

'An hour is all I'll need, and I'll be gone' Sam said, 'and I promise I won't break any more of your stuff. Now, if you'll please join me in the living room, I'll let you know what I think is going on here.'

Sam, Alice and Elena took their seats by the fireplace in the living room. The fire had now died down to just a few crackling embers. Lloyd stayed standing in the doorway, staring at the floor in disbelief, his dumb-founded gaze fixed upon Sam's chalk pentagram.

'You've drawn on my carpet,' he said in a voice that was so monotone and devoid of emotion it was marginally more terrifying than when he was shouting.

'Necessary to ward off negative energy and malicious spirits. If I'd drawn these symbols in the dining room, you'd still have a complete set of china,' Sam said. Lloyd just glared back at him.

'Anyway,' Sam started to explain, clasping his hands together, 'a poltergeist that breaks kitchenware, plays with the lights and leaves foreboding messages on mirrors, suddenly ups its game and starts throwing books at people and causing serious damage in the dining room. This started out as a fairly benign haunting, but it seems our arrival has agitated things.'

'From the moment we walked through your door, she knew why we were here, and she's trying to scare us off,' Alice prompted.

'So far, so obvious... But poltergeists don't tend to change their behaviour just because of who they're haunting. Some are malicious and go out of their way to cause harm, and others are just the nuisance pranksters of the spirit world. This one I thought would be the latter, but she's now on the offensive,' Sam said. He could see the perplexed looks on the Turners' faces. 'My theory is that the spirit that haunts this hous-' He was interrupted mid-sentence as the lights began to flicker again. The four of them looked around the room. Alice readied herself for something to happen.

'Bloody fuses again...' Lloyd mumbled.

The lights went out completely, and an eerie stillness descended on the room. The grandfather clock stopped ticking. The final embers of the once-lit fire ceased crackling. The room was plunged into darkness. Then nothing happened. No books flew off of the shelves, no crockery spontaneously broke itself, and no furniture was up-turned. Sam stood up in nervous anticipation. Alice held her breath. It felt as if time had come to a stand-still. Nothing continued to happen.

After a few moments had passed, the lights suddenly burst back to life, lighting the room up again, and the grandfather clock resumed ticking. With a relaxed sigh, Sam sat back down. 'It's fine,' he said as he took his seat, 'we're safe as long as we're in this room.'

They had only just settled back down when a terrified scream echoed throughout the house, and the Turners were out of the door in an instant.

Following the sound of the scream, Sam bounded up the stairs with Alice not far behind, and darted into the bedroom of Charlie Turner. Inside, a calmer looking Lloyd was now stood at the foot of a bed while his wife knelt by the side of it, cradling their son. Sam hovered in the doorway, as the child repeated through terrified sobs 'they're going to get me.' He looked up from his mother's arms and saw Sam and Alice stood in his doorway. He didn't seem to be too concerned about Alice's presence, but it was clearly an unnerving experience for the little boy to see a tall man he had never met before, in a coat and hat and clad all in black, standing in his doorway and looking at him with a quizzical stare. Charlie tightened his grip on his mother and cried.

'Make them go away.'

'It's all right, Charlie. They're here to help get rid of your nasty dreams,' Elena said soothingly. Charlie still clung tightly to her. Sam shifted where he stood, looking more than a little awkward.

'Yes,' he said, and looked as if he was going to say something else, but decided not to. Alice gently pushed past him and knelt down by the side of the bed, next to Elena.

'Hey Charlie, I'm Alice.' The little boy stared back at her with big, watery eyes. 'Can you tell me a little about your dreams?' she asked softly. Charlie shook his head, burying his face in his mother's shoulder.

'He's had them almost every night for weeks now,' Elena said, gently stroking her son's hair, 'always around this time, a little after midnight. He dreams he's being chased by monsters-'

'What kind of monsters?' Sam interjected.

'Shadow monsters,' mumbled Charlie.

'It's just a dream, son, they can't get to you. Go back to sleep,' Lloyd said. He still stood at the foot of the bed, looking disconnected from the rest of them. Charlie seemed less than convinced that his dreams could not harm him.

From his position in the doorway, Sam surveyed the room. If Lloyd Turner seemed disconnected from everything else going on, Sam Hain was on a completely different plane of existence. He scanned his eyes over the entirety of the room. *Curtains closed, unmoving; no breeze, windows shut; comfortable temperature, double-glazing,* he mentally catalogued what he could observe of the room. *Wardrobe doors closed, mirror covered, night-light on. Muted décor. Nothing present in the local vicinity conducive of usual externally produced nightmares.* A twitch of a smile flickered across his lips. *Conclusion:*

spooky things.

'Alice?' he said, gesturing with his head for her to join him in the doorway.

'What is it?' She stood up and made her way over to the door. 'Think you've got something?'

'Maybe. Do you feel anything about this room?' Sam asked, lowering his voice almost to a whisper.

'Not really, why?' She shrugged.

'Just try to focus in on it for a minute. Do you sense anything?'

She closed her eyes and tried to tune in with her surroundings. It was hard for her to go on her first impressions of the room. Anything she felt was immediately superseded by the situation; a crying child, a probably-still-angry Lloyd Turner, and the feeling that they shouldn't be there. She felt deeply uncomfortable with being in this little boy's bedroom, in the house of complete strangers, one of whom had been ready to throw them out only a few moments previously.

'I'm sorry,' she eventually said, opening her eyes again, 'I can't *feel* anything. I guess I just can't get past the feeling that we're intruding.'

'*Intruding.* Yes, good word, that's it...' Sam mused. He turned to leave the room, his overcoat billowing out as he span around. 'Mister and Misses Turner, please join me back in the living room. Bring Charlie with you, I suspect the boy needs a nice mug of hot chocolate.'

'I could do with one, too,' Alice muttered to Sam as they left the room.

Once the Turners had congregated in the living room, Sam closed the door and started pacing around the room. Lloyd and Elena seated themselves in the armchairs, with Charlie balanced on Elena's lap and nursing a mug of steaming hot chocolate. He seemed happier now, although he still regarded Sam with a wary eye.

'Mister and Misses Turner,' Sam announced, once they had made themselves comfortable, 'I don't just suspect that your house is haunted – that much is evident – but I believe you have unwittingly moved into the house of someone who has not yet moved out.' Perplexed looks were exchanged around the room. Lloyd Turner stood up, standing toe to toe with Sam.

'I don't know about you, Mister Hain, but I don't see anyone else here.' Sam had never really noticed Lloyd's height before, but now he was stood mere inches away from him, Lloyd seemed to be towering over him.

'Mister Turner, are you familiar with the late Louise Haversham?' Sam asked, trying to straighten his posture and stand as tall as he could. He still felt short.

'What do you know of the Havershams?' Lloyd asked, an accusing look in his eyes.

'She's listed as the most recent resident, before yourselves, at this address,' Sam said, producing his phone from his pocket and showing him a web page from directory enquiries. He didn't want Lloyd to find out they'd been looking through his desk; that was a sure-fire way to get kicked out, if the dining room fiasco hadn't been enough already.

'Yes. She lived here before we moved in. House was sold after she died. We bought it from her son,' Lloyd replied.

'Would I be correct in the assumption that Louise Haversham left this property to her son in her will?' Sam asked, knowing that it was stated in the contract, and he took a few steps back from Lloyd.

'I believe so.'

'According to this,' Sam said, flicking over the page on his phone, 'this was valid as of the end of September. So Louise Haversham was still living here about three months ago. Are you aware of when she passed?'

'No,' Lloyd replied flatly, 'we saw this place on the market last month, and put an offer in almost instantly.'

'So if this is correct, then Misses Haversham has been gone for between two to three months now. I suspect that once the deed to the property had been signed over to her son, he put the house on the market, and you bought it. My theory is that her spirit wasn't ready to move out when the sale went through – she still isn't – and she's letting you know that you're not welcome in her home.'

'That'd be why I felt like we were intruding,' Alice mused aloud.

'Exactly. Our arrival only signified more of an intrusion to Misses Haversham, and she knows we're here to help you with everything you've been experiencing. She probably fears we're going to force her to move on, so she's trying to get rid of us. Not all souls go quietly into the night.'

Lloyd scoffed, sitting back down and casting a sceptical glare at everyone else. 'What rot! You really think that a dead woman is trying to kick us out because she thinks she still lives here? That's impossible.'

'Well then, I ask you to come up with what you think is a more reasonable conclusion. In my experience, the impossible has a certain integrity to it. No matter how impossible something may be, it can be so bloody-minded that it makes itself possible. Or, at least, very, very improbable,' Sam said. He felt less intimidated now that Lloyd had sat back down. 'Now, if you'll give me a few moments more, I think I can have this whole ordeal resolved.'

He made his way to the door and opened it. Alice stood up to join him, but just as he was passing through the doorway he turned around and faced her. 'No. Alice, wait here with the Turners. If she sees two of us looking for her, she'll start throwing things again. I'll be back before you know it.'

'Oh. Fine,' Alice said, feeling more than a little dejected. She'd been the one who'd found the documents after all, and she had also seen the ghostly woman who she was sure was the soul of Louise Haversham. Sam probably wouldn't even know the ghost's name if it weren't for her. Regardless, she sat back down in the armchair and watched as Sam disappeared out of the door.

She and the Turners sat in awkward silence for a short while.

'So... Weather's turned out better than expected tonight, huh?' she said, trying to break the tension that now hung in the room. Elena simply 'hmm'd' in agreement. Lloyd just stared blankly at her. Charlie sipped his hot chocolate.

Chapter IV

Cautiously walking up the stairs, Sam made his way to the last known location of the Turners' haunting: Charlie's bedroom. It seemed darker than it had before. The glow from the boy's night-light cast eerie, misshapen shadows up the walls. Simple objects like a chest of drawers became vast, shadowy monsters. He was surprised he had not noticed it this way earlier. If this was how it always looked when Charlie was going to bed, he could see why the boy suffered from nightmares so frequently.

That, and the ghost that haunted the house, of course.

The floorboards creaked loudly as he set foot in the room, and Sam tried to tread more carefully as he made his way further into the room. A similarly loud noise came creaking from the opposite corner of the room. Slowly, Sam approached the spot where the noise had come from, reaching into his pocket for the probe. The crystal at its tip fizzled. Something about the room made him feel uneasy, more on edge than before, and he peered over his shoulder. There was nothing but the shadows and the glow of the night-light.

He leaned in towards the corner, casting the probe over the chest of drawers. He traced around the dinosaur toys which decorated the top of the chest, following the ebb and flow of the crystal's pulsating light. Its light emanated intensely, almost becoming a good substitute for a torch, and Sam thought he saw something moving, writhing, in the dark space between the chest and the wall. He peered in closer, pressing his head against the wall.

There was a sudden, loud bang. Sam jumped back in surprise, and wheeled around to see that the door behind him had slammed itself shut.

'So, we're playing it like that, are we?' he muttered beneath his breath, slowly approaching the door. He pulled at it, twisting the handle, but to no avail. The door had firmly shut itself, and was not willing to let him go. He turned back around into the room, and sighed an exaggerated sigh. The ends of the bed-sheet waved gently as if a breeze had blown through, but Sam could feel no draught. Absolute silence had descended upon the room.

'Louise?' Sam called uncertainly into the darkness. 'Louise Haversham, are you there?' Nothing happened. For quite some time, things continued to not happen, but Sam stood patiently, waiting for a sign that the spirit of Louise Haversham was willing to talk with him. The probe's tip lit up like a lightbulb, glowing vibrantly, and Sam looked at it with intrigue. He couldn't remember the last time it had picked up on a presence so strong, and just as he was about to take this as a sign that he had opened dialogue with the spirit, two pillows were hurled at him.

'Louise, I understand why you're upset,' Sam started, attempting to reason with his invisible assailant. The bedsheets began to writhe like a bag of eels who were particularly angry to be in a bag. 'Let's just remain calm about this, I think we can help you...'

He has it all wrong, a voice seemed to echo in Alice's head. She felt herself tense, her body shifting into a rigid upright posture, and she glanced at the Turners. They were behaving as if they hadn't heard anything, and by the looks of it they hadn't seen her react to it in any way either. For a brief moment, she thought she must've been imagining the voice in her head, but then it spoke again. *He doesn't understand.* It wasn't like hearing someone speak, and it wasn't like having a thought. It was something like the two things, and somewhere in between them, yet entirely unlike anything she had ever experienced. She didn't know what to do. Leaning her head back against the armchair, she closed her eyes and tried to focus on the voice. It didn't say anything else.

Who are you? she thought, and in an instant her mind's eye was flooded by images of the property deed contract and the spirit of Louise Haversham. She tried to focus on the apparition she had seen in the Turners' study, concentrating on engaging the voice in conversation. *Is this Louise?* There was no reply, but Alice felt as if she was right. There was another stretch of silence, but eventually the voice came again.

Yes. He has it wrong. Not me. Them.

Them? Who are they? Alice asked in her mind.

Shadows. Darkness. They're coming... The voice uttered.

Darkness is coming? Alice felt an affirmative wave flow through her.

Through the portal. The portal is open.

What portal? Where? What?

I came with a warning to deliver. They're coming. The voice was starting to feel more and more flustered. *They're coming.* It seemed to scream inside her mind and, jolted by the force of the scream, Alice lifted her head, her eyes wide open. The Turners stared at her for a second, confused and concerned.

It was then that Alice noticed something was amiss. Smoke had started filtering into the room in thick, black plumes. It swirled up and around, moving in an almost snake-like fashion, not like smoke at all, and Alice felt a deep sense of uneasiness. It began to spin violently around, circling her and the Turners, and as it came closer she could see that it wasn't smoke at all. It was like a school of eels. Oily shadows swarming around and around, but at no point did they cross the boundaries marked out by Sam's chalk symbols.

Alice had seen something not too dissimilar in her dreams around the time she first met Sam. She looked at the Turners, but they didn't seem concerned in the slightest. It was as if they were not even aware that plumes of smokey, oily, flying eels from another dimension were swimming around them. The only one who seemed to actually see them was Charlie, who tightly clung to his mother in mute fear while he watched them swirl around the room. Neither Lloyd or Elena seemed to notice Charlie's concern.

'How much longer do you think it'll be?' Lloyd mumbled. What little patience he had was wearing incredibly thin.

'Hopefully not much longer,' Elena replied, 'but I'd rather he did his job properly and not rush it.' Lloyd scoffed at this, evidently not convinced that Sam was performing any kind of job at all.

The shadowy entities continued to swirl around the room, completely unnoticed by the Turners.

'I'll, uh... I'll be back in a second. Just going to check on Sam,' Alice said, standing up and moving cautiously towards the door. The Turners nodded in acknowledgement.

She looked at the symbols drawn on the floor. The shadows had yet to cross them. Sam was right, it did keep them at bay. Alice withdrew the pendant from around her neck and clutched it tightly to her chest, standing just short of the swirling darkness. She hesitated, swaying slightly on her feet as she tried to step over the boundary and through the swirling darkness which surrounded them. She took a deep breath, and plunged herself into the shadows.

The Turners watched with curiosity as Alice took her bracing breath and made a single dramatic step forward, as if her step was leading to some leap of faith, before walking out of the room with hurried and wobbly steps. To them, it seemed as if she thought she was stepping out onto a tightrope. Lloyd shook his head. 'Strange girl.'

The shadows were not quite as thick out in the hallway, and with every step forward she took, Alice could see them parting in front of her. She stopped holding her breath, and knew that for as long as she held on to the pentacle around her neck, they could not harm her. Wading through the smoke-like eels which now covered the floor, she made her way towards the staircase. The shadowy beings slithered and writhed, curling around bannisters, crawling up the walls and across the floor. More swooped down through the air as she was making her way up, parting just in front of her and weaving around. She struggled to suppress a shriek, letting out a squealing whimper, but she carried on.

The upstairs was mostly empty of these entities, as if the majority of them had headed downstairs, which made Alice feel much more comfortable. When she reached the door to Charlie's bedroom, it was shut. She turned the handle and pushed, but it seemed to be jammed shut.

'Sam, you in there?' she called, her head pressed against the door.

'Yep,' came the response.

'Can you let me in?'

'Umm... I'm a little indisposed at the moment.'

'For God's sake...' Alice muttered, and she shoved herself against the door. It opened with a sudden and unexpected ease, and she stumbled into the room. She looked around, and for a moment she couldn't see Sam anywhere, but then something drew her eyes upward. On the bedroom ceiling, pinned by a duvet, was a rather disgruntled looking Sam.

'Louise and I had a bit of a disagreement,' he said. 'I said she should just accept that someone else now lived in her house, and she threw me up here.'

'It's not Louise,' Alice stated, taking a few cautious steps into the room.

'Who've I been talking to then?'

'I don't know, weird oily-shadow eel things! They're everywhere. We need to do something. I think Louise told me they were coming from a portal somewhere.' She looked up at the occult detective being held captive by a gravity-defying duvet, and in her mind's eye she could see the faint outlines of smoke-like beings pinning him to the ceiling.

'Ooh,' he mused, 'a portal. Of course...'

'Apparently,' Alice nodded. 'Now what do we do? How can I get you back down?'

'They took the transphasic probe,' he said, wiggling around inside the duvet and eventually producing an arm from within its folds. He pointed down at the floor, and Alice could see the wand-like device. She darted over to it, picking it up and waving it aloft.

'Now what?'

'Point and hum!'

'Point and hum?'

'Point and hum!'

Alice pointed and hummed. She could feel the device gradually starting to hum too, vibrating in harmony with her, and the crystalline tip began to glow brighter and brighter. The device's humming intensified, eventually growing to such a volume that Alice could no longer hear herself over it.

'You can stop humming now, it's attuned to you, just think about whatever is keeping me up here and force it to release me,' Sam said, and Alice stopped humming.

She turned her thoughts to the things that were pinning Sam to the ceiling, focussing on them disappearing. The device carried on humming for a few moments and, with a judder and one final, high-pitched sound, it fell silent. It was as if someone had turned on an extraction fan, as the shadowy forms Alice thought she could see were suddenly dissipated. There was a momentary flash of violet light as the beings broke apart. Almost instantly, Sam fell from the ceiling, enveloped in the duvet and plummeting head-first onto the mattress below. There was a soft thud, and a plume of feathers rose up from the impact. From amidst the feathery cocoon, Sam's head emerged, grinning up at Alice.

'Good work.'

'What on Earth is this... This... Oojamaflip?!' Alice asked, throwing the thing back to Sam. It landed on the bed just in front of him. He grabbed it, getting up off of the bed in the most ungraceful manner.

'What do you think it is?' He asked in response, holding it up in front of her.

'A kind of techno-wand type thingy?' She didn't know, otherwise she wouldn't have asked. As far as she had been concerned, it was just a thing that glowed and made high-pitched noises when there was stuff. Now it was a thing that glowed, made high-pitched noises, hummed and could disperse shadow-eels.

'It's a multi-functional transphasic energy probe. It utilises the crystal's dominant oscillatory rate to detect variances or fluctuations in the Akashic Field. It can also interact with the Field, using Akasha energy to project and enhance the user's magickal will. You hum, it resonates and bonds with your psychic signature and frequency, and interfaces with your thought patterns,' he explained as he dusted the loose feathers off of his coat. He marched purposefully towards the door, paused, and turned back to Alice. 'So, yes. Techno-wand.'

The probe glowed steadily as Sam walked out onto the landing, waving it around in front of him like he was trying to fend off a particularly persistent wasp. Clutching the pentacle close to her chest, Alice followed him.

'You do know that the stuff you say makes no sense whatsoever, right?'

'It probably doesn't, but that doesn't stop it from being right.' He continued to wave the probe around in front of him, and Alice could see the shadows parting ahead of him just as they had done with her and the pentacle pendant.

'So how *do* you know this stuff?'

'I told you, I had a Guide. Now are we going to spend the rest of the night playing Twenty Questions, or shall we seal off this portal?' Sam stopped in his tracks, and took a few paces backwards. The transphasic probe glowed a peculiar shade of purple and made a disconcerting buzzing noise. He took a few steps forward again, and the buzzing ceased. Stepping back, the buzzing started up again. Pointing it upwards, the buzzing became more high pitched.

'The loft,' Sam said, pointing to the loft hatch at the other end of the landing, 'it's in the loft.' He made his way over to it, and stood directly beneath the hatch. 'Still got the pendant?' He asked, turning to Alice. She nodded. 'Good, hold on to it.'

'It's got me this far, I'm hardly going to let it go now,' she said, still clutching on to it. 'You could've used it earlier, why didn't you take it with you?'

'I wanted to make sure it'd keep you safe while I was trying to sort things out... I thought I was talking to a misunderstood spirit, not entities from beyond the void.'

Sam reached up and pushed the hatch. It made a clunking sound, but nothing happened. He pushed again and the door came swinging down, knocking his hat off in the process. He ducked down, grabbing his hat, and looked up into the loft. It was pitch black. Pulling the ladder down with a loud *ker-clunk*, he led the way, climbing up into the blackness beyond, transphasic probe pointing ahead of him.

In the darkness of the loft, Alice fumbled around with

her phone to turn the torch on. Light emanated from the phone and illuminated the room directly ahead of them. The loft was surprisingly spacious: the roof was high enough for Sam to stand almost upright, and there was plenty of room to move around. Bags and boxes littered the area, strewn about almost haphazardly, and a mound of black plastic bags were congregated around the base of a limbless mannequin, like offerings to a strange idol.

Standing just within the lip of the hatch's opening, Sam pointed the transphasic probe around the space. It pulsed and glowed and buzzed, and Sam slowly followed the direction it was guiding him. He beckoned to Alice to shine the torch in his direction, and as the light panned across the room it revealed the other things in the loft: more boxes and bags, pieces of an old bookcase, and then nothing. It was not so much that there was nothing of note there, quite the opposite; it was literally a gaping hole of nothingness. A space entirely devoid of anything, like a hole in the fabric of reality. Alice's eyes struggled to make sense of it, and her head began to ache. Try as she might, Alice couldn't even begin to comprehend it. Her torch couldn't shine a light on it, and she couldn't even look at it.

'What am I looking at? Is that the portal?' Alice asked, her voice quavering slightly. She couldn't wrap her head around what was in front of her, and she had to turn away from it.

'You're not looking at anything. It's the Void. The vast expanse of the unknowable which exists beyond reality. Just try not to look at it too much, it could drive you just a little bit mad.' Sam kept his gaze fixed on Alice, trying to keep his eyes from looking directly at it as he stared obliquely. 'We can't even begin to comprehend it, it exists beyond our normal senses, and yet our brains still try to fathom its existence. Or rather, non-existence. Something must've generated a massive amount of energy in the Akasha to rip a hole like this...'

Sam lifted the transphasic probe and pointed it at the Void portal. It glowed a peculiar shade of indigo again, and started to screech irritatingly. Alice looked back to see what was happening, but immediately snapped her head away from it. It was as if the act of simply trying to look at it burned the inside of her mind like the worst of migraines. The screeching techno-wand didn't particularly help matters in the headache department either. A weird sound, almost like a muffled rushing of wind and running water, burbled from the Void's "surface", and from the corner of her eye Alice could see it shifting and swirling like water down a drain.

'Hold on to the pentacle, and whatever you do, do not let go!' Sam said, and he turned to look directly at the portal. The Void glared back at him, and he squinted to try and focus on it.

'What are you doing?'

'I'm fixing it. Just hold on to the pentacle!'

The beings of shadow began to rapidly rise through the floor of the loft, twisting and writhing through the air. They spiralled up and around Alice, brushing past her legs and spinning around her head. She clutched the pentacle pendant tightly and stood her ground, suppressing the urge to run screaming from the loft. The things coiled around Sam, wrapping themselves around him and almost completely concealing him from Alice's sight.

As they continued to twist their way around the two of them, she felt a twinge in her stomach and looked down, watching with silent horror and disbelief as some of them passed through her body. She winced at the sensation. Then she felt the pull. It was a sudden tugging, pulling on the pendant and drawing it in towards the Void like the suction of a hoover. The smoke-eel things coiled around the hand Alice was clutching hold of the pendant with, and the pull increased. She held on tightly until her knuckles turned white, refusing to let go of it.

Clouds of the smoke beings were suddenly sucked towards the Void portal, spiralling into the seeming nothingness, swirling around and around as they fell into the event horizon. The entities started to fall off of Sam and Alice, being pulled away from them and into the ever-waiting, gaping maw of Void space. The pull on Alice seemed to grow stronger. Pressure began to build up in her head, as if she had been hanging upside down for quite some time, and she was drawn inexorably towards the Void. She could almost see it now, as the smoke beings were dragged into the swirling chaos, but still what lay beyond was impossible to see. She could feel the unusual coldness of the Void approaching. She could feel herself being pulled in closer and closer, and she looked back. Shadows flew past her head, clouding her vision, but she could see Sam a short distance behind her.

'Do something!' She screamed, but no noise came from her mouth. Her cries fell silently into the Void. The chain around her neck snapped, and she struggled to hold on to it. The pentacle began to slip from her grasp, dangling from the end of its chain and leading her in towards the portal. She dug her feet deeper into the floor, bending her knees to try and stop the inevitable, but to no avail. She was being sucked in and there was nothing she could do about it.

Thank you, a voice echoed in Alice's mind, *thank you for listening.*

Suddenly, Alice was pulled off of her feet. She could feel herself falling straight towards the portal. Everything seemed to come to a stand-still, as if time had come to a stop, and Alice was convinced that this was the last moment she would ever have. She closed her eyes, and awaited whatever was to come next.

With the slurping noise of the last remaining water going down a drain, the Void portal collapsed. Alice hit the floor with a thud, no longer being drawn in towards the gaping nothingness, and looked up to see the nothingness starting to recede. It fell in on itself, spiralling away and compressing down to a single point the size of a pin-prick. And then, nothing. But not the same nothingness as before. It was now just a normal loft space, without any Void portals or smoke-eels.

Alice stood up. The pendant fell limply in her hand, succumbing to normal gravity now the Void was no longer sucking her in. She breathed a long sigh of relief, and turned around to face Sam. He was gone, his hat resting on top of the mannequin's head. 'Sam?' she called out uncertainly. 'Sam?'

'Hello,' came the familiar voice, and Sam bounded up from the floor in the same spot the Void portal had been.

'Bloody hell, I thought you'd been sucked in!'

'Thankfully no, but look,' he said, holding up a crystalline object. It was an oval, quartzite stone, the right size to fit in the palm of a hand, and was perfectly formed. Around the circumference of the crystal was a series of intricately carved symbols, and in the middle of it was a weird spiral-like pattern. 'Void crystal,' Sam announced, 'always wanted to see one of these. And you were right, you know.'

Alice looked perplexed. 'About what?'

'Louise. She came to warn the Turners of the portal, but when they wouldn't listen she had to try a more direct tactic.'

'So that was-'

'She helped plug the portal. Now as long as this stone remains inert, it won't be coming back.' Taking out a handkerchief, Sam wrapped up the Void crystal and pocketed it. 'It's in safe hands now,' he said, retrieving his hat from the mannequin and giving it a cursory 'thank-you', and started heading back down the ladder out of the loft.

'Where's Louise now?' Alice asked. She tried to listen for the voice in her head and tried to feel the presence of the spirit of Louise Haversham. She couldn't feel or hear anything like she had before. Sam turned and looked at Alice, an apologetic uncertainty in his eyes.

'I don't know. She's probably returned to the ether now... She used the portal to interact more easily with the world, but now it's closed she probably can't come through so easily,' he said, 'she'll be around, though.'

'Do you know how, or why, that Void crystal thingy was here?' Alice asked.

'I'm afraid I don't know that either,' Sam said with a resigning sigh. He pulled back the handkerchief slightly to show Alice the crystal. 'Not every day you see one of these things. Weird magick, even by my standards.'

Everywhere was refreshingly clear of smoke-eels and shadow-snakes. The house now looked like a normal house to Alice, with no entities dwelling just outside of her normal perception, and she felt like she could finally breathe properly. The first light of dawn was peering in through the window above the front door, casting bright beams of light on the once dark hallway.

'Wait, hang on, why's it light? What's the time?' Alice looked perplexed.

'I don't know,' Sam said, and he consulted his pocket watch, 'it's about two o'clock.'

Alice checked her phone. It said the time was 01:57.

'It can't be... Look outside! It looks like it should be about eight o'clock,' Alice said. She wasn't wrong; the sun was very rarely up at two o'clock in the morning.

'Temporal displacement?' Sam wondered. 'Maybe the Void portal sucked in localised time, too? What felt like minutes to us could've easily been hours everywhere else...'

'Well that's not at all confusing,' Alice said.

'Anyway, not a word of what went on up there to the

Turners. They had a poltergeist problem, and we fixed that problem. They needn't know about the Void or entities or missing time. Just that things are back to normal.'

'Okay,' Alice nodded, and she opened the door.

'Good news, Mister and Misses Turner!' Sam announced, flinging his arms wide open. 'Your problems are solved.'

'About bloody time,' Lloyd grumbled, standing up and immediately making his way out of the living room.

'Thank you, Mister Hain,' Elena said, and she rolled the now-asleep Charlie over, propping him up against the arm of the chair. 'Charlie's certainly calmed down, so whatever it is you've done has worked.'

'Bollocks!' came a shout from the hallway, and the form of Lloyd Turner shot past the living room door in the direction of the kitchen. 'What's the time? We must've bloody fallen asleep. I'm going to be late!'

Elena looked confused. 'What on Earth's he on abou-' She stopped mid-sentence as she noticed the daylight flooding into the hallway. She made her way over to the living room window, and pulled open the curtains. Sure enough, a bright winter's morning greeted her. 'I guess we must have nodded off for a while there...'

'Sorry to have kept you all up for so long,' Sam said, 'it took a while, but I don't think you'll be having any more hauntings any time soon.'

'Not a problem, Mister Hain. I appreciate whatever it is you've done here. Let me brew you both some tea, you're probably more exhausted than us,' she said, and she made her way out to the kitchen. Sam wasn't going to turn down an offer of a cup of tea, even if he had somehow inadvertently caused this family to lose six hours.

Sam and Alice were saying their final goodbyes to the Turners as they prepared to take their leave. Lloyd had disappeared upstairs to hurriedly get ready for work. Elena seemed incredibly grateful, despite the visible tiredness written across her face, and was shaking Sam's hand enthusiastically. Charlie had remained silent for most of the time, drifting off to sleep every now and again with a wobble of the head before waking himself up again. He had just nodded off again, his head swinging in an arc and back up as he awoke, and he looked up at Alice.

'Morning Charlie,' she said, walking over to him. She wasn't brilliant at working with children, but she felt he deserved to hear something about the night's occurrences too. 'How are you?'

'Tired,' he replied, blinking dazedly at the daylight, 'but okay.'

'Last night,' Alice started, kneeling down beside him, and she paused as she worked out how best to broach the subject. 'Last night, you could *see* them, couldn't you? The, uh, the things. The shadows.'

'They were always in my dreams. The old lady helped me get away from them.'

Alice smiled. 'Yeah, I imagine she did.'

'I wasn't worried,' he added quickly, 'I knew your friend would keep me safe.' Alice looked over at Sam, who had seemingly managed to acquire a croissant without even leaving the room. Flakes of pastry were scattered down his front.

'Yeah... I've not known him long, and I sometimes have my doubts, but he knows what he's doing.'

Charlie looked over at Sam, and tapped Alice's knee. This bright and friendly child was a far-cry from the nervous, scared boy she had first met a few hours previously. 'No, silly. Your other friend. The man who held the shadows back.'

Alice stared confusedly back at Charlie, not really sure what to say. Her confusion slowly transformed into a look of perplexed wonderment. She remembered being

Charlie's age, and how her imaginary friends would deal with the monsters beneath her bed, and helped her escape from her nightmares. The more she thought about it, the more she was starting to question whether they had been imaginary after all. She was about to say something when Sam came over and tapped her on the shoulder.

'Come on, we best be off.' He brushed the croissant flakes from his chest, and Alice looked up at him with a dumb-founded expression. 'It's been a long night for all of us, and I think it's about time we got out of the Turners' hair.'

'Bu-'

'Misses Turner – Elena – it's been a pleasure. If you ever feel like there's something metaphysical bothering you and your family again, give me a call.' He extended a hand, holding out his business card.

'Thank you, Sam,' Elena said, 'and you too, Alice.'

Alice stood back up. 'Yes, a pleasure meeting you, Elena. And tell Lloyd we said goodbye too, I don't think he'll be seeing us before we go.'

'I will. He may seem the grumpy sort, but he means well,' she replied, but it sounded more like a poor excuse. 'Take care, and thank you again.'

As they walked down the path and away from the house, Alice turned to take one last look at the place. She couldn't quite explain why, but it seemed lighter than it had when they first arrived the night before. It could have simply been the fact that she was seeing it in the light of day for the first time, but she felt it was more likely because of what they had been able to resolve there. Elena and Charlie were stood watching them out of the living room window, waving. She waved back at them, and for the briefest of moments Alice thought she could see the faint shape of Louise Haversham with them. She smiled to herself, and turned to follow Sam.

'Come on,' he said in an unusually cheery voice for a man who had been awake all night (especially one who had been closing Void portals), 'let's get some breakfast at one of those cafés. They're probably open by now. They might even have clocks that haven't been temporally dislocated, too.'

The café was significantly emptier than it had been the night before, but no less warm and comfortable. A rosy-cheeked Alice reclined luxuriously on one of the cushiony sofas, her coat and scarf draped over the back of the seat. She sipped from a large mug of hot chocolate, which was piled high with whipped cream and marshmallows, and a decadent slice of rich chocolate cake sat on the table next to her. She was tired. She had not slept, had almost been sucked into another dimension, and had apparently been temporally dislocated by a Void portal, but none of that mattered right now. She finally had the hot chocolate and cake she had wanted the night before, and to her this was the perfect way to end the arduous night.

Sat opposite her, leaning over a small ceramic plate, Sam indelicately munched on another croissant. The flakes scattered out across the table with each bite, landing in his tea, clinging to the wool of his coat, and going anywhere that was not the plate positioned immediately beneath him. He had kept his coat on, despite the warmth of the café, and Alice briefly wondered how he would cope when spring eventually sprang. He had at least removed his hat, though, revealing the chaotic mass of hair that was contained beneath it.

As she sat across from the occult detective, Alice realised there was no going back now. There was no longer any room for scepticism; she had stared into the Void and witnessed things she never thought she'd experience. These things which she previously believed only existed in the realms of fantasy were now a part of her reality. She now saw Sam in a different light, too. What had once seemed like the weird ramblings of a strange man were now the words of experience from someone who saw the world in a way like no other. Alice was pleased she had joined him on this adventure.

'Wha' you thinkin' 'bout?' Sam mumbled through a mouthful of croissant.

'Oh, just stuff,' Alice said with a smile. She had been thinking about what Charlie had said, too, not able to shake the thought of imaginary friends maybe not being quite as imaginary as the name would suggest. 'I was thinking,' she started hesitantly, worrying if it might sound stupid. She suddenly realised how many things Sam must say on a daily basis which sound stupid. 'The Turners' son, Charlie... He said he knew my friend would keep him safe.'

'Well, I'm glad to have been of service,' he replied, taking a large mouthful of tea which puffed his cheeks out, and gulped loudly.

'He didn't mean you. He meant someone else... Charlie said that there was a man who held back the shadows. Kind of like I dreamed my imaginary friends did when I was growing up. Does that sound mad? It just seemed a bit, y'know...?' Her sentence trailed off.

'Not mad in the slightest. I believe I said to you when we first met that imaginary friends are probably spirit guides. Children are more open to such things, they don't worry about whether or not it makes any sense in the "real" world.' Sam made air quotations as he said this. 'After all, magick is an art of the mind and soul. What people might dismiss as an over-active imagination is likely a world they've simply forgotten about in their day-to-day lives. Not all, but most. Just because you're no longer a little girl who dreamed of friends no one else could see doesn't mean they're not still there, in a sense,' he said. 'I can see you're starting to remember, though.'

In that moment, for reasons she couldn't quite explain,

Alice thought Sam seemed impossibly old. His face was still that of a man in his late twenties, but his eyes looked like those of a wise, millennia-old soul. Despite the strange eccentricities Sam Hain often exhibited, Alice could feel that at his core there was a man far wiser than he would ever like to let on.

She smiled and nodded with a contented 'hm,' and took a sizeable mouthful of chocolate cake.

When she finally got back home, Alice threw herself onto the sofa and closed her eyes. She hadn't realised quite how tired she was until she was back in the comfort of home. She was just floating off to sleep when a sudden bang startled her awake.

'Ah, look who's home! Where were you all last night? You look exhausted,' Rachel said. She put the kettle on and started to make the pair of them some coffee. Alice simply lay back down on the sofa, closed her eyes and softly laughed.

'I don't even know where to begin...'

SAM HAIN
OCCULT DETECTIVE

THE GRIMDITCH
BUTCHER

Prologue

That Wednesday had been just like any other for Douglas Norton.

He had shut the shop at six o'clock, cashed up the day's earnings, binned the produce which was no longer fit for sale, and then stopped for a couple of pints with the lads at *The Hog's Head* before heading home. This was a regular routine for Douglas. He and his friends had a habit of going for a drink after work every Wednesday and Friday, stay for a pint or two and have a quick game of pool, and then head home. The walk home was an easy one for Douglas, and rarely took him longer than fifteen minutes from door to door, unless he needed to stop off at the corner shop along the way. He would always walk the same route, following the roads and alleys as if he was on autopilot, and then settle down in front of the television when he got in. He was comfortable being a creature of habit.

Tonight, Douglas did not need anything from the corner shop, and he had started to make his way back home from the pub not long after nine o'clock. He walked along the high street and onto one of the residential roads, turning left and into the gravel alleyway which ran along the back of a terrace of houses. It was the quickest route home, cutting out a few of the roads and leading around the back of the terrace, past the garage, and down into the cul-de-sac where he lived. To one side of the narrow pathway stood the monotonous plain brick façade of the backs of the houses. The brickwork was only occasionally broken up by graffiti or a downstairs-bathroom window. To the other side, suburban gardens hid behind tall wooden fences, and trees peeked their leafy heads over, reaching down to any passers-by below. At either end of the path stood two lamp posts, but there were no other lights along the length of the alleyway. The path was so long and winding that, for the most part, the road ahead was shrouded in darkness.

The gravel crunched noisily beneath his feet as he walked along. The night was a lot colder than it had been earlier that week, and Douglas briefly regretted not bringing a coat with him. The past few days had been unusually warm for January, but today the weather had decided it was still very much in the depths of winter. A chilling wind came blowing down the alleyway, and Douglas clutched his arms around himself to brace against the cold. It was then that he heard it.

It was not a noise he had expected to hear down the often quiet, empty alleyway, and it was certainly not a noise he had heard before. It was like a low, guttural growl, a rumbling roar echoing off of the alley's walls. Douglas felt his body tremble with the noise, as if a low-flying aeroplane had just soared overhead. Then, as suddenly as it had came, the noise went. Everything fell completely silent. An eerie stillness hung in the air.

He turned around to see what on Earth could have produced such a sound, but he couldn't see anything. The alleyway behind him was pitch black. Dark and empty and silent. Presuming it had just been a weird effect caused by the wind blowing through the alley, or maybe the rumble of an oncoming storm, he turned around to carry on his way. Without explanation, Douglas felt a sudden, strange, searing sensation pierce through his stomach, shortly followed by the feeling of something warm and wet. He looked down.

His white shirt being stained crimson red with blood was the last thing Douglas Norton ever saw.

CHAPTER I

The breakfast news was very rarely a source of good morning entertainment. On-going news stories would be briefly covered, broken up by smaller local interest pieces, followed by several iterations of the weather and the ever pessimistic coverage of traffic on the M25.

Alice watched the footage of motionless cars with very little interest as she chewed on a piece of slightly blackened toast. She only really had the television on to keep an eye on the time to make sure she wouldn't be late for work, but at least she now knew how long some people had been waiting in traffic whilst driving into central London. She was particularly grateful not to be one of them.

'All right, I'm off,' Rachel announced as she walked through the living room, throwing on her jacket, 'I'll see you in a couple of days, I suppose.' She was going away on a mandatory two-day course of team-building exercises for work. Alice did not envy her.

'Have fun!' Alice chimed sarcastically. 'It won't be as bad as you think...'

'The body of a man was discovered in an alleyway in Grimditch earlier this morning,' the newsreader announced, his voice just as flat and unmoving as his face, *'police on the scene of the murder are trying to piece together-'*

'A group of incredibly dull people for fake meetings, role-playing interviews, and getting teams to try to build bridges out of straws and tape. It's going to be an absolute riot,' Rachel retorted, rolling her eyes. 'How drinking-straw-architecture is in any way connected to customer service, I'll never know.'

'Look at it this way,' Alice said, swallowing the last bite

of mildly burnt toast and standing up, 'it'll probably be better than working on the refunds desk for two days.'

'We'll see,' Rachel said doubtfully, and she hugged Alice goodbye, 'I'll see you on the other side.'

'See ya,' she said, and Rachel walked out of the front door, slinging her overnight-bag over her shoulder as she left.

'-is the third incident to have occurred this month.' The newsreader straightened himself, maintaining a cold and unblinking stare down the camera. 'Now here's Tom with the weather.'

'It's looking grim, Jim,' announced Tom with the Weather, pointing to a map of London which had little cartoon clouds with sad faces on them.

Alice peered at the bottom-left side of the television screen to check the time. 07:13. She gulped down the last of her cup of tea, and headed to the bathroom to quickly clean her teeth before having to leave. As much as she did not envy Rachel's team-building days, she also wasn't too enamoured with the idea of spending the next eight hours standing behind a till accepting a seemingly endless barrage of refunds and exchanges. She had just started to clean her teeth when she heard a knock at the door.

'Fuhgut sum-thun?' Alice foamed through a mouthful of toothpaste as she pulled the door open, expecting to see Rachel there. However, standing in the doorway was not Rachel, but the familiar figure of Sam Hain, his greatcoat flowing down to his ankles and the rim of his fedora tilted over his eyes, clutching a crumpled newspaper beneath his arm.

'Have you seen the news?' he asked, holding up the paper and entering the flat. He glanced at the television, which was now recounting the story of a hamster who had climbed up a drainpipe, and – assuming this meant Alice had been paying attention to the rest of the news that morning – sat himself down on the sofa. 'Ah, excellent, you have. I won't need to fill you in then.'

'Wuh?' Alice frothed. 'Hol' on.' She darted off to the bathroom, spitting out the minty foam and quickly rinsing her mouth out before returning to the living room. She watched the news for a second to try to catch up with what Sam was saying. A hamster had climbed up a drainpipe and, despite having caused a blockage and survived a barrage of attempts to unblock it, had been reunited with its owner. 'Right, so what's got you interested in this story about a hamster?' She couldn't quite fathom the importance of a rodent in the drainpipe, but from what she had come to know of Sam Hain, anything was possible.

'No no no,' Sam said, unfurling the newspaper in front of him, 'nothing to do with hamsters. This.' He pointed a finger at a news article, a page-long piece about a recent string of murders in the east end, headlined with the tasteful title "The Grimditch Butcher". 'You haven't been following this then?'

Alice shook her head. 'Nope. And?' She didn't much care for sensationalist news coverage of murder victims.

'And? And what?! Three dead, all in similar circumstances, in the past month! And one of them was found in the early hours of this morning.'

'Why am I not surprised you get excited about murder?'

'It's not the murder itself, it's this.' Sam took out a sheet of folded paper from his inside pocket, and laid it out in front of Alice. Printed on it were pictures of the previous two murder cases, the bodies of the victims prominently displayed in the centre of each image. In each case, the bodies were laying on their backs, limbs sprawled out and their clothes stained red around the abdomen, a pool of blood coagulating around them. Any police involvement had mostly been cropped out of the images, so each one focussed largely on the bloody corpse, although the occasional officer's elbow or hand still found its way into shot.

'Elliot Ferguson, a candlestick maker, and Brian Mayweather, a pastry chef, were both found dead within these past few weeks. Both in similar circumstances. And now, there's been a third.' Sam detailed, indicating to the bodies pictured.

'Wait, hold on. Did you say "candlestick maker"?' Alice asked.

'Well, yes. Elliot Ferguson was a candlestick maker.'

'Is that even a real profession? Aren't candlesticks made in factories now we're not living in the middle ages?'

'Well, yes, I suppose so, but that's not the interesting point! What links these victims?' Sam said, pointing to the pictures again.

'They were stabbed in the stomach...'

'Yes, and...?' Sam gestured, as if somehow waving his hand over and over would lead Alice to the answer.

'There's obviously something weird about it, otherwise you wouldn't be looking at me like that.' Alice looked back at the pictures, but didn't say anything more about them.

'No? Okay then, see the stab wounds, here and here,' Sam pointed, 'do you notice anything about them?'

Alice looked at them. Dried blood stains, a deep brownish-red colour, marred the victims' clothing, torn away at the abdomen and ripped like they had been ravaged by a wild animal. But the wounds were not quite like that of an animal attack. There was something deliberate, almost intricate, about the cuts in the flesh. The wounds spiralled and swirled, with smaller cuts which looked like symbols around them. 'They're like patterns,' she said.

'Yes, but, these aren't just any patterns,' Sam sounded far too enthusiastic for someone who was looking at pictures of formerly-living people. He pointed at the patterned wounds again. 'These symbols, they look like sigils to me. They're symbols of power, used for evoking and manifesting a spell-caster's intent.'

'What intent?'

'That depends on the one who is casting them. They can be invoked to do anything, from making it rain and boosting lottery chances, to inflicting pain and summoning demons. Very powerful magick in the right – or wrong – hands. And these people... Well, these aren't just your run-of-the-mill murders, and they're certainly not a part of a ritual spell to attract health and prosperity. This is blood magick.'

Alice stared at the images for a while longer before looking back up at Sam. 'And you're thinking we should go and investigate a murder which is more than likely linked to powerful, sacrificial blood magick rituals?'

'Absolutely,' was his simple reply.

'To be fair, I don't even know why I had to ask,' Alice said, looking for her shoes. 'So what do these sigils mean?'

'I have no idea,' Sam said frankly, 'but I have a plan to find out.'

'What's the plan?'

Sam stood up, straightening the lapels of his coat. 'We'll take a cab to Grimditch, we'll be there in about quarter of an hour. The magickal footprint of this will still be fresh, we'll be able to sense any disturbance in the Akasha. With any luck, the coroner won't have moved the body to the morgue yet, and I can get a proper look at the carvings in the latest victim.'

'Yes, with any *luck*...' Alice said, pulling on her boots. She wasn't particularly enthusiastic about the idea of starting her day with a corpse, but she couldn't deny there was a strange sense of intrigue to see it from Sam's unique point of view. There was something almost exciting about a magickal murder, although Alice was sure she would probably change her mind quite quickly when face-to-face with the reality. She double-knotted her laces and stood up.

'All right then, let's go,' Sam said, making his way out of the door. Alice started to follow.

'Wait. You may want to lose the hat at least before we go anywhere,' she said.

'Why?'

'You want to go to a crime scene, and you're dressed like you're on your way to a fancy dress party as a film noir detective. If you were any paler, you'd actually be in black and white.'

Sam stood still for a moment, contemplating her suggestion. 'The hat stays,' he announced, as if coming to an important conclusion, and marched off down the corridor and towards the stairs.

The black cab drove smoothly down Islington high street. The traffic seemed to be surprisingly light for that time of the morning, and the taxi driver had mostly kept himself to himself, not really engaging in small-talk with either of his passengers. Sam appreciated both of these things.

'Bollocks!' Alice suddenly exclaimed, causing the taxi driver to jump slightly in his seat.

'What's the "bollocks"-ing for?' Sam asked, still gazing vacantly out of the taxi's window.

'I'm meant to be at work in ten minutes,' she said, pulling her phone out of her pocket. They had just driven past the Angel underground station, which – had she have been going to work-work rather than off on some supernatural-murder-mystery-work – Alice should have been boarding the tube at that very moment. She tapped at her phone's screen, coughing and making a strange wheezing noise. 'How do I sound?' she croaked, suddenly sounding as if she were on her deathbed.

'Like you're dying of a horrible debilitating virus,' Sam replied bluntly. He could hear the muffled ringing of the phone, shortly followed by the clicking of someone the other end picking up the receiver. Alice thrust a finger up in front of her pursed lips, staring at Sam, and she put the phone up to her ear.

'Hey,' her voice creaked like the floorboards of a dilapidated old Victorian townhouse, 'I'm so sorry about this, but I'm afraid I won't be able to make it in to work this morning.' She coughed violently down the phone to drive home her point. It was a miracle she didn't force a lung up in the process. 'I'll take some flu medicine or something, and I should be able to come in this afternoon if you set my shift back a bit?' She followed this with an exaggerated sniff and a half-hearted splutter.

'God no, you sound dreadful,' came a voice from the phone, *'just rest-up and get better, okay. Liz can cover your shift for the next few days.'*

'Oh, thank you so much,' she wheezed, 'I'll see you Monday.' She hung up, but not before choking out a few extra coughs away from the phone for added authenticity. 'There, that's that,' Alice announced with her usual cheery and not-at-all-flu-y voice, and put the phone back in her pocket.

'You are a woman of many talents, Miss Carroll,' Sam said with a subtle smile.

The taxi driver rolled his eyes. *Oldest trick in the book,* thought he.

Grimditch was an unusual place. It was a small region in the east end of London, but despite being a part of the city it felt more like a village or hamlet; just without any surrounding countryside, and with a strip club immediately next door to a fast food establishment. There was a single high street, populated by a few corner shops, a butcher's, a pharmacy, and a generous amount of run-down looking pubs and nightclubs. This street then linked to the surrounding housing estates, and beyond those stood several bland, towering blocks of flats, looming like concrete giants over the district below.

Sam and Alice exited the taxi a short distance from the alleyway where the body had reportedly been found, and started to make their way towards the scene of the murder. Alice's first impressions of the place were hardly positive. It didn't help that the weather had forgotten about the early Spring it had been promising, and instead decided it was going to be cold and overcast. Large, grey clouds hung low over Grimditch, and a bitter wind swept through the streets. At least the place was living up to its name.

As they approached the alleyway, Sam quickened his pace to a purposeful stride, marching with conviction up the gravel pathway. His coat swished back and forth rhythmically. Alice jogged a little to catch up, and matched his pace. The alleyway was an enclosed space, Alice thought, with the houses towering over her on the left, and gnarled trees leaning over the fences to her right. She wouldn't feel comfortable if she had to walk down this alley on her own. Doubly so now that someone had been murdered here.

Ahead of the two of them, a small congregation of police officers were gathered around a cordoned off area of the pathway. Behind the cordon stood a large white tent, completely concealing the site where the body had been found. Sam cut a confident swagger over to the police, making sure he was a few paces ahead of Alice. As he drew closer to the cordon, a sergeant stepped forward, holding his hand out to stop them from going any further.

'Sir, madam, I'm going to have to a-' the sergeant started, but Sam quickly cut him off.

'Arthur Doyle, consulting detective,' he said with an

authoritative tone and a quick wave of what Alice presumed was a fake police ID, 'and this is my colleague.' Sam gestured in Alice's direction.

'Joan... Joan Wilson,' Alice offered hesitantly, stepping forward and extending her hand to shake that of the police sergeant. He simply stared back at her, ignoring her out-stretched hand.

'We were dispatched to aid in the investigation,' Sam concluded, and attempted to push past the sergeant.

''scuse me, sir,' the sergeant said, placing a firm hand on Sam's chest, holding him in place, 'I wasn't told we were expecting an extra set of hands. We have everything under control here. May I ask who sent you?'

Alice could see the cogs whirring in Sam's head as he tried to come up with a convincing cover.

'Anderson. Homicide desk,' he said determinedly. He didn't have a clue if Anderson was a real person or not, or – if he was indeed real – whether or not he worked on the homicide desk. It was a gamble, but Sam often found that if he said things with enough confidence and authority then people tended to believe him.

There was an unnaturally long pause, and Sam was starting to feel nervous. Maybe the sergeant knew Anderson. Maybe the sergeant *was* Anderson. Maybe there wasn't even an Anderson, and this man knew it! He tried to maintain his authoritative composure whilst he waited for what felt like an eternity for the sergeant to pass his judgement.

'All right then, go on through,' said the sergeant with a nod, and he waved Sam and Alice on through.

'Thank you, sergeant,' Sam replied, making his way past the cordon, lifting the "Police Line Do Not Cross" tape over his head as he ducked beneath it, and walked towards the tent. He breathed a sigh of relief.

'You do realise that impersonating an officer of the law

is a criminal offence, don't you?' Alice hissed at him when she was sure they were not in earshot.

'Trust me, this isn't the first time I've bluffed my way through something. I know what I'm doing.' It was true, he had bluffed his way through things before, but stating he knew what he was doing may have been a bit of an exaggeration.

'I'm sure. Is that how you got your hands on a fake police ID?'

'When you've seen a few IDs, you can replicate one to a passable standard, provided they don't look at it for too long. Comes in handy with freelance detective work,' he replied, nodding in greeting to one of the guards posted outside of the tent, and pushed his way through the entrance.

The scene inside had been carefully preserved for further investigation, with a small number of little yellow placards placed around key details. The gravel path had been kicked and scuffed around, with signs of disturbance – presumably caused by the dragging of feet – leading away from the middle of the path and towards the grassy verge. The blades of grass were stained a deep, rusty red, painted as if with a single oily brush-stroke in one particular direction. Towards the body itself.

It was a surreal sight, seeing this thing which had once been a person now laying sprawled out by the side of the path like an old discarded rag-doll. The legs were positioned not unlike that of the stick-man on a wet floor sign, with the arms also spread in a weird, angular way. In the middle of the victim's white shirt was a large rip, surrounded by a crimson-red stain. The collar and shoulders were also stained with blood, and red flecks marred the sleeves of the shirt, but that was where the body of evidence ended. Where one would normally expect to see a neck and head, there was nothing but a bloodied stump.

Alice turned away from the sight, feeling her stomach churning more and more with every second she spent staring at the headless body. Instead, she knelt down by a leather wallet, marked with a yellow placard numbered "2", and pretended to examine it with great interest. An uncomfortable lump formed in her throat, but she swallowed it and tried not to think about it too much.

Sam made his way over to the officer who was stood over the body, picking up a pair of rubber gloves from the nearby table as he went. 'What's the situation?'

'You the DI?' the officer asked, straightening himself up as Sam approached.

'I am.'

'What's with the get-up?' He looked Sam up and down with a sceptical expression.

'What do you mean?'

'You just look like what my son would dress up as if he was going to a Halloween party as a detective, that's all. Would've thought you'd want to wear one of the regulation jump-suits or something. Anyway...' The officer turned his attention to the headless body. 'One victim, found earlier this morning, deceased for around maybe ten or twelve hours now. Was found on this verge, partially concealed by a pile of leaves,' the officer reeled off as if reading from a shopping list. 'Victim was found headless, and with a substantial abdominal wound. No sign of any theft; victim still has his phone, his wallet, his keys... So we can rule out a mugging. There's no evidence of much of a struggle, either. A bloody hand-print was found on the wall next to the body, presumably where the victim attempted to regain his balance before...' He trailed off, and ran his index finger across his neck, miming decapitation. Sam didn't really understand why the amateur dramatics were somehow better than saying "beheaded."

Alice tried to conceal her revulsion as she listened in on

the description, and distracted herself by focussing on the wallet and its contents. She felt distinctly uncomfortable about the whole situation. Not only was she a few feet away from a headless body, but she was also now rummaging through its wallet. She flicked through the collection of credit cards and café loyalty cards, and she peered into the change pocket; amongst the standard loose change were a couple of crumpled old receipts, some commemorative coins, a token with a golden logo on the front, and a half-torn lottery ticket. Nothing of any interest.

Sam grimaced as he looked down at the body. 'ID?'

'Hard to get a positive ID without a head 'n' all, but according to the driver's license and credit card in his wallet: Douglas Norton, forty-two years of age. We're now awaiting clearance to search his residence and workplace.'

Sam nodded. He looked down at the body with a morbid fascination, and his eyes traced the trail of scuffed gravel and the occasional streak of blood back towards the middle of the path. From what he could tell, the body had been dragged at least eight feet from its initial position.

'Looks like the victim was initially injured here,' Sam said, stepping back towards the point where the scuff marks came to an end. Or rather, as he inferred, a start. There was a small pool of dried blood at his feet, leading off into a smeared trail which grew heavier and heavier until it joined with the body. 'There's significantly less blood here, probably from the initial stab wound. Presumably these marks are from where the victim was dragged, and then decapitated here.' He walked back over to the body and knelt down by the side of it, pulling the pair of rubber gloves on with a satisfying snapping sound. 'If I had to hazard a guess, I'd say that the murder weapon wasn't removed from the man's abdomen until he had been dragged back to this spot here.'

What the hell am I doing here? Alice thought to herself. She didn't have the stomach for bloody beheaded corpses, or any blood for that matter. She had enough difficulty watching hospital-based soap operas (although admittedly the state of the patients were not always the worst things about those series).

Poring over the body, Sam gently pried away the torn and tattered fragments of shirt from around the stab wound. The cotton was crusty with dried blood, and required some convincing to come unstuck from the browning congealed tear in the stomach, but Sam could start to see that his suspicions were right. 'Al-... Joan, could you come and look at this please?'

It took a few seconds for Alice to realise he was actually talking to her, and a few seconds more to try to find a way of not looking at the dead body. 'I'd rather not...' *Please don't make me. Please don't make me. Please don't make me.* 'I'm, uh, busy over here.' She flapped the wallet about a bit.

'It's important,' Sam said, peering at her over his shoulder.

Bugger. She stood up from her rigorous inspection of the wallet and tentatively made her way towards him. And Douglas Norton. The headless, bloody body of Douglas Norton.

'Note the pattern of the abdominal wound,' Sam said, pointing to one of the many things in the vicinity of the one place Alice was trying her best not to look. Still, she looked to where he was pointing. The wound was not just any wound. A large bloody hole, presumably the entry wound, was where the belly button would have been on a non-cut-up person, and from there the pattern cut into the flesh spiralled outwards, forming a grotesque and unearthly symbol. The symbol twisted and turned at strange angles and seemed to be surrounded by other smaller symbols, but Alice had to look away before she could even begin to make sense of its shape. She swallowed heavily.

'Like the others?' she asked in a hushed tone, and Sam nodded morosely.

'You mean the other cases this month?' the officer enquired, standing behind them and peering over their shoulders. 'It does bear some similarities with the others. This is the first headless one, though.'

'Any sign of the murder weapon?' Sam asked, standing up. As he turned to face the officer, he slipped the transphasic energy probe into Alice's hand. She felt the cold metal of the TechnoWand in her palm and held on to it. As she clasped it, she thought she felt it vibrate in response.

'No, I'm afraid not. Same with the previous cases, too,' the officer explained, 'the killer may not have hidden the bodies well, but aside from that the scenes have been clean. No prints, no weapon, no evidence of any kind other than the body itself. All we have to go on are these strange patterns. My guess is that our killer likes scaring people, so he leaves the bodies in plain sight with a little signature to sign his work, but still cleans up anything which might lead us to him.'

While the officer was distracted with Sam, Alice slowly moved the probe over the body. She assumed that was what Sam had wanted her to do, anyway. She watched what she was doing out of the corner of her eye, squinting with disgust and trying her best not to think of the fact that her hand was now no more than a few inches away from a beheaded corpse. It seemed to be working, though, as the crystal at the probe's tip glowed intermittently, accompanied with a dull vibration through its metal body. *Definitely something out of the ordinary here then...*

The officer's radio started to blare a static crackling noise, and a voice almost entirely indiscernible shouted something through it. The voice mumbled and crackled its way through a garbled sentence, and the officer nodded.

Police officers have a unique ability to make sense of garbled communications which no-one else can understand. Second only to train conductors. 'Copy that,' the officer stated, and turned to face Sam. 'You'll want to start making your way back to the high street, we've got a warrant to search the victim's workplace.'

'Where are we heading?' Sam asked.

'The butcher's shop,' replied the officer, and spoke into his radio again. 'I'm sending *Sam Spade* your way.'

Maybe I am a bit too film noir... Sam thought as he and Alice were led towards one of the police cars. Alice handed the probe back to Sam and gave him a subtle nod.

Standing outside of the butcher's shop, Sam and Alice stared at the scene which lay before them, dumbfounded. Alice stood in silence, her mouth hanging open in shock. She turned away from the sight, retching. The police had only just opened up the front of the shop, revealing the horrific image it had been hiding.

There, sitting prominently in the middle window of the butcher's shop, surrounded by hanging porcine carcasses and select cuts of beef, sat the severed head of Douglas Norton, his mouth a-gape and a shiny red apple clasped between his teeth. His eyes were wide-open, but were partially concealed by a pair of sunglasses, and a Hawaiian-style sun-hat rested upon his head. A wreath of fake pink flowers were wrapped around what had once been Douglas Norton's neck.

'Well, at least that solves the mystery of the missing head,' Sam said.

CHAPTER II

The smell of meat hung heavily in the air of the butcher's shop. It was as if the stench of death was clinging to every surface. It was not a pleasant aroma by any means, made all the worse by the knowledge that the severed head of a man was now sat in the window. Alice had elected to stay outside for a while to catch some air, at least until the head had been removed from the scene, while Sam jumped straight on in to carry on with his investigation.

It was fairly standard in terms of butcher's shops; animal bodies hung down from the ceiling on meat hooks, morbid displays of body parts decorated the window, and a selection of complementary sauces lined the shelves on the back wall. Sam found the whole thing repellent; exactly why people still wanted to eat the meat after shopping here was beyond him. Through the door towards the back of the shop was a large walk-in freezer, filled with frozen goods and the rather haunting image of rows and rows of pig carcasses. But nothing seemed to be out of place, broken or disturbed in any way. Aside from the human head which now decorated the shop front, it was a perfectly normal butcher's shop.

'Looks like we have ourselves a phantom,' one of the officers remarked idly as he peered around the shop, taking down a few notes in his pad.

'Pardon?' Sam said, suddenly looking up from where he had been studying the severed head. He was more than a little surprised. It wasn't every day the Metropolitan Police considered something supernatural was involved in a case.

'Phantom suspect,' the officer replied. 'No witnesses, no murder weapon, no evidence of a break in... No evidence of any kind. We've not got much to work with here.

Whoever did this was able to make themselves vanish, leaving no evidence other than those sick symbols.'

'Ah,' Sam replied. He was a little disappointed that he hadn't found a new associate with access to actual search warrants. He carried on examining the severed head, taking great care to not touch it.

The head of Douglas Norton was ghostly pale. His eyes were glazed over, as if staring into a void beyond the veil of reality. It was a haunting sight to behold. Sam had had very little experience with dead bodies, even less so with decapitated heads, and he was starting to regret wanting to be on a case involving a proper murder. It always seemed like an exciting prospect to him, but now he was actually investigating one he was not enjoying it quite as much as he had thought he would. *Reanimated corpses, yeah,* he thought, *the undead risen? Of course, not a problem! But an actual dead-dead person...? Blimey.* Supernatural cases were often exciting and intriguing, sometimes even fun, but now that human lives were clearly at stake...

Speculating about murder cases by piecing together the evidence supplied by the news had been a hobby for him, but that and having the severed head of a murder victim actually in front of him were two very different things. He shook the thought from his mind as he tried to turn his focus back to Douglas Norton's head.

It did not really betray any marks of the paranormal, although he wasn't too sure what he had been expecting from it. It was eerie and off-putting, but aside from that he wasn't really coming to many other conclusions. The most he could say was that yes, this head had at one point been connected with the body in the alleyway, and as far as he was concerned there was something more to this than met the eye (in his line of work, wasn't there always?). Whatever that something more was would have to wait, however, as the officer was now approaching him with an expectant look on his face.

'So what's the verdict, detective?'

Sam swallowed quite audibly as he tried to think of a quick and passable answer. 'Well, uh, as you can see,' he started, and pulled back the wreath of fake flowers wrapped around what had been Douglas Norton's neck, 'the head was severed along here.' He pointed to the very evident place where the neck ended and the body promptly failed to begin. The officer nodded.

'Hmmhmm. I can see that.' The officer was clearly unimpressed with his deduction, and gestured for Sam to continue.

'To be honest, officer, it's too early to say anything conclusively,' he said, 'as you said, whoever did this knew how to cover their tracks. This joint is clean.' *"This joint is clean",* Sam thought to himself, *maybe try not to borrow too many clichés from crime dramas...* 'You know, severed heads not withstanding,' he added, looking back at the head. 'Maybe the coroner might have more luck inspecting the victim and his, uh, dislocated head?'

'Okay, we'll have the head dispatched to join the rest of the victim,' replied the officer, signalling to another to come over and collect the head. It was hastily placed inside a cooler and carried outside to a nondescript black van, which had just pulled up in front of the butcher's shop.

'Now that's interesting...' Sam mused as something out of the ordinary caught his eye. Where the head of Douglas Norton had been sat was a bloody mark. It was not simply a matter of the blood from the severed head leaking onto the surface and drying there, it was far too precise for anything like that. It was a spiral shape, radiating anti-clockwise and drawn in blood, with five smaller shapes – sigils – dotted around the outside of the spiral. It was more than a little reminiscent of what had been carved into the Void crystal found during the night in Knightsbridge.

'Please send my colleague in, officer,' Sam said, peering closely at this new revelation. As the officer walked away to call in Alice, Sam whipped out the transphasic probe from his breast pocket and quickly waved it over the patterned blood stain. The crystal turned a shade he could only describe as purple-black. It could not really be said to have glowed, as the colour it turned seemed more like an absence of light than anything else. He raised a curious eyebrow as he examined the weird, shadowy aura the crystal was now generating.

'Has the head gone?' Alice asked as she was led in by the officer, slightly averting her eyes and prepared to suddenly cover them just in case she saw a body-part which really should have been attached to a body. Sam quickly pocketed the probe, and beckoned for Alice to come over.

'It's fine, the head's on its way to the coroner. I just wanted you to have a look at this,' he said, pointing down at the bloody spiral. As Alice approached, she could see why he had called her in.

'That's what I think it is, isn't it?' she asked, knowing full well the answer.

'I'm afraid so,' Sam said with a nod, 'and thank you, officer...?'

'Smith. Officer Smith,' replied Officer Smith.

'Thank you, Officer Smith. Oh, also, get the rest of forensics in here. We're going to need to dust for prints.' After years of watching crime dramas, he had always wanted to say that sentence.

'I'll have a team sent in ASAP.'

As Officer Smith walked away, Sam turned back towards the spiral and sigils. He stared at it silently for a long time, lost in thought, before turning his attention to Alice. 'Alice, listen, I very rarely say this... Actually, I can't remember the last time I had to say this to anyone, but,' his voice was uncertain and concerned. His eyes couldn't quite seem to decide where to look as he spoke, and ended up settling with gazing down at his shoes. 'But you're going to have to leave.'

'What?' Alice asked, taken aback. 'Is it because I couldn't stand to be in the same room as that severed head? Because I think that's a perfectly normal reaction to have to severed heads.'

'No, it's nothing to do with that. What we're facing is... Look, human lives are at risk, and I really don't know what to expect next. If this means what I think it means,' he said, pointing to the sigils, 'then it's connected to the oncoming darkness. Whatever was behind the Void portal, and everything that happened to you on Halloween, I don't know what or why, but...' He sighed, and fixed her with a serious stare. 'I don't want to put you in any unnecessary danger on this case.'

She looked deep into his eyes, and could feel his concern. She had never really thought about him being emotionally vulnerable, but in this instance she could see and feel his worry, even if she didn't quite share his concern for her safety. 'What, and you think that I'm just going to leave you to it? I've come this far, I may as well stay with you and see this through to the end,' she said. 'Besides, if it is connected with that thing that ended up inside my head, then I'd like to give it a piece of my mind! Figuratively speaking.' She could see Sam was not particularly happy with that idea. He continued to stare at her, silently, wearing a worried expression on his face. 'Okay, the minute things look like they could be taking a turn for the worse, I promise I'll get out of the way. Very quickly.'

Sam nodded begrudgingly. 'Good,' he said, although he didn't seem to mean it, 'I told you when we first met that it's not all quite as fantastical and magical as people might think, but I never thought you'd have to witness something like...' He held her by the shoulders for a moment, but soon released them, swallowing his anxiety and clapping his hands together. 'Anyway!' He span around, looking around the butcher's shop.

'What are you thinking?' Alice asked, trying to get back in on the case. Now that the head of Douglas Norton had gone, and there was not a decapitated body in sight, she found it was easier for her to think about what they were there for, rather than constantly being distracted by the macabre sights.

'Well, let's examine the evidence we have so far. The decapitated body of Douglas Norton, a local butcher, is found in an alleyway near his home. His head is then found at his workplace,' Sam began to reel off enthusiastically. 'His abdomen was marked with a sigil, and the Void sigil was found beneath his severed head. Now, it doesn't seem that there was much of a struggle where the body was found, and there's no evidence of a forced entry to the butcher's shop. What would that suggest to you?' He span around again, pointing at Alice to answer his question as if this was some kind of murder mystery pop-quiz.

'That Douglas trusted whoever killed him? He wouldn't have struggled against his attacker, because he wouldn't have seen it coming. He must've also trusted whoever it was with a set of keys to the shop, because his keys were still... Still with his body. So maybe a co-worker?' She was uncertain as to whether or not she was right, but it was the first thought that popped into her head.

'A sound theory, but the attacker could easily have taken the shop key off of the keyring. Nevertheless, Mister Norton was stabbed in the front – not from behind – and *then* decapitated, but didn't seem to put up much of a struggle. And they knew enough about him to know he worked here, and what time he would be heading back home. It's likely that whoever it was was someone he recognised and probably trusted, like a friend or associate.' Sam said, and he continued to case the interior of the shop. He still couldn't see anything else of interest. Yet he could not shake the feeling that he was missing something important.

'And what about the symbols? Why have all three bodies been found with the same sigil?' Alice asked.

'Same murderer, same motive,' he replied, gazing absently out of the window.

'Which is?'

'Haven't the foggiest.'

'Brilliant.' Alice had hoped for something a bit more insightful, especially from a self-proclaimed detective.

'All I do know is that they were cast for some dark intent.'

'Three murders with mutilated corpses; a dark intent behind it? You surprise me!' She pulled a sarcastic "I'm-incredibly-surprised" face.

'There must be a reason the murderer chose these three victims... This is more than a murder of convenience, especially now that Mister Norton's head was found here,' Sam said, although he seemed to be pondering things out-loud more than talking to anyone directly. 'No... Your run-of-the-mill killer wouldn't go to the effort of decapitating his victim and leaving the head in the window display, it's too... Unnecessary. Not to mention the sigil carvings in all of the victims, too. That's more than just a signature or a boast.'

'So what are you thinking? That someone wanted these men out of the picture for whatever reason?'

'Yes, and not just any reason. One doesn't cast a sigil without an intent, and this symbol wasn't carved into the Void crystal for no reason. There's definitely something supernatural behind all of this, and I think I know what it is.'

'Which is?' Alice was getting tired of Sam's vague musings.

'Well, we haven't got all of the evidence yet, but it's a good starting point. These victims were targeted for a reason, and from what I can tell they didn't have much in common. Other than their deaths. So what if... Mister Norton here, and the other recently deceased, were part of a cult and perhaps – perhaps – they were the unwitting sacrificial goats in a blood magick ritual they didn't even know they were participating in. Using blood magick to cast Void sigils would, to me, suggest trying to bring some physicality to something metaphysical. Which isn't a particularly good plan.' He spun on his feet and made a bee-line for the door.

'So what now? We go in search of a murderous cultist maniac practising some kind of dangerous dark magick?'

'No,' Sam said, turning to face Alice, 'we're going to talk to people, ask around, see if anyone knows whether or not Mister Norton or his fellow victims were involved in some sinister and arcane organisation. *Then* we're going to go in search of a murderous cultist maniac practising dangerous dark magick.'

Outside the butcher's shop, Officer Smith was talking with the man behind the wheel of the black van. The man seemed to be wearing a well tailored black suit, and a pair of dark sunglasses covered his eyes. Sam thought this was odd for two reasons. Firstly, such a fine suit was not really suitable for handling severed heads. Secondly, it was not remotely sunny enough to be wearing sunglasses. He gave Officer Smith a cursory wave as he and Alice walked by, but Smith and the other man were too busy to notice. Instead, Sam approached two of the other attending officers.

'Excuse me. Hi. I was just wondering, have you managed to identify any potential suspects, maybe familial or social connections to the victim yet?'

The officers stared back at him with stone-like expressions. 'Isn't that your job, detective?' one of them asked him flatly.

'Well, yes, but I've been investigating the victim's workplace, not sifting through files,' Sam said indignantly, reasserting himself as the one in charge here. He straightened himself, sizing up to the two officers, and clutched at his coat's lapels. 'An ID was found on the body at the initial crime scene. A background check should have been run by now.'

One of the officers nodded, and reached down for his radio. 'McKenzie to dispatch, have you got backgrounds on the Grimditch body?' The radio squawked an incoherent response through the static. 'Copy that,' he said after several garbled sentences. Sam still could not get his head around how any of these policemen were able to understand what was being said. 'Ex-wife, Felicity Bamford. Lives a few roads away from the victim's house. We've yet to notify her of her ex-husband's passing.'

'Thank you, Officer McKenzie,' Sam nodded, 'if it's all the same to you, I'll be the one to break the news to her. I have a few questions I'd like to ask her.'

'Yes, sir. She lives at 74 Prior Road,' Officer McKenzie said. 'Mind your backs,' he added, as the black van slowly approached them, and Sam and Alice stepped out of the way for it to pass.

'Thank you,' Sam said after the van had driven off, 'be sure to inform me as soon as we have a search warrant for Mister Norton's property.' He was actually starting to quite enjoy the proper-police-detective act, severed heads notwithstanding. Sam handed Officer McKenzie a slip of white paper with a telephone number scribbled across it. It was not his actual phone number, of course; Sam liked to have a second, disposable phone on hand for whenever he found himself in a situation which most people might consider less than legitimate. This was one such occasion.

'Come on,' he said to Alice as he started to walk down the road, 'we've got bad news to break.'

CHAPTER III

Sam and Alice made their way up the garden path to the front door of Felicity Bamford's home. It was a fairly old looking house, probably having stood on this road for at least seventy years. The wooden window frames were decaying, their white paint peeling away to reveal the damp wood beneath, and the blue door was starting to show signs of weathering. Sam knocked rhythmically on the door, and stuck his hands in his pockets as they waited. A few moments passed, and the door slowly creaked open. A woman's face peered tentatively around the corner. 'Hello?' she greeted them warily.

'Felicity Bamford?' Sam asked, inching his foot towards the threshold.

'Yes...?' Felicity Bamford replied with a nod.

'I'm Sam Hain, and this is my friend and associate, Alice Carroll-'

'Hello,' Alice chimed in.

'Hi,' Felicity said with a half-smile.

'- we're working with the Metropolitan Police,' Sam continued, pulling out his fake police ID, 'your ex-husband was Douglas Norton?'

Felicity nodded uncertainly. 'Yes,' she said, confused.

'We have some bad news. May we come in?'

'Oh Christ...' Felicity took a step back, her face now wrought with concern. 'What's Doug done?'

'Not much, he's dead,' Sam said matter-of-factly. Alice regretted not suggesting to him that maybe she should be the one to break the delicate news. The words "delicate" and "Sam Hain" rarely fell within the same sentence. Except for that one.

'Wha-? How?' The colour drained from Felicity's face, turning ashen and wan.

'Miss Bamford,' Alice said, taking a step forward and pushing past Sam, 'if we could please come in we'd just like to talk to you for a bit. We're terribly sorry for your loss.' She shot a quick, scolding look at Sam.

'Yes, very sorry.' Sam nodded in agreement, but he sounded more like a toddler who had just been told off than a man offering his condolences.

'Oh, of course. Sorry. Please, come in,' Felicity said obligingly, opening the door wide for them. Her face was now almost as white as her house, and she had a distant, worried look in her eyes.

Felicity led Sam and Alice into her living room and directed them to be seated. It was a fairly sparse room, of cream carpet and walls, the furniture pointing towards the television, and a modest array of ornaments sat atop the mantelpiece above the gas fireplace. Felicity hovered around Sam and Alice for a brief moment, not sure what to do with herself.

'Can I get you two a cup of tea?' she eventually asked, her voice trembling.

'No, it's quite all right,' Alice said, and gestured for her to sit also, 'are you okay? Maybe I can get *you* a cup of tea?'

'I'm fine. Really,' Felicity said, lowering herself into an armchair, 'I'm just... You know?' Alice nodded sympathetically.

'So when was the last time you saw Douglas?' Sam asked, leaning forward and attempting to soften his voice.

'Only last week. We tried to stay friends after things didn't work out, but... Things are never quite as they used to be, I suppose. How did it... How did it happen?' Felicity asked.

'We're not quite sure of all the details just yet, but we're dealing with a murder,' Sam said.

'*Murder,*' Felicity whispered involuntarily with shock.

'Indeed. I'll spare you the details,' he said, 'we just need to ask you a few questions, if you can answer them as best you can.'

Alice reached out and held Felicity by the hand. She could feel her shaking. 'I know this is difficult, but please try and stay calm and remember everything you can about last night.'

Felicity nodded, 'okay.'

'Well, first of all, where were you last night?' Sam asked, pulling out a pen and notepad. He stared intently at Felicity.

'I was here, at home,' she replied.

'Was anyone here with you last night?' Alice asked. 'The police want to cover all angles, and we'd like to save you any unnecessary stress.'

'Um, no. No. I was here alone.'

'Listen, Miss Bamford, I'm not here to interrogate you, or catch you out or whatever. I'm following my own... let's say *unique* line of investigation, and I'm just looking for information which could point me in the right direction. I trust you – I do – but the police will need something to support your alibi, otherwise they'll label you a suspect.' Sam said. 'I believe that your ex-husband's murder is connected with the two other deaths which have occurred this month, and the police can't ignore the similarities between the cases. If you have anything which might prove you either weren't responsible for Douglas Norton's murder-' Felicity let out a slight whimper at the words '- or have a solid alibi for the nights of any of the other victims, it'll help you immensely.'

'I remember when I heard the news about the first one,' she began to explain, 'because I thought to myself, *Christ, that's where I live!*

'Where were you when you heard the news of the first murder? What were you doing around the time of Elliot Ferguson's death?'

'I was on a team-building weekend, up in Peterborough-'

'Oh, how frightfully dull,' Sam interrupted. 'I'm sorry, carry on.'

'When you find out that someone was murdered just down the road from where you live, it makes you grateful you're not at home. You don't feel quite as safe in your own town when that happens.'

'And the second murder. Brian Mayweather, I believe. Where were you when that happened?'

'That was around the 10th, wasn't it?' Felicity asked, and Sam nodded in confirmation. 'That was the night of Doug's party. His birthday was on the 8th, and he invited a group of friends to join him at *The Hog's Head* on the Friday night for drinks.'

'And the others who were there can confirm this?' Alice asked.

'Yes. I can give you their details if you want?' Felicity said. She was starting to settle down a bit more, probably because the questioning was keeping her occupied and distracted from the shock of Douglas's passing.

'That would be most helpful, thank you Miss Bamford,' Sam said. 'I know that you and Douglas have been separated for a while, but were you aware of Douglas's whereabouts last night?'

Felicity hesitated momentarily, gathering her thoughts. 'Not as such, no,' she replied uneasily, 'but he used to go to the pub every Wednesday and Friday night and meet up with some friends. At a guess, I'd say he was there.'

'Would you happen to know who he was with last night?' Sam probed.

'I don't know everyone my ex-husband was friends with, detective. He was friendly with almost everyone in

Grimditch.'

'You say "almost",' Sam pried a little more, 'was there anyone Douglas was not friendly with?'

'Oh no, I don't mean it that way,' Felicity answered, somewhat flustered, 'I only meant that I don't *know* everyone in Grimditch.'

'Okay, I understand. But if you can think of anyone who might have wanted your ex-husband dead...'

Felicity shook her head morosely. She and Douglas had had their ups and downs, but even in the heat of an argument she wouldn't have wished this upon him, and she certainly couldn't think of anyone who would have wanted to kill him.

'No,' she uttered, 'a lot of people liked Doug. He was the local butcher, always friendly and happy to see his regular customers. He was very sociable. I can't think of anyone who would want to...' Her sentence trailed off.

Sam had been taking notes of everything Felicity had been saying, nodding and hmm-ing attentively. He scrawled the last few notes into his moleskine notebook before looking back up at her. 'Now this might strike you as an odd question, but was your ex-husband involved in any kind of group or organisation? Maybe like a society, or gang, or something?'

'A gang? No, no, he was never part of a gang or anything. As I said, he met up with a group of friends at the pub a couple of times a week, but that was it.'

'Do you know if he was involved with the occult in anyway? Applied the arcane arts? Meddled with magick not meant for mortal men?' Sam enquired, particularly fond of his last sentence. *I might use that one more often...*

'What? What kind of-? N-no, of course not. Why?'

'We suspect it may have played a part in his murder, and those of the other victims this past month.' He reclined into the soft, cushiony back of the sofa, appearing to write down some more well-considered thoughts in his notepad. In fact, he was now just doodling; it helped him think. He scribbled a rough copy of the sigils found on Douglas's body, and eyed them with a wary eye.

'Well, he did have an interest in conspiracy theories and secret societies, but it was only an interest of his. I don't think he was ever *involved* in any, not anything that would put his life at risk. He and Pete used to talk about crazy conspiracies all the time.'

'Who's Pete?' Alice asked. Sam stopped scribbling and looked up, intrigued.

'Pete Jones. He and Doug worked together for a while. Pete left the butcher's to work at a delicatessen down the road, but he still popped in to help Doug out and cover the shop if he needed to,' Felicity paused for a moment, but Sam's eagerly enquiring face pressed her for more information. 'They'd talk at length about all kinds of weird stuff.'

'Such as...?'

'Oh I don't know, I never really listened to any of it. The usual conspiracy stuff I suppose; secret organisations running the world, controlling the state of the economy; aliens working with the American government, and spaceships disguised as clouds.' Felicity giggled to herself, remembering some of the mad things Douglas used to say. Her fond memories started to bring a little bit of colour back into her otherwise pale face.

'Any idea where I might be able to find this Pete Jones? We're going to need to speak to him also.'

'He'll probably be at work at the delicatessen. You don't think he's responsible, do you? He's a bit of a joker and can be quite pig-headed, but he's a good man.'

'No. Well, not yet. Too soon to say either way, really. We just need to build up a profile of your ex-husband's life, it might help us draw some connections and come close to identifying his killer. Anyway,' Sam said, pocketing his notepad, 'thank you for your cooperation, Miss Bamford. Again, we're terribly sorry for your loss.'

As Sam stood up, he noticed something on the mantelpiece. It was a small, circular stone, probably no larger than a fifty-pence piece. Carved into the front of it was a symbol, an angular hieroglyph with a right-slanting line at the top, and a long vertical line stretching downwards, ending in a two-pronged fork shape. The carved symbol had been carefully painted in gold, making it stand out from the slate-like stone, and Sam thought he vaguely recognised it from some ancient culture. *Possibly Egypt*, he thought. He couldn't explain why it had caught his eye, but he felt compelled to take a closer look.

'That's an interesting stone,' he remarked, and walked over to the mantelpiece to have a better look at it. It was curiously, almost unnaturally, smooth, and the more he looked at it the more he was sure it was an Ancient Egyptian symbol. He felt like he had seen it somewhere before at any rate.

In fact, now that he was sure it was Egyptian, he could see other pieces of Egyptian symbolism and memorabilia around the room, such as the statue of a serpent-like creature, and another which was a weird amalgamation of creatures, with the head of a crocodile, the forequarters of a lion and the hindquarters of a hippopotamus. *Ancient Egypt had some cool looking gods.* 'Been to Egypt recently, by any chance?' he asked, turning back to face Felicity.

'No, I haven't. My boyfriend went last month though,' she replied casually, 'Ryan came back with a suitcase full of weird little trinkets like that.'

'If you don't mind me asking, did Ryan and Douglas get on? You said you tried to stay friendly with Douglas after the divorce, so that must have caused some tension with you and your boyfriend?'

'Not really, the two of them actually got on quite well. They had a lot of things in common. They'd even go for a pint together sometimes.'

'Hmm, then he's a better man than me! I wouldn't want to go for a drink with my ex's new boyfriend,' Sam said. 'So, just to be sure, Ryan wouldn't have any motive to kill Douglas?'

'No! Of course not.'

'Okay, just checking,' Sam said, a sceptical tone in his voice, and he turned to leave. 'Thank you again for your cooperation, Miss Bamford. We'll be in touch when we have more information or if we need to ask you any more questions.'

'Oh, all right,' Felicity replied, and she stood up to escort Sam and Alice to the front door. She opened the door for the two of them, and with a wave goodbye she said, 'thank you for letting me know, detective. I appreciate what you're doing. Just get this guy.'

'It's very much my intention to,' Sam replied without even turning around to face her, and with a casual wave over his shoulder he carried on striding down the path. Alice put her arm reassuringly around Felicity's shoulders as she went to leave, and handed her a piece of paper with several numbers written on it.

'I quickly looked up the details for some local bereavement counsellors,' she said as Felicity took the paper, 'I'm sure the police will have somebody for you to talk to, too, but I thought... You know.'

Felicity nodded and smiled slightly. 'Thank you,' she said, and Alice thought she could see Felicity's eyes welling up with tears. With a quick hug and a final goodbye, Alice stepped down the stone steps and walked down the garden path to join Sam.

'So what's the plan, Batman?' Alice asked once Felicity had shut the door. 'We've got a couple of names now, where shall we start?'

Sam gazed off into the middle-distance as he thought for a moment. 'Hmm, yes. Pete Jones and Felicity's new boyfriend Ryan... We'll start with Mister Jones. If Douglas Norton was dabbling in conspiracies and the occult, Pete Jones would probably know.' He started to walk down the road, only to suddenly stop after a few steps, and he turned to face Alice. 'And don't call me Batman. If I were a comic book character, I've always fancied myself more of a *Constantine* type.'

'But that doesn't even rhyme!' Alice said.

'Doug's... dead?' Pete Jones said in utter disbelief, resting his head in his palm as he leaned on the counter of the east London delicatessen. He was a middle-aged man, succumbing to the effects of a gradually greying and receding hairline, and his face was creased with grief. His apron and gloves were marred with flecks of grease, and Sam and Alice had immediately been able to identify him by a badge which read "Hello! My name is Pete" secured to his apron with a small, gold pin. 'How?' he asked after a few moments of silence.

'We're attempting to find that out, Mister Jones. We spoke with Felicity a few hours ago, and she suggested that you might know more about Douglas's recent circumstances. When was the last time you and he saw each other?' Sam asked. He leaned against the delicatessen's counter, and immediately regretted it when he felt an unidentifiable cold liquid seeping into the elbow of his coat.

'Well, we used to work together, but ever since I took the job here we've met up like twice, three times a week,' Pete said.

'Yes, Felicity mentioned that. But when did you last see Douglas?' Alice asked. She didn't repeat Sam's mistake of leaning and putting her elbow in some anonymous fluid, and instead decided to stay standing upright.

'Last night. Ryan and I met up with him at *The Hog's Head* for a couple of pints,' he replied. 'Guess that was shortly before...'

'I'm afraid so, yes,' Sam said with a solemn nod. 'Was there anything that stood out to you last night? Someone at the pub who you might not have seen there before, maybe someone who left at the same time as Douglas?'

'No, not that I saw. Most of the regulars were in, nothin' out of the ordinary,' Pete replied.

'And what about Doug? Did he seem off-colour, a little distracted or worried about something?' Alice asked.

'He looked tired, but other than that, no.'

'Hmm, okay. And you mentioned that a Ryan was there with you last night. Would this perchance be the same Ryan as is currently in a relationship with Miss Felicity Bamford?' Sam enquired with an inquisitive raise of the eyebrow.

'Yeah, Ryan Nicholls. That's how Flick met him; me, Doug 'n' him go way back.'

'As I understand it, you liked to discuss things of a slightly unconventional nature?'

'What, Flick told you 'bout the things they like in the bedroom?' Pete seemed genuinely shocked, and more than a little embarrassed.

'Um, no... No. She mentioned the conspiracy theory stuff, though.' Sam shifted uncomfortably.

'Oh, right. Pretend I didn't mention bedroom stuff. Shouldn't be tellin' officers of the law about a man's private bits.'

'I wouldn't mind ignoring the subject, either,' Alice added.

'Anyway, conspiracy theories, the occult...' Sam

prompted.

'Wasn't anythin' really. Just discussed ideas and theories about stuff, shared things we'd read online. Was just interesting to think about, really.'

'And have you or Douglas ever practised the occult or dabbled in magick?'

Pete was silent for a few seconds, a look of confusion across his face. 'No, no. Why, y'think that could have something to do with Doug's death? That's madder than some of the tinfoil hat crackpot theories we'd read about!'

'I have my theories, Mister Jones. So neither of you belonged to any secret societies or cults or anything?'

'What, and if we was you think I'd tell ya?!' Pete said with a half-hearted smile. Sam simply stared at him. 'Nah, course not,' Pete added, 'was only jokin'.'

'What about Ryan Nicholls? What can you tell me about him?' Sam asked, taking down a few hastily scrawled notes into his notebook.

'He's a banker, works in the Shard. Doug sometimes felt like Flick had traded him in for a wealthier man, but he seemed alright with it.'

'And there was no bad blood between them? No hard feelings about having been with the same woman?'

'Nah. For a man and his ex's new fella, the two of 'em got on like a house on fire. There'd be the occasional comment, but they was just joshin'. And Flick and Doug still got on alright after the divorce.'

'So you wouldn't say that Ryan would want to have Douglas killed?' Alice asked.

'No, he wouldn't. He's not that kind of guy. Yeah, sure, in a soap opera or somethin' then they'd've been arch-enemies, but it wasn't like that at all.'

'An-' Sam started to say, but was quickly interrupted.

'And no, before you ask, Ryan is not in a cult or some

master voodoo sorcerer.'

'I wasn't actually going to ask that, but thank you for the additional information, Mister Jones,' Sam said. 'I was actually going to ask where I might be able to find Ryan now. You and he were with Douglas last night, and I'd like to ask him a few questions too.'

'Oh, well he's out of town on business today, but he'll probably be at home tomorrow,' Pete replied, scratching at the back of his head awkwardly. 'How's Flick handlin' things, anyways? She holdin' up alright?'

'She'll be okay, she was very taken aback by the shock when we broke the news to her, and she'll need to take time to mourn,' Alice said, and Pete nodded with a solemn agreement, 'I left her with the numbers for several bereavement counsellors, and I'm sure the police will have some contacts too.'

'Could I, uh... Could I also have the numbers of them counsellors?' Pete asked hesitantly, and his already ruddy complexion turned slightly redder. Alice nodded, and handed him a piece of paper. Evidently she had made a couple of copies just in case. Pete muttered a 'thanks' and quickly pocketed the paper.

'Thank you for your time, Mister Jones,' Sam said with a courteous tip of the hat, and he proceeded to walk towards the door.

'No worries, guv'. I hope you get the guy,' Pete said, regaining his composure.

As they were about to walk out of the delicatessen, Alice turned around. 'Sorry, one more question Pete?'

'Yeah?' He looked up from the counter.

'Did you happen to know any of the other murder victims from around this area? Have you lost any other friends or colleagues this month?'

'Yeah, I knew Brian. Mayweather. He used to join us down the pub for a couple of pints on a Friday. Things've been quieter since...'

'I'm sorry, it can't be easy for you. Both Douglas and Brian were found in very similar circumstances, as was the other victim,' Alice stated.

'I... I didn't know that. You think they were got by the same guy?'

'It's a theory we haven't ruled out,' Sam replied, 'now, we've got work to do.' He strode purposefully out of the door, and beckoned for Alice to follow.

'Two good friends gone in the same month...' Pete said morosely to himself as Sam and Alice left the delicatessen. 'Christ.'

Standing outside of the delicatessen, Sam quickly checked the time on his phone. It was now early afternoon, and he still hadn't heard anything about a search warrant for Douglas Norton's house. Aside from questioning Ryan Nicholls, it was the only thing Sam could think of which might lead him close to some sort of an answer. Something about the case made him feel uneasy, and it wasn't just the murder. There was something else, something important he was missing, but he couldn't quite put his finger on it. A gust of wind came blowing down Grimditch high street and threatened to steal Sam's hat. He clung on to the wide brims and tipped it further down in front of his face. No force of nature was going to take his beloved hat.

'Why didn't you want to ask him about Brian Mayweather?' Alice asked as she stepped out of the shop and joined Sam. 'Surely that would've helped us in some way?'

'Probably not. We already know Pete Jones is not a man for great detail, and he'd already confirmed that Mister Mayweather used to join them at the pub, prior to his untimely demise. But where does that leave Elliot Ferguson in this picture? The fact that only some, not all, of the victims were friends means we can't rely on there being a social connection. If we can solve why one was murdered, we may well have the reason for the remaining two as well, and that will in turn lead us to a conclusion,' Sam surmised.

'If you say so, I just thought it might be worth following up. So, what's the scheme, Constantine?'

'I like that one!' Sam said with an approving smile. 'Well, we can try to get in touch with Ryan Nicholls, which might be difficult with him out of town. Seems a little convenient he was around yesterday, but not today...' He paused to think for a moment, staring up into the light grey sky as he tried to come up with an idea. 'It'd be an idea to rummage through the previous case files for both Ferguson and Mayweather, they might provide us with a connection. We'll need to head to the police station anyway to start trying to get in touch with Mister Nicholls.'

'Okay, where's the station?'

'I have no idea...' As Sam went to reach for his phone to check a map, he felt his pocket vibrate. Pulling out his phone and unlocking it in one quick motion, he opened his new message. *Have the warrant for Douglas Norton's house,* the message read, *meet outside 26 Becknall Crescent. -Smith*

'Looks like we're going to Douglas's for afternoon tea,' Sam said.

CHAPTER IV

Douglas Norton's home was not much to look at. It was a small house, a simple two-up-two-down building with a small patch of grass for a garden towards the back of it. The police had already arrived by the time Sam and Alice got there, and they were busy investigating the inside of the house. Not wanting to miss out on any of the snooping around, Sam immediately bounded up the door step into 26 Becknall Crescent.

Inside, Douglas's house was in a state of disarray. House-keeping was evidently not one of his strong points. The carpets were thick with dust and darkened in spots from trodden-in dirt, and the coffee table in the middle of the living room was covered with scrunched up receipts, loose change and torn-open letters; a half-full and long abandoned coffee mug sat resting on top of this pile of scrap paper. None of the furniture matched, clearly bought for function over fashion, and there was no discernible sense of order or tidiness to the place.

Sam started to case the room, looking around and scanning for anything vaguely useful in his particular line of investigation. It was clear that Douglas Norton didn't consider his home-life a priority, but Sam hoped there might be some evidence around here which would confirm a connection with the supernatural. He started to rummage through the piles of paper on the coffee table, turning over outstanding bills and bank statements with little interest, and picked up a copy of the *Evening Standard*. It was a couple of days old, marked with the occasional coffee stain, and open with the crossword facing upwards. Some of the words had been filled in, each letter appeared slightly shaky, as if written on a train or in a car, but evidently Douglas Norton hadn't had the time to finish it.

Sam stared at the paper, and was momentarily distracted when he absent-mindedly started to wonder about the frankly obscure and cryptic clue for 20 Down, *Earl in indiscriminate use of rubber.*

'Hey, have a look at this,' Alice said from the other end of the room, leaning over a table with another inexplicably large pile of paper, 'looks like Douglas left his laptop on.'

Douglas's laptop had indeed been left turned on, charging and sitting on stand-by. As Alice opened the laptop up, the screen came to life. It was already signed into Douglas's user account, the front window of his butcher's shop set as the desktop background. In the image, sitting prominently in the middle window and surrounded by hanging porcine carcasses, was a pig's head. Its mouth was clasped around a shiny red apple, and its eyes were partially concealed by a pair of sunglasses. A Hawaiian-style sun-hat rested upon its head, and a wreath of fake pink flowers were wrapped around its neck. Sam peered over Alice's shoulder at the screen.

'Huh. How's that for irony...'

'I know, right! What is it you say about coincidences?' she said, turning to him.

'That there's no such thing, the Universe is rarely so lazy?'

'That's the one. Yeah, it can't be coincidence that this is exactly what happened to Douglas...'

'Not at all. Almost a fitting send-off for Mister Norton, don't you think?'

Alice didn't respond, she just carried on looking at the screen, sifting through the recently used programs. At the very top of the menu sat a short-cut to Douglas Norton's emails and, out of investigative curiosity, she clicked it.

Douglas Norton's email account was as much of a mess as his house. His inbox was flooded with spam emails, unopened newsletters and social media notifications. But in amongst it all was something which stood out considerably, and immediately caught both Alice's and Sam's attention. It was an email conversation, no subject line, between three correspondents; Douglas Norton, Elliot Ferguson, and Brian Mayweather.

Sam pointed to the screen. 'Click th-'

'Yeah, yeah, I saw that, just opening it...'

The conversation opened in a new window, showing the email thread between the three men. The first message was received on the 2nd of January. Some of the emails in the thread were now missing, presumably deleted from the conversation for reasons best known only to the person who deleted them, but what remained of the email exchange read as follows.

From: elliotferg@mail.com
To: brian.mayweather@mail.com, norton72@mail.com
Subject: Re: no subject
I've been thinking about the artefact.....I don't know what it is about it, but it fascinates me in a disturbing way. There's something haunting and unsettling, almost other-worldly about it, I can't explain it. It's only been sat on the shelf a couple of days, but it makes me feel uneasy whenever I look at it. Feels like it's watching me, you know?

From: brian.mayweather@mail.com
To: elliotferg@mail.com, norton72@mail.com
Subject: Re: no subject
You're just imagining things, it's fine. We're not even sure what it represents yet. When I'm next at the Lodge, I'll dig through the archives and see if I can find any references to it. In the meantime, we just need to keep it somewhere safe.

'Check out Brian's user image,' Alice said, as she stared at the screen. Brian Mayweather's profile picture was a black square with a simple gold pattern in the middle. It was an angular shape, with a right-slanting line at the top and a long vertical line stretching downwards, ending in a two-pronged fork shape. 'I've seen that somewhere before.'

Sam nodded in agreement. 'Felicity Bamford's mantelpiece...'

'I think there was something like that in Douglas's wallet, too,' Alice added, thinking back to the beginning of the day. The token in Douglas Norton's wallet did bare a striking resemblance to the piece on Felicity's mantelpiece, and in Brian's user image. 'Another not-at-all-coincidence?'

'Certainly not,' Sam replied. He reached over Alice's shoulder, tapping impatiently at the arrow keys to continue reading the rest of the emails.

From: elliotferg@mail.com
To: brian.mayweather@mail.com, norton72@mail.com
Subject: Re: no subject
OK but can we please not keep it in my house? I cant even stand being in the same room as it any more. Dont want to sound mad, but I think its evil. It whispers to me at night in my dreams. Can we please move it somewhere else?

There was a gap in the thread, as if several of the intermediate emails had been deleted from the conversation. The messages picked up again on the 5th of January.

From: norton72@mail.com
To: elliotferg@mail.com, brian.mayweather@mail.com
Subject: Re: no subject
The Regents like to use scare-tactics so we don't take any of their precious artefacts. It's mostly harmless. We're getting close, though.

From: brian.mayweather@mail.com
To: elliotferg@mail.com, norton72@mail.com
Subject: Re: no subject

I'll take it back to mine after the next session, see if I can get anything else from it.

The thread ended there, with no further contact evident between the three parties; although, with the amount of missing messages in-between, any further emails may also have been deleted. However, there was one additional email outside of the conversation, dated the 9th of January. Alice clicked on it and began to read.

From: brian.mayweather@mail.com
To: norton72@mail.com
Subject: no subject

Doug, it got Elliot, and now it's coming for me. I can hear something banging on the door, and trying to break in. Every night I can hear it clawing at my windows. I can't see it, but I know it's there. It's hiding in the shadows, watching, waiting. It's that damn artefact... We should never have given that blood offering. I think it wants more. We've got to get rid of it. I've sent the artefact to your shop, hopefully it going through the post will put it off the scent.

'Rub a dub dub, three fools in a tub. And who do you think they be?' Sam chanted in a sing-song kind of voice.

'The butcher, the baker, the candlestick maker...' Alice mused as she continued to glance over Douglas Norton's inbox.

'Turn them out, knaves all three!' he declared with a flourish. 'Looks like they were all meddling with something they really shouldn't have been meddling with. Blood offerings, never a wise move. Give a drop of your blood to a demon, and it will just keep on wanting more. Offer your life-force to an entity powerful enough, and it won't hesitate to come after you and claim its tribute. Especially if they were toying with something they didn't know anything about.'

'What are you thinking?' Alice asked, turning away from the screen for a moment to look at Sam.

'Some kind of supernatural souvenir by the sounds of it, most likely an Akashic artefact,' he replied, stroking his chin in thought.

'Akashic artefact?'

'An artefact imbued with Akasha energy,' Sam said helpfully. 'It might bestow some kind of metaphysical or supernatural power, or change the energy of an area around it with its mere presence. If they were giving blood offerings to a demonic force through this thing... Who knows what they could have unleashed. And who are these "Regents"?'

'Hang on, there's something to Pete in the sent folder,' Alice said, and she opened the email. It was dated yesterday, the 22nd of January.

From: norton72@mail.com
To: p.jones@mail.com
Subject: favour

Pete, I need you to come to the shop soon, maybe this Friday after a pint, to pick up something. It's something more than either of us could've imagined! I'll explain more at the pub later, but you won't regret it. Thanks, bud, I'll owe you one.

'See? Told you we should've questioned Pete a bit more,' Alice said triumphantly, an "I told you so" look crossing her face. Sam nodded in agreement.

'All right, you're right. Looks like we'll have to pay Mister Jones another visit then; he knows more than he's letting on.'

'That might be a little difficult,' came the voice of Officer Smith from somewhere behind them, and Sam quickly closed Douglas's laptop. 'We tried to call him in for an official statement, but we can't find him anywhere. He's not at work or at his home. We're running a trace on his Oyster and credit cards now to see if he's travelling anywhere, and we've got feelers out looking for him.'

'Any word on Felicity Bamford or Ryan Nicholls?' Sam asked.

'Miss Bamford has been very obliging, and her alibis check out. We've yet to reach Nicholls at work or on his mobile, seems he always disappears around these times.'

'Wait, what do you mean "always around these times"?' Alice asked curiously.

'Nicholls has always been a contact for each of the deceased, so we've had to bring him in for questioning on a number of occasions. But every time he's been away on business the day after the incident,' Officer Smith explained. 'Seems suspicious to me, but his alibis have been consistently solid, and there's no evidence whatsoever which can pin him to any of the murders. I guess he's just a very unlucky guy.'

'Hmm, seems off to me too, but unless we have something solid to go on there's nothing we can do,' Sam mused. 'If it's all right with you, officer, I'd like to review some of the previous case files and see if I can find anything which can give us a lead.'

'Sure thing, detective. I'll have a ride dispatched shortly,' replied Officer Smith, and he walked away mumbling into his radio.

Outside of the house, Sam waited for the police car to turn up and take him to the station. He was trying to think of the best course of action to take. With both Ryan and Pete nowhere to be found, they were now feeling their way around in the dark. He was just clinging on to whatever he could find which might lead him towards a conclusion. He could not shake the feeling that he was close to something, building up a picture of the circumstances surrounding the deaths, but no solid answers.

If what these men had been doing had caught the attention of something, and that something had been summoned through blood offerings, Sam wondered, gazing pensively up at the grey skies, *would that something not seek to claim every drop of blood it could get? Would it be satisfied with taking just the lives of the ones who summoned it, or would it crave more?*

'Alice,' Sam eventually said, returning his focus back down to Earth, 'while I'm digging through the files, stay here with the police. Start going through all of Douglas's emails, see if you can find any further reference to the artefact, or to the Regents.' He returned his gaze to the sky. 'Plus, I'd be happier knowing you're safe here for the moment.'

'Okay, and then what?' Alice didn't feel like he was trying to cut her out of the case this time; she was actually quite pleased he was trusting her with conducting one side of the investigation while he was busy with another.

'I'll give you a text when I'm done, and we'll reconvene later,' he said, and waved to the police car as it turned the corner into Becknall Crescent. 'I'll see you later. Keep in contact if you find anything.'

'I will,' Alice replied, 'see you in a bit.'

The message had come through about three hours after Sam had left for the station. It was brief and to the point.

Meet at butcher's after dark. Will explain more later. -SH

CHAPTER V

Alice pulled her jacket tightly around herself as she walked down Grimditch high street. The cold night air was especially bitter this evening, and the skies were pitch black. Not a single star was in sight. Small groups of people milled about the streets, marching from pub to bar to club on a Thursday night crawl. Occasionally an eerie stillness would fall upon the night, as the people disappeared and the roads were left feeling empty and quiet. Alice didn't really know which one she would rather, the creepy empty streets or the equally creepy stares she was getting from groups of men on a night out. She was relieved when she saw the familiar figure of a man in an overcoat and wide-brimmed hat leaning against a lamp post. Sam looked more noir-like than ever, silhouetted against the dim orange glow of the street light.

'Evening,' Sam said as Alice approached, and he took a few steps forward from the lamp post. 'How'd you get on?'

'Not too bad, actually,' Alice replied, and she waved a memory stick in front of him. 'I've downloaded Douglas's emails, but they don't really add much more to what we read earlier.'

'Nothing more about the Regents?'

'Not really, the Regents are only mentioned a few times in passing. But, I did find out more about that symbol.'

'Oh?'

'I did a quick search for it. It's the Was Sceptre, an Ancient Egyptian symbol held by Gods and Kings. Apparently it represents power, dominion, and – you've probably guessed this – regency.'

'Interesting...' Sam mused, gazing up into the starless

night, lost in thought. *How deep does this rabbit hole go?*

'What'd you find out?'

He snapped out of his reverie. 'Well, it turns out that both Mayweather and Ferguson had similar tokens to the ones found in Norton's wallet, and Nicholls's piece on Bamford's mantelpiece. If the Was Sceptre is the logo of the Regents, then I think we have a solid connection between the three victims and Ryan Nicholls,' Sam said. 'Also, Ryan was consistently away on business the day after each murder. As Smith said, his alibis check out. Every time he returned to town, he was brought in for questioning, but there's never been enough evidence to tie him to any of the cases, aside from him being generally suspicious and cagey. However, the day after each of the times he's been questioned, the houses of the victims have been broken into and ransacked, but nothing was taken or missing from the victims' personal effects. The detective reports from each of these incidents indicate that the perpetrator was looking for something, but couldn't find it.'

'So why was Douglas's house – well, it wasn't "okay", it was a mess – but why hadn't it been broken into too?'

'Ryan Nicholls is out of town, the break-ins only occurred after he returned. I'd like to talk to him about those when the police bring him in tomorrow.'

'Why are we meeting back here then?' Alice asked, looking up at the butcher's shop. It looked strange and eerie in the dim evening light, illuminated only by the light from the lamp post. As she peered through the window, she could see long, haunting shadows stretching towards the back of the shop, disappearing into the darkness.

'Douglas's email to Pete indicated he had something here. I felt like something was off when we were first here this morning, and it wasn't just the severed head. We're missing something important, and I think that artefact is here, somewhere,' Sam said. He walked towards the door of the butcher's shop, quickly taking a cautionary look over each shoulder, and leaned forward to pick the lock. Alice peered around nervously. She heard scraping, turning, prying, and then a satisfying click. Sam stood up and grinned at her.

'Shall we go in then?'

The little bell jingled cheerily as Sam slowly pushed the door open. The place was partially lit by the street lights outside, but towards the back of the shop was nothing but a thick veil of darkness. That distinct smell of a butcher's shop, of dead flesh and slowly decaying meat, hung heavily in the air, and Alice felt her stomach turn as the pungent aroma hit her nostrils.

'Remind me why we're breaking into a smelly butcher's shop under the cover of night?' she whispered to Sam.

'Because,' he replied, not bothering to whisper, 'I can conduct *my* investigation properly without the police peering over my shoulders.'

'I know, but... Couldn't we have at least stuck roses up our noses?'

'Bit prickly.'

'Just the flowery bit, idiot! Just to take the edge off of this smell.'

Sam progressed further into the shop, drawing the transphasic energy probe and using it to light the way. It wasn't much more effective than a candle flame, but it was better than nothing. He began to peer around the counter, passing the light of the wand over it.

'Look for something out of place,' he said, looking over to Alice, 'Void crystal, sigil stone, an old yo-yo covered in runes... Anything which might be an Akashic artefact.' Alice was already looking around for something along those lines, although she hadn't really considered a rune-inscribed yo-yo.

Approaching the back of the shop, Sam held the wand out ahead of him like a torch. The pitch blackness was gently illuminated by the crystal's glow, highlighting the charcuterie. He peered closely at each item, from specialised sauces to cuts of beef, probing for anything abnormal. A pig's head appeared to be hung on the wall at about head-height, and as Sam passed the light of the probe over it the glow became a little bit brighter.

Without warning, the pig head's nostrils flared. Its jaw flapped and its eyes blinked as if waking from a long slumber. It shook its head, its jaw and ears flapping peculiarly, and it groaned a spine-chilling groan. Sam staggered back, his eyes wide. He kept the wand pointed firmly at it.

'Woah-oah-oah!' he exclaimed, walking backwards into a table. Alice turned to see what the fuss was about, and her mouth hung open in an expression caught somewhere between awe and terror. The pig head was not just reanimated, but it had begun to move forward, as if staggering on unsteady legs. As it walked into the faint light coming from the street lamps outside, it became clear why. From the neck down, the pig's head was not just a pig's head; it was a human body, standing about six foot and its clothes stained with blood. It wore a little name badge, splattered with blood, which read: "Hello! My name is Pete." The pig's dead, unseeing eyes blinked like something which didn't quite know how blinking worked.

'This is weird...' Sam said uneasily. He kept the probe trained on the shambling, pig-headed corpse of Pete Jones.

'Th-this is hideous!' Alice exclaimed as she took a few staggering steps backwards towards the door. The mere sight of the monstrosity sent a wave of fear and horror coursing throughout her body; the only reason she was not sprinting down the road at this very moment was because she did not want to turn her back on the gruesome creature for even a second. She tried to move away even

further, but she felt as if her body had been rooted by her fear.

'Halt right there!' a voice shouted from somewhere behind them. 'Hands in the air, now!'

Alice immediately put her hands in the air, trying to angle her head to face whoever was shouting at them. She could not quite make out who it was, but from what she could see in the darkness they were wearing a police uniform. Sam simply stayed facing the creature before him, probe pointed at it in defence.

'I'd really much rather not,' he said.

'I said hands in the air, now!' screamed the voice, and the jingle of the doorbell echoed through the room as the door slowly shut.

'Officer McKenzie, is that you?' Sam asked, thinking he recognised the voice.

'Smith ordered me to keep an eye on you. I followed you here, "detective." I knew something was off... What are you doing h-' The voice of Officer McKenzie cut off mid-sentence as he stumbled over his words. The sight of the pig-headed man had caught him off-guard. 'What the hell is that thing?!'

'You have come too far,' spoke the pig's head, its mouth flapping awkwardly. It appeared to be speaking, but the voice which spoke to them was deep and reverberating, echoing around in their minds. It continued to limp its way forward.

'I don't exactly know,' Sam said in response to Officer McKenzie, keeping his eyes trained on the thing which had at one point been Pete Jones. 'What are you?' he asked, trying to maintain his composure while the shambling pig-man corpse marched towards him with undead intent.

'I am beyond your comprehension,' came the pig-man's response.

'Try me,' Sam said, standing straight as he challenged the

creature, 'you're not my first being of inexplicable horror.' It stopped advancing and stood, swaying uncertainly.

'I transcend your very understanding, mortal. I exist in a world far beyond your own,' it spoke, its jaw flapping peculiarly like an amateur ventriloquist's dummy.

'Like the Void?' Alice asked, swallowing her fear and lowering her arms. She figured that with a demonic pig-man in front of them, Officer McKenzie was not likely to be interested in herself or Sam any more. She took a tentative step forward. The undead pig head swung unnaturally, turning to face her.

'I can sense your mind, grasping in its ignorance. There are planes of existence so far beyond your understanding that you cannot even begin to imagine their reality.' Alice felt the words swim around her brain, and her blood ran cold. She could feel the malevolence of whatever this was emanating from it, filling the room and enveloping everyone in it. As she stared into its dead eyes, she felt a wave of terror wash over her again, a fear so deep her stomach began to churn. The more she locked eyes with it, the more she was overcome with the vile reality which stood before her. For a brief moment, she thought it took pleasure in her fear.

Suddenly, two loud gunshots rung through the air. Immediately dropping to the floor, Alice took cover behind a table. She could barely hear anything over the ringing in her ears. She looked up and could see Officer McKenzie standing there, his gun pointed out directly in front of him, and two bloodied bullet holes in the chest of Pete Jones's apron. Another shot was fired, and another, but still the unearthly creature stood resiliently, seemingly unharmed by the bullets.

Officer McKenzie's eyes widened. 'Oh fu-' he slowly mouthed to himself.

'Your efforts are futile,' the voice echoed in their minds, clearly and unhindered by the deafening ringing from the

gunshots, *'you only damage the vessel, you can not harm me.'* Officer McKenzie swayed uneasily as the voice overwhelmed him and he promptly collapsed to the ground, unconscious.

'You're not even really here, then,' Sam said, ignoring the police officer who had just fallen to the floor, 'you're just using that abomination of taxidermy as a conduit.'

'This shell is merely a vehicle for my being,' intoned the voice in response.

'So this is just an avatar for your consciousness? A connection that links you from your realm to ours. A connection that can be broken.' He kept the probe pointed at the pig-man, and the crystal glowed and pulsed with energy.

'Your words are as meaningless as your existence, human. You know not the magnitude of what you face,' it said, and the pig-man took an unsteady step forward, its arms raising slowly. There was a sudden burst of light from the end of Sam's wand, and almost instantly the pig-man's body crumpled and fell to the floor, like a puppet with its strings cut.

Sam breathed a sigh of relief, and turned to Alice, who was now struggling back on to her feet. 'I severed the link, it's g-'

'You rudimentary creatures of blood and bone,' intoned that same deep and dark voice, interrupting Sam and seemingly reverberating throughout the room, *'you are incapable of understanding. I am bound to your realm by more than the mere physical. You cannot even begin to grasp the nature of my existence.'* The pig-man body lay motionless at Sam's feet. Its jaw did not flap and its eyes did not blink, yet the voice still bellowed in their minds. Alice felt a shiver run throughout her body, and judging by the look on Sam's face he had felt it too. He tightened his grip around the transphasic energy probe.

'Tell us then,' Sam spoke, 'tell us who we're facing.' There was a sinister chuckle in the darkness, a noise which sounded unlike any earthly laughter, but no answer came. 'Are you responsible for the deaths of these people? Is this your doing? The Grimditch Butcher?'

'That is how your sensationalist tabloids refer to me,' the voice sounded almost amused by this, *'a name to give form to their darkest fear. Death. An inevitability of all physical life, your kind so easily succumb to entropy, and yet you try to ignore it, to escape it. I merely expedited the end of their mortal journey. Fitting that you should come to face me here, in a house which trades in death. But that is not what I am.'*

'So what should I call you?' Sam asked, but it was more of a demand than a question.

'Fallen Angel. Dark God. Demon. I have been given many names and titles across the millennia, but in the end, what you choose to call me is irrelevant. I simply am.'

'But why?' Sam addressed the room, attempting to confront the disembodied voice, 'why did you murder those people?'

There was a momentary pause before the voice spoke again. *'Because I desired it,'* came the reply.

'Really?!' Sam exclaimed incredulously. 'Just because you wanted to?'

'They were toying with powers beyond their ken. Their clumsy, primitive attempts to harness the power they held in their hands summoned me to this realm. They offered me each a drop of their life blood as tribute, in exchange for knowledge, for power, but they were not so willing when I thirsted for more. Thus I claimed what I desired. I got what I wanted; they did not.'

'And what gives you that right? What makes you think that you can just take human lives at your will?' Sam spoke sternly. His eyes were fixed into a solid glare, and his jaw was clenched. It was the first time Alice had really seen him burning with anger.

'You humans consider yourselves superior to the other species of your world. You claim to have the right to take the body of an animal and do with it as you please because you are superior. So too do I.'

Alice took a step forward and clenched her fists. She spoke into the darkness of the room, addressing their invisible tormentor. 'That's different,' she started to say, and Sam gestured desperately for her to stop, but she continued regardless, 'killing a human is a lot different than killing an animal. We use animals for food, you can't do that to a person.'

Sam stared at Alice, the glare still firmly fixed on his face. The dark voice chuckled again, and Alice froze on the spot. Her body started to feel numb, and her stomach continued to churn nauseatingly. She felt as if every fibre of her being was squirming in the presence of this shapeless horror.

'And why not, young Alice Carroll? Humans consider animals lesser than themselves, only because your kind deem them to be so. Just as my kind deem you to be lesser than us. I feasted on the essence of those men, as you might feast on the flesh of an animal. And with each life I claim, with every drop of blood drained from their hearts, my power grows.'

Sam took a step towards Alice, standing directly in front of her. As he did so, she could feel the entity's nauseating focus shifting away from her. 'What she means is that human beings have a greater capacity for intelligence than the animals of this world who are not quite as cognitively developed.'

'Is that not just a matter of perspective? As a man deems himself more intelligent than a pig, would a pig not consider itself more intelligent than a rat? A lion is more

developed for the hunt than a gazelle; would you deny it its right to feast on prey?'

Sam remained silent. He did not wish to be drawn into the entity's twisted games.

'Our knowledge of the universe is greater than yours. We are not bound to a single plane of existence by such flawed vessels of flesh and bone as you are. Your kind are born into this world, you wither and die. We have no beginning. We have no end. We are infinite and eternal. Compared to us, you are nothing.'

'It's funny,' Sam said, although by the tone of his voice he found nothing funny about it, 'that for such an allegedly superior being, so far beyond my comprehension, that you lack even the remotest sense of morality. You see this Universe as a playground, its inhabitants only for your twisted amusement.'

'The forces of this Universe bend to my will. You do not yet understand your place in the vastness of eternity, mortal.' The voice was cold and dispassionate, and the butcher's shop seemed to shake with its words. Jars of condiments rattled on the shelves before falling to the floor and smashing.

'And you call that superior reasoning? A truly superior being would not think it its place to toy with lesser beings, it would see its responsibility to help make this Universe a better place; to help others, not terrorise them!'

'You are vermin. Bacteria. We will cleanse this plane of your existence.' The voice no longer sounded so measured. It spoke with wrathful intent.

'Do you know what I think of you? I don't think you're so superior at all. You talk big, but I think you're overcompensating. You're just a parasite, leeching off of the life force of other beings. A parasite with delusions of grandeur! That's why the sigils were cast in the bodies. Without feeding on their lives, your power in this realm would fade.' Sam was now shouting his words at the butcher's shop ceiling.

'*You only delay the inevitable. I am the herald of your destruction.*'

In the darkness, unseen things began to move and shuffle, unearthly noises calling out from the black. Alice glanced around nervously as the noises drew closer and closer, and Sam peered into the darkness to see what was coming. He swept the probe across the room, and the crystal's glow illuminated things he would rather not see. Shambling corpses marauded from the dark corners of the butcher's shop; the cut-up and hollowed-out pig bodies one normally sees hanging from the ceiling or in the window of a butcher's were making their way across the floor. Their short had-been-limbs dragged the carcasses forward.

'*You are in my domain now. You creatures, so small. So inferior. You thrive in the light of day and shy away from the dark, clinging to your insignificant rock, adrift in the cosmic void. Before the Universe there was only the Void, and when the last sun dies out only darkness will remain.*'

With a sudden burst of unnatural energy, one of the bodies launched itself at Alice. It propelled itself through the air, knocking her to the floor. She yelped, struggling beneath the weight of the carcass. It had her pinned down. She kicked and flailed her arms, striking the thing in a bid to free herself, but to no avail. It held her down, writhing around and exuding the foul stench of decaying meat.

A bolt of purple energy shot across the room, hitting the pig carcass and throwing it off of her. Alice turned to see what had happened, and she saw Sam standing just off to the side, the transphasic energy probe pointed in her direction and a look of triumph on his face.

'I was really hoping I wouldn't miss!' he said with a grin.

'*You will die here. All of your kind will perish. This speck of dust you call Earth will be your tomb, and my kind shall retake our rightful place as the masters of this Universe.*' The voice sounded as if it was raging against them, screaming in their minds with fury and hatred.

'Not if I can help it!' Sam shouted back, and another burst of purple energy erupted from the wand. It struck another of the carcasses, sending it flying back into the wall with an unpleasant and meaty thud.

'*Confidence born of foolish arrogance. You fight against the inevitable, Sam Hain, like dust struggling against a cosmic wind,*' the voice boomed throughout the room.

One of the pig-like husks threw itself towards Sam, and he fired another bolt of energy at it. It hit its mark a short distance from his face, throwing the body backwards and splitting it in half. Flesh exploded and tore from the magick's impact.'Alice, keep looking,' Sam instructed, glancing over to her, 'it's got to be here! We need to finish this.'

'What am I looking for?!' Alice yelled back, running from the reanimated pig bodies which were slowly trying to follow her. They may have only been crawling after her, but she felt as if she was trapped in a living nightmare. She prayed she would wake up soon and have a normal Thursday, but she knew that was very unlikely to happen.

'Trust your instincts. Find it. Whatever it is. You'll know it when you see it.' He pointed the wand at Alice's pursuers, and a wave of energy pushed them back, but still they carried on moving forward, their stubby limbs carrying them as fast as they could crawl.

'*Your efforts are futile. You cannot break the cycle.*' The voice sounded almost mocking.

'Cycle? What cycle?' Sam asked. He noticed the pig bodies slowed their advance when he asked the entity the question.

Alice made a dash for the shop counter, getting behind it and crouching down to hide from their attackers. She knew it would not help – she could sense that it could see, or feel, everything in that room – but at least, for the moment, it made her feel a little more protected. It was then that she looked up and saw the cash register.

'The cycle has continued for longer than you could possibly fathom. The pattern repeats itself time and time again. All of this has happened before, and all of this will happen again.'

'What cycle? Answer me!' Sam shouted, throwing his arms wide open as if inviting the being to take a piece of him.

'Know this as you die in vain. The time of our return is imminent. Darkness is coming. The Old Ones shall awaken from their slumber and blacken the skies of your world. You will know your doom.'

Alice hastily tried to unlock the till, tapping numbers at random in the desperate hope she would hit upon the right combination. Nothing happened. She looked up nervously and saw more of the reanimated meat making its way towards her. The room seemed darker than it had before, and she could barely see what she was doing. She tried to suppress her fear and attempted to focus on the right combination.

'You resist, but you will fail. The time will come, and your kind will beg to serve us!'

Sam managed to repel another of the husks with an energy burst, but the energy flowing through the crystal was waning. It sputtered with each progressive shot, and he could feel himself becoming more and more drained. He leapt up on top of one of the tables, giving himself the high ground over their attackers. 'Now would be a *really* good time for some divine inspiration, Alice!'

8. 1. 7. 2. The numbers flashed through Alice's mind, and she knew she had the answer. *Douglas's birthday, 8th of January, 1972. That must be it...* She hit the keypad, and with a triumphant *cha-ching*, the till's cash-draw flung open. There, in one of the compartments, sat a peculiar object. It appeared to be a smooth stone, perfectly ovular, with a series of unearthly symbols carved into its surface. The symbols glowed in the darkness of the butcher's shop. In the centre of the stone was engraved a spiral pattern, and even though Alice knew it was not possible, she thought she could see the stone emanating a black, shadowy taint. As she tentatively picked up the strange object, she noticed it easily fit in the palm of her hand, and with a hopeful throw she chucked it in Sam's direction. 'Catch!'

Sam staggered as he attempted to catch the stone, almost losing his footing and falling off of the table in the process. He had only just managed to catch it, clutching the stone between his fingers. He held it up above his head.

'You see this?!' he cried out in triumph, waving the strange stone around, taunting the entity. 'After all that talk, all those grandiose statements, now *I* will be the one to end *you.*' His voice was tainted with a dark vengeance Alice had never heard before, and she was not in a hurry to ever hear it again. Sam cast the engraved stone onto the floor, and pointed his wand at it.

'You consider this a victory, mortal? You've changed nothing. You have the attention of those infinitely greater than yourselves. You will know pain.'

'That may be so, but you won't be around to see it. Give my regards to your Dark Masters. Bye-bye.' The crystal at the probe's tip began to glow violet, crackling and sparking as it charged up.

'You are arrogant. You cannot kill me. I always survive. I am eternal. My essence lives on in the bleeding hearts of

men, in their sorrow and their hatred and their fear. I thrive in your darkest nightmares. You can not destroy me.'

The wand erupted with a bright purple beam of energy, tearing through the air, sparking and hissing as the energy beam spiralled towards the stone and striking it with a sudden burst of violet flame. The stone shattered into countless fragments, leaving nothing more than a scorch mark and its scattered shards. The voice echoed in their minds no more.

There was a sickening thud as the reanimated animal corpses fell to the ground, and Alice breathed a sigh of relief. Sam jumped down from the table and ran over to her, throwing his arms wide and taking her in an embrace. He could feel her body trembling.

'Are you okay?' he whispered.

'I'll be all right,' she uttered through uncertain breaths. 'It was right, though, you know. That entity, it was right. You may have destroyed the artefact, but it's not gone. I could feel it. It's still out there, somewhere, filled with nothing but fury and hatred.'

Sam nodded silently. He knew it was still out there; they always were. But presently that didn't matter. What mattered now was that it was cut off from their realm, unable to return. Unable to cause more harm. And that, to him, was victory enough.

'Come on,' he eventually said, releasing her from his embrace with a firm pat on the shoulder, 'let's get out of this place.' He made his way towards the door, stepping over the still-unconscious body of Officer McKenzie and, with the cheery jingling of the little bell, Sam opened the door.

'What about him?' Alice asked, pointing back to the policeman laying prone in the middle of the butcher's shop, surrounded by bits and pieces of animal flesh.

'He'll come to, sooner or later. And I don't want to be around when he does... An unconscious police officer, coming round on the floor of the butcher's shop with the two people impersonating officers of the law, who have been meddling in a murder investigation, with another dead body and no substantial evidence pointing to a real, physical, human suspect? I don't think he'd be too pleased! And suggesting that a demon from another dimension committed these murders... Well, that's a one-way ticket to prison or a psychiatric hospital.'

He stepped out into the cold night air of Grimditch and took a deep breath. He held the door open for Alice while he rummaged around in his pockets, looking for something. He pulled out a battered box, and withdrew a crumpled cigarette from the packet. Sam lit the cigarette and took a long, deep drag, exhaling a cloud of smoke into the air.

'Since when do you smoke?' Alice asked incredulously.

'Since I had a shouting match with a demon and had to fend off a selection of reanimated charcuterie. That kind of magick isn't easy, it really takes it out of you.' He took another long drag on the cigarette. 'Now come on,' he said, 'it's late. We'd better be going.'

The taxi ride back to Islington was quiet and uneventful. Sam spent the majority of the time staring out of the window, lost in his thoughts. He turned the evidence over and over in his head, from sigils carved in human flesh to the unearthly artefact and its demonic connections. And the talk of Regents in Douglas's emails, what part did they have to play in all of this? All Sam really knew was that, although whatever they had just encountered was no longer here, this was only the beginning of something more.

Alice too had been lost in thought, although she was not quite as preoccupied with the sinister portents of the day.

Seeing the decapitated body and severed head of Douglas Norton seemed like a distant memory, and only now was she starting to see the strangeness of what had just befallen them. Looking back, she was overcome with horror and revulsion as images of mutilated corpses, animated porcine carcasses and the shambling pig-headed man flooded her mind. Her stomach churned with the mere memory, and she shook the images from her mind's eye. Instead, she started to wonder what she had done to deserve any of this, and exactly why she had been drawn into this man's strange and terrifying universe in the first place.

The cab stopped with a subtle jolt as it pulled up outside of Alice's house. None of the lights were on, save for the dim glow of the hallway light; presumably all of the other tenants were either still out or asleep by now. Alice bid a quick thank you to the driver, and stepped out onto the curb. Sam also stepped out onto the street with her, signalling the cabbie to wait for him for a moment.

'Thank you for joining me today,' he said in a perfectly normal fashion, as if they had just been out to dinner or some other completely normal activity, 'it's been... interesting.'

'I'm not sure that's the word I would use, but sure. Interesting,' she replied.

'You know what I mean,' Sam said with a smile, but his face immediately shifted back to a serious expression. 'Listen, if you need anything, if anything happens, I-'

'I know,' Alice cut him off, 'but if I can survive the Little Butcher's Shop of Horrors, I'm sure I'll be just fine in my own home. Thank you, though.'

'You're starting to wake up and see the world for how it really is, Alice. You're experiencing things in a way many people can't even begin to imagine. But some of these things really don't like people being aware of them...'

'Well thank you so much for that,' Alice said

sarcastically, 'it's not like I was planning on getting any sleep tonight anyway!'

'Just be mindful,' Sam said, 'you know how to reach me. Have a good night.' With that, he got back into the taxi.

'Good night,' Alice reciprocated, and she waved as the taxi drove away, down the road and around the corner, into the night. She took a long, deep, calming breath, and opened the door to the house. She made her way up the stairs and into her flat, and headed straight for bed. Alice did not sleep well that night, laying awake and staring up at her ceiling. When eventually she did fall asleep in the small hours of the morning, she dreamed dreams of malignant, shapeless beings lurking in the shadows, and of the dazzling white light from which they tried to hide.

The following day, Alice tried to put the thoughts of the events of Grimditch out of her mind. She was surprised she wasn't quite as scarred by the image of corpses as she thought she would be, but still she felt a lingering sense of uneasiness. Try as she might to forget, flashes would dance across her mind's eye, and she would remember with haunting clarity the words the disembodied voice had spoken. And that ever present phrase which warned that darkness was coming. She could not easily forget, and what she once called reality now seemed to be a desperate distraction from the actual real world.

That Friday evening, Alice was sat watching the television, eating dinner. She was experimenting with a vegetarian burger and, much to her surprise, it did not taste like damp cardboard. In fact, she thought, she could get used to it. Maybe even enjoy it.

There was a rummaging sound from outside, and the lock in the front door clicked as a key turned. The door flew open, and Rachel walked in. 'I'm back,' she announced with a weary but almost triumphant voice, dropping her bag on the floor with a dead thud.

'Hey, how was it?' Alice asked, craning around to see Rachel.

'Ugh, don't ask. I'd rather forget the whole thing,' she said, and Alice knew the feeling well. 'So, what's new? Anything interesting happen while I was away?'

'I'm vegetarian now,' was Alice's simple response, and she lifted the not-cardboard-y veggie burger up as proof. 'Cup of tea?' she asked, putting her plate down and standing up to make her way out into the kitchen.

'That'd be wonderful,' Rachel replied, following her. 'So what's this about vegetarianism?'

'Police have released the image of a man they suspect to be involved in the recent Grimditch murders,' the newsreader on the television announced to the now empty living room. *'Reports indicate that this man may be guilty of concealing vital evidence and perverting the course of justice, as he was sighted at key locations during an investigation while masquerading as a police officer.'* A photo-fit image of a man who looked not entirely unlike Sam Hain appeared on the screen. *'The Metropolitan Police warns that this man, who goes by the name of Arthur Doyle, may be dangerous and must not be approached. If you have any information regarding this individual and his whereabouts, please inform your local authorities. Now here's Tom with the weather.'*

'Forget about that early Springtime we were promised, Sally,' said Tom with the Weather, surrounded by cartoon clouds with sad faces, *'it looks like we're not out of the dark yet.'*

Sam Hain

Occult Detective

The Regents

PROLOGUE

He knew they were following him. They had been ever since he had left the café. He had seen them there no more than half an hour ago, sitting only a few tables away from him. Not that he had really been paying much attention to them at the time, they had just been on the peripheries of his vision. But now that he was aware they were following him, he could not help but notice there was something strange about them.

It wasn't much past ten o'clock when Sam Hain had walked into the café. He had ordered a large cup of tea (English Breakfast, dash of milk), paid for it with a fistful of coins, and sat down at his usual table by the window, looking out onto Hampstead high street. He had idly watched people wander back and forth past the window, going about their day, and he sipped his tea. This had always been his favourite place to come and relax.

It had been a couple of weeks since Sam and Alice had investigated a string of murders in London's east end. His involvement, and subsequent resolution, of the case had inadvertently landed Sam on a list of suspects when the police learned that he was not, in fact, a detective hired by Scotland Yard after all. *This is the thanks I get for banishing a murderous entity*, Sam had thought when he first saw the photofit approximation of his face on the news. *It's not my fault they were expecting the killer to be human.*

Thankfully, the police never knew his true identity, and after almost two weeks of only leaving the house to make a few stealthy, disguised runs to the corner shop (as well as a few cloaking spells for good measure) Sam was starting to feel confident that he was not in any immediate danger. The news had pretty much forgotten the whole thing after a couple of days, after all, and he'd had no trouble with the authorities since then. He decided, rather wistfully as he gazed up at the cloudy skies above Hampstead, that he could take this time to sit and drink his tea in peace. So he did.

For the rarest of moments, Sam was able to relax and forget all of the burdens of his life; of the ghosts and demons and other paranormal phenomena he had to regularly deal with in his weird world. He idly thought about calling Alice for a friendly chat, maybe invite her out for dinner, and the idea of something so perfectly normal in his far from normal life made him smile. He sat back in the café's chair, contented. For once, Sam Hain could enjoy his cup of tea and not worry about anything out of the ordinary happening at all.

Only a few short moments later, probably no more than a minute or two, two men had entered the café and sat themselves down a few tables away from Sam. The men wore identical black suits, clearly expertly tailored, with slim-style silk ties. Their eyes were covered by narrow pairs of sunglasses, the lenses seemingly opaque and as black as their suits. They both appeared to be in their forties, their faces worn and chiselled like stone. One of them was tall and slender, his short hair slicked back with more gel than was probably needed, while the other was slightly shorter and stockier, his hair thin and receding. Sam had thought very little of them at the time, not giving them more than a cursory glance when they had sat down.

However, now that they were following him down the street, he cursed himself for daring to relax. He thought back to how they had entered the café, and realised they hadn't even ordered anything. They had simply walked in, sat down at a nearby table, and stared ahead in complete silence. Both of them had been facing him, and he couldn't seem to remember hearing them talk to each other. Now here they were, no more than ten feet behind him, following him down the road.

Maybe I'm just overthinking things, Sam thought to himself as he quickened his pace. *It's the middle of the day, what harm can they do?* He took a quick glance over his shoulder. There they were, the two men in their well-tailored suits, their eyes concealed by dark glasses, walking in eerily perfect unison. *Don't be so paranoid, why would they be following you?*, he tried to reassure himself, but he couldn't shake the uneasy feeling. He rounded the corner onto a cobbled alleyway, grey brick buildings enclosing the narrow passage ahead of him. *Secret service? Demonic possession? Two men who really dislike my hat? Oh Christ...*

About half-way up the alleyway, Sam leaned against the wall and waited, his eyes trained on the corner from which he had just come. If they were following him, he thought, they would turn into this alleyway too. If not, and this had all been sheer coincidence and utterly unnecessary paranoia, they would walk on past without even glancing in his direction. He wanted it to be the latter. He wanted them to just walk on past so he could carry on with his day, but he had a sneaking suspicion that that would not be the case.

It wasn't long until the two men came into view. Sam's heart sank. They turned the corner and stood staring at him. Moving away from the wall as calmly and casually as he could manage, feeling like he was about to be in a Wild West style shoot-out, Sam tipped his fedora hat towards the two men. They both nodded back at him in unnatural unison.

'Oh, good,' Sam said under his breath, 'they are following me.' Turning around, he continued to walk up the alleyway, gradually walking faster and faster until, before he knew it, he had broken into a run.

His feet pounded the cobbled street as he ran, carrying him forward as if by a will of their own. His greatcoat billowed out behind him, and Sam would probably have enjoyed how dramatic he must have looked in that moment were it not for his sudden rush of fear and adrenaline. Behind him, he could hear two sets of feet starting to run in pursuit. He tried not to think of the two men chasing him down. He thought he had seen the bulge of a gun concealed beneath each of their jackets, but maybe in his panic he was now just imagining things. He was running blindly, no escape plan, no idea where to go other than somewhere – anywhere – where they were not. Another side alley was coming up on his right, and he turned into it without a moment's thought.

A busy antique's market took up most of this Old London style street. *Bollocks.* He kept on running, weaving his way through the crowd of shoppers browsing the stalls, hazarding a quick glance behind him every now and again. The men were still in pursuit, but the throngs of people antiquing were proving to be an obstacle for them. One of the men thrust an elderly woman out of his way as he charged through the crowd, sending her staggering into a display of 1920's china teacups. There was an audible gasp from several people, followed by the sound of smashing crockery. Neither of the men stopped or even turned around. They just carried on moving forwards.

Ducking into another passageway, Sam hid himself amongst the bins in what was presumably the back courtyard of a shop. It was dank and unpleasant, and the smell coming from the bins would normally have made him retch. He was too fixated on not being found to notice the stench. If they found him there, he had no way of escape. They would have him cornered. As much as he wanted to know who they were and why they were following him, he had a feeling he did not want to find out on their terms. A trickle of sweat ran down the side of his face.

Peering from between two large black bins, Sam looked

out into the courtyard. It seemed empty, but as he moved to get a slightly better view he could see them. The two men jogged around the corner and into the courtyard, their ties flopping as they ran, and they came to an abrupt stop no more than a few feet away from his hiding place. They stood stock still, surveying the area. Sam held his breath, desperate not to make even the slightest of sounds. He felt his entire body tense up.

The two men stood there for a while, their bodies motionless but their heads slowly turning as they looked around, like eerie sentinels. It felt as if an eternity had passed for Sam, but after just over a minute one of the men put his finger to his ear, pressing on a wireless earpiece. He nodded a single stoic nod, and the two men turned and strode out of the courtyard, rounding the corner and walking out of sight.

Sam Hain breathed a sigh of relief, emerging from amongst the bins and dusting himself off.

Bloody hell...

CHAPTER I

'Okay,' Rachel said as she paced around the living room, swapping her phone from one ear to the other. 'Yeah, yeah, sure. That sounds good to me. Okay, cool, we'll see you there. By-e!' She hung up, slipping her phone into the back pocket of her jeans.

'So what's the plan for tonight then?' Alice asked. She leaned over the back of the sofa, twisting around to face Rachel.

'We're going to meet the rest of the girls at the Red Lion, probably catch a show or something, have a few drinks and go from there,' Rachel said. 'Sound good to you?'

'Sure, what've they got on this evening?'

'Didn't say. Probably just casual stuff. Knowing Chantelle, she'll be in a low-cut dress and caked in fake tan, the tart!' Rachel cackled.

'No, not the girls. The Red Lion. What've they got on this evening, show-wise?'

'Oh. I don't know. Some fringe performance art thing, I think.'

'Right,' Alice mused. 'What time are we heading out?'

'About eight.'

'Okay. Afterwards we could head to-' Alice was cut off mid-sentence as her phone vibrated loudly. 'One sec.' The phone vibrated again, moving itself an inch along the coffee table. She instinctively slid her thumb across the screen and tapped her messages.

Constantine Road. Come as soon as you can if you're free. -SH, read the first message. *Actually, free or not, come anyway. It's important*, read the second. Alice put the phone down on the arm of the sofa as she stood up, glancing around for her shoes.

'After the Lion we could head to the Steam Passage,' Alice finished, 'it looks like quite a nice place for a drink.'

'Yeah, we can do.' Rachel nodded in agreement as she too started flipping through the notifications on her phone.

'Anyway, I'm heading out for a little bit,' Alice said, slipping on her converse shoes. She flicked and gently tousled her hair in front of the mirror.

'Alright, where are you off to?'

'Just going to meet a friend in Hampstead. I'll be back in time to get ready for tonight.'

'Okay, see you later, then. Have fun!' Rachel gave a little wave as Alice threw on her denim jacket and walked out of the door.

Alice had been thinking about going for a walk anyway. She wasn't one for staying in the flat all day, and paying a visit to Sam was more than enough of a good reason to head out for a while. She had never seen his house before, and she didn't know what she should expect from the home of a man whose life was far from normal. The thought of it and what peculiar oddities lay within made her curious to say the least.

The weather that day was, contrary to the forecast, surprisingly pleasant. It wasn't warm by any stretch of the imagination, as the winter wasn't yet ready to yield to spring, but the air no longer carried with it a biting chill. However, Alice did have to pull her jacket tightly around herself to brace against a particularly brisk gust of wind. The sky was grey and overcast, but peaking out from between the thick grey clouds, she could see glimmers of blue sky beyond.

As she walked along the road towards Islington high street, Alice noticed that the trees lining the road were beginning to look a little greener, and the first new buds were starting to sprout. After the long, cold months of winter, the world was slowly coming back to life. Spring was just around the corner, she could feel it. Alice had always considered herself a spring spirit, preferring that sweet spot between the cold winter months and the baking summer heat. It made the world feel fresh and full of life.

The tube, on the other hand, was not, and could never have been described as "fresh" or "full of life" even at the best of times. As Alice boarded the train at Highbury and Islington station, she was immediately greeted by the stale air of the carriage, and she began to glance around for an empty seat with as few stains as possible (which is a challenge to say the least). As it turned out, much to her surprise she did not need to look far. The carriage was almost entirely empty. There were only two other people on board, both of whom had their heads down, reading the Metro with bored expressions on their faces.

The train jolted and lurched awkwardly as it pulled away from the platform, causing Alice to ungracefully stumble forward and into a seat, almost spilling the chai latte she had picked up on the way to the station. She took a sip of the thick drink and grimaced as she attempted to work out exactly how she felt about it. On the one hand, it was sickly-sweet and creamy, and on the other it was quite spicy with decidedly more than a hint of cinnamon. The aftertaste was less than desirable, so she took another gulp, only to repeat the cycle. She found it to be slightly more pleasant after the third sip, and she concluded that it was probably an acquired taste.

It was a relatively short journey to Hampstead Heath station, and before she'd even had time to untangle her headphones, Alice found herself stepping off of the train and onto the platform. The gate beeped merrily and swung open as Alice brushed her Oyster card against the scanner and, walking through the expectantly open gate, she made her way out of the station. Sam's flat was only a short walk from the station, and this was probably one of the rare occasions when Sam would say something was "literally around the corner" and it actually was; as opposed to being a mile or two away, which was often the case.

Alice walked out onto South End Road, passing the small fruit and vegetable stand which sat immediately outside of the station's entrance, and she started to head down the road. People were milling about the local cafés and shops, several others were walking their dogs towards the heath, and a surprising number of red buses seemed to be chasing each other around the pedestrian island towards the end of the road. Despite this part of Hampstead more closely resembling a small village, it was alive with city life.

Passing the corner shop at the end of the road, Alice turned left and began to walk along the rows of red brick houses which lined Constantine Road until, halfway down the road, she reached the address that Sam had given her. The doorway was up a set of concrete steps, framed by a wild growth of ivy which wound its way up the pillar one side of the door, across the wall above, and down the pillar on the other side. A large concrete dragon sat at the foot of the steps, proudly holding a shield between its talons. Had she been in any doubt that this was the right address, Alice felt this was a bit of a give-away. She walked up to the door and knocked.

The door tentatively began to open, and through the widening gap the face of Sam Hain could be seen peering out. 'Oh good, it's you,' he said with a smile the instant he saw it was Alice, and he swung the door wide open to let her in.

'Hello,' Alice said with a sweet smile, and she quickly wiped her feet on the doormat as she stepped inside. The hallway ran the full length of the house, all white walls and cream carpet, and Alice was surprised that a man as unusual as Sam would have such a conservative taste in decor. Two doors ran off from the right side of the hall, and two staircases – one heading to the first floor, the other down to the basement – were at the far end of the hall. The house was a lot bigger than she had first expected from the outside. 'How do you afford to live in a place like this?' she asked, almost incredulously. Judging by the size of it alone it had to be an expensive property, doubly so considering its location so close to Hampstead Heath.

'He doesn't,' came the voice of a particularly stern-sounding woman from one of the doorways, presumably leading to the living room. 'He's already two months behind on the rent.'

Sam looked up at the ceiling and visibly rolled his eyes. 'Landlady,' he said dryly, 'I rent the basement flat.' He leaned towards the living room door and called out, 'all things in due time!' The voice from the living room did not reply.

'Right then,' Sam announced, before lowering his voice to almost a whisper, 'I think I'm on to something big, and you're going to have to try not to think I've gone mad.' His eyes were suddenly wider and wilder than usual. Then, as if he had just flicked a switch, he returned to normal. He clapped his hands together. 'But first, I'm going to have a cup of tea. Do you want anything?'

Alice nodded uncertainly. 'Okay... I'm feeling a little bit nervous now! But yeah, please, a cup of tea sounds perfect,' she said.

'Okay, two teas, coming up. My temple is just downstairs,' Sam said, and he began to lead the way down the stairs at the far end of the hallway. As she walked past the open door, Alice glanced in to say hello to the landlady, but all she saw was the back of a white-haired woman's head, happily occupied watching a daytime soap opera.

Alice followed Sam down the steep, bare-wooden

staircase. She could see a single door at the bottom, a wooden pentagram hanging on the front of it, and a brass plaque in the very centre of the door which read "Sam Hain - Occult Detective". A large wooden sign rested above the door frame, emblazoned with the words "Abandon hope, all ye who enter here", which Alice thought was not the most welcoming of signs.

'Here we are, then,' Sam said, producing a large, rustic-looking iron key from his pocket and turning the lock. He swung the door open and started to make his way towards another door at the back, which presumably lead to the kitchen. 'Make yourself at home, I'll be back in a minute.'

The door opened on to the middle of a fairly large room with bare, dark oaken floorboards and faded dark turquoise walls, mottled and marked with age and wear over the years. Alice stepped through the door and immediately found a creaky floorboard. To the left of the entrance was what looked like the dining room; an oak table with four chairs positioned around it sat perfectly in the middle of that half of the space, with a wrought iron candleholder twisting around itself in the centre of the table. To the right was the living room, where a worn looking sofa and mismatching arm chair were at right-angles to each other, sat on the nearest corner of an ancient looking rug. A coffee table stood in the middle of the rug, directly between the sofa and a fireplace. Diagonally across from the door was the television, covered in dust.

The walls were lined with tall, dark wood bookcases which seemed to overlook the entire room, looking as aged and worn as the walls and floorboards. On a number of the shelves were strange ornaments and artefacts, but most were packed beyond capacity with numerous books, piled up and crammed in however they would fit, with tomes and volumes the likes of which Alice had never seen before. There were, of course, some more recognisable pieces of literature – a handful of contemporary books, a number of classics – but there was also a generous amount of slightly more obscure titles.

The room did not look decrepit by any means, but nor was it pristine. It put Alice in mind of a mysterious old house with a peculiar twinge of Victorian and Gothic design. She hadn't really known what to expect from Sam's taste in interior design, but she wasn't too surprised by it.

Alice made her way into the living room area and, out of curiosity, she decided to have a quick flick through some of the more unusual books on Sam's shelves while she waited for him.

The Magical Creatures Bestiary was the first volume she pulled off of a shelf. The book contained an exhaustive list of fairy tale animals, lovingly illustrated and filled with information about various kinds of magical creatures, some of which Alice could faintly recall from childhood bedtime stories. Next to this was something titled *How to Bag a Jabberwock*, a practical guide to monster hunting – also illustrated – which did not focus so much on the fairy tale element as much as it did on the hunting of mythical creatures, as though jabberwocks and manticores and werewolves were game for some fantasy blood-sport. There was also a hefty tome of almost encyclopedic lengths, *A Guide to the Supernatural World*, which was presumably about everything metaphysical (some items in the guide had had their paragraphs scribbled over, and Sam's handwriting scrawled next to it brazenly exclaiming "*WRONG!*"). The shelf below was littered with an array of magickal works, including books by Aleister Crowley and John Dee, and a red leather-bound volume called *A Guide to High Magick*. Something about these books seemed almost sacred. Enchanted.

On the wooden coffee table in the middle of the room sat the familiar sight of Sam's self-penned guide to all things weird, the book Alice had once referred to as

"Demonology for Dummies". An ink-pot and black feathered quill sat next to it, and as Alice opened the book she found that on the first page Sam had written in calligraphic style the words *Encyclopedia Arcanica*. She nodded approvingly, thinking the title had a slightly more respectable tone to it than her unofficial one, and flicked through the pages. She noticed he had made a few amendments to some of the previous entries. She suspected that he often needed to make revisions to what he thought he knew; there was bound to be no shortage of surprises when it came to the weird and wonderful world in which Sam Hain lived.

After quickly flicking through the *Encyclopedia Arcanica*, Alice put the book down and glanced over towards the fireplace. She thought she saw something glinting on the mantelpiece out of the corner of her eye, and when she turned her attention to it she saw that the mantelpiece was adorned with an array of strange and abnormal looking things she could not even begin to fathom. Odd twisting ornaments and alien-looking artefacts covered the mantel from end to end.

The particular thing which had caught Alice's eye was a clear quartz crystal skull, glistening in a beam of sunlight which was coming in through a small gap at the top of the window where the street-level was just about visible. Compared to some of the other things on display (including several stones engraved with unusual runes, statues of strange figures she did not recognise, and an old, spherical glass pocket watch), the crystal skull was not the most outlandish thing in the room. Alice picked it up. It was a weighty thing, made of solid crystal, and just the right size for her to hold comfortably in one hand. She gently stroked its perfectly smooth surface with her thumbs before putting it back down.

Above the mantelpiece, stuck in place with tape and blue-tac, several sheets of paper covered a large portion of the wall. They had been arranged to form one big, abnormally-shaped sheet. The paper was covered in scrawled notes and printed-out images, with pen lines linking from point to point to point. One piece, towards the top of the would-be mind-map, had a picture of a dark cobbled street, the date "31st OCTOBER" written in block capitals above it. *The night I first met Sam...* Alice mused. A number of almost illegible notes referencing the veil between worlds were scrawled around the date, as well as a couple of photographs of eerily dark and empty streets and shadowy, unearthly forms. "Darkness is coming?" was written by the side of it.

The words "darkness is coming" recurred quite a few times across the pieces of paper. There was also a photograph of the Void crystal they had found in the loft on their night in Knightsbridge (notably missing from the artefacts on display in the room), two images of the late Douglas Norton – both when he was alive and after, in two separate pieces – and numerous notes about Sam's methods used in fending off "shadow eels" and a "pig-headed demon". There were sub-notes attached to these, reminding Sam to come up with better names for them. At the centre of all of the pieces of paper, in the very heart of the arrangement, was a map of central London. Sam had circled each location where these previous cases had taken place. Islington, Knightsbridge, Grimditch... There were some other marks across the map, small crosses presumably denoting some of Sam's other exploits.

As Alice took a step forward to take a closer look at Sam's notes, she felt something beneath her feet. It was cold and smooth, but it wasn't the marble tiling surrounding the fireplace; it felt rounded, and irregularly shaped. She took a step back and looked down. At her feet was an intricate pattern of two concentric circles, formed by the even and symmetrical placement of crystals. Orange, black and teal stones formed the circles, with quartz points facing outwards in all directions leading out from the centre like the spokes of a wheel. A single larger piece of quartz stood in the middle of the pattern. Leaning against this central stone was the metallic, shiny wand-like shape of Sam's transphasic energy probe. Or TechnoWand, as Alice still liked to think of it.

'Careful,' came Sam's voice from somewhere behind her, as if he was warning a child from something dangerous, 'try not to disturb the grid too much. It keeps the Thing away.'

Alice turned to look at him, a puzzled expression on her face. 'What's "the Thing"?'

'I don't know. I just call it "the Thing".' Sam widened his eyes as if to convey a sense of awe and mystery, but it simply came off as cartoonish.

He raised a cup of tea up in the air as he made his way over, and sat himself in the armchair. Alice smiled at him appreciatively, walking over and taking the tea before sitting down on the sofa. It may have looked like an old and worn sofa, but it was surprisingly comfortable.

'So, why will I think you've gone mad this time?' Alice asked. She sounded almost blasé about it, and took a sip of her tea.

'I think I'm being followed,' Sam confided. Of all the things he had said since they first met, Alice thought, this was possibly the sanest.

'By who? Or what?' Alice leaned forward, intrigued. Her mind immediately jumped to thoughts of demons and dark spirits.

'Men in Black,' was Sam's simple reply.

'Like the Will Smith movie?'

'I'm not joking, Alice. The Men in Black are after me.' His face was the sincerest Alice had ever seen it, and she thought she detected a hint of fear behind his otherwise stoic eyes.

'Okay,' she said slowly, 'why are they after you?'

'I don't know,' Sam said, and his voice seemed to quaver, 'I don't know...'

'You don't think it might be because you impersonated a police officer to gain access to a murder scene? The authorities might have assigned agents to find you. One of those photo-fit thingies of your face was on the news. They want anyone who knows anything about you to come forward.'

'I know. Thankfully, I've been able to lay relatively low, and know a few things about keeping myself anonymous when I need to. Hiding in plain sight, that sort of thing. But no. No. Even if it were, they wouldn't be quite so... Creepy.' He could not think of any other word to describe them. The two men in Hampstead had had a decidedly creepy air about them when they had been following him, distant and almost ethereal, as if they were part of an entirely different world than the rest of the town. Were it not for the old woman and all the broken crockery, he would wonder if anyone else had even noticed them.

'What makes you think they're after you? You might just be paranoid.'

'I'm not paranoid. I thought I was, but they've been following me,' he said, and he leaned in closer to her. 'Alice, listen. I don't know who or what I can trust any more. I don't even know how safe I am in my own town. I can count the people I trust on one hand.' He held up his right hand and waggled his fingers about a bit, before reaching for his cup of tea. 'You're one of them, by the way.' She knew he meant it.

'Who do you think they are, these Men in Black?'

Sam gulped down a mouthful of tea and sighed, placing his cup back down and clasping his hands together. He rested his chin on his clasped hands and stared off into the middle-distance. 'I really don't know. Secret service, maybe. They looked the government type. MI-5, MI-6... Which one's the agency which deals with internal threats?

That one.' He unclasped his hands, and began to drum his fingers impatiently on the table as he thought. 'The thing is, with everything I've been looking into, we could soon find ourselves in something far deeper than I could have imagined.'

'What do you mean?' Alice asked.

'The Regents,' Sam stated.

Alice immediately thought back to the events at Grimditch. The corpses, the esoteric symbols and the hint of a cult all came flashing back through her mind. They had discovered that a group called the Regents had been connected to the events in some way, but that was all they knew. Who the Regents were, what they do, and how they were involved still remained a mystery. The unwelcome memories of Grimditch and the decapitated body nauseated Alice, and the image of the entity wearing the body of Pete Jones with the head of a pig made her feel sick to the pit of her stomach. Whenever she thought of Grimditch, the thoughts would grip her mind like a vice; it would take a long time for her to forget. She shuddered involuntarily, and broke herself out of the traumatic trance.

'I've been trying to do some digging to find out anything I can about them,' Sam carried on talking, seemingly oblivious to the fact that Alice had spaced out for a moment, 'but I haven't been able to find anything remotely informative. I've asked an old friend to help, he was always more knowledgeable about cults and secret societies. He'll have access to the right information. He should be joining us shortly.'

As if on cue, there was the sound of feet coming down the creaking stairs, shortly followed by a knock at the door. Before Sam could stand up to answer it, the door opened and a man in a grey twill suit with a satchel slung over his shoulder walked in. His hair was shorter and more controlled than Sam's (that was hardly difficult), and Alice estimated he was probably in his late twenties. She couldn't really tell, though; guessing people's ages wasn't something she considered to be her strong point.

'Alright, Sam,' said the man as he closed the door behind him.

'Good to see you, James,' Sam replied, standing up and walking over to greet his visitor. He held his hand out to shake, but his greeting was met with a fist. James held his arm outstretched, fist clenched, anticipating Sam to reciprocate with a fist-bump. The two stood stock still, staring at one another wordlessly, their arms extended towards each other with mismatching gestures, waiting for the other to do the same. James gave a nonchalant shrug of the head, and Sam yielded, scrunching his open hand into a fist and gently punching James's.

'Hi,' said Alice, once the whole awkward greeting had concluded.

'James, this is Alice. Alice, meet James Mortimer,' Sam said, waving his hands chaotically between the two of them as way of introduction.

James Mortimer was a tall and brooding man with a name to match. He stood probably a couple of inches taller than Sam and had a vaguely intimidating presence about him, but not in the same kind of way so frequently referenced in erotic novels. Alice held out her clenched fist, but instead of another fist-bump James delicately took her hand, unfurled her fingers and gave her a quick peck on the back of the hand.

'So you're Sam's new protégée I've heard so much about. A pleasure,' he said with a smile. She wasn't too sure how she felt about being called a "protégée", but she decided she would let it slide just this once.

'Good to meet you,' Alice reciprocated, 'I've heard literally nothing about you.'

'Oh, come on, Sam, my man! You mean to tell me you haven't shared the stories of our most excellent adventures?' He turned to face his old friend with a look of mock offence.

'What, like the time we found an enchanted mirror and you were convinced you were the... Oh, how did you put it? "The fairest of them all"?' Sam smirked and raised an eyebrow at his old friend.

'Not the stupid ones, the exciting ones! Remember Manor House?'

'We said we'd never talk about Manor House again,' Sam said, forcing his face into the most serious expression he could manage, and speaking with a tone so stern it would be the envy of any middle school teacher. James and Sam then solemnly nodded at each other in unison, suppressing the urge to smile at their stupid performance.

'Anyway,' James announced, pulling a tablet computer out of his satchel and flicking his finger across the screen, 'to business.' He sat on the sofa next to Alice as he continued to poke and prod at the tablet, opening files and sliding documents around the screen. 'I've been researching those Regents you mentioned, Sam.'

Sam sat back down in the armchair and leaned forward. 'And? What did you find?'

'Not a lot,' James said distantly, his focus still on the screen, 'officially, they don't exist.'

'They bloody do!' Sam interjected, before slowly sinking back into his armchair, realising that his outburst probably made him appear more paranoid than he already was. 'I have the files from the Grimditch case...'

'Exactly, officially they may not exist,' James continued, 'but there are several accounts of them and their activities. At first, I thought they may have just been a small-time cult, but talk among conspiracy circles implies they're much bigger.'

'As in, above the government?' Sam asked.

'Quite possibly,' James nodded, 'certain reports I've seen

from conspiracy theorists suggest the rabbit hole goes much, much deeper. Some believe they're a governmental department for paranormal research, others that they are entwined with or even above the government, influencing events as they see fit.' He poked at the screen and pulled up a file. 'There are a number of occult symbols associated with them, which apparently surround their places of operation. The All-Seeing Eye, Torch of Prometheus, that sort of thing. One account even depicts the same symbol you found in connection with them.'

Alice and Sam peered over his shoulder to take a look. On the screen was a shape they both recognised; an angular hieroglyph with a right-slanting line at the top, and a long vertical line stretching downwards, ending in a two-pronged fork shape. The Was Sceptre. The symbol of the clandestine Regents.

'Yeah. That's the one,' Sam said.

'At this point, I'd take anything we find with a pinch of salt, though. This guy claims he was involved in something called the Voidwalker Project, supposedly they were sending test subjects through quantum gateways. Allegedly, many of the test subjects were driven mad,' James shrugged. 'His report reads like the ultimate conspiracy theory. He even says that any information leaks are suppressed, whistleblowers are silenced, and the Men in Black tie up their loose ends through any means necessary.'

'If that's the case, how did this person share this information?' Alice asked. She was sceptical at the best of times, especially when it came to crackpot conspiracy theories. Then again, she had not really believed in ghosts and demons before she met Sam.

'Like I say, pinch of salt,' James said casually.

'Plausible deniability,' Sam muttered, almost as if he was talking only to himself. He stared at the coffee table with a far-off gaze in his eyes.

'What do you mean?' James asked, looking at his friend with concern.

'Plausible deniability,' Sam repeated. 'The Regents don't officially exist, right? So they must keep a tight lid on things to keep the truth of their existence from getting out, silencing leaks and deleting information. But they let the most mad, out-there theories and information slip. The most unhinged voices are heard. They eliminate the legitimate threats, and the remaining leaks are branded the ramblings of a madman, or works of fiction, and they fall into obscurity. Anyone who winds up believing it simply gets labelled as another crazy. If anyone suspects anything, they can point to these theories and state they're nothing more than paranoid delusions.'

'That rant is a prime example!' James said jokingly, but Sam did not seem amused.

'James, this morning I was enjoying a perfectly good cup of tea, and ended up being chased by two men in very good looking black suits,' Sam said. 'You say that account said that the Men in Black come to tie up the loose ends? There is no doubt in my mind that that is exactly what I was running from. After everything involving the Regents surrounding Grimditch, I wouldn't be surprised if my,' he paused and looked at Alice, '*our* involvement stepped on a few toes.'

James nodded silently. His friendship with Sam Hain went back to their college days. As a couple of teenagers, they and a group of their friends used to go ghost hunting in abandoned houses and cemeteries, progressively delving deeper into the occult. Sam had gone down the route of magick, investigating the paranormal and demon hunting, while James had been more interested in researching the history and influence of secret societies and cult practices. Their interests in the esoteric may have diverged, but they both respected each other's expertise, and sometimes their two worlds would converge. Now, James thought, was likely one of those moments.

'Okay,' he eventually said, putting down his tablet and meeting Sam's gaze, 'if the Men in Black are looking for you and you really have caught the attention of the Regents, you're going to have to lay low until we know what's really going on.'

Alice had remained quiet all of this time, listening to the two of them discussing the conspiracies surrounding the Regents, and she was trying to get her head around the madness of what they were saying. It all sounded so ludicrous, and if any of it was indeed true, it was almost too huge to comprehend. She had witnessed the paranormal with her own eyes, she had spoken with spirits and she had stood alongside Sam as he fought off dark entities. In a way, she could almost believe that an esoteric supernatural organisation was pulling the strings from behind the curtains. She could certainly think of quite a few politicians who seemed to be anything other than human, and it wouldn't come as much of a surprise to her if she were to learn that a handful of them were beings from another dimension. But to consider that she and Sam might be caught up in the machinations of a cabal seemed unreal, and more than a little bit frightening.

'Try clearing your name,' she said, and both Sam and James looked at her quizzically. 'If you go to the police and clear your name, maybe the MiB will get off your back? You didn't do anything wrong-'

'I impersonated a police investigator to gain access to evidence in a murder case,' Sam interrupted, 'which they probably wouldn't be too happy about. They'd see it as potentially perverting the course of justice. Especially when they haven't got any solid evidence to identify the killer, largely because it wasn't from this particular plane of existence.'

Alice looked at the floor for a moment. 'I see your point,' she said, 'I'm at a loss for ideas, then.'

'And what if it was the Regents who put me on the list of suspects in the first place? If they're above the police, and they know about what happened, maybe they want to bring me in and silence me,' Sam stared at Alice and James with wild eyes. 'If their ranks really do go as high up as the government, or beyond, then we're all just puppets to them. But people like us see the world for how it really is. We have no strings for them to pull. So they come after us, to shut us up or make sure we don't get in the way of their games.'

Alice stared at him, unblinking. For the briefest of moments, she thought that he had completely lost it. Perhaps he was losing the ability to distinguish between the world he knew and the rest of the... Well, it wasn't so much the real world as it was the "normal" world (the metaphysical world is just as real as plants and animals and mortgages, but decidedly more interesting and fantastical and entirely not normal). Maybe he was starting to see the demons everywhere, even where they were not.

'See, I thought you'd think I was mad,' Sam said, his eyes darting between her's as if he was scanning her, reading her thoughts. 'I don't need you to believe me, Alice, I just need you to trust me. I don't know what they want with me, but they could very well come for you too. Just be on your guard. Please.'

Alice nodded silently, and she leaned forward, taking his hand in hers. 'As mad as this all sounds – and it really does sound absolutely bloody bonkers – I trust you. I do.'

Sam's face turned into the picture of relief, as if a great weight had been lifted off of his shoulders. 'Thank you,' he simply said. 'If I'm right, I dread to think what they might want from me. From us. And I hate the thought of anything happening to you.'

Alice nodded understandingly.

'Listen,' James said sombrely, 'we don't even really know what we're dealing with yet. The little information I've been able to scrape together about the Regents could just be the ramblings of another crazed conspiracy theorist. Just lay low, watch your backs, and don't do anything stupid.' He slid his tablet back into his satchel and zipped up its pouch. 'I'll keep digging. All we can do is try to get to the bottom of this, and hope that we find the answer before the answer finds us.'

Chapter II

The weather had taken a turn that evening. Gone were the light skies and gentle breezes, instead replaced with a torrential downpour and rolling dark clouds looming over the city. The rain drops fell thick and fast. The skies turned black.

As she walked back alone in the heavy rain, Alice's mind wandered to Sam's ranting about the Regents. *Could he be right?*, she wondered, half considering it. She had not believed him about the supernatural and metaphysical entities when they had first met, after all, and had very quickly learned that it was not all as absurd as it had sounded. She wondered if it could be the same now, if the world really was being governed by hidden organisations directing things from behind the curtain.

It wasn't long before Alice was thoroughly drenched. Her mousy blonde hair turned brown in the downpour, and her clothes, damp and heavy, clung to her body. A cold wind blew down Constantine Road, but it felt like an arctic blast which cut through to the bone against her wet clothes. Alice ran her fingers through her rain-soaked hair and quickened her pace to the station.

'Need a lift?' came a voice from somewhere behind her, and she turned around to see a sleek black car pull up alongside her. The man behind the wheel had wound down the window, and was leaning out towards her. He was very well dressed, presumably driving home from working at some high-end job. 'You shouldn't be out getting drenched in weather like this.'

Alice politely declined the man's offer, saying she was heading for the tube and was only a minute or two from there. He insisted he give her a lift, or she would catch her death of cold in this weather, but she assured him she would dry off as soon as she got back home. The man had eventually driven off, although when Alice reached Hampstead Heath station she was sure she could see his car parked on the curb a little further up the road.

She stood beneath the shelter on the platform, huddled among the other disgruntled travellers trying to stay out of the rain. A few errant drops of water snuck through the roof of the shelter, landing in thick droplets on the heads of the people below. When the train arrived, Alice stepped onto the crowded carriage, cold and completely soaked through. She squeezed herself into a small gap in amongst a throng of similarly drenched Londoners. As the train began to move, she grabbed a hold of the pole and resigned herself to standing and waiting for Highbury and Islington.

Sam had left the house for just a few moments to buy some food for that evening. For the sake of simplicity, he had headed to the Marks and Spencer no more than a ten minute walk away to buy one of their ready-made vegetable lasagne. It took him twenty minutes to walk there, as – owing to his paranoia – he had taken a less than direct route. He didn't want to run the risk of being followed again.

He wondered, as he peered over someone's shoulder into the freezer compartment, whether he was being too paranoid. Maybe he was seeing things where they were not (reading about cults and conspiracies can do that sometimes). He thought about the men in the tailored suits, and how they had followed him and chased him through the side-alleys of Hampstead. There was no doubt that they were after him, and he knew that he was better off being on his guard than being too complacent. Taking a lasagne from the shelf of the freezer, Sam began to make his way towards the rows of self-service checkouts. He started to think about Alice, and wondered if she had got back home okay. He decided that when he was in and the lasagne was cooking, he would text her to make sure she was safe and sound. Or was that a bit excessive?

'Unexpected Item in Bagging Area.'

He sighed, removed the lasagne, stared at the screen impatiently, and replaced it on the checkout.

'Unexpected Item in Bagging Area.'

He muttered a series of irate-sounding words at the machine, and tapped at the touch screen with so much force he may as well have been punching it. Today was not the sort of day he felt comfortable being out of the house, not unless it was for something absolutely necessary like a frozen lasagne, and now it seemed that the self-service checkout was conspiring against him.

'Please wait. Help is on the way.'

What if it actually was conspiring against him? *You're getting paranoid, now*, Sam told himself as he stared at the machine, waiting. *Or am I?* He told himself to focus, to stay calm and buy his lasagne. He would be home in less than ten minutes, put his dinner in the oven, and sit down to see what was on TV that evening. A simple M&S checkout was not going to push him over the edge.

The sound of footsteps coming closer and closer reached his ears, and Sam turned around to see one of the members of staff approaching him. She was in her late teens, dressed head-to-toe in company-issued clothes and looking almost swamped by her fleece. She flashed him a well-trained customer service smile, while her eyes remained emotionless and unchanging. 'How can I help, sir?' she asked.

'Unexpected Item in Bagging Area,' the checkout machine chimed in helpfully.

'It's been rigged,' Sam said plainly.

'Rigged, sir? I'm sure there's just a mistake. Let me just-' She was about to override the machine's warning message, but Sam interrupted her.

'It's been rigged to hold me up and delay me... But you already knew that, didn't you?' Sam's eyes narrowed as he inspected the assistant, who stared back at him with a mixture of fear and confusion.

'I... Sorry?'

'You're one of *them*, aren't you?' A voice in the back of his mind told him he was being irrational and that maybe he should not be berating M&S staff, but he ignored it. The assistant stared back at him, perplexed, and she leaned around Sam to fix the machine. It was then that she spotted the problem.

'Sir, you've left your wallet in the bagging area. You're the unexpected item.' She smiled again to try and lighten the situation.

Sam looked down and saw his wallet sitting alongside the lasagne, and his face flushed a rather vivid shade of red. He looked sheepishly back at the assistant, muttered a 'sorry' and a 'thank you', and desperately tried to pretend he hadn't just made an arse of himself.

A cheer rose up from the crowd filling the theatre above the Old Red Lion. The production had been a postmodern take on Romeo and Juliet, in which the same actor had played the parts of both Romeo and Juliet, supposedly as a statement on the character's (and presumably actor's) love of himself. The Montagues and Capulets were also played by the same group of actors, as a comment on the internal conflict caused by trying to raise such a troubled, narcissistic teenager. It was almost a good idea, in theory, but only almost; in execution, it was entirely different.

The cheer from the audience was likely due to the fact that the play was over. Not that the actors would ever know that. Their next production was to be a version of Hamlet, in which Hamlet is also his own father and his uncle.

Following the rest of the audience downstairs, Alice made her way into the pub below. It was relatively crowded downstairs, as the throng of the audience began to fill out the space. It felt like a very traditional pub, with fading red carpets and mahogany furnishings, and the bar was alive with clientele clamouring for drinks. The general hubbub of a packed out bar filled the air, glasses chinked, and laughter and cheers soared above the chatter of the crowd. Alice walked up to the bar, standing beside Rachel, and ordered a bottle of passion fruit cider.

'So what'd you make of it?' Rachel asked, a quizzical eyebrow raising above her right eye.

'It was... Interesting,' Alice replied. It was the politest way she could describe the performance.

'Didn't understand a word of it, me!' Rachel said with a giggle, and she took a swig from her cider.

Alice's bottle of cider, along with a pint glass filled with ice, was placed in front of her. The golden liquid bubbled over the ice cubes as Alice poured her drink, and she took a sip of the sweet and refreshingly crisp beverage. She peered around to see where the other girls were, and could see Chantelle, with her platinum blonde hair and unseasonably tanned skin in a very tight and very low-cut red dress, heading towards a table in the corner, where Jess was already seated with her glass of Chardonnay.

'Fancy coming clubbing with us in a bit?' Rachel leaned in towards Alice, and took another swig from her bottle. 'It's kind of boring here.'

Alice disagreed. She much preferred the atmosphere of a good pub to the thumping music and eccentric light show of any club. She would rather sit around chatting with friends over a few drinks than all of the shot-fuelled dancing and not being able to hear each other over the music. 'Nah,' she eventually said to Rachel, 'I'm not sure

I'm really in the clubbing mood.'

'Oh, go on, it'll be fun! Chantelle and I were saying how dull it is just to sit around, and then Jess said about this club night going on and-'

Rachel continued talking, but Alice had zoned out of the conversation, for just over Rachel's shoulder she had noticed something. Two men in well-tailored suits had entered the pub, their thin black ties falling in a perfectly straight line down to their buttoned up slim-fit jackets. They both wore dark sunglasses which only covered their eyes, which was weird for ten o'clock on a Saturday night. As Alice surreptitiously watched them (it wasn't difficult; they stood out like sore thumbs in amongst the crowd of the pub), she noticed they that did not order a drink, or talk, or mingle. They simply walked in and sat down, facing in her direction. Something about the two of them made her feel incredibly uneasy.

One of the men turned to the other, and nodded silently. Neither of them moved their mouths to speak. That wasn't the only odd thing Alice noticed about them. They seemed to be entirely separate from everyone else in the pub, moving through the crowd unhindered. Their existence seemed to jar with the rest of reality. There was an otherworldly aura about them, almost as if they were not quite as much a part of this world as they appeared.

'Actually, you know what, why the hell not?' Alice declared, not really sure whether Rachel was still explaining the club plan or not, and she clinked her drink against Rachel's before taking a big swig. 'We'll leave in five, yeah?'

She didn't care where they went; all Alice wanted was to get away from the men who had just entered. She could not shake the thought of what Sam had said earlier, and, she reasoned, heading to a packed club was a good place to lose them. If, indeed, they were following her.

It was pitch black in the alleyway. Sam peered cautiously around the corner and out onto the road, keeping himself pinned as close to the wall as possible, lurking just outside of the pools of light cast by the streetlamps. His hat was askew, his coat wet and marred with flecks of mud, and the vegetable lasagne in his Marks and Spencer's bag was defrosted. Headlights veered around the corner, driving along the road in his direction, and Sam ducked back behind the wall. He flattened himself against it, and took a quick glance out of the corner of his eye. It was the nondescript black van again, driving slowly past.

He had left the shop about two hours ago and started to head home when he had noticed the two men in suits approaching. He had doubled back inside, feigning he'd forgotten to buy something else, and kept a cautious eye out. Sure enough, the men in suits had entered too and seemed to follow him up and down the aisles from a discreet distance. He hmm'd over a bottle of Cabernet Sauvignon, checked the price of a packet of crisps, and was eventually able to lose them in the bakery section (managing to abscond with a cheese twist at the same time). He fled as quickly and as casually as he could manage, and was back outside in no time.

However, it wasn't long before the two men were stood outside the shop, fingers pressed to their ears, presumably as something in their headsets spoke with them. They nodded in silent unison, and started to follow Sam down the road. Once again, he found himself quickening his pace. His mind raced as he worked out whether he could lose them and still get back home safely. The two men didn't bother to speed up to catch him, they simply followed Sam at a methodical and even pace. They looked similar to the men in the café, but he couldn't be sure whether they were the same agents.

But he knew they were agents. Men in Black. There was no doubt in his mind. Any doubts he had about whether something sinister was going on, any attempts his rational mind made to try and reassure him he was being paranoid, were dispelled. They were definitely still following him. He checked over his shoulder and there they were, striding after him with purpose. He carried on walking as fast as he could manage without having to break into a run. If he started to run from them, Sam thought, it would provoke them into giving chase, and he did not foresee that ending in his favour. He wondered why they hadn't already done that, why they didn't just run after him and try to tackle him to the ground. The thought was quickly brushed aside; more than anything he was grateful that they hadn't made much of an effort to catch up with him. It bought him more time to plan his escape.

The familiar and normally safe sight of home was just across the road from him. The outside light had been left on, causing the green of the ivy around the door and the red brick wall to glow vibrantly in the darkening twilight. It was like a beacon calling out to him; a beacon he would have to ignore for the moment. He longed to be at home, relaxing in front of the TV, in the comfort of his living room, and – most importantly – not being followed by secret agents. But there was no way he could just walk up to the door and let himself in, not when they were tailing him. Sam put his head down and carried on walking, all the while his brain raced to think of a way he could try to lose them.

With the glaring of headlights and screeching of wheels, a black van pulled out of the road directly ahead of Sam, causing him to jump. In many ways it was a standard black transit van, although its tinted windows were entirely blacked out, and it bore no license plates. The van took a sickening swerve around the corner and with the jolting of brakes it came to an abrupt stop alongside Sam. The side door clicked and began to slide open. Without a moment's hesitation, he ran.

Sam's feet pounded the pavement, his coat billowing out behind him in the wind and his boots splashing through the puddles. His face was drenched by running head-long into the rainfall. He no longer cared about remaining discreet, or whether he would provoke them into further action. Running was his only chance. He glanced over his shoulder and saw the other two agents approach the van and jump into the back. Beaming white headlights loomed ominously across the street as the van made a U-turn, veering around to give chase, and with a sudden roar from the engine they were in pursuit. Now that their mark was on the run, they were picking up speed and rapidly closing the gap. Sam desperately prayed he would be able to outrun and lose them.

It seemed that Sam's prayers were answered, as within moments he realised he was coming up to a footpath which lead over a bridge to Hampstead Heath. Darting to his left at an almost perfect right angle, Sam sprinted up and over the footbridge and carried on running into Hampstead Heath, disappearing in the darkness of the dwindling daylight.

He didn't stop running for quite some time. Even though the van couldn't have pursued him over the footbridge, there was every chance the Men in Black would be following him on foot. Having bought himself maybe a few precious moments more by escaping over the bridge, Sam wasn't going to slow down until he had put a good amount of distance between him and them. He carried on running up Parliament Hill, his legs throbbing with each laboured step, his breathing heavy and uneven, as much from exertion as anxiety. His boots were caked in the fresh mud of the heath, and his clothes were soaked from the rain. Sam stumbled into a copse of trees part-way up the hill, and slumped down behind one of the trunks.

He had watched them from there, hidden behind the trees and concealed by the dark of night. His pursuers had indeed got out to follow him on foot, but evidently lost sight of him soon after the footbridge. They were still at the base of the hill, wandering around with their torches casting cones of light across the heath. The light from the torches never reached Sam; in his position, he was entirely out of sight. He watched them for ten minutes, although to Sam it felt infinitely longer, before he felt it safe to start making a move again. The agents were still lurking around where he had come from, but they were starting to slowly snake back towards Constantine Road.

It was not easy navigating Hampstead Heath in the dark. Sam had been here several times before, often absent-mindedly wandering around the park, but by night it was like treading the grounds of a familiar yet entirely unrecognisable world. His eyes had adjusted to the night as much as could be expected, but still he could barely see where he was going. He tripped and stumbled along in the pitch black, not daring to use his phone as a torch in case someone saw its light.

Rain pelted the already sodden earth, and the occasional arc of lightning streaked through the pitch black skies, briefly lighting up the way ahead with a distant growl of thunder. For almost an hour Sam Hain had wandered, venturing further into the heath than he had intended, and after walking in a large, looping arc from Parliament Hill, Sam was nearing home again. Walking alongside a large pond, almost perfectly black beneath the night's sky, Sam had risked a glance at the map on his phone, and he discovered a shortcut through a small alleyway onto South Hill Park Gardens.

It was this alleyway he now found himself in. He watched as the black van disappeared out of sight, presumably to loop around again on a patrol. Not sure of when he would next be presented with the opportunity, Sam made a mad dash around the corner and down the road. He was only a short distance from Hampstead Heath station now, and he would be home in five minutes if he made good pace. Stepping out onto the main street which ran past the station, Sam's heart was beating faster than ever. His eyes darted around, looking for any signs of the Men in Black. He hated feeling so exposed, but there was no other way than along the road. At least with other people on the street and a steady stream of passing cars and buses, Sam could try to disappear amongst the crowd, disguised beneath the canopy of rain-drenched umbrellas. Whenever he could, he would keep as far from the road as possible, taking a less visible route around to Constantine Road.

It wasn't long before Sam was bounding up the steps to the front door. With shaking hands, he thrust his key into the lock and slipped inside, closing the door quickly behind him. His landlady wasn't in, and most of the lights were off, but he was home. Sam dropped the plastic bag to the floor; amidst the fleeing from the Men in Black, he had crammed the bag with the M&S lasagne into his coat pocket as best he could, and now what was meant to be his dinner was a horrible, defrosted and soggy mess. He leaned against the inside of the front door, allowing himself to slowly slide down it until he was sat on the floor, and let out a long, exasperated sigh.

The club was not even remotely what Alice had wanted from her Saturday night. The floor was sticky, the music obnoxiously loud, and the place was packed full with people dancing in a haze of energy drinks and alcohol, plus other substances. She and the girls had sat down at one of the tables towards the back of the club, and had tried to talk with each other over their drinks. It was mostly futile, no-one could hear each other over the music, unless they were literally screaming directly into each other's ears, and they eventually gave up on conversation.

Rachel had got up to dance, a slightly unbalanced dance,

owing in part to her unnaturally high heels as well as the neon coloured shots she had downed as soon as they had arrived. Alice watched with the fascinated curiosity of a wildlife expert watching a newborn giraffe learning to walk. She tottered around the dance floor, waving her arms and clearly having a fantastic time.

Chantelle followed shortly after her, taken by the hand and led away, giggling, by a particularly muscular and typically handsome man in his late-twenties. Her body wiggled seductively in her red dress as she followed the man, her hips swaying to the sound of the beat, before he scooped her up in his arms and swaggered to the centre of the dance floor.

The music thumped on, and multicoloured lights strobed and danced across the black silhouettes of the revellers in the dark of the club. Jess had excused herself and disappeared to find the toilets, leaving Alice sat at the table by herself. She finished the last of her vodka and coke, and she toyed with the idea of getting another drink. She didn't feel drunk enough to jump in and start dancing yet, but if she was going to be here in this club anyway she may as well enjoy herself. Half-melted ice cubes clinked merrily as she vacantly swirled them around at the bottom of her glass.

'Can I buy you a drink?' a monotone shout came from somewhere to Alice's right, and she turned to see a man standing next to her. He looked at her and smiled a winning smile.

'Sorry?' Alice shouted back, leaning in a bit closer.

'Can. I. Buy. You. A. Drink?' The man repeated himself, making sure to speak slowly and loudly so she could hear him.

Alice looked back up at him, and she noticed that he was actually quite attractive; beneath spiky light brown hair, his face was chiselled and defined like a carving of a Greek god, with prominent high cheekbones complementing his strong jaw. A thin, perfectly trimmed subtle layer of stubble peppered his chin. Even in the dark she could see his opalescent blue eyes. Then she noticed something else. Beneath the cuff of his sleeve he had a small tattoo, and she was able to clock the rough shape of it before he adjusted his sleeve to hide it. It was a vertical line, a right-slanting line at its head, and two prongs at the bottom. She swallowed heavily as she felt a new bout of panic – or was it paranoia? – sink in. It could just be a tattoo, of course, but was she really willing to run that risk?

She looked back up at the man. He wasn't dressed like the men Sam had described at all – instead of the well-tailored suits, he opted for a casual shirt and ripped jeans – but Alice was feeling distinctly uneasy. He certainly wasn't the same as the men she had seen in the pub, but seeing that symbol had sent a frisson of fear running down her spine. If there was one thing she had learned, it was to trust her instincts.

'Sure,' she said after a short pause, leaning in a bit closer towards the man.

'What do you fancy?'

'Surprise me!'

The man walked off towards the bar, his gait strangely measured and completely asynchronous to the music blaring through the sound system. She watched him walk away, and tried to get her thoughts straight. *Am I just being paranoid now too?* It was certainly possible, she wouldn't have thought much about a man offering her a drink on any other day, but she couldn't get the thought out of her head that something more sinister was at play. *Bloody Sam, can't have a normal life!*

When she was sure he wouldn't be able to see her, Alice quickly picked up her bag and made her way back towards the stairs of the club. She didn't have time to say to her friends that she was heading back home – even if she did, it might not be a good idea – she just wanted to disappear into the night and leave all this conspiracy paranoia behind. She snaked through throngs of people dancing, weaving her way as quickly as possible through the crowd and checking behind herself to make sure he wasn't following. He was not; he was still at the bar, completely unaware that Alice was making a hasty escape.

A remix of Pharrell Williams' *Happy* came blaring through the sound system, and Alice quickly made her leave of the club.

The rain fell heavily on Islington that night, and the walk home was longer and darker than Alice had thought it would be. She kept checking over her shoulder, eyeing every passer-by with the utmost suspicion. Her mind raced with everything Sam had said. His fear, his paranoia. She understood it now. Thinking back, she remembered the man in the sleek black car who had offered her a lift. Then she thought of the Men in Black look-a-likes at the pub, exactly as Sam had described them, and with an unsettling vibe about them. And now the man in the club, with his tattoo so reminiscent of the Was sceptre. What if it was all in her head? Maybe Sam and James's talk of conspiracies was getting to her, and she was starting to see threats where there weren't any. She tried to talk herself out of the paranoid delusions, but Alice knew that something did not feel right. She tried to listen to the voice of reason, but after everything she had experienced that day, something told her precisely the thing she didn't want to hear. Sam was right.

She walked up to the front door of her building and let herself in. It was deathly quiet inside and the lights were off, which hardly helped Alice with her sense of uneasiness. Closing the door behind her, she started making her way up the stairs to her second floor flat. She could not wait to get into bed, get some rest and reassess things with a clearer head in the morning. Maybe Sam or

James would know something else by then.

Keys jangled and her bag landed with a soft *thoomp* sound as Alice threw them both onto the sofa. She stripped her rain-soaked denim jacket off, flinging it over one of the hooks by the door, and she started to undress as she headed towards her bedroom. Picking up a towel she had left on her floor that morning, Alice quickly dried herself off with it before slumping down on the bed. She had just closed her eyes and could feel herself sinking into the soft enveloping rolls of her duvet, when her phone jolted her awake. She eyed it suspiciously, and saw across the screen the words "Sam Hain is calling".

'Hello?' Alice said as she answered the call, sounding more confused than she intended to.

'Hello,' the voice of Sam Hain said, 'you okay?'

'Sam, it's almost one in the morning,' Alice replied, 'why're you calling? You hate phone calls!'

'I know,' he said bluntly. Whether he meant he knew it was almost one, or he knew he hated phone calls, Alice wasn't sure. 'I just wanted to check, uh, make sure everything was all right... Have you had any, y'know, "incidents"?'

Alice knew what he meant, and for a moment she considered lying and telling him that she'd had an entirely uneventful evening. After all, neither Rachel, Chantelle or Jess would have been aware of what Alice had noticed. If she was only seeing these things because Sam had unintentionally put the thought of it in her head, then she was reading into things that did not need any reading into. But she knew on some level that that wasn't the case.

'Yeah,' she said sombrely, 'yeah.'

'Me too,' Sam said. A silence hung on the phone line for a short while. 'What happened?'

'These two guys, exactly how you described them, turned up at the pub earlier. I don't know, I think they were watching me. They didn't order a pint or talk to anyone. They just kind of stood there.' She paused. 'You're right, though. There's definitely something off about them.'

'Yeah, sounds like them... Creepy, sinister-looking bastards, aren't they?'

'There was also a man driving near your place in the afternoon who offered me a lift home. I didn't think much of it at the time, but looking back something was strange about that too – no-one in London is friendly enough to offer a stranger a lift! And another offered to buy me a drink at the club. They were all exactly as you described them... Well, except for the guy in the club, but he had a tattoo which looked like the Wazz sceptre.'

'Was sceptre.'

'Whatever.'

'But nothing else?' Sam asked.

'No. Why?'

'Okay. You realise that drink was probably going to be-'

'Spiked? I don't know, I suppose it crossed my mind, I couldn't tell if I was just being paranoid. I left there as soon as I could.'

'Good. And you're home safe and sound now?' He sounded relieved.

'Yeah, I am,' Alice replied, 'how about you?'

There was another sizeable silence before Sam answered.

'I was followed again,' he eventually said, 'four of them, at least. And a black van, tinted windows, no license plate. I took them on a run around the houses and through the park. Took me bloody hours to lose them.' He sighed. 'Ruined my lasagne.'

'Right,' she said. She tried to think of something else to say, something probably a bit more reassuring or proactive, but nothing came to her. She couldn't get her head around the reality of the situation they found themselves in, it was just too mind-boggling. But their experiences could not be chalked up to something as simple as paranoia, no matter how many times Alice tried to convince herself that was all it was. The more she considered the reality of it all, the more futile their situation seemed. 'So what are we going to do? Any word from James?'

There was nothing but silence the other end of the line. She waited to hear if Sam would eventually say something, but she couldn't even hear him breathing now. She looked at her phone screen, and the call had abruptly ended.

'Hello?' Sam said into the silent telephone. 'Hell-ooo?' The landline crackled, and went dead. Nothing. Not even the dull hum of a dialling tone.

He put the phone's handset down on the base unit and furrowed his brow. What if something had happened to Alice? His stomach twisted with worry. A low growl of thunder rolled overhead, which relaxed Sam a little bit; the weather had probably knocked out the phone line. It didn't do much to put his mind at ease, but he could at least try to call Alice from his mobile or text her. The living room curtains briefly flashed with light. This was followed by another noise, a loud rhythmic knocking, which Sam thought was a very peculiar sound for thunder to make. The knocking came again, and reluctantly Sam made his way to the front door.

Peering through the door's viewer, Sam could see a man in a fluorescent jacket standing on the doorstep. He had a lanyard around his neck, and looked very unhappy to be there. He wondered why this man was knocking on his door at this time of night and, with trepidation, Sam slowly and cautiously opened his front door. He left the chain across the latch, allowing the door to only open a couple of inches, and he peered through the gap.

The rain was building into a torrent, and the skies rumbled ominously. The man on the doorstep was a very wet looking man. His fluorescent jacket sounded almost like it was crackling as raindrops fell and bounced off of it, and a plastic hood was pulled over his head.

'Phone line repairs,' the wet man said, 'seems to be an issue on your line.' He held up an ID, which was hanging around his neck on a lanyard, and Sam inspected it. The man was indeed a telephone engineer.

Sam stared at him with confusion and suspicion, and blinked incredulously several times before he eventually spoke. 'What?'

'I said-'

'No, I know what you said. Why are you knocking on my door at one o-bloody-clock in the morning?'

'Crossed signals at the exchange,' the telephone engineer explained, 'been working on the junction box a couple of houses down in this bleedin' weather. I noticed a fault on your line, and seein' as your lights're on, thought I'd fix the issue.' The man smiled at Sam, who simply stared morosely back at him.

'I have had an incredibly long day. If there's a fault with the landline, I'm sure it can wait until the morning. Thank you.' Sam nodded and offered a small wave through the gap in the door.

As he was about to push the door shut, he heard a noise which sounded uncannily like the telephone engineer saying 'oh screw this', shortly followed by a much clearer sound of a boot kicking the door. Hard. The latch and chain flew off of the front door as it burst inwards, and before Sam had a chance to make sense of what was going on he felt a sudden and sharp pain hit the side of his skull. Darkness quickly swam in around him as he lost consciousness.

CHAPTER III

The sound of a humming engine filled Sam's ears. The world was still shrouded in darkness, his eyelids too heavy for him to open them, and his head pulsed in agony. He tried to piece together what had happened, but he couldn't even begin to get his thoughts straight.

The next thing he became aware of was the sensation of leather pressed against his right cheek. It was warm, and he could feel it sticking to his skin. Lifting his head slightly, he peeled his cheek away from the leather and went to rub the side of his face, but discovered that his hands were firmly bound together behind his back.

There was a clinking noise, as if two glasses had been knocked together, and the sound of hushed conversation came from somewhere in front of him. Slowly struggling to peel his eyes open, Sam tried to gauge his surroundings.

He was greeted by the sight of the inside of a limousine. It was brightly lit by several small spotlights, and two rows of black leather seats ran up the full length of the limo, contrasting with the sparkling white marble floor and mirrored ceiling. At the far end, just behind the driver's area, was a polished chrome mini-bar. Sam found himself staring sideways down the length of the limo from the very back seat.

What on Earth is going on?

Immediately ahead of him, not too far from the mini-bar, Sam could see two men in suits sat opposite each other. They were mid-conversation, keeping their voices low as they sipped from slender flutes of champagne. As Sam's vision started to come back into focus properly, he was sure he recognised the two of them from the café that morning. He could sense there were another two men sat either side of him too.

'Looks like our friend's coming round,' said the man on the left. He was the stockier of the pair, with the receding hairline.

'Wakey-wakey, sleepy-head,' chimed the one on the right, who was the taller, more slender of the two.

Sam struggled to sit up, discovering his feet were bound together too, and managed to shift himself into an almost upright position. Neither of the two men, nor those either side of him, bothered to help. 'Were-um Ah?' Sam managed to slur, and he shook his head the minute he heard and felt the words tumble sloppily from his mouth.

The Men in Black stared at him vacantly.

'Where. Am. I?' Sam repeated, making sure he was articulating his words properly. His tongue felt like an old sponge.

'You're in a limo,' stated the man on the right. He took another sip of his champagne.

Sam swallowed hard. His head was throbbing, and the world around him was still decidedly blurry, but he was determined to struggle through his mental fug. He wanted answers and, although he had not wanted to find out on their terms, now was as good a time as any. 'I can see I'm in a limo,' Sam hissed bitterly at the man, 'but why?'

'So we can have a little chat,' he replied. Sam stared at him as if to prompt him to continue talking, but the man took a casual sip from his champagne without another word.

'So, let me guess,' Sam said after several moments of silence, 'Agent Smith? Agent Jones?'

The stocky man on the left looked up. 'Yup,' he gruffly replied.

'Well, which one?'

'I'm Smith, he's Jones,' the slender man said, gesturing to

his compatriot sat opposite him.

'You sure we should be just giving him this intel?' Agent Jones said, leaning towards Agent Smith.

'They are only code names, agent. There's not much our guest can do in his current predicament, is there?'

'He still knew our code names somehow. Evidently he's more cunning and resourceful than they gave him credit for.'

'Actually, I'm not,' Sam interrupted, and both of the agents stared at him. 'Lucky guess, really.' He smiled a half-sheepish, half-wry smile, hoping he was maintaining a sense of bravado, concealing how he really felt. Internally, he was bricking it.

'So what do they want us to do with him now?' Jones asked Smith.

'We're to present their proposal to him. Nothing more. It's up to him whether he'll choose to comply with their suggestions.'

Sam shifted awkwardly in the seat. It was quite distracting having his limbs bound and unable to move properly. 'Um, hi, I am still here,' he said, leaning towards the two agents, 'who are these "they" you keep mentioning? What do "they" want with me?' He would have used air quotations, had his hands not still been firmly tied behind his back. Probably for the best, really; he doubted they would have appreciated him miming air quotations.

'*They* are our employers,' said Smith, intentionally vague.

Now that Sam's vision was almost back to normal, he was sure he could see the bulging outline of a gun beneath Agents Smith and Jones's suits. This did nothing to put his mind at ease. It no longer hurt quite as much to move around, so he turned to face the two men sat either side of him. He noticed the man on his left also wore an identical suit with matching gun-bulge. The man on his right, however, looked very different to the others, and more than a little familiar. He wore a bright fluorescent vest, and a telephone engineer's ID hung around his neck.

'You're not really a telephone engineer, are you?' Sam said to him.

'No,' replied the man who wasn't a telephone engineer.

'I apologise for our forceful methods,' Agent Smith started to say, leaning back in his seat, 'but you left us with very little choice.'

'What, I didn't like being stalked by secret agents, so you had to assault and kidnap me? I can see how you didn't have a choice...'

Agent Smith simply sipped his champagne, and sighed a luxurious sigh. 'It got you here though, didn't it? No need to thank us for the luxury.'

'Yeah, I appreciate the thought of abducting me in a limousine – very premium – but it would be nice if I wasn't all tied up. I'd quite like to feel my feet again.' Sam twisted his face into a sarcastic smile. When in doubt, or in mortal danger, always try to be charmingly sarcastic: that was his new motto. Even if he was still shaking inside.

'All in good time,' said Agent Smith with a smug smile creeping up his face.

'Thing is, Sam, you're a liability,' Agent Jones said. 'You, and your line of work.'

'My colleague is right. If you carry on the way you have been, we might need to get involved. And I can assure you, you really don't want us getting involved.' Agent Smith raised his glass to Sam, and in unison all four agents nodded.

'Listen, I've been conscious for – what, five, ten minutes? – and everything you've said so far has just been irritatingly and intentionally vague. I want answers. No, more than that, I demand some bloody answers.' Sam was quite impressed with himself. From where he sat, he sounded commanding, full of conviction, not a shadow of doubt in his heart. He hoped it seemed that way to the agents, too. 'Now, who are you people? MI-5? MI-6?'

All four agents suddenly burst into laughter. Sam looked around at them, confused. *What'd I say that was so funny?* He may not have been in on the joke, but he felt a little at ease that they were laughing at something. At least they had human emotions underneath those perfectly tailored suits and calculated facial expressions.

'No, no. We'd never affiliate ourselves with those idiots,' Agent Smith said, his face slightly pink from laughter.

'You'd never catch one of us leaving confidential documents on a train!' Agent Jones exclaimed, and they all started laughing again.

'Let's just say that our employers are decidedly more... in control of things,' Agent Smith twirled his hand around as he explained. 'You see, our interests and yours aren't all that dissimilar, Sam. All we ask for is a little cooperation, to allow us to get on with our work uninterrupted.'

'Carry on as you are, though,' Jones interjected, 'and you'll only get in our way. Neither of us wants that now, do we?'

Sam stayed silent this time. He simply stared back at the two of them waiting for them to continue. Asking questions would clearly get him nowhere.

'Your little fiasco in Grimditch really interrupted a project of ours,' Agent Smith said.

'Aha,' Sam said almost a little too triumphantly, 'so you *are* the Regents?'

'No, we are not the Regents,' said Agent Jones, 'we simply work for them.'

'And you say I got in the way of your project in Grimditch?' Sam scoffed. 'What I saw was the beginning of a situation which could easily have spiralled out of control into a god-damn bloodbath! I think our interests lie in very different directions if that was one of your "projects"...'

'Rogue agents,' Agent Smith replied with a dismissive wave of the hand and an almost too nonchalant attitude, 'they took an artefact from the vaults and used it for their own purposes. To say they had it coming, well...' He raised his hands in a "what can ya do?" kind of gesture.

'Why permit them to continue, then? Why did I get in the way if these men had gone rogue?'

'The Regents were intrigued,' Agent Smith said with glee, 'it's not every day one can observe a Class Five Animating Possessor uninhibited.'

'The Pig-Headed Demon?' Sam clarified.

'Yes, as you oh-so eloquently put it, the Pig-Headed Demon.'

'We were ordered to allow the AP to continue without obstruction until its actions posed a legitimate threat,' Agent Jones added. 'You brought an untimely end to what was panning out to be a very promising project.'

'You don't think those men losing their lives and a demon possessing one of the corpses posed a threat?' Sam lowered his voice. Any sense of fear or paranoia had left him, most likely due to his righteous indignation and the sudden surge of adrenaline running through his veins. 'If you think what was happening there, what was going to continue happening there, was acceptable, then I'm afraid you are sorely mistaken. You didn't see what it was like. I saw the bodies, I saw the look on Douglas's ex-wife's face when she heard of his death, I saw that *thing* using people as its grotesque meat-puppets. Someone had to bring it to an end.'

'Don't try to be too sanctimonious about it, Sam. We knew about everything that was going on; we were there, observing events from the ground level,' Agent Smith said. That was when something clicked in Sam's memory, and he stared at Smith for a moment. As his eyes focused on Smith's face, he knew he recognised it from somewhere.

'I thought you seemed familiar, *Officer* Smith,' Sam said, and internally he kicked himself for not recognising the principle police officer who had been on every scene in the Grimditch case.

'Same alias, same face, different uniform,' Agent Smith nodded in confirmation. 'Playing the part of such a prosaic pedestrian plod felt like a bit of a demotion, but the Regents were insistent I was there to oversee the unfolding of events. Our involvement had to be entirely unobtrusive, unremarkable, so as not to influence the course of events or the intelligence we gathered, and we were prepared to pull the plug on the whole operation when necessary.'

'Human lives were lost!' Sam exclaimed. His righteous frustration was now behind the steering wheel, while his anxiety was sat by the side of it trying to reign it in a bit, desperately hoping he didn't antagonise them too much.

'The men who lost their lives were expendable. They turned their backs on the Regents and tried to pursue research into that artefact – and that entity – on their own, for their own purposes. We could've stopped them from the start, but we allowed them to continue, and in exchange we got a hint of the results we were hoping for. Witnessing what that Class Five was capable of was fascinating. You should consider it a miracle that the whole situation was as tame as it was.' Agent Smith quaffed the last of his champagne. Sam held his tongue.

'We want the same thing as you,' said Agent Jones, adopting an almost gentle tone, 'to keep the people of this world safe. For thousands of years, the Regents have been the guardians of arcane knowledge on Earth, and we've been there to keep the praeternatural world under wraps, under control. But to do that, we need to better understand the forces we're dealing with. Harnessing the power of the Akashic field; interdimensional travel; the quarantine, containment, and elimination of demonic threats. These pursuits naturally come with great risks, but they are risks which must be taken. Surely you've seen the signs yourself, whispers from the void that a darkness is coming... We need to be prepared.'

'All we're asking is that you take a step back. Stop prying into our organisation, and stop interfering in paranormal events with little regard for what we could achieve if we see them through to the end. All we need is that things remain as they are, and upstarts such as yourself stay out of our way.' Agent Smith had suddenly taken on a menacing tone, and he glared at Sam, his eyes seemingly burning into him.

'Right,' Sam said, 'we'll just have to agree to disagree then.' He swallowed hard, and felt his heart sink into his stomach as he dared to stand his ground. *Will they kill me for this?* 'I will not sit idly by while innocent lives are at risk, or when something from beyond this world needs to be dealt with. You carry on with your "experiments", I'll still do everything in my power to protect the ordinary from the extraordinary.' He was kind of proud of that last sentence, and in a brief moment of whimsy he considered it being his new slogan.

'I had hoped you'd listen to reason. Very well, never mind,' Agent Smith said coldly, and he casually gave a quick flick of his hand. Sam felt a sharp pain in the back of his head again, and his world was once again engulfed in darkness.

CHAPTER IV

Alice awoke early the next morning with a troubled mind. Not with the hangover she had expected to have, but with worry. She had been trying to call Sam back ever since the phones had cut out, but his landline was off the hook, and he didn't answer his mobile. She text him, but he hadn't replied. It wasn't unusual for him to be difficult to contact, but something about this occasion made Alice's stomach uneasy, especially after their conversation the day before. Something did not feel right.

She had tried to talk to Rachel about Sam's sudden disappearance; either for help in reaching him or for reassurance that he was probably okay, she didn't know. Rachel had not been much help.

'Is 'e your new lover?' she had slurred in the early hours of the morning when she came stumbling in from the club.

'It's nothing like that,' Alice had tried to say, but Rachel continued to tease her.

'*Alice and Sam, sittin' in a tree-*' Rachel chimed in an irritatingly sing-song voice. She could probably have tolerated her if she had been drunk too, but when sober, Alice found Rachel to be an incredibly annoying drunk. She had decided to leave Rachel to it at that point, and went back to bed. Sleep did not come easily for her that night, as she lay awake with conspiracies running riot in her mind. When she did eventually succumb to sleep, her consciousness slowly drifted into that place somewhere between wakefulness and dreaming. In these waking-dreams, she saw Sam being taken by the Men in Black, bound and tied and in the back of a car, being taken to some sinister underground chamber.

She hoped Sam would be in contact in the morning. She hoped to wake up to find a message saying "sorry, drifted off" or "sorry I couldn't call you back, but…"

Alice woke up to find no such message. She was worried. Thankfully, Rachel was in a much more sedate mood that morning, but she was still just as unhelpful.

'I think I remember you mentioning him last night… New boyfriend?' she said with a wry smile.

'No, I said last night it was nothing like that.'

'Oh. So why are you worried? Men will only message you when it suits them, especially if they know there's no chance for anything else. He'll be in touch when he wants to,' Rachel said, as if she was imparting sagely advice. There was a momentary pause while she squeezed her eyes tight and put her hand to her forehead. 'Ugh, my head! I had *so* much to drink last night.'

'He disappeared in the middle of a call last night. He wouldn't just hang-up without saying goodbye or without sending a message, he's not like that,' Alice replied, ignoring Rachel's traditional drinking boasts. 'What if something's happened?'

'Like what?' Rachel asked. Her motionless face showed she didn't really want to know, and was more preoccupied with her hangover-induced self-pity.

'I don't know, I just have a bad feeling,' Alice said, thinking of all the things which could have happened but would sound far too insane to say out loud. *Secret agents, conspiracies, assassinated, abducted*, she thought, *attacked by a demon, possessed…*

'You really need to relax, everything's bound to be fine. "Bad feelings" often don't mean anything,' Rachel said. She craned her neck around to look towards the kitchen. 'I don't suppose you're thinking of brewing a pot of coffee, are you?'

'I'll stick the kettle on then, shall I?' Alice said, making her way towards the kitchen. *If you'd seen the things I'd seen*, she thought, *you wouldn't say that bad feelings don't mean anything.*

After having a couple of cups of coffee – the strength of which gave Alice a caffeine high and coffee shakes, and restored some life to Rachel's hangover-face – Alice quickly ate a cereal bar and got dressed. She wasn't hanging around any longer waiting for Sam to get in touch, she had to go and make sure he was okay.

'I'm going to meet the others for a nice greasy breakfast at the caff around the corner, if you want to come with us?' Rachel had offered when she saw Alice slip into her dress and throw a jacket around her shoulders. She politely said no, and made her excuses before leaving. She wasn't going to tell Rachel that she was going to Sam's house to check on him; she would only say she was making a big deal out of nothing. She didn't particularly want to be grilled on her relationship with him when things were already mad and difficult enough to explain.

Alice arrived at the house on Constantine Road around mid-morning, clutching her jacket around her. The cold wind was particularly biting that morning. The streets were darkened by the rainfall the night before, and puddles of water gleamed and reflected the grey skies above like murky mirrors.

Sam's house seemed eerie and imposing in the weird, greyish-white light of the day, but there was something else which really put Alice on edge. As she approached the house, she saw that the door was ajar. Tentatively pushing the door open, Alice took a cautious step into the hallway. 'Hello?' she called out, but no-one answered. The house felt eerily deserted. Heading towards the stairs down to Sam's flat, Alice peered in the rooms which lead off from the hallway, but there was no sign that anybody was home; neither Sam or his landlady.

Her footsteps echoed and the floorboards creaked as she cautiously made her way downstairs. The door to Sam

Hain's basement flat was shut, but as she tried the handle, Alice discovered it was unlocked. Gently pushing the door open, she stepped inside and peered tentatively into the room. Immediately Alice noticed something was amiss. Sam's coat and hat were still hung up on the antique coat stand. At first she guessed he must have left in a hurry, but she knew him better than that: he would never leave his hat and coat behind, not even in an emergency.

There was a hauntingly empty air about the place. As she took a few more steps into Sam's living room, Alice felt like the hairs on the back of her neck were standing on end. An unnerving feeling tingled at the back of her mind. 'Sam? You there?' she called out again, but already knew she would receive no answer.

Her dream from the night before flashed through her mind. Visions of Sam being taken by the Men in Black, bundled into a car and taken to an underground lair. She started to wonder if it had really been just a dream, or something else. Something more. *What do I do?* She paced, lost in her thoughts. *What can I...? How...?*

'You can start by trusting in your particular talents,' a voice came from behind her. Alice jumped and whirled around, only to see James Mortimer standing in the doorway. Despite his slender build, James seemed to take up the whole of the doorway.

'How did you...? What're you doing here? Where's Sam?' Alice asked in a barrage of questions as her thoughts all attempted to jostle to the forefront.

'Same as you,' James said, stepping into the room and sitting down on the sofa. 'I don't know what's happened or where Sam is, but something is very wrong.' He gestured to the hat and coat hung up, Sam-less and abandoned. 'I figured I'd find you here, though. You're one of the few who'd know something was amiss.'

Alice nodded uncertainly. She went to sit in the armchair, but hesitated and hovered by the side of it for a while. Nervous energy compelled Alice to stay standing. Too many thoughts were running through her head all at once, and pacing around the room seemed like the sort of thing someone with too many thoughts would do. 'He suddenly cut out on the phone last night, and I haven't been able to contact him since. You don't think-?'

'That he was right?' James stretched his arms, and clasped his hands together behind his head, leaning back against one of the mismatched throw pillows. 'I don't know. I've known Sam a long time, and he's been right about even stranger things before. This,' he said, gesturing around the room and its conspicuous lack of Sam Hain, 'I'd say at least suggests he wasn't wrong.'

'Yeah. Definitely,' Alice said, sounding almost distant as she spoke. 'They came for me too, last night. The Men in Black. At least, I think they did, I'm not sure. I might've just been imagining things, but... No. I don't think I was.'

James leaned forward. 'What happened?'

Alice recounted the events of the night before. She told James everything that had happened, from the seemingly otherworldly men in well-tailored suits – exactly as Sam had described them – at the pub to the Was sceptre tattoo on the clubber who offered her a drink. The more she looked back, the more it began to dawn on Alice that had it not been for Sam talking about conspiracies and the Men in Black that day, these would have been wholly unremarkable events. But there was more to it than that; the sense of fear and dread Alice had felt was not just conjured up by seeing two men in black suits. There was a distinct presence to them, an otherness which she couldn't quite put her finger on. Whatever it was, they gave off an aura which had made Alice feel uneasy.

James listened to her tale intently, but whether any of it surprised him or evoked any thoughts or feelings at all was impossible to tell. His face was unchanging, sat with the same neutral expression, and Alice started to wonder if he was even listening. She finished recalling the previous night, adding that had it not been for Sam's ranting, she might have disappeared exactly as he had.

'That's good,' James said, and when Alice shot him a strange look he added, 'that you had your wits about you. It'd be easy for you to overlook them and carry on as normal – anything for a quiet life – either dismissing it as needless paranoia or not even noticing anything is wrong at all. But you had the acuity to know something was up. That's a vital skill to have, especially when Sam Hain is a part of your life.'

'There's also... No, that's not important,' Alice started, but stopped herself mid-sentence. She thought it best to leave the story with only the solid facts. 'The point is, our phone call suddenly cut out, and since then I haven't been able to reach Sam at all.'

'Alice, if there's one thing I've learned, it's that there's nothing that's not important. Everything is interconnected in one way or another, whether we realise it or not,' James said, and Alice could almost hear Sam's voice echoing those words. 'What was it?'

Alice waved her hand dismissively. 'It was just a dream. I didn't sleep well last night, but I had one of those half-asleep dreams that Sam had been tied up by the Men in Black and shoved in the back of a limousine. They were taking him to some kind of supervillain lair underground. After everything else, it was probably just all of the built-up stress.'

'On the contrary,' James stood up, 'Sam told me you were a latent psychic, and I see what he means now. You probably don't even realise it yourself half of the time.'

'I'm not entirely sure I realise it now, to be honest.'

'Hypnagogic clairvoyance.'

'Hypnagogic clairvoyance?' Alice echoed.

'It's like having a vision during the transitional state

between wakefulness and sleep. Those strangely vivid dreams, especially when you're half-asleep, which you can't shake the feeling were somehow quite profound, even if they didn't make much sense.'

'Dreams, basically.'

'It's no secret that dreams can give you some insight into your life, even if it isn't apparent at first. Some dreams can show you something more, though.'

'So you're saying you think that that was more than just a bad night's sleep, and I somehow managed to remote-view Sam being abducted,' Alice said, and her tone was laced with scepticism.

'It's a theory. It's worth looking into, at least. Can you remember any specific details? Any idea where they went to get to this underground lair?'

Alice shook her head. She could only recall the dream in brief flashes. Sam was tied up in the back of a limo, surrounded by Men in Black, and taken somewhere which put Alice in mind of old wartime bunkers. There was nothing which particularly stood out as a clear and distinct detail, and she forced herself to remember more of the dream. Try as she might, the dream fragments refused to give up any more information. 'I'm sorry,' was all she could say.

Running his hand through his hair, James slowly wandered over to the window. There wasn't much to see out of it, mostly just the sight of a wall, but the very top of the window could just about see the street level, which allowed for a small amount of natural light. He gazed up and out through the small space, to the white-grey skies beyond. He felt like they should have had something more to go on, but instead they were now missing one detective. There was only one thing left which, although it was not his favourite idea, might help them get that bit closer.

'You remember I mentioned that conspiracy theorist

yesterday?' James said, his gaze still focussed outside the window.

'The escapee test subject? Yeah, I do...'

'I'm going to reach out to him, see if he's willing to share the information he claims to have. You never know,' he said, turning around to face Alice, 'if his intel's genuine, he might be able to shed some light on what you saw in your dream.'

'And if he doesn't agree?' Alice almost hated the tone of her question, but she was feeling more than helpless. Everything seemed so futile in that moment, pessimism came easily. It clearly gave James pause for thought too, as he stared at the floor in silent contemplation for a moment.

'Then we keep on digging until we strike gold,' he said, 'but we'll worry about that if this doesn't pan out. While I make contact, you need to keep a low profile until we know more. We can't risk anything happening to you too.' When he noticed the worried look in Alice's eyes, James quickly added, 'not that anything will happen to you.'

Strangely, this did not do much to assuage Alice's worries.

James had insisted he give Alice a lift back to Islington. Even though he had stressed he didn't believe she was in any immediate danger, he thought it was best to err on the side of caution. She had agreed. The events of the night before had unnerved her to say the least, and with Sam now nowhere to be found, Alice felt even less secure. If they could take Sam from his own home, where was safe?

The drive back to Islington was a short one. The traffic had been very forgiving, and Alice was back home within quarter of an hour. She and James had sat in awkward silence for most of the journey, occasionally trying to make idle small talk to fill the time, but they both had their minds set on bigger things. It was hard to focus on anything else. Alice kept probing her memory for more snippets from the dream, anything which might give them some kind of answer. Nothing new came to her. Only an uneasy feeling which twisted and turned in the pit of her stomach.

That afternoon, Alice stayed at home. Partially because of James suggesting she keep a low profile, but also because leaving the house felt like an insurmountable challenge. Instead, she tried to unwind as much as she could given the circumstances, but that was another challenge in and of itself. She had picked up a book and tried to read and relax, but she couldn't get into it. Her mind kept wandering to the Regents, the Men in Black, and Sam Hain. She lay on the sofa, flicking through the TV channels to find something she could lose herself in. There wasn't much on, but she watched one of the afternoon films. It was nothing more than a bit of light entertainment, but she felt like it was what she needed to calm her nerves; which it did, for an hour and a half. When the credits began to roll, the fear and uncertainty crept their way back in.

No matter what she tried to do, she could not shut off from everything that was going on. She was a mess of nerves, but outwardly all she could express was a quiet and despondent moodiness.

Rachel, thankfully, did not try to pry into her friend's moody state, and instead allowed her her personal space, except to bring her a cup of tea and a family-size bar of chocolate for emotional support. Alice smiled a thank-you, but as much as she appreciated the gesture, it was going to take more than tea and chocolate to fix this particular situation. Not that that stopped her from enjoying the whole bar.

It was not until early that evening that she began to feel like things may be starting to look up. James had text her, and the seeds of a plan were beginning to grow.

Chapter V

The conspiracy theorist had agreed to share what he knew with James, on one condition: the conversation would have to be conducted in person. He did not trust most forms of communication, believing they were being monitored, and rathered they met face-to-face to discuss things. The man had introduced himself through a message as Cypher, followed shortly by another message which mentioned a Caesar salad and a string of seemingly random letters: *zrrg ng ternfl fcbba pnss rqtjner.*

James was no stranger to deciphering encoded messages, and he had made short work of this one. It was vague, but it was simple enough to point James in the right direction, and he set out to meet Cypher immediately.

The Greasy Spoon Café, as was its name, was a fairly dingy affair. On a street somewhere in North London, surrounded by independent taxi companies, corner shops and a launderette, the Greasy Spoon lived up to its name. An old and weathered sign – which looked as basic as the café itself – stretched across the front of the café, and large windows covered the entire street-facing wall. In the windows, the Greasy Spoon boasted a few of its menu options, including "All-Day English Breakfast" and "Coffee".

The sound of a small bell chimed as James pushed the door open and stepped inside. The four other occupants of the café stopped what they were doing and stared at James with suspicion. Sat in the corner, a grizzled old man with a long beard and tired eyes peered over the top of his newspaper, and then resumed reading. Two men, both wearing orange hi-vis jackets and dusty overalls, briefly stopped eating their fry-ups to look up. Towards the back of the café, a bald, weathered-looking man in an old army coat was hunched over a steaming cup of coffee. He did not look up, but he shifted nervously in his seat. *He must be the guy*, James thought.

He started to make his way towards the back of the café. Stood behind the counter, a friendly-faced man in grease-stained chef whites smiled at James as he walked past. James felt like he was overdressed for this kind of place, his pristine grey suit clashing with the off-white floor and stained wooden tables. Nonetheless, he nodded to the man behind the counter and with a wave he simply said, 'coffee, black.'

'Right you are, guv. Cup o' worm dirt, comin' up,' replied the server.

James slid himself into the seat opposite the man in the army coat, who made very little effort to greet him. 'Are you the man they call Cypher?'

The question caught the man's attention, and his head snapped up to face James. His eyes were manic and bloodshot, and they darted back and forth as if he was having difficulty choosing where to focus his gaze. 'Who's asking?' he asked aggressively.

'I'll take that as a "yes", then,' James said with a smile, and he extended his hand. 'Mortimer. James Mortimer.' The man who went by the name of Cypher ignored James's hand, and instead stared at him with wary eyes.

'You're that chap who wanted to talk about *them*,' Cypher said, and when James nodded he added, 'mad bastard.'

'Here you are, friend, your wakey-wakey juice. That'll be two squid,' the server announced with a warm smile, placing a large white cup in front of James. It was filled to the brim with a steaming black liquid which looked more like oil than coffee, and from certain angles it even had the same opalescent shimmer as oil.

James gave the server a cursory 'thank you' as he handed

him a two pound coin. He took a sip of the coffee, only to discover that it had very little taste to it. It simply tasted of scolding hot water and a bitter earthiness. *Worm dirt indeed,* James mused as he stared into his cup. All the while, Cypher kept his gaze on James as if he was analysing his every move.

'Now,' James said, looking up from his disappointing coffee, 'it seems our meeting couldn't have come a moment too soon. Yes, I want to talk about *them.* I've read over a couple of your leaks, but I'm hoping your unique insight can help me with something.'

'No one wants help from a crazy old coot like me,' Cypher said derisively, not taking his eyes off of James. Something about the wild but distant look in his eyes told James that this man was not all-there in the traditional sense, but there was still a keen mind ticking away somewhere inside the paranoia-twisted psyche. With a pained chuckle, Cypher took a gulp from his own coffee cup. 'Here to finish me, is it?'

'I'm sorry?'

'Put me outta my misery, silence my gob for good,' Cypher continued, his unbreaking and unblinking stare still fixed on James. 'Make it look like I topped myself, am I right? Crazy ol' conspiracy nut couldn't take his paranoia no more, decided to end it all.'

James stared at him with a mixture of confusion and disbelief. He had expected his meeting with Cypher to be an unusual one, but he was not quite expecting this. 'I think you misunderstand me, I'm-'

'You're not fooling me,' Cypher interrupted, 'I've had more dealings with your kind than I can count. Your games won't work with me. I know what you are.' Without warning, Cypher grabbed James's hand and in a single swift and remarkably precise motion he stabbed a knife into James's palm and cut along the soft flesh. James yelped in pain and forcefully pulled his hand back from the lunatic, instinctively reaching for a napkin and holding it against his unexpected wound.

'What the?! Jesus! What the hell was that for, you maniac?' James exclaimed. Several of the other café patrons looked up to see what the commotion was about, but almost instantly decided to turn a blind eye and not get involved.

His body surged with pain and anger as the shock subsided. Droplets of deep red blood dripped onto the table, and he had to press the napkin firmly against the cut across his palm to stem the bleeding. The formerly white napkin started to turn crimson. Cypher stared in disbelief. 'For Christ's sake, man, you look like you've never seen blood before,' James spat.

'I... I-I'm sorry,' Cypher stuttered, suddenly looking confused and frightened. He was transfixed by James's bleeding hand, gazing at the blood in disbelief. 'I thought- I didn't think...'

'You didn't think what?' James's eyes seemed to turn black as he glared at his unexpected assailant.

'I didn't think you'd bleed.'

'Well what the shit did you think was going to happen?'

Cypher continued to stare, but he was no longer looking at James or the freshly drawn blood. He looked like his mind was no longer in the café with them, as if his consciousness had mentally checked out and retreated to the back of his mind. 'You're real. You're... human?'

James nodded a slow and sarcastic nod. 'Yes... I'm human. Were you expecting someone else?'

'I thought you were one of, you know... *Them*.'

'The Men in Black?'

'You look like they do. All prim and proper in their pretentious suits,' Cypher replied, and he seemed to spit his words with venom. He suddenly snapped out of his distant stare, and looked up at James. 'Thing is,' he said, leaning forward and lowering his voice to a conspiratorial whisper, '*they* don't bleed.'

'What do you mean?'

'I mean exactly how it bloody sounds. Prick us, do we not bleed? Because they sodding well don't. Listen, I've been runnin' from those creepy sons of bitches for years now, always havin' to watch my back. Can't trust no-one these days.' He leaned back into his seat and took the last swig of his coffee. He was notably more sane-looking than a moment ago (benefited by the fact that he was no longer wielding a knife), even if his words were still barbed and bilious. 'When you strode in all tall 'n' toffee-nosed, I pegged you as one o' them. I wasn't just gonna bolt out the door, see, that plays into their hands.'

James looked down at his own hand as Cypher babbled on. Thankfully, the knife had not cut deep, and although it was absolute agony, the napkin was managing to stem the bleeding. He adjusted his grip on his hand, and quickly applied a clean napkin to the wound.

'Now, when you're confronted by somethin', what do you do? You got two choices; fight, or flight, innit? So I was always runnin', hidin', until one day they had me cornered. Only two of 'em, and way I saw it, I could take 'em. I couldn't run, so figured I'd at least go down swingin'. So I pulled me pen knife on them, and when one of the bastards tried to get too close, I stabbed 'im!' The table jolted as Cypher mimed himself stabbing an invisible agent. Repeatedly, with slightly more passion than telling the story really warranted, and certainly more than James was comfortable with. 'But me knife just came back out, clean as anything. No blood on the blade, or on their poncey easy-iron shirts, not even a reaction as you might expect from someone who's got a knife in their gut. So sorry I cut you up some, I really wasn't expectin' you to be an actual person.'

For a madman, Cypher seemed genuinely apologetic

about stabbing James in the hand. If it weren't for the still searing pain in his palm, James would almost have considered putting the whole event behind them. As it happened, he wasn't even in the mood to say something to vaguely accept the apology. 'If you can't hurt them, then how did you escape?'

'Well I fuggin' twatted 'em, didn't I?' Cypher replied with a triumphant laugh. 'They might not bleed and you might not be able to kill 'em, but you can still stun 'em with a swift punch in the face. They might look it, but those Men in Black ain't exactly what you'd call human.'

'What would you call them, then?' James asked, intrigued. His hand throbbed, and he wrapped it around his coffee mug, hoping that the heat would help to quell the pain. 'If,' he added, 'you trust me more since cutting my hand open?'

'They're creatures born out of necessity. The Regents needed people to do their dirty work for 'em, see? But people-people, like me 'n' you, we have flaws. We have emotions, consciences. We crack under pressure, we feel pain, we-'

'Bleed?' James interrupted snarkily, and he gave Cypher a wry smile.

'Yeah. Basically, we cock up and are kind of crap sometimes. To err is human, after all. And there are quite a few in the organisation that are human, but them Regents don't want no mortal screwin' up their wetwork and accidentally lettin' things slip. Not when it comes to the real important stuff. That's where these Men in Black come in. They have these creepy automaton buggers do their biddin' for 'em, like little worker bees. Buzz buzz buzz.' Cypher traced patterns in the air with his fingers as he continued to make buzzing noises. 'Drones to serve the Hive. They can buzz off for all I care!'

'I must admit, your story intrigues me, Cypher. You've had far more experience dealing with them than I have,'

James said, trying to ignore Cypher's occasional buzzing noise. Through what could be seen as the ramblings of a lunatic, James felt like he was getting somewhere. 'Do you know what they are, precisely? These Men in Black drones?'

Cypher could only offer a shrug in response. 'Beats me. All I know is they ain't exactly from this particular terrestrial plane of existence, if you catch me drift. Upset the Hive and they'll come and sting ya. Trust me, you don't wanna get stung by them.'

'So I gather. I can't say I've had any encounters with them myself, and the more I'm learning about them the happier I am about that. In fact, I knew next to nothing about the Regents until I read your leaks.' James swilled the coffee around his mug thoughtfully.

'I ain't surprised you never heard of 'em before. Not many have, they make sure of that. The Regents pull all the strings from behind the curtain, and if one of their little puppets don't dance right, then...' He drew his finger across his throat and grimaced to drive home his point.

'And you got away from them alive?'

'Obviously. I'm 'ere, ain't I?'

James shook his head and made a noise that was somewhere between a laugh and an exasperated sigh. 'I mean, how did you escape from the Hive without getting... stung?'

'Ah. I just been lucky, I guess. Every few months I 'ave a bit of a ding-dong with their chaps in black. They try to take me back, and I give 'em the slip. Ain't no force in Heaven or Hell gonna take me back there.' And Cypher was gone again, his focus slipped away and he stared at nothing in particular with a far off gaze.

'Hey, are you still with me Cypher?'

'Yeah, mate, yeah,' Cypher said, suddenly snapping back to reality. 'Sorry, Voidwalker side-effects. Reality ain't quite what it seems when you been through that.'

'Through what, precisely?' James asked, leaning across the table. 'What was the Voidwalker Project?'

'Mad bastards,' Cypher replied and he shook his head. 'Somethin' to do with extra-dimensional research, portals to other realities, that kind of thing. People like ol' muggins here were their little guinea pigs. Sending us through their portals, using magic nodes to send our minds astral travellin', see if we didn't come back with our psyche's snapped in half. I've seen all kinds of mad shit. I've seen that void between worlds, that infernal howlin' abyss. And them words, echoin' across that void, that some kinda darkness is comin'. It ain't right.'

'And you got away from that intact? It's incredible you're still here to tell the tale.' James had more than a hunch that maybe Cypher's mind had not quite made it back from its extra-dimensional travels in one piece. But if Cypher had managed to break free from one of their facilities and been able to evade the Regents and the Men in Black for so long, he clearly still had some of his wits about him. He seemed cognizant enough to be of some use in helping Sam Hain.

'You don't need to patronise me, friend,' Cypher said solemnly, 'I know I ain't all there in the 'ead no more. Can't odds that when you're made to hop across alternate dimensional realities, like a mouse runnin' around a maze in some lab. I still got me wits and me mind, it's just them signals between mind and brain that have gone a bit skew-whiff.'

'I'm sorry, I didn't mean for it to sound like that. There's no doubt you've still got a firm grasp of your wits; you managed to break free from their facility, and have stayed ahead of their game, avoiding capture or worse.' James sounded genuinely impressed. It must be no mean feat evading the Men in Black – especially if it was true, as Cypher said, that they weren't human – let alone escaping from the Regents' facility. If they held enough sway to manifest their own unnatural operatives, and were powerful enough to conduct things like the Voidwalker Project, he could not imagine that breaking out was a walk in the park. 'So how did you escape? It can't have been easy.'

Cypher stared into his now empty coffee cup morosely, and stayed silent. After a while, he looked up again. 'No, it wasn't.' His words were clear and simple, and it was probably the sanest, or most serious, his voice had sounded all afternoon. 'I was bein' held in one of their detention facilities. When they wasn't sendin' us into hell, they kept us locked up below ground. Nothin' much to say about that hovel, just some concrete bunker for their little lab rats and worse. The ones who had already lost their minds were the lucky ones, blissfully deluded, least they weren't aware they was stuck in some concrete cell day-in day-out.

'One day – I dunno when precisely, time is an immaterial construct we perceive to make sense of our linear reality, but it's a fair bit more fiddly than that – anyway, one day, this alarm starts goin' off. *Bweee-ooo! Bweee-ooo!* And I kinda twig, "hullo, somethin's goin' on here." So I press my 'ead against the door and see if I can hear anything. Course, I can't hear a chuffin' thing, cells are soundproof 'cept for the alarms. Then, the door begins to shake, see, and the sound of the lock being opened. Door swings open, and there's this chap in an 'ospital gown with wires comin' outta 'is head. Another Voidwalker.

'Well I didn't waste no time, I joined the blighter and ran. Turns out there'd been some kinda containment breach, something had come back with my escapee friend and them agents were scramblin' to send the bloody thing back.'

'What was it?' James interrupted. He was getting impatient, and he was desperate to get to some information which might be useful in finding and rescuing Sam. *Still*, he thought to himself, *Cypher's intel is certainly informative.*

'You think I hung around to find out what all the excitement was about? Bollocks to that! I ran. There's only a handful of agents in that place, so most of 'em were busy tryin' to stop a transdimensional incursion while we made a break for it. One of 'em spotted us, and tezzered my pal, but I managed to stay hidden. I was lucky enough to get out. Had to keep all stealthy-like, obviously, didn't want no other suit spottin' me. When I got topside, I found meself in that royal park. Regent's Park, that's the one. Nice place when the weather's good.'

'Regent's Park?' James repeated, almost incredulously. 'The underground facility you escaped from was beneath Regent's Park?'

'Yeah, funny that. You'd think they'd name it somethin' less conspicuous.'

'So if you got out, you'd know how to find the way back in?'

'Why the titty-lovin' Christ would you want to know how to get in?'

'One of my friends, well, my oldest friend, believed he was being followed by the Men in Black yesterday. I've known him long enough now to know he wasn't just being paranoid. It turns out he was involved in a situation that was connected with the Regents-'

'Oof, nasty stuff.'

'And this morning, he's nowhere to be found. His flat is empty, and he suddenly dropped out of contact late last night. There's no doubt in my mind that what he feared would happen, has happened,' James said, his voice betraying his concern.

'Then they've probably taken him to the Hub,' Cypher said, and his face contorted apologetically. 'Your friend ain't comin' back out.'

James slammed his fist on the table, and instantly regretted it as pain seared from the wound in his hand. He had been so distracted by coming close to a revelation that he had almost forgotten that this man had greeted him by stabbing his hand. Wincing, he pulled his hand back slowly and gently nursed it under the table. 'That's not good enough,' he said, his voice mixed with anger, pain and desperation, 'you got out in one piece, even if your mind didn't. There must be a way.'

'Very different kettle of fish. There was some kind of hellbeast clawing its way out of the abyss, the Men in Black were distracted! Barring another monster attack, they won't be so easy to get by. It'd be suicide.'

'Just tell me how to get to this Hub. I'll worry about whether it's suicide or not.'

Cypher stared at the table for what felt like an eternity, and he would murmur incoherently to himself every now and again, as if he was debating whether he would help or not. He felt sorry for James's situation, and for what had happened to his friend, but he was not sure he could burden the guilt of sending someone to their doom. No matter how well-intentioned. But then an idea struck him, a terrible idea which stoked a fire in his heart, and a darkly satisfied smile crept across his face.

'One condition,' he said, 'I come with you.'

'Don't be absurd! You just said it would be suicide.'

'The only life I can remember was either spent in their dingy little cells, or runnin' from their creepy goons. I got nothin' to lose. If you pull this off – and I jus' reckon you might, you crazy git – then I can get some of me own back.' Something glimmered in Cypher's eye, a kind of maniacal glee which unnerved James slightly. But maybe someone who already knew about the facility, someone who was knowledgeable, if more than a little unhinged and fuelled with revenge, was exactly who they needed.

James extended his non-cut hand towards Cypher. This time around, he took it and shook his hand firmly. 'Okay, you have a deal,' James said, 'but first and foremost, this is a search and rescue operation. There will be no heroics, no unnecessary risks. Understood?'

'Yes, boss!' Cypher exclaimed and gave him a wonky salute. 'Meet me in the north-west corner of Regent's Park, ten-a-clock tonight. I'll take ya to the Hub and into the mouth of hell. We'll get your buddy out.'

'Thank you,' James said, and he was hit by a wave of relief now that things were moving forwards. He had the man with inside knowledge on their side and by tomorrow morning, he told himself, Sam Hain would be safe and sound. Then he was hit by a wave of anxiety when the reality of infiltrating a secret organisation sunk in, but he tried not to think about it.

Standing up from the table, James returned his coffee mug to the counter of The Greasy Spoon, for which the server thanked him, and he turned to face his unusual co-conspirator. 'It's been a pleasure, Cypher,' he said, 'surreal and unexpectedly painful, but a pleasure.'

'No troubles, friend,' was Cypher's simple reply. With that, James strode towards the café's door and left.

He paused for a moment outside, pulling out his phone and quickly tapping out a text to Alice. He would go over the details with her later on, but for now he thought she should know that things were looking up. At least, as up as they could be looking, given the circumstances.

I've met with the guy and he's been a great help. Will tell you more later, but for now things are looking positive. -James

Sam awoke to find himself laying in the middle of a room. It took him a while to come to his senses again, but after he was able to piece together the events which had lead to this moment, he realised where he was. He was in a prison cell.

It was cold and uninviting, not that cells could ever be said to be warm and welcoming. It was a small concrete cubicle, only a few meters wide and a few meters deep, but the ceilings were fairly high. If this were listed on a London property website, they would make a big feature out of the high ceilings, regardless of the state of the rest of the place.

In the corner towards the back of the cell was a foam mattress, no more than an inch thick, with a single thin blanket draped over the top of it. Whoever had placed Sam in this cell had not had the courtesy to place him on his would-be bed. Not that he minded, though, because the blanket was clearly old and there were several stains on it which Sam did not dare imagine what they might be. In the opposite corner sat a metal bucket, presumably the makeshift toilet. Mercifully, the bucket was empty.

Struggling to his feet, Sam staggered towards the door. His feet and hands were no longer tied, but he could still feel the soreness from where he had been bound. Everything hurt, and it was an effort just to stand, but he was not just going to lay back and accept his fate. Lifting one bruised hand up, he slammed on the metal door of the cell.

'Hello?! Anyone there?' he shouted through the door, slamming it with his palm as hard as he could. The metal clanged and echoed in the cell as Sam repeatedly hit the door, but there was no other noise. Eventually, when his hands were starting to feel even more bruised and swollen, Sam relented.

He slumped to the floor, defeated.

CHAPTER VI

'I'm bloody well coming with you, James!' Alice shouted at the man in the grey twill suit, who was trying his best to ignore her as he made his way towards his car.

He had met with her in Islington that evening to let her know everything he had learned from Cypher, and to inform her of their plan of action. He had asked her to stay at home, where it was safe, until the mission was complete. She refused. At great lengths, James had told her about the underground facility, Cypher's story, and not least the allegedly unkillable, inhuman agents who act without remorse, and emphasised exactly why it was imperative she stayed out of harm's way. Again, she refused. He asked her if she heard him say the bit about the unkillable agents, and apparently she had.

She's either incredibly stupid or incredibly brave, James had thought. As Sam Hain's accomplice, it was almost certainly the bravery. He could respect that, and he admired her willingness to take part in something so dangerous, potentially putting herself at risk for the good of another. That wasn't going to make him change his mind, though.

Unlocking the doors of his car, James stood by the driver's side and watched as Alice jogged across the road, catching up with him. 'Alice, I've already said to you, it's too dangerous. Please, go home.'

'Why is it too dangerous for me, but not too dangerous for you, hm?' She didn't mean to be so confrontational, especially when the idea of what they were about to do scared her beyond belief. After everything that had happened since Sam had told her that he was being followed, Alice was feeling more than highly strung. She hadn't been able to focus on anything all day, just waiting to hear whether James was on to something; the stress and worry and helplessness of the situation was consuming her. She wasn't just going to sit idly by when she could be out helping to rescue Sam.

'Listen,' James began, attempting to sound as calming and reassuring as possible, hoping he didn't sound patronising, 'Sam wouldn't want you getting yourself into any unnecessary danger. He couldn't bear losing someone like you. And I wouldn't be able to forgive myself if anything happened to you, too.'

He was right. Sam would not want Alice endangering herself, and she knew it. But she also knew that Sam needed their help, and as far as she was concerned there was no room for debate. She was going to help. In her mind, there was not an alternative.

'James, I've had a shadow being live in my head, I've stared into a Void portal, I have looked into the eyes of a butcher's decapitated head and I have been attacked by re-animated pig carcasses,' she rattled off as she opened the passenger-side door of the car, 'it's not my first adventure. I'm coming.' There was no excitement or intrigue with this adventure, though. Only a terrifying sinking feeling in the pit of her stomach, and her heart beating heavily in her throat.

The car doors slammed shut as Alice and James seated themselves. With an exaggerated and exasperated sigh, James turned to face Alice and smiled warmly. 'You know, you remind me of my sister,' he said, 'she could be infuriatingly obstinate sometimes, too.'

'Is it really being obstinate when it's the right thing to do?' Alice retorted with a slight smirk.

'Yup, just like Lorna,' James muttered, and he turned the key in the ignition. The car growled to life and they snaked out into the stream of traffic, heading down the road and towards Regent's Park. Towards the Hub.

They pulled up on Prince Albert Road on the north-west side of Regent's Park a little after ten o'clock. The drive had been a relatively short one, and the two of them had spent most of it in silent nerves and quiet contemplation. Neither James or Alice were looking forward to what they were about to do, but they both knew what had to be done. The crumpled up greatcoat in the backseat of the car, with the fedora hat resting on top of it, served as a constant reminder.

Waiting on the corner of Avenue Road, by two pillars which marked one of the gateways to the park, stood a bald man in an old army coat. He waved cheerily at the car as they arrived and parked on the opposite side of the road.

Before getting out of the car, James turned to face Alice. She carried on staring directly ahead, presumably preparing herself as much as she possibly could.

'Ready?' he asked.

'As I'll ever be,' Alice sighed, and they both stepped out of the car, making their way over the road to meet Cypher.

'Alright, mate,' Cypher greeted James, and he tipped an imaginary hat towards Alice. 'Enchanté, m'lady. I'll be your tour guide for this evenin'.'

'Alice, this is Cypher,' James said, waving his bandaged hand towards the bald man.

Alice eyed him warily. From what James had told her about their confederate, she was not looking forward to placing her trust in an unhinged escapee. She was nervous enough about the whole situation as it was, without throwing a madman into the mix. She affectionately referred to Sam as mad, but overall he was harmless (if, to put it politely, unique). It worried her that this Cypher was decidedly further along the madness spectrum. Smiling politely, she gave the man a cursory 'hello.'

'Now listen, you ain't got nothin' to worry about, darlin',' Cypher said, 'we're going to get your friend out of there all hunky dory.' He leaned forward and touched her arm reassuringly. 'I've got a plan!'

Cypher had explained his plan as they walked over the bridge crossing the canal, which ran along the perimeter of the park's northern side, and onto the Outer Circle road. From the road, they would climb over the small iron fence into a densely wooded area, using the foliage for cover during their approach. Bearing east beyond the trees, they would stick to the shrubbery around the northern edge of a rugby pitch until they reached a footpath. There would only be a small group of trees between them and the Hub at this point and, Cypher emphasised, moving close to the ground and using what cover they could find would be imperative. From this small cluster of trees, the entrance to the Hub would be visible, and they could assess the next phase of the plan: infiltration.

They had agreed to the plan and, checking over their shoulders to make sure that no-one was watching, one by one they hopped over the iron fence and into the thicket. Beyond the fence, the trees and shrubbery were wild and overgrown, and the trio had to wade through the dense undergrowth as they snuck themselves over the perimeter of Regent's Park. Twigs snapped and dead leaves crunched underfoot with each careful, trudging step. Alice clutched Sam's hat close to her and, for reasons she could not quite explain, she found holding onto it was somehow reassuring.

It wasn't long before they had cleared the thicket and found themselves on the edge of a clearing which stretched away into the darkness. The dark shapes of trees marked the horizon, silhouetted against the clear night sky, dotted with the faint light of countless stars. In the distance, the warm golden lights of London glowed almost in defiance of the cold bluish-black of night.

Under the cold white glow of the moon, they could just about make out the well-kept grounds of what must be the rugby pitch. Directly ahead of them, and no more than a hundred yards away, was another smaller cluster of trees and the very faint hint of a concrete footpath. Cypher signalled for them to move around the outside of the rugby pitch, sticking close to the treeline, and to keep low. Crouching, they slowly and carefully arced around the pitch and towards the path, looping around behind trees where possible, until they eventually made it to the pathway.

The terrain was irritatingly flat, and the only cover they had on their final approach was from the small, sparse cluster of trees which separated the footpath from the Hub. Had it not been nearing midnight and they were under the cover of the darkness, the three of them would have been clearly visible. Cypher gestured towards the trees and flattened himself against one of the trunks. Alice and James followed suit. One by one, they peeled away from their trees and scurried towards the next ones, advancing forward until it was eventually in sight.

On top of an artificial-looking mound sat the Hub. It was a squat, circular structure, made mostly of glass and metal, and it put Alice in mind of a spaceship from an old science fiction film, almost like a classic flying saucer. Despite its sci-fi appearance, the UFO-like glass building was in fact a café during the day. Beneath it, a large opening was cut into the side of the mound, leading to a small concrete tunnel into the space beneath the Hub. Standing just within the entrance of this concrete passageway, Alice saw two men. Both were tall and slender, wearing finely tailored black suits, and narrow sunglasses covered their eyes. Their appearance was all the more unsettling tonight, standing stock still and staring straight ahead like statue-esque sentinels.

Alice mimed to James and Cypher, gesturing around the

tree to where the guards were stood and holding up two fingers. Creeping around the trees to a position just outside of the Men in Black's vision, the three of them huddled together.

'There's two of them, three of us,' Cypher whispered chirpily.

'You're not suggesting a full-frontal assault, are you?'

'Why not? It'll be easy-peasy-lemon-squeezy. Listen, we get closer to the buggers, then we rush 'em! Bish-bash-bosh, and they's out like a light. Luvvly jubbly!'

'Does he always talk like this?' Alice turned to James, raising a concerned eyebrow.

'I'm afraid so, yes,' James said frankly. 'It's not too late, Alice. You don't need to follow us in.'

'Actually, I think it might be too late now,' she said. Her eyes did not meet James's. Instead, she was staring beyond him and towards the Hub with a shocked expression. When he turned, James noticed that Cypher was no longer by the side of them, and with a sinking feeling in the pit of his stomach he heard a distant shout.

'Alright, chaps! Which way to the top secret base?'

Cypher had sprinted right up to the two Men in Black, and seemed to be tauntingly dancing in front of them before breaking into a run further away into the park. One of the agents gave chase, sprinting after him at full pelt.

'Shit!' James spat, and without another word he too broke into a run, arcing around outside of the remaining agent's vision, quickly making his way from the trees to the side of the Hub. It was a narrow window of opportunity, but James knew he had to act fast to make the most of the situation. With only one agent between them and the Hub, the odds were a little more in their favour. And Cypher had forced his hand by jumping straight in, so it was now or never.

Skirting around the edge of the mound, James started to

approach the agent from behind. He moved quickly but quietly, and when he was an arm's reach away he tapped the agent on the shoulder. The Man in Black turned around stoically, only to be met with a right hook to the face. He immediately crumpled and fell to the floor, unconscious. Kneeling down, James fished around inside the agent's jacket for anything which might be useful, and retrieved a keycard from the breast pocket. With a beckoning wave, James gestured for Alice to come over.

'That was all very sudden,' Alice said as she jogged over to the entrance of the Hub, 'what's the plan now? What about Cypher?'

'I can only assume he knows what he's doing,' James muttered, although that assumption seemed like a bit of a stretch. He hesitated for a moment. He had noticed the grip of a handgun sticking out of a holster around the agent's waist, and after a moment's consideration James took the weapon. It was shiny and sleek, but he didn't bother inspecting it further and simply secured it beneath his belt. Better to go in there armed than to come back out unarmed and be met by a man with a gun and a black eye. Standing up, James brandished the keycard he had found to Alice. 'Now,' he said, 'we let ourselves in.'

Inside, the area beneath the Hub wasn't much to look at. Concrete corridors lined with storage lockers led blandly to the central circular area directly beneath the café. In the middle a spiral staircase wound upwards to the café above, and around the circular space several doors ran off into other rooms. The Hub was certainly larger than it would have suggested from the outside. Peering cautiously through the doorways, James and Alice discovered two very empty function rooms, but nothing of any interest.

There was, however, one door which separated itself from the rest. At a glance, it wasn't any different from the others; a simple grey door with two circular windows, but instead of having a number on the wall by the side of it, there was the familiar hieroglyph of the Was Sceptre. Beneath the symbol was a simple card reader.

'Not very secretive, is it?' Alice mused as they approached the door.

'I suppose they don't have to be. If you've come this far, you either know what's behind this door, or you don't even give it a second thought.' James tapped the keycard against the reader by the side of the door. It beeped merrily, followed by the *click* of a door unlocking.

They stepped through the door into another concrete corridor. This one was even more desolate than the last; completely empty, save for the elevator waiting for them at the end of the corridor. Alice and James set foot in the elevator and, almost as if operating on autopilot, she pressed a button. Other than the standard range of buttons (doors close, doors open, emergency, and the mysterious unmarked fourth button which could do anything from calling maintenance to transporting you all the way down to the seventh circle of Hell) there were only two operational buttons: Up and Down. It was the latter which Alice pressed. The elevator doors closed, and with a jolt they were heading down.

The journey down seemed to go on forever, probably not least because of Alice and James's rising anxiety, but also because they were heading quite some way underground. It wasn't like taking the lift down to the food court in Oxford Street's Marks and Spencer as much as it was like trying to get to the twentieth floor of a high-rise building; if that building were structurally inverted and almost exclusively underground.

Alice had imagined her apprehension would slowly dissolve as she got more involved with the infiltration, as she often overcame her fear when on a case with Sam, but this time was different. A solid lump stuck in her throat and her stomach felt heavy and uneasy. She was starting to feel numb and lightheaded, and she nervously toyed with

Sam's hat in her hands. Despite his peculiarities and haphazard approach, the occult detective always seemed to have things under control in the end. This was a situation far from Sam's – or, indeed, anyone else's – control, and Alice felt like they were in over their heads.

Stood by the side of her, James idly nursed his bandaged hand. He was lost in his own thoughts. The minute the doors opened, they would find themselves in the heart of a Regents' facility from where, if Cypher's story was anything to go by, very few people returned to see the light of day. The thought of that was driving James forward, to defy the odds and get his friend out, but it did not make it any easier. The sensation of the gun tucked into his waistband was not providing him with any reassurance.

The elevator came to a stop, and the doors slid open.

Peering out from just within the doors, James and Alice were unsurprised to be greeted by the sight of yet another corridor. What did surprise them was that it looked decidedly older than the floor above. The off-white plaster walls were cracked and stained in places, and where it had started to peel and crumble away it revealed it was covering brickwork which looked even older. It vaguely resembled an old World War II bunker or a disused Underground station. Fluorescent strip lights lined the arched ceiling, casting an incongruously bright light on the dingy hallway. The place gave Alice a sense of deja vu as images from her dream echoed in the back of her mind. It was more than eerily similar.

It seemed to be just as deserted as the level above, with no sign of the Men in Black – or anyone else, for that matter – in sight, which came as a welcome relief. On either side of the corridor there was a small alcove, each with a doorway, and further along two more hallways ran off to the left and right. At the far end there was a set of double doors, and James suspected that this was where they needed to be heading.

They held position for a moment, staring out and into the corridor, watching for any signs of activity. When James felt confident that they were not about to be ambushed, he tapped Alice on the arm and led the way out of the elevator. They hurried forwards in silence, eyes and ears open for any hint of danger, and even their lightest of footsteps put them on edge, fearing they would be discovered at any moment. Alice was starting to feel as if she was in a nightmare she couldn't wake up from, sneaking through this place so far underground, with its eerily decrepit hallways. It was a far cry from the glass, metal and concrete of the modern building above. The fear of being discovered was all the more palpable now, and she was certain that even the slightest mistake would not only cost them the opportunity to find Sam, but ensure that they would never see the light of day again. The thought did not instil her with confidence.

The doors at the end of the corridor began to open, and without a moment's hesitation James ducked into one of the alcoves, dragging Alice with him. She almost yelped in surprise as she felt herself being pulled off-balance, but caught herself before she could make a noise. James pushed her tightly against the inside of the wall, and he flattened himself against it too, holding a finger to his lips.

Footsteps. At first it sounded like one person walking, but as James listened closely to the echoing footfall he could hear it was two people walking in almost perfect unison. The footsteps were coming closer. And closer. James's lungs felt tight in his chest. He didn't risk glancing around the corner to see how close they were, but they sounded much too close for his comfort. Glancing at the door to the side of them, James carefully pulled it open just enough to slide in and ushered Alice inside. He closed it just as carefully, slowly easing the handle upwards, and he was relieved when the latch didn't click as it slid into place.

The room they now found themselves in was large, dimly lit by a couple of flickering light-bulbs, and packed full with boxes and crates. Narrow pathways wound through the piles of boxes like a maze, and James and Alice snaked their way through, deeper into the storage room. Peering out from among the boxes and the shadowy recesses were ancient statues of unearthly looking beings, made all the more sinister in the low light of the room. Some bore screaming demonic faces, others more composed and regal but far from human in appearance, and some resembling rejected concepts for Egyptian gods. Alice tried not to look at them. It wasn't just that they looked as if they would be at home in the British Museum's Exhibit of Creepiest Deities, but she had the very distinct impression that they were staring at her.

'Come on,' James whispered, 'I think I can see a door behind the hippalectryon.' It was a sentence he had never even considered he might say, but he wasn't wrong. Around the corner, on which stood the statue of a creature which bore the front half of a horse and the hind of a rooster, there was another door. They made their way towards the door – Alice eyeing the rooster-horse suspiciously as they crept past it – and, cautiously, James pushed it open and slid out into the corridor.

They were now just around the corner from the double doors. It was still and quiet in the corridor again, the sound of footsteps no longer echoing off of the walls, and after a moment of listening out for any noise James began to lead the way. He stuck close to the wall, almost skimming along it until he reached the corner. Pinning himself against the wall, James could almost see back down the corridor they had entered from. The lift's doors were closed, and he assumed that whoever had been coming down that corridor had taken it back up to the surface. He tilted his head to the side and cautiously tried to look around the corner.

The double doors were open, leading into a large ovular chamber. It was brightly lit and looked like it had fared better over the years than the rest of the facility; the white walls seemed almost new, and the floor appeared to be a large metal walkway. It opened up in the very middle of the room, presumably overlooking the chamber's lower level. Computer banks, terminals and desks ran around the edge of the central opening, and on the far wall there was a large display which appeared to show a map of London. Numerous lights and blips flashed across the map. Silhouetted against the display stood two figures with the poise and stillness of suit department mannequins. They didn't appear to be facing towards the corridor, their attentions focussed on the display, and James saw the opportunity. He scurried around the corner and into the chamber, crouching behind the first group of desks.

Without thinking, Alice followed suit and almost froze when she noticed the two figures on the opposite side of the room. She quickly ducked down and joined James behind the desk, where he greeted her with a finger held against his pursed lips. Slowly, he glanced over the top of the desk. They were still there, facing the display and with their backs turned to them, seemingly unaware of the two intruders.

James quickly skirted around the end of the desk, keeping low while he advanced along the row of terminals before taking cover behind the next work station. He was now halfway across the chamber, and he couldn't have been more than ten yards away from the two agents. They remained stock still, monitoring their display. If he stood any chance of finding where Sam was being held, he would need to access one of the computers, and he knew he couldn't risk that when the Men in Black were present. He glanced back around towards Alice, and signalled for her to stay where she was. She nodded in fearful agreement. She felt glued to the spot anyway, and hiding beneath a desk seemed like the safest place to be.

James took another quick glance over towards the agents, and felt his hand graze the grip of the gun. Carefully, he withdrew it from his belt. If push came to shove, he would be ready.

For the first time since picking it up, James inspected the weapon. It was quite unlike any handgun he had seen before. The body of the gun was sleek and curved, and made of brushed steel or chrome, giving it an almost science fiction inspired finish. Above the grip was a switch and two light emitting diodes, and there was no sign of a traditional firearm's hammer. Where one would normally expect the gun's barrel to be was instead a long transparent cylinder, revealing the unusual firing mechanism inside. Five copper rods ran along the length of the inside of the cylinder, culminating at the muzzle. A large quartzite stone was held in place between these rods, which stretched the length of the cylindrical chamber, from the crystal's base – secured within the body of the gun, just above the trigger – to the point, which incorporated itself into the muzzle. James eyed the gun curiously. It almost looked like a weaponised version of Sam's energy probe wand. He flicked what he presumed was the safety switch.

The gun made a short, high-pitched whining noise before settling into a consistent gentle hum. One of the little diodes lit up green.

This was shortly followed by a very similar noise, and the measured voice of a man saying 'don't move.'

James looked up to the see the tall figure of one of the agents standing over him, and the same otherworldly gun pointing at his head. He knew the agent would pull the trigger before he even had a chance to raise his weapon in response, and as much as he was intrigued by how this device worked, he thought it best if he was not on the receiving end.

'Looks like we have an intruder,' the agent said flatly. 'How did you get in?'

'How'd ya think he got in? In-tru-da window?' an unexpectedly chipper cockney voice called out from the direction of the corridor. There was the loud crackling buzz of electricity, and suddenly a bolt of white-purple energy shot across James's vision, striking the agent squarely in the chest. He promptly vanished in a plume of smoke, which seemed to surprise the agent in his final fleeting moments of corporeality almost as much as it had surprised James.

The beam continued to crackle and buzz as the stream of energy arced above James's head. Sparks flew and the nearby computer terminals popped and sizzled, and James took shelter beneath one of the desks. He looked around urgently, trying to see if he could spot Alice. Through another hail of sparks he could see her, also huddled beneath a desk and hugging her knees. There was a shout from the remaining agent, and a reciprocating beam of energy briefly fired back before both streams of lightning ceased. The lights of the chamber flickered uncertainly in the ensuing calm. Everything fell silent.

'Looks like I got 'ere just in time, hey?' The voice broke the silence, and the grinning face of Cypher appeared as he knelt down by the desk. He was met with the terrified, wide-eyed face of Alice. Her lips trembled involuntarily as she managed a small and nervous nod. 'It's alright, love, I vapourised 'em both!' Cypher said, waving the strange gun cheerily, and although he meant it in a reassuring way, it was anything but.

Alice was uneasy on her feet as she unfurled from beneath the desk. Cypher had held out his hand to help her up, but it wasn't until she was standing that she realised how much she had actually needed the support. Her whole body was shaking as fear and adrenaline coursed through every fibre of her being, her knees were weak, and she felt as if her legs had turned to jelly. Lurching forwards, Alice steadied herself and clutched one of the desks for balance, squeezing her eyes tightly shut. The mayhem had finished almost as quickly as it had started, but it was going to take longer than that for her nerves to calm down. She struggled to catch her breath as another wave of panic washed over her, and she tried to focus on taking regular, deep breaths, and not how close to death she had just been.

A couple of yards away, James was staggering to his feet too. He seemed more dazed and confused than anything else, and he welcomed the sight of Cypher with a lacklustre wave. He quickly looked around the room, swaying as he turned his head one way and the other. There was no trace of the Men in Black whatsoever. No bodies, no suddenly empty suits, not even a pile of ash. Nothing. It was as if they simply ceased to be.

'Ah, see you nabbed yourself one of these beauts too, hey Jimmy-boy,' Cypher said, casually waving his gun about as if it were a flag. James flinched every time the muzzle was vaguely pointed in his direction. 'Got mine from the bastard who chased me. Lovely bit of kit.'

'You... You vapourised them?' Alice uttered.

'It's alright, they ain't real. Not like you or I. They're thoughtforms them Regents willed into bein' to do their dirty work. They ain't people, strictly speaking; they exist only to serve their purpose, like worker bees and investment bankers. Give 'em a zap and *poof*, the idea is gone.'

'You can't kill an idea, though,' James said.

'Ah, you're a canny one,' Cypher replied, waving finger-guns in James's direction, 'you're quite right. Can't kill an idea; ideas exist in a realm beyond the physical. But you can disrupt 'em. You can knock one of them Men in Black bastards out with enough force, and with a blast from one o' these tezzers of theirs you can vapourise their manifestation. The core idea of the Men in Black ain't gone, mind you, they'll rematerialise eventually, but you can hinder 'em and blast 'em out of this plane of existence for a little while.'

James nodded dumbly. He hadn't quite believed Cypher at the café when he had said that they weren't real, at least not to the full extent. It sounded too absurd to believe that the Men in Black were ideas given form, but seeing the agent evaporate in front of his eyes was as close as he was likely to get to solid evidence. Although "solid" probably wasn't the most accurate adjective, given the context. Even so, with that knowledge, it was still no less unsettling to witness the agent vapourising, and going by the pale look on Alice's face that explanation didn't do much in the way of putting her at ease either.

'So, if we got caught in the...?' Alice waved her hands around as she tried to find the words. Her mind was more than muddled from the panic, and she was struggling to get her thoughts straight. Even though they were now safe from the brief crossfire, having to cower beneath a desk while men fired lightning bolts from pistols at each other was not an experience that was going to be leaving her any time soon. 'Would we be, y'know, gone?'

Cypher shook his head emphatically. 'Oh no, not gone. You'd be unconscious for a bit and have a wicked bad headache and muscle-ache when you came to, maybe some nasty burns where you was hit, but not gone. It's a stun gun more than anythin', but got just enough ampage to disrupt thoughtforms. Although,' he added, and tweaked one of the switches on the gun, 'up the output and ya can kill an elephant stone dead.'

While Cypher was busy explaining the functionality of the gun to a very on-edge Alice, James took the opportunity to access one of the computer terminals. He tapped rapidly at the keyboard as he sifted through the directory, searching for anything relevant. Several folders and documents were password encoded, but he did get access to a file which seemed to display a map of the facility. The first thing which struck James was how similar in shape the floorplan was to the Ankh, an ancient Egyptian symbol of life. Considering the Regents identified themselves with another ancient Egyptian symbol, he didn't think it was all that surprising. The second thing which struck him was that, marked on the lower level immediately beneath them, was a label which simply read "containment".

James looked up from the computer screen and turned to face the other two. Cypher was waving the "tezzer" gun around while explaining in great detail the welt he had on his back after he was zapped by the Men in Black one time. Standing opposite him, a very pale Alice stood with her arms crossed and had the expression of someone who has just realised they're about to be hit in the face by a cricket ball. 'Are we right above the cells?' James asked, interrupting Cypher's story much to Alice's relief.

'Yessir, we gotta head down there.' Cypher pointed to the large opening in the middle of the floor of the chamber. Railings ran around the perimeter of the opening, and at the far end of the room a flight of steps led down to the level below. From where they were, the three were able to peer over the railings to the lower level. There were fewer terminals and desks below, only a couple of pieces of machinery and relays which connected to the computers on the upper level. A tangle of cables wound their way around the room and towards the centre where, at the very heart of the chamber, stood an unearthly shape.

A small dais was raised up from the floor, and from it four narrow, curving prongs stuck out, arching upwards and inwards. The very points of the prongs culminated in the middle some ten feet above the ground, making the structure's overall shape almost resemble the outline of an egg. At a glance it seemed to be carved from a black stone, but where the smooth surface reflected the light of the room it appeared to shimmer and gleam with hints of deep purples and turquoise greens. It was like looking at the surface of the water in a clear and deep ocean. There was something ethereally beautiful about it, yet also something forbidding and disquieting. At the base of the prongs, the extraordinary met the ordinary, and great metal clamps were secured around the otherworldly monument, with wire and cables snaking around it.

It was an unusual thing to behold, its eerie and alien form jutting out from amongst desks, computers and cables, almost like something poking its way through from another universe.

'This is what they're here for,' Cypher announced as if he were a tour guide, 'this gert thing. Sounds like an amazin' idea on paper; shame it snaps fragile human minds in 'alf like twigs.'

'Something about it seems familiar, somehow,' Alice said as they drew closer to it. She could make out the shapes of strange symbols carved into its base and along the prongs, a string of angular sigils which looked like nothing on Earth. In the centre of the monument's base, a spiral-like pattern wound around itself. 'What is it?'

'No-one really knows,' he replied, 'but they're doin' their damnedest to learn its true purpose. So far, it works by rippin' an 'ole in the fabric of reality as a kind of interstitial cross-dimensional gateway.' He walked up to the monument and slammed his hand against one of the prongs. The structure stood firm, barely even acknowledging the force of Cypher's hit, but beneath the black stone surface a cloud of purples and greens rippled like droplets in a pool of water.

Ripping a hole in the fabric of reality... Alice mused as she stared, transfixed by the rippling colours. There was something unsettling about the otherworldly structure, but also something terrifyingly alluring. It was then, as she looked into the depths of the rippling beneath the solid stone, that she realised why it seemed familiar. She glimpsed the gaping nothingness that she and Sam had found once before, the wound in reality which had been torn open by a Void crystal. The engravings on the monument here were more than reminiscent of the symbols carved into the crystal. 'This is a Void portal,' Alice said aloud as the revelation dawned on her.

'The lady knows 'er stuff, hey,' Cypher replied with a wink, 'you're spot on, love. This is Project Voidwalker. Bane of my fugged up life.'

'They use this thing to open a gateway, and then... They send you through it? How does it work?' James asked, intrigued.

'Nah, they don't open no gate, nothin' so neat 'n' tidy. They zap it full of power and punch a bloody great hole through dimensions, like jabbin' scissors through cardboard.' Cypher looked at the gateway of Project Voidwalker with disdain. Its smooth black surface seemed to stare back at him coldly. He shook his head as if an insect were bothering him, and he turned to start making his way towards a door at the far end of the chamber. 'Detainment cells are right through 'ere.'

Cypher led them away from the gateway and into the cells. The corridor was dark and dank, its plain concrete walls occasionally broken up by the doors to cells. Most of them were open, and as the trio walked past each room they looked in out of curiosity. Each cell was incredibly small, and aside from the thin mattresses laid out on the floors, the cells were entirely empty. Anyone detained in them would have nothing but the four concrete walls. That would have been their world.

'Bloody hate this place,' Cypher spat. He skulked ahead of James and Alice, leering into each room they passed. One door refused to open as Cypher tried it, and after a few inquiring pushes he decided to slide the viewing grate open and peek in. No sooner had he put his face to the now-open grate, Cypher jumped back and slid the cover shut again. A moment later, there was a very loud metallic thud from the other side of the door. 'Don't think ya friend's in that one,' he announced, wide-eyed.

Tentatively, James and Alice approached the door and slid the viewing grate open again. The grate didn't allow them much of a look into the room, and in the dim light they could barely see anything. Then, at the back of the cell, Alice spotted the shape of a person. The person was huddled up in the corner, but when they sensed they were being watched they looked up. It was at that moment that Alice instinctively clutched hold of James's sleeve and let out a slight whimpering noise as she tried to suppress a scream.

The person looking back at them was not quite a person. Outwardly, it appeared as human as anyone else, but it stared back at them from the dark with vibrant yellow eyes. The pupils were thin black slits, and when the thing blinked, it blinked sideways. The almost human-looking face started to contort into an unnatural smile, until the creature's grin literally stretched from ear to ear, revealing rows of razor-sharp teeth. It snapped and hissed at them, and James quickly pulled the grate shut again.

The door banged several more times as the thing threw itself at the inside of its prison.

'What the hell was that?' Alice asked, her voice wavering. She was suddenly feeling quite sick and light-headed again.

'Voidwalker,' Cypher said dispassionately. 'Sendin' folk through that portal, there's no tellin' what's gonna happen. Some go mad, have their minds snapped in two, but sometimes people come back... Changed. That,' he said, pointing towards the metal door, which now emitted a low snarling sound, 'that ain't human. It may look it, but somethin' else has piggybacked its way 'ere.'

The other occupied cells hardly seemed any better off. Of all the doors in the corridor, which looped around the operations chamber, only five of them had anything in the cells behind them. As they checked each door, sliding the grates open to look inside, they were greeted by a series of snarls, hisses and woops. Alice had to keep reminding herself that the nightmare would be over as soon as they found Sam. Seeing, even hearing, these things which were not quite human was making her skin crawl, and she was relatively sure her heart was now going into overdrive. Upon the fifth door they looked into, they were greeted with a surprisingly courteous 'oh, hello!'

'Sam!' Alice exclaimed, and a sudden rush of relief washed over her. Cypher began to fiddle with the locks and bolts, the clanking metal echoing throughout the corridor as he unlocked the door. Eventually, with the final bolt removed, the door swung open.

'Alice! Thank God you're here. I've been clicking my heels together, saying "there's no place like home" for ages!'

Alice could tell he was just putting on a jovial front, and in his eyes she could see the glistening of tears welling up. He lunged forward, flinging his arms wide and taking her in a tight embrace. It was a hug of sudden, inexorable relief. She couldn't begin to imagine the desperation he must have felt being trapped in that cell, but the rush of relief was not lost on her, and she returned the hug with an equally tight grip.

'And you brought my hat too!' he exclaimed when he eventually released her from his arms. Alice had almost forgotten she had been carrying Sam's hat with her; she had been holding onto it for so long now it hadn't really occurred to her. She handed it over to him, and he perched it on his head. He finally was starting to feel more like himself. All that was missing was the coat, and he would feel whole again.

Stepping forward, Sam took James's hand in a firm shake, before pulling him in for a hug too. 'Honestly, you have no bloody idea how happy I am to see you both. It is

terrifyingly boring in that cell. There's nothing to do. Not even one of the Men in Black spooks for company.' He turned and saw Cypher standing by the door. 'And you...' Sam scrunched his face and sucked the air through his teeth as he racked his brains trying to recognise the bald man in the military jacket. The silence in the middle of his sentence was beginning to stretch on for too long, and Sam concluded it was more than likely that he didn't know who this man was. 'And you... Person. Thank you for whatever it is you did.'

'This is Cypher. He provided the intel, helped us get inside, even saved our skin not that long ago,' James said in way of introducing their accomplice. Cypher took an elaborate and exaggerated bow.

'At ya service, sir!' He extended his hand and shook Sam's enthusiastically. 'I spent more time in this place than I'd care to tell ya, so helpin' another soul outta here seemed like the least I could do.'

'Then I'm incredibly grateful for your help too, Cypher,' Sam said, and he tipped his hat to him. He turned to face all three of them, and he was almost overwhelmed by the feelings of relief and joy such a simple sight could bring. 'I feared they might have got to you as well. Inside those four walls, after a while it's impossible to imagine you'll ever see the light of day again, let alone the people close to you. I-'

'There they are! Get them!' A shout from down the corridor cut Sam's sentence short. Two Men in Black had appeared through one of the doorways and reached for their weapons. They fired.

'I'll finish my sentence later,' Sam said as a bolt of purplish energy zipped past them, scorching the wall behind his head. 'Run!'

They ran. Cypher and James drew their guns too, and fired over their shoulders at their pursuers. The beams hit far from their mark and sparked harmlessly off of the concrete walls. At the very least it slowed down the agents' pursuit. The Men in Black fired back, taking potshots at the escapees as they fled. Beams crossed, and the colliding energy flared in sizzling balls of light at the heart of the crossfire.

'Why do you have ray guns?!' Sam shouted. Energy bolts flew chaotically around them. Beams buzzed and crackled with electric ferocity. Sparks erupted from the walls.

Agent Smith took extra care in lining up his next shot. With any luck, he thought, he would stun Sam Hain and put a burning hole through that stupid hat of his. *Might even kill him*. He aimed, and pulled the trigger. White-purple energy arced from the gun's muzzle, cutting its way through the air with a crackling buzz. With mere moments to spare, the four escaped through the door into the main chamber, slamming it shut behind them. A shower of sparks burst as the beam hit the metal door, leaving a burn mark at exactly head-height. Smith cursed under his breath and continued the chase.

On the other side of the door, Cypher tipped over a server bank as a temporary barricade, heaving it against the chamber's door. It would not hold the agents back for long, but they needed all the time they could get. Sam had momentarily slowed to take a look at the Voidwalker gateway in the middle of the chamber. He gawped perplexedly at the unearthly structure. 'Is that an interstitial cross-dimensional Void gateway?'

'Funny time to ask questions,' Cypher retorted, and he fired a stream of vibrant energy into the core of the gateway. Electricity began to surge up the prongs, winding around them like ethereal serpents. It started to hum ominously. Connected cables and machinery sparked violently, and a couple of the computers on the lower level blew out, smoke rising from the terminals.

The four of them reached the top of the stairs and looked back down towards the entrance of the cells. The doors shook and rattled as the agents tried to force their way through, but the server bank was proving to be quite stubborn. It had moved less than an inch, although it was slowly scraping bit by bit across the floor with each subsequent ramming of the doors. The computers and machinery below were the very image of devastation, and at the heart of it all the gateway seemed to be glowing.

Wasting no time, Cypher ran over to one of the computers on the upper level and began typing frantically. A window which appeared to display technical readouts popped up on the screen, and several of its meters had escalated from green, straight through amber, and threatening to break into the red at an alarming rate.

'What're ya waitin' for, for Chrissakes? Get movin'!' he shouted, as Alice, Sam and James hovered, hesitating by the way out, waiting for him to follow.

'What are you doing?' Sam demanded. 'In a couple of minutes they're going to get through that bloody door. We need to leave. Now.'

'In two minutes, that ain't gonna matter, friend. I got some unfinished business with these chaps.'

'What's going to happen in two minutes?' James asked, and he ran back towards Cypher.

Alice looked nervously down at the doors as the agents on the other side were continuing to ram their way through. A gap was starting to appear in the doorway. They would be through in no time. She clutched on to Sam's arm.

'You won't be 'ere to find out, that's what!' Cypher exclaimed, and he tried to shoo James away. 'By the by, mister Hain, I wiped that there arrest warrant thing off their server. The Fuzz shouldn't be troublin' you,' he nodded his head back towards the ever-opening door, 'can't say as much 'bout them bastards.'

'Thank you, Cypher,' Sam said. 'Really, thank you.'

'Been a pleasure, sir, now get the buggery outta here. You ain't got long.'

Alice nodded and gave her thanks as well, and she started to lead Sam away by the arm, pulling him along and towards the lift back to the surface. They hadn't made it this far, having gone through everything they'd had to endure, only for it all to go terribly wrong again. She was going to make sure of that.

'Sorry 'bout ya hand, again,' Cypher said, turning to James, 'jus' don't want ya thinkin' I's the kinda man who goes about stabbin' people in the 'and all the time.' He flashed him a quick smile.

'Cypher, what happens in two minutes?' James insisted. Ribbons of energy coursed along the structure of the Voidwalker gateway and, unless he was mistaken, James was sure it was building up to something.

'I turned off their poncey safety measures, rigged that thing to overload. The fugger's gonna blow any minute now, takin' this God-forsaken shit 'ole with it.'

The door eventually burst open, and immediately agents Smith and Jones began firing up at James and Cypher. They both ducked down, narrowly avoiding the energy beam as it streamed over them, and Cypher fired a quick warning shot in the general direction of their adversaries. More crackling of electricity filled the air, and an alarm started to sound as the gateway's readings fluctuated wildly in the red. There was a loud boom, and a quick look down to the level below revealed that the gateway was active. A swirling vortex had formed between the prongs, and bolts of lightning lashed out from its centre and around the room.

'You're bloody mad-'

'I know that,' Cypher interrupted.

'We're not leaving you here.'

'Don't you be worryin' 'bout me, Jimmy-boy. This ain't

me first cross-dimensional rip, after all. I'll keep 'em busy while you 'n' your friends get out, alright? Never know, me and them monstrosities in those cells might find some peace when this place goes kablooey.' Cypher glanced around the corner and saw the agents trying to make their way up the stairs, and fired another warning shot in their direction. 'Looks like I can finally get me revenge on the bastards. Now go on, off ya pop, you ain't got long now with all this chin-waggin'.'

James hovered in a stunned silence, while the crackling and booming cacophony of the Void gateway's overload started to take its toll on the chamber. The walls were cracking and the ceiling was threatening to collapse, all the while the swirling maw of the Void grew larger, unleashing a raging storm from its heart. Another bolt of energy from the Men in Black's guns surged past James's head, and Cypher pushed him towards the exit.

'Thank you for everything you've done,' James said with a pained smile, 'you mad bastard.'

'I'll see you on the other side, my friend,' Cypher said.

That was the last James saw of him. He sprinted for the elevator at the end of the corridor, and without explaining to either Sam or Alice he shoved them into the lift and slammed the button. Before the doors could close, they heard one last shout coming from the chamber: 'Come on, ya wankers! Bet Voidwalkin' don't seem like such a bright idea now, does it?'

The elevator doors closed, and they felt it start moving up back towards the surface. A few moments later, a muffled but deafeningly loud boom ripped through the air, shaking the lift and almost knocking its occupants off their feet. Then all was silent. James sunk despondently into the corner and stared at the floor.

Kneeling by the side of him, Alice gently held his hand, and for the first time that evening she allowed herself the emotional breakdown she had been holding back. Tears started to roll down her face as the fear, the relief, and the panic overwhelmed her all at once. Sam instinctively crouched beside her, putting his arm around her and cradling her head to his chest. The ride back to ground level was the longest any of them had experienced.

The cold night air was crisp and fresh on their faces when they eventually emerged from the Hub. On the surface, Regent's Park looked entirely unchanged. There was no sign that the explosion below had had any effect on the outside world. Up here, everything seemed so still and quiet. Sam stared up at the twinkling stars and took a deep lungful of the fresh air. It felt good to be back in the real world again. He almost said as such, but thought better of it given the circumstances.

'He was a good man,' James said, 'completely unhinged, but a good man.'

'Mad as a box of frogs,' Sam agreed solemnly. 'Cypher sacrificed everything so we could get out alive, and he managed to take that place down with him. The mark of a true, good – if a tad crazy – man. He gave his life to save mine. You all risked everything to break me out. I won't forget that. And I'm sure the Regents won't forget what happened here in a hurry, either.'

'He didn't need to die. There was still time. I should've... I should've dragged the obstinate git out with me!' James kicked a wall out of frustration, but it didn't give him the release he was hoping it would. 'I barely even knew him, but it was my fault. I brought him into this, and it got him killed. Too many people suffer because of cock ups like that. It's not right, damn it!' He kicked the wall again, still with no effect other than hurting his foot.

'We couldn't have done it without him,' Alice said sombrely, and she placed her hand on James's arm, 'he helped us more than we could've expected. He didn't need to; he wanted to. You can't beat yourself up over that, there was nothing more you could've done.'

Silence hung heavily in the air. James stared vacantly at the grass. His skin was pale and his eyes black, a curious mix of remorse and anger written across his face. 'I still could've pulled him out with me.'

'I mean no disrespect to the guy, but he wasn't all there, was he?' Alice remarked. 'It was what he wanted. Maybe... Maybe he found his peace. And he helped rescue Sam, and destroyed that horrible place at the same time. That's pretty good if you ask me.'

James nodded sagely. Alice was right; Cypher had given his all and did what he felt to be right. 'Yeah, I suppose,' he said, 'I can't help but feel like I dragged him into this, but he was more than ready to lend a hand. And after everything those bastards did to him... He got his revenge though, taking them down with him. Hopefully he found some solace in his final act.'

'Still, it doesn't feel like this is over,' Sam mused, staring at the star-studded sky. 'Smith said something about them being more in control of things... This isn't the last we've heard of the Regents, I'm sure of it.' An involuntary shiver shook Sam's body, and it occurred to him that he was still missing his coat. 'Anyway, let's get going, shall we? It's bloody freezing out here.'

The walk back to the car was a quiet and sombre one. The three of them walked in silence, their minds caught somewhere in between the nightmare they had just been through and the relief that the ordeal was finally over with. At least getting back to the car was easier now that they weren't having to sneak through the undergrowth surrounding Regent's Park, and they could walk along the paths and pavements with ease.

When they had got back to the car, Sam had taken his coat from the back seat and draped it over Alice like a blanket for the drive back to Islington. She had started shivering uncontrollably – whether it was the cold or she was in shock, he couldn't tell – and he figured he could cope without it for a while longer. The weight of the coat had surprised Alice, it was a lot bigger and more unwieldy than it looked, but it was warm and comforting. She sat curled up in the back seat of the car, and watched the glow of the streets rush on by.

These roads, so frequently bustling with traffic, were strangely empty and serene at this time of night. In some ways it was good to get back to the normal world, but she knew it would take a while for her to shake the disquiet and uneasiness from that night. For the time being, though, it was over. Sam Hain was safe and, in spite of everything, she and James were okay too. She was thankful for that.

With a slight jolt and the clunking of gears, they pulled up outside of Alice's home. James twisted in the driver's seat, craning his neck around the headrest. 'Thank you for everything, Alice,' he said, straining to face her properly, 'and I'm sorry for everything I've put you through. We soldiered on through, though, hey. You're a star.' He smiled a half-hearted smile, and although he meant it, it was difficult to hide the shadow of remorse. 'You've found a good one, Sam,' he added, turning to his friend who was busy watching a spider which had made its home in the wing-mirror, 'hopefully she'll help keep you out of trouble.'

Alice smiled sweetly back at him, uttering a thank-you and wished him a goodnight, and she unfurled herself from the coat. Shakily, she stepped out of the car and began to make her way around to the front door. She was searching for her keys in the dim light of the street, cursing that nothing could ever be easy when all she wanted to do was get inside and crawl into the safety of her bed, when she heard the sound of feet bounding up behind her.

Turning, she saw Sam Hain standing in the orange glow of the streetlight, looking much more like his usual self. His hat perched on top of his long, curling hair, slanting slightly over his face, and his greatcoat billowed around his ankles in the light breeze.

'There aren't any words for me to tell you how grateful I am,' Sam said, 'so a simple "thank-you" will have to do.' Expressing genuine gratitude was evidently not something which came easily to Sam Hain, but there was a sincerity behind his eyes and a kindness in his voice which told Alice more than any string of words could. A simple "thank-you" was all he needed to say.

'Just don't go getting yourself kidnapped, you twit!' She playfully slapped him on the chest, and Sam's mood seemed to brighten a bit.

'Easier said than done, apparently,' he replied with a wry smile.

'Would you-?' they both began to say in unison, but cut each other off mid-sentence. After a brief moment of almost painful politeness, insisting to one another that the other should finish their sentence first, Sam eventually relented.

'I, uh, was going to ask... Would you mind if I stay here? Just for a little while. It's just that with Men in Black abducting me from my place in the middle of the night, it's probably not wise if I go straight back home. I'm in no rush to repeat this whole ordeal again any time soon, and it'll be safer if I lay low for a bit. I can just crash on your sofa. If you don't mind, of course? I'll be no trouble at all!'

This last part was not entirely true. Although it could not be said that Sam Hain himself was trouble – he certainly tried his best not to be – it was more the fact that trouble always seemed to inexorably follow him wherever he went.

'Of course,' Alice said. She felt relieved by his request. 'Actually, I was going to ask you if you wanted to stay here too. I thought you might not feel safe being back there yet, after what happened... And, to be honest, after tonight, I don't think anywhere feels safe.' She looked at Sam sheepishly. She had never been very good at admitting when she felt vulnerable, but tonight was an exception, and all Alice wanted was a sense of security.

He nodded understandingly. 'Yeah, me neither.'

While Alice continued to rummage for her keys, eventually producing them triumphantly and unlocking the door to the building, Sam was saying his goodbyes to James. 'Honestly, I can't thank you enough. What you lot put yourselves through to get me out was nothing short of incredible. And... I'm sorry, about Cypher. If I hadn't been in that stupid mess, none of this would've happened.'

'Hey, when a shadowy secret society is out to get you, there's only so much you can blame yourself for,' James said, managing a smile, 'besides, I'm the one who got Cypher involved. His sacrifice wasn't in vain, though. I'm going to have to keep telling myself that one, too.'

Bidding a final goodbye, James slowly pulled away from the front of the Islington townhouse. Filled with gratitude, Sam watched the car drive off down the road and around the corner, disappearing into the night. He turned and walked back towards the house, where Alice was stood waiting for him in the open doorway.

'Mind if I put the kettle on?' Sam asked as he stepped over the threshold and started to follow Alice up the stairs to her flat. 'It's been over twenty-four hours since I last had a cup of tea. The Regents have no idea how to treat their guests.'

Epilogue

Rachel woke up the following morning to the incessant and irritating beeping of her alarm. She dozily tapped her phone and dropped it onto the pillow next to her, wrapping her duvet around herself and curling up into a ball. Five minutes later, her phone started beeping again, and with a moan of frustration she rolled out of bed. She sleepily swayed as she made her way out of her bedroom, and caught sight of herself in the mirror, her half-awake face gazing back at her and framed by a mess of long brunette hair. Mornings were not for her.

The crisp light of dawn was creeping in through the living room window, casting dust-mote filled beams into the room, but she barely even noticed how nice the morning was as she trudged into the kitchen. She filled the kettle with water and flicked the switch down. Rachel habitually adjusted the waistband of her thong and lazily scratched her buttocks. With a loud and luxuriating yawn, she raised her arms high above her head and stretched herself out as much as she could, causing her t-shirt to ride up above her navel. She concluded she couldn't really be bothered with making a proper breakfast this morning, and instead pulled a packet of pain au chocolat out of the cupboard.

The kettle began to hiss and occasionally made a banging sound, as if to reassure her that it was putting some real effort into boiling. Operating on autopilot, she tipped a spoonful of coffee granules into a mug and poured the boiling water in immediately after. She shoved one of the sweet rolls into her mouth, flakes of pastry scattering down the front of her t-shirt, and with coffee in hand she started back towards the living room.

She picked up the remote and flicked the TV on. A news report was detailing what was suspected to have been a gas explosion in the area of Regent's Park, which had disturbed a number of local residents in the small hours of the morning. The situation, the news reporter assured viewers, was under control and had not caused any harm or property damage.

It was only then that something startled her into wakefulness.

A low, guttural noise, somewhere between a moan and a growl, rumbled from somewhere in the room. Rachel froze, and she was sure her heart had skipped a beat. She was suddenly on edge, her heart pounding heavily in her chest, and she cast a wary but still sleep-blurred eye around the room. She turned around. There, on the sofa, was a shapeless black mass, heaving and shifting unnaturally. The form jolted suddenly with another groan, and a very human foot emerged from one end of it. She began to back away from it slowly, and as Rachel's eyes began to focus on the shapeless form she started to make sense of it. It wasn't shapeless at all; it was a man, his feet hanging off of one end of the sofa and his head – a mass of unruly dark hair – hanging off of the other. A large black greatcoat was draped over him like a blanket, and a fedora hat lay forlornly on the floor by the side of him.

Rachel very quickly abandoned her coffee and breakfast. Pulling her t-shirt down as far as possible, barely covering her thong and buttocks, she scuttered out of the living room as fast as she could and into Alice's room. She shook her friend gently, and then a little more forcefully, awake.

Alice, who was no more dressed and far less awake than her flatmate, stared up at her with bleary eyes. 'Wuh?' she managed to utter, her voice quiet and croaky.

'Why is there a strange man on the sofa?' Rachel asked, almost accusingly.

'Huh? Oh, he's... He's not that strange when you get to know him, really.' Alice rolled over and snuggled back into her pillow, asleep.

Sam Hain
Occult Detective

The Eye of the Oracle

PROLOGUE

Wednesdays, Tim Carmichael had decided, simply were not his days. This one, in particular, had been especially peculiar.

There was invariably a stressful atmosphere in Parliament on Wednesday mornings. Staff rushed about the place like a swarm of confused insects, making preparations for Prime Minister's Questions; politicians were ushered hither and thither, while servers with trays of tea and biscuits dutifully followed them; journalists gathered on the green outside the House, and running news crews set up their equipment. This had happened almost every week for over fifty years, and yet somehow no-one had quite managed to figure out how to make it all run smoothly.

Tim – or rather, Timothy Frederick Carmichael the Second of Worcestershire – had been seated on the backbench of the Opposition for that week's parliamentary debate. He both loved and loathed it. On the one hand, it gave voice to the Members of Parliament to raise their questions directly to the Prime Minister, and for the Opposition to challenge the Government's stance on certain current affairs. A vital aspect of democracy, Tim thought. On the other hand, the debate would often play out like an argument between two sides of a pantomime audience. Questions and statements would often be deflected with a chorus of jeers and jibes, shortly followed by uproarious laughter and cacophonous shouts from either side. Some MPs had even stopped attending amidst noise complaints, and others had tried to call for a more measured and less theatrical debate.

It did not work.

Tim would sometimes find himself cringing with

embarrassment when the debate would descend into what he could only describe as an unruly primary school class. It could be entertaining to witness, like bloodless gladiatorial combat, and he was sure that was why the sessions were broadcast on the BBC, but he often wondered what the public must think of the people who run their country when they roar with laughter or bellow the rafters down. Especially when debating important subjects, like national health care, or the economy and spending of the national budget. But it wasn't his place to question that. Instead, he would be resigned to the backbench until he was called to speak.

This particular Wednesday had proven to be even worse than usual. Debates and questions of the Government's stance on certain international policies, foreign affairs and the ever-increasing amount of budget cuts to vital sectors had very quickly devolved into personal jibes at the opposing party leaders, met with a chorus of 'ooooh's and over-the-top cackles. No progress was made, and no clear answers were provided to any of the serious and pressing questions. Anyone could be forgiven for thinking that they had accidentally stumbled into a political satire show rather than a parliamentary debate. Even Tim's own query ("how can the Government substantiate an increase in taxes, housing costs and tuition fees, while rejecting the proposition to raise the national standard minimum wage?") had been met with laughter, applause, and a remark about why the Right Honourable Gentleman should concern himself with taxes now, when he had never seemed to worry about paying his own in the past.

Dejected and despondent after the day's debates, Tim had decided to take a walk along the Southbank to clear his head. He looked out over the Thames as he walked, carefully weaving his way through the crowds of tourists who gathered there for some of London's most famous sights. Street performers flanked the constant flow of the crowd, who would stop to watch them perform, often getting distracted by the performances and standing to watch right in front of Tim's path. He was somewhat used to weaving and dodging and occasionally bumping into crowds, but today of all days he did not have the patience for it. It was not until he caught sight of his father – Timothy Carmichael Senior – in amongst the throngs of people, stood watching someone dressed as Charlie Chaplin in the shadow of the London Eye, that he started to feel the pressures of the day begin to lift.

He and his father stopped for a coffee at one of the cafés along the Southbank, and Tim had unloaded about his day. He talked of how he had thought going into politics would mean he could contribute something, affect some positive changes, but those who held more sway in Parliament would not listen, and how he felt that he was no more than a puppet having his strings pulled for a show much larger than he realised. Timothy Carmichael Senior sat and patiently listened, sagely nodding his head, just as he always had done. Although he did not impart any particularly useful advice, simply listening and understanding had helped to alleviate Tim's worries.

After talking for what felt like several hours, but was in fact only about an hour, Tim began to make his way back home. 'Keep true to yourself and fight for what you believe to be right,' his father had said as they parted ways, and as simple as that statement was, Tim found solace and strength in those words. He hailed a taxi outside of Waterloo, and thought about what it was he was really fighting for, what changes he could affect in his current position, as he rode to his house in Notting Hill.

The house in Notting Hill was officially regarded as Tim's second home, and he only ever stayed there when he was in town for parliamentary business. His wife and children were still at home in Worcestershire, and although he missed them and would have preferred a normal family night, he had work to do. Paperwork needed catching up on, policies needed reviewing, and he had new propositions to draw up for public sector funding which would have to be presented at the next cabinet meeting.

Nothing about this particular Wednesday had seemingly been out of the ordinary, and certainly nothing noticeably strange or unusual for Tim, except for one thing. One niggling little detail which kept him awake until the early hours of Thursday morning. It was the fact that his father had been dead for almost ten years, and, Tim considered, it would have been very difficult for him to have had a conversation over coffee that afternoon.

CHAPTER I

They gazed lovingly into each other's eyes, their arms wrapped around one another in a tight embrace. Leaning slightly forward, the man's lips gently brushed against the woman's. The light of the sun cast a golden-orange glow over the pair as it began to set, a rainbow arching across the sky behind them.

'The Lovers,' spoke the voice of an older woman, as she placed the tarot card down on to the velvet clothed table in front of her with a satisfying papery flipping sound. She looked up from the table to fix a grey-eyed stare on her client. Her eyes seemed to glint, and the corners of her lips twitched, with a humoured air. 'A woman who is close to your heart, a soul with whom you share a special bond which transcends this world. There's a special young lady in your life now, hmm?'

Sam Hain met the old woman's gaze, looking down to the cards which were laid out before him, and back to the old woman again. From beneath a tangle of thick, silver-white dreadlocks, behind a pair of large, round glasses and set within tired-looking sockets, her icy grey eyes stared back at him. They seemed to sparkle with a youthful joie de vivre, completely incongruous with her aged face.

'In a sense,' he said, casting his eye over the entwined naked pair depicted on the card, 'but not quite in the way you're implying.'

'Oh,' she said, lowering her voice conspiratorially, 'the cards would suggest that there is something more at play than a mere "in a sense" as you claim.' She smiled knowingly. The multitude of wrinkles which lined her face creased and deepened, prominently crinkling in a way which made her skin resemble a satellite image of Norway. She casually waved her hand across the cards which were spread out between them. 'Pick another.'

None the Wiser they called her, and not without good reason. To say that her soothsaying prophecies were wrong would be unfair; that her fortunes were often inaccurate or annoyingly vague would be much more precise. 'I may not have told them the whole truth,' None the Wiser would say if anyone questioned her divinations, 'but I told them exactly what they needed to hear.'

As the crone and matriarch of an order known as the Priestesses of Phoebe, None the Wiser was revered by those in the sisterhood as the one closest in communion with their tutelar Titan. She was deemed the zero-point of the priestesses' powers; the progenitor of their order, and the font of their wisdom and prophecy. She would often seclude herself for prolonged periods of time in her temple – a studio flat in Bethnal Green – shrouded in the smoke-veil of burning cedarwood and bay laurel leaves. In these times, she invoked the essence of Phoebe. There were those who even suspected she was merely a vessel through which Phoebe communicated with her followers.

To the order, she was All, and she was None, and she was Wise. She was None the Wiser.

She also wrote horoscopes for the Sunday newspapers.

To Sam Hain, however, whether she was the wisest of the oracles, a Titan incarnate, a skilled soothsayer, or an old crone with a penchant for telling comfortable truths, it did not matter. Her prophecies had often proven themselves to be true to him, and so far in Sam's dealings with None the Wiser, her hit-or-miss ratio was leaning very much in favour of hit. He pulled another card from the deck.

Amidst a dark and stormy sky, a grand tower stood atop a craggy mountain; tall, proud, and imposing. A lighting bolt struck the tower, toppling its upper levels, as flames burst from its windows.

'Change,' None the Wiser's voice groaned, whining not unlike an old engine which refuses to start up, 'chaotic change.' Again she fixed her steely eyes on Sam, running the tips of her fingers across the card. Something about her seemed different, exuding an aura of otherworldly mystique. 'The Tower is as it is. It is what you know, or what you think you know, or what you do not realise that you know. And soon it will pass that you do not know what you think you know.'

Sam stared at her with a forced expression of understanding. 'I... See?'

'Ah, you do not! But you will. For the lightning strikes in a burst of clarity, destroying what you once knew, and it may seem like all has fallen to chaos and devastation... But from the destruction of the old comes the birth of the new; revelations which will change your view; the flames the phoenix rises through.'

'The rhyming really cleared that up for me, thank you,' Sam said flatly.

'Good, then I am glad. Rhymes are not always so easily had.'

Pulling two more cards from the deck, Sam placed them in front of None the Wiser. One, a man lay face-down in the sand, his face turned towards the sea, with ten swords embedded in his back. The other, a golden wheel – engraved with a sigil of ancient symbols – turning in the sky, flanked by the embodiments of Aquarius, Scorpio, Leo and Taurus, and held aloft by Anubis and a Sphinx.

'The Fates, they turn and turn and turn again! Your journey through these cards has gone from light to dark to light once more. The Lovers share that you have a union, or a reunion, with one who is close to your heart. The Tower's destruction reshapes the world around you, tearing away the veil, and bringing new insight. The Ten of Swords pierce your back, a warning of deception, to be wary of betrayal, of spiritual wounds. And then the Wheel of Fortune spins around, with you as its axis, the Fates in your favour. Change is afoot, darkness is coming, but you will emerge from these tribulations triumphant.'

With a sudden jolt, None the Wiser slammed the palms of her hands on the table. Her body slumped forward. She stared at the floor for an unsettlingly long time, and Sam peered at her, curious and slightly concerned. He was about to give her an investigatory prod to make sure she hadn't just shuffled off her mortal coil when she slowly began to raise her head again. Her eyes were no longer piercing and steely, but more of a very murky grey.

'So,' Sam probed as the mystic returned to the land of the living, 'what does that mean? Good? Bad?'

None the Wiser glanced back down to the cards, taking a moment to analyse them as if this were the first time she had seen them. She shrugged non-committally. 'Some good, some bad. Bit of a mixed bag, really.'

'Since when has life been any different?' Sam said, a wry smile creeping up his lips. He was used to his fortunes being a mixed bag.

'Pull me three more,' None the Wiser spoke, waving her hands like a parlour magician above the deck, 'there is one more thing which remains to be seen.'

Sam did as he was asked, reaching out to the deck and pulling three cards from it at random. The art to these sorts of things, he believed, was to not think about it and just act on instinct. He laid them out before him: the first, the Moon, gleaming silver, high in the night sky; the second, nine wands, forming a staircase to the Moon; the third, seven wands in a circle, lightning striking at their heart. None the Wiser pored over the imagery spread in front of her, croaking a contemplative 'hm' noise.

'That which is not seen in the light of day, the shadow realms beyond our perception. There your answers lie. It will be an uphill struggle to find these answers, but it will be worth it, and things will not be the same as they were before.' Again her face crinkled as she beamed a smile to him. 'I sense you have a new case underway?'

Returning the smile, Sam's eyes lit up with a look of excitement, like a child who has just heard the chime of the ice cream van. 'A case? It's about bloody time! What is it?'

None the Wiser's face sunk back to neutral, her wrinkles evening out. 'That I can not say,' she said, 'but you will know it when you find it. Or when it finds you.'

He nodded, and began to stand. 'Thank you,' he said, slowly moving around the chair and pushing it back under the table, 'as ever, you may not be the clearest of Guides, but your words are helpful nonetheless.' Placing his hat upon his head, Sam turned to leave the small room – which was draped in all manner of mystical, occult and cabbalistic decorations – by the bead-veiled door he had entered.

'Ah-ah-ah,' None the Wiser chimed in a mock-scolding tone. 'In exchange for my wisdom, you must cross my palm with silver, my boy.' She held out her hand, veined and wrinkled, and turned it over to present her palm. Sam reached into his pocket, rummaging around to the sound of jingling coins and rustling paper. He pulled out a crumpled twenty-pound note.

'Since when has anyone ever paid you in an offering of silver?' he asked, half-joking, as he placed the note in her hand.

'It has happened on occasion, but the folk who still pay their offerings in silver and gold do not often walk in this realm as you mortals do.' She folded the note and placed it by the side of a crystal ball, which seemed to reflect and refract the printed image of the Queen's face into weird, unearthly patterns. 'Twenty pounds will do, as you present it to me as if it were an offering of silver.'

The beads clattered together as Sam pushed the strands of the veil aside, ducking slightly to avoid getting tangled in them. Quite why anyone would hang beads in their doorway was beyond him, but much of None the Wiser's way was beyond him. It was all part of her appeal, he thought.

'Remember, Sam Hain,' her voice came creaking like floorboards from behind him, 'the Eye of the Oracle is watching. With the turning of the Wheel of Fortune, it may be more awake than before.'

Sam nodded a sagely nod. He wasn't going to ask her what she meant, she was being intentionally vague, and he didn't fancy having to part with another offering of currency to find out. He left, ironically, none the wiser than when he had arrived. One thing was certain, however; if her prophecies were as accurate as they were vague, he was in for an interesting time ahead of him.

Stepping out onto the street was a stark contrast to the world from which Sam had just emerged. From what had felt like a secluded chamber, adorned in metaphysical wares and draped in rich cloths and tapestries, illuminated by the light of a multitude of candles and shrouded in the smoke of incense, Sam found himself on a busy street in Bethnal Green. The sun was high in the vibrantly blue sky, and the warmth of early-spring wrapped itself around him. Coming out of that darkened room into the light of day felt like it was burning his eyes, and he squinted as he reached into his jacket for his teashade sunglasses.

Pushing his way through the crowds which bustled their way down to the Underground station, Sam resigned himself to a journey on a sweltering tube train. The weather may have been hot outside, but the London Underground had a way of turning itself into a veritable pressure cooker. He removed his jacket, slinging it over one shoulder as he boarded the train, and leaned against the inside of the doors as the tube began to fill up. It was not the nicest form of transport, but Sam prided himself on knowing the routes like the back of his hand.

He had zoned out for a good ten minutes of the journey, lost in his own world inside his head, so that each passing station and turn-over of passengers all melded into a single blur. It was only at Bank that he snapped back to reality, squeezing his way through the stationary passengers with a muttered 'excuse me' and 'sorry', and out onto the platform. Bank station was, by anyone's standard, a confusing labyrinth of tunnels and stairs and platforms to other Underground lines, and was invariably busy. The crowds moved at that unique pace reserved exclusively for London commuters, somehow meandering at a leisurely pace while also being in a rush to get somewhere else, and Sam found himself plodding along in the middle of them.

The droves of people all seemed to meld into one, homogeneous mass; a single current moving like a river through the winding tunnels, with a handful of others running against the flow as they rushed to their platforms like salmon swimming up-stream. However, in amongst this faceless crowd, something caught Sam's eye. Something he recognised. Several people ahead of him, standing out amidst everyone, bobbed a head of mousey-blonde hair. A pastel pink bag hung lazily off of one shoulder, and a light crop-top hugged the woman's body. She walked with an airy grace, a quietly contented stride which seemed to be at odds with everyone else around her.

As if sensing Sam was looking at her, she turned and smiled a wide, beaming smile at him. Her light blue eyes glistened happily, and Sam felt his heart skip. He blinked, confused, uncertain, at the young woman, before managing a hesitant smile back. It had been a long time since he had seen that face, that warm and welcoming smile, and without a second thought Sam began to force his way through the crowd, weaving as best he could to catch up with her. She glanced over her shoulder, a smile gracing her lips, as she turned a corner.

'Wait!' he called out to her, his voice more of a desperate plea than he would have liked, just as she disappeared out of sight. He hurried around the corner, mere meters behind her. But when he turned the corner, she wasn't anywhere to be seen. He stood still as the throngs of people continued to flow around him, glancing around and inspecting each and every face in the crowd. Nowhere. Nothing. It was as if she had simply vanished.

Of course, Sam thought as he began to solemnly plod towards the escalators, *it couldn't have been... Not really.* Although, as much as it defied all reason, he sensed that there was likely more to this apparent apparition than a simple case of mistaken identity.

The rest of the journey passed by without anything else of note, and soon Sam found himself alighting at Angel in Islington. This was partly out of habit; for a couple of weeks he had been staying with Alice in her flat while he kept a low profile, so as not to draw any more unnecessary attention to himself. After the Regents' spooks had kicked his front door down for a not-so-friendly chat and intervention in his paranormal activities the month before, he had thought it wise to stay away from home for a little while. However, Sam knew he couldn't keep himself in the shadows for long – if he did, he was essentially allowing those who would put a stop to his work to win – and he considered it was about time he moved back into his own flat. Especially if a new case was afoot. Now that None the Wiser had mentioned it, he could feel it in his bones.

Or maybe that was just him itching for something new and interesting to sink his teeth into.

CHAPTER II

It was an unusually hot day in Islington. The weather, as anyone who has lived in England will attest, can be an unpredictable and fickle thing, and the city had been gripped by a sudden springtime heatwave. The skies were clear and a vibrant shade of blue with barely a cloud in sight, and the people moved sluggishly under the baking heat of the sun. Islington Green was littered with impromptu sunbathers, taking in the unexpectedly hot weather and lazing in the sun like dazed bumblebees, sipping iced coffees, not in much of a rush to do anything. Those who were in a rush – the men and women who had just left work, many still in their office suits – managed to build up a sweat from even the most minor of activities, clinging to the shadows as they walked from A to B, beads of sweat glistening on their brows.

Alice walked along the high street with a spring in her step, her golden hair bouncing and gleaming in the sunlight, her floral summer dress swaying gently in the breeze-less air. The warmth of the sun caressed her skin, and felt as if it was reinvigorating and re-energising her soul. Despite what had been a pleasantly short shift, getting to leave work around mid-afternoon, it had seemed like an impossibly long day to her. After simply standing behind a till beneath the store's fluorescent lights (while most people were out enjoying the weather instead of clothes shopping) for six hours, Alice felt like this was exactly what she had needed to lift her spirits.

Quickly stopping off at a café along the high street, she bought herself a chilled drink to enjoy on her way home. She sipped on the syrupy crushed ice, which was refreshingly cool and tasted like some kind of indeterminable tropical fruit hiding beneath a large amount of sugar. It was perfect, Alice thought, savouring the flavour of a chemical-approximate of what fruit might taste like. Turning the corner on to the road she lived on, Alice couldn't wait to get home, unwind, probably take a cold shower to refresh herself, and figure out how to make the most of such a lovely afternoon.

Most people, she considered, would be out enjoying themselves. Some of her friends were already thinking about arranging barbecues for the weekend. She thought about perhaps taking the opportunity to bathe in the sun for a while, almost not caring that her flat only had access to a garden shared and overlooked by the other residents of the building; it was too sunny to waste it worrying about neighbours seeing her in her underwear. Afterwards, in the evening, she could meet up with friends for a few drinks in the park or get some cocktails in a trendy East London bar. Rachel would certainly like that idea, and Alice wondered about inviting Sam Hain along as well; she thought that he didn't seem to get out much, not in the normal sense anyway (not that he did anything in the normal sense, come to think of it), and might enjoy doing something not supernatural for a change.

Alice walked up the stairs to her flat, grateful to be home, and stepped through the front door. Flinging her bag onto the sofa, she called out into the seemingly empty flat. 'Rach, you home?'

'She is,' replied a voice from the kitchen, and the head of Sam Hain appeared from around the corner. He grinned broadly at her. 'Good, you're here too! Cup of tea?'

'I am!' Rachel's voice echoed from her bedroom.

'Nah, I'm alright thank you. It's a bit too hot for tea,' Alice replied, 'I-'

'It's never too hot for a good cup of tea,' Sam interrupted, his head disappearing back into the kitchen.

'I thought you were going back to your place now things

have quietened down?' Alice asked. She realised it may have sounded as if she wasn't pleased to see him, and hastily added, 'not that you're not welcome.'

'I am,' he said, emerging from the kitchen, delicately stirring his tea, 'or rather, I was.' He sat himself down on the sofa, resting the cup on the arm of the seat. After staying with Alice for a few weeks, Sam was feeling rather more at home there. 'I'll be out of your hair soon, just needed to pick up the last of my bits and pieces beforehand.'

'Don't worry about it,' Alice said, seating herself on the sofa next to him, 'don't feel like you need to rush off. You're welcome to stay here if you need.'

'Thank you, Alice, I do appreciate you putting up with me. I know it's not been the easiest situation, harbouring a potential fugitive who might still be hunted by a clandestine organisation of supernatural secret agents.'

Sometimes, Alice found, she had got used to Sam's surreal situations and strange sentences. Not that it was ever normal – not by a long shot – but she had come to expect a certain degree of weirdness to come out of his mouth whenever he spoke. However, it was sentences like that which reminded her just how unusual things were at times. She nodded her head slowly. 'What are friends for, hey?'

'Besides,' he said, staring into his tea, 'a case is coming. I can feel it.' He quickly downed the remainder of his tea, and placed his hand over the rim of the cup. In a swift motion, he turned the cup upside-down, leaving a cluster of tea leaves in his palm. He squinted at them, bemused. 'Huh.'

'What is it?'

'I don't know. I can't read tea leaves.' He scraped the damp mess back into his cup. 'I thought they might have been a bit clearer than just a shapeless lump. I really should get None the Wiser to teach me...'

'Who's None the Wiser?'

Before Sam had a chance to answer the question – although what little he knew would only make matters more confusing – Rachel emerged from her bedroom, brandishing her laptop. 'I've found it,' she declared triumphantly. 'Found the thing I was telling you about.'

'Is this that Big Celebrity Love Trap Jungle Karaoke Date thingy?' One could almost hear his eyes roll as he spoke. When he had arrived at the flat, Rachel told him that Alice would likely be back home soon, so he decided to wait. In that time, he listened to Rachel talk about some kind of reality TV show which stranded celebrities he had never heard of together in a jungle and set them up on dates, made them sing famous pop songs in front of a panel of judges, and the winners got married or signed a record deal or something. He wasn't sure; he hadn't really been listening. Reality TV all seemed the same to him: mostly boring. All he had really taken in was that there had been some big drama between a children's television presenter and a politician over a bottle of wine.

'No, no,' Rachel said, 'the weird thing. It's the kind of weird, stupid shit you'd say has something to do with ghosts.'

Sam raised an eyebrow at her as she placed the screen in front of him. The video started playing, and Rachel quickly fiddled with the volume controls so they could hear it better. Alice leaned in and peered over Sam's shoulder to watch.

The video showed Timothy Frederick Carmichael the Second of Worcestershire, one of the backbenchers in Parliament, at a table outside of a café along London's Southbank. Two cups of coffee sat in front of him, and although the chair opposite him was vacant, the politician seemed to be engrossed in a very engaging conversation with an invisible companion. He gesticulated wildly as he talked, staring wide-eyed at the empty space in front of him, before pausing and nodding his head silently as if listening to their reply. The recording, which had been uploaded the night before, had since gone viral and been picked up by several major news networks. The MP – or rather, now former MP – had been made to take involuntary leave, citing health issues as the reason for stepping down from his seat.

'Well,' Sam said, his voice betraying his intrigue over the video.

'Well?' Rachel probed, clearly pleased she had found a way to engage the occult detective's interest. Her previous attempts of talking about reality TV and celebrity gossip had failed.

'Well, what if...' Sam mused. 'What if he's not gone mad, as the commenters seem to suggest. What if...' He paused, trying to think of something other than a ghost. 'He's talking to an invisible wizard? Or...'

'Or?'

'Or a ghost.'

'See! I knew you'd say it was ghosts.' Rachel poked him, mockingly.

'Or an invisible wizard! Don't discount that possibility,' he retorted with an equally mocking tone.

'Hang on,' Alice interjected, 'why does it specifically have to be an invisible *wizard*? We can't see it, it could be an invisible anything.'

'Because,' Sam said, his voice sounding assured as if his logic was infallible, 'if it's not a wizard, how else would it cast a spell to make itself invisible?'

'My bet's on the ghost, to be honest,' she replied, before something caught her eye. On the sidebar of related videos, there was another with the title "WOMAN POSSESSED ON SOUTHBANK!!!" which had been uploaded that morning. 'What's this one?' she thought aloud, and clicked on the link.

The next video showed a tourist prancing along the Southbank. She skipped ahead of the person recording, spinning around in front of the London Eye with her arms spread wide and a beaming smile across her face. She continued to skip her way along the walkway, occasionally stopping to pose for the camera or take in the sights. Street performers juggled, human statues stood as still as stone, unmoving and unflinching, buskers played music and sang songs to enraptured crowds. For a short video, it captured the spirit of the Southbank.

And then it happened. The woman danced her way towards a sculpture. It was a strange thing, a vaguely ovular shape which had been split down the middle, with a circular hole cut through the very centre of it. It was through this hole that the woman's face appeared, peering through from one side of the statue to the other. She grinned into the camera, but her smile quickly faded and her eyes rolled back into her head. Her knuckles turned white as she gripped either side of the statue, fingers clasped around it like claws. She took a rasping breath, and a voice which did not sound like her own came tumbling from her mouth.

'*Nehw eht diov snekawa dna ssenkrad snigeb ot esir, esoht ohw netsil ot eht swodahs yam eveileb rieht derepsihw seil,*' she said in a tongue which did not sound like it should be pronounced by any human being, while the person filming continued to utter 'oh my god' repeatedly. Her eyes snapped back to fix the camera with a solid and unsettling stare. 'Darkness is coming,' she intoned, 'Sam Hain.' With that, the woman fell backwards, struggling to her feet and visibly shaken by the experience. The video ended.

The next suggested video was of a cat falling down some stairs, which proceeded to autoplay.

'That was...' Sam began, but he wasn't sure how to finish

his sentence. He simply covered his mouth with his hand as he tried to process what he had just seen.

'Interesting? Weird? Creepy?' Alice offered as suggestions to finish the sentence. Sam simply nodded; any of them would do.

'Probably just a coincidence, right?' he said, his voice tinged with a nervous and naive hopefulness.

'What have you always told me about coincidence?'

Sam sighed reluctantly and resigned himself to replying like a schoolchild reciting an important lesson. 'There's no such thing...'

'You told me the same thing when I had to pay off my credit card on the same day I won the exact amount I needed on the lottery,' Rachel chimed in. 'The Universe is rarely so lazy, or some Zen hippy crap like that. Didn't help.' She folded the laptop shut and held it under her arm. 'I won't pretend to understand exactly what it is you do, Sam, you're a strange person who does a lot of strange things-'

'Thank you,' he interjected.

'But you're caught up in some really weird shit, mate. I can't tell whether it's really cool, or really freaky.'

'In my experience,' he said, 'it's a little bit of both.' He sat there for a short while in a stunned silence, staring vacantly into the middle distance.

'So,' Alice eventually said, 'I guess a relaxing evening is off the cards?'

'I don't think such a thing is ever on the cards for me,' Sam said. 'Fancy a night out on the Southbank?'

The Southbank was a hive of activity that night. As the sun began to set over the city, casting an orange glow across the Thames, crowds of people milled along to the various bars and restaurants which lined the riverside.

Some of the street performers had started to pack away their gear, while the lilting lyrics of a busker serenaded the passers-by with her guitar and soulful singing. Queues still snaked around the base of the London Eye, waiting to watch the sunset from a capsule which could oversee the entire city.

'Something feels weird,' Sam said as he strode purposefully through the crowd. He held his transphasic energy probe ahead of him, looking at it intently. The crystal at its tip glowed a strange shade of green. No-one seemed to pay any attention to the man waving around a glowing TechnoWand; Sam assumed they would likely think he was another eccentric costumed performer, and he would just blend into the crowd. He was right.

Alice looked at him quizzically. 'You're only just thinking this now?'

'Well, no. Obviously Members of Parliament talking with imaginary friends and a possessed tourist with a very pointed message for me within the same twenty-four hours is a little odd. But this is even odder.' He pointed the probe in Alice's direction, giving it a slight wave and a wiggle. 'See this?'

'You're waving it right in my face, so yes,' she said, brushing the TechnoWand aside. 'It's doing its glowy thing it does when there's weird stuff.'

'Exactly, but look.' He brought it back up to her face. The crystal continued to glow a colour which resembled the green of glow-in-the-dark paint. 'This isn't some simple spectral scene, not an intentional incursion. This is like walking into a paranormal pocket. A region of unfettered weirdness.' He spun on his heels and darted away, cutting a path through the crowd. Following close behind, Alice hurried after him.

Ahead of them, the sea of people seemed to part and give way to an open space. The crowd moved in a circle around the space, as if the spot had been reserved and marked off for one of the performance artists. It was like an invisible cordon was in place, and people were walking around the perimeter. There, standing in the absolute centre of the open space, stood the monument.

It was an odd, curvy thing, sculpted from bronze and standing no taller than chest-height, on top of a small black plinth. It looked as though it had once been almond-shaped, although one side had been mostly hollowed, as if the metal had been scooped out, leading to a hole in the very centre of the statue. The hole through which the tourist had peered through. The piece was split into two, a perfect cut dividing it straight down the middle. It appeared entirely harmless; simply another art installation along the Thames walkway.

The thing which struck Alice as strange, though, even stranger than the statue and Sam's speculations, was that the space was not as empty as it had first seemed. A series of lights, not unlike the little solar-powered lanterns one might place on their lawn, circled the statue. They glowed a fluorescent royal purple, and were linked together by a tangle of cables. A single wire snaked out and away from the circle of lights, leading to a laptop which sat on the floor in front of the statue. Hunched over the laptop was the figure of a man. He wore a grey twill suit, and seemed too preoccupied with whatever he was looking at on the screen to notice Sam and Alice approaching him.

'Well, well, well,' Sam announced loudly, an exuberant and happy lilt in his voice, as he approached the man.

The figure peered over his shoulder, and the face of James Mortimer was looking back up at them. 'Sam, my man, I didn't expect to see you!' He stood up and offered his friend a fist-bump in greeting. 'Alice,' he added, leaning around Sam to shake her hand. 'How are things?'

'Weird and confusing,' he replied, 'you?'

'Same,' James said with a casual nod in the direction of the statue. 'There was a spike in Akashic energy here a day or so ago. I've been analysing this statue here, trying to work out what and why, and it seems to be in a state of quantum flux. High levels of Akasha are emanating from it, and even more currents are being drawn to it like some kind of weirdness magnet. I guess that's what brought you here too?'

'Are you saying that I'm drawn by the natural law of weirdness magnetism?' Sam said, putting on an affronted face.

'Yes,' he replied with an air of frankness, 'aren't you always? It's a happy coincidence you two are here, though. Three heads are better than one!'

'I don't think coincidence has anything to do with it, James,' Alice said with a knowing tone.

'Almost certainly not. The Universe didn't lead us here on a mere whim. It's all connected, and with an energetic disturbance this prominent...' Sam mused, pacing around the statue and slowly waving the probe as if it were a mini metal detector. The probe glowed and pulsed a sickly pale green. 'What do you make of it?'

'It's strange, Sam,' he replied as if that was all the answer it really needed. He crouched down in front of his laptop again, intently studying the display on the screen and nodding his head in contemplation. 'It's like we're at the point of intersection for several different currents of energy. Extra-dimensional properties collide and combine together, and this statue is the epicentre. In effect, it's amplifying these energies, and they seem to be bleeding through into our dimension. Watch.'

James took a pen from his jacket pocket, and gently tossed it in the direction of the statue. The pen wobbled slightly, but rather than start on a downward curve towards the ground as a normal, law-of-gravity-obeying pen would, it instead corrected itself in mid-air and shot with alarming speed towards the statue. It flew like a projectile hurtling through the air, before coming to an abrupt stop in the middle of the hole at the statue's heart. Staring at the floating pen, it reminded Sam of a magic trick which used magnets to create the illusion of levitating objects. The pen continued to hover there for a short while, before promptly vanishing from existence.

'Ooh,' Sam said with an awed sense of understanding, 'it's an interdimensional cross-rip.'

'And in real words that means...?' Alice asked.

'Well,' James said, flipping his laptop around for Alice to see the screen. 'This is reality as we know it in our dimension.' He pointed at a graph which plotted an X, Y and Z axis. 'We perceive everything in three dimensions. But, compare it to the dimensional properties coming from the statue...' He pointed to a new graph. Except it wasn't a graph; at least, not something one would immediately recognise as a graph, or present at a board meeting. It was a chaotic mess, like someone had just taken a whole pack of coloured pencils and scribbled in spirals and wavy lines over and over again.

'That doesn't look very scientific, it looks more like something my two year old nephew would scribble.'

'That's the terrifying bit. This, despite looking like a child's scribbling, is actually completely, one-hundred-percently, mathematically accurate.'

While James was busy trying to explain the unexplainable, Sam stood with his arms folded, contemplating the statue. It fascinated him. For such a convergence of energy to cause an interdimensional cross-rip was inconceivable; doubly so that everything else around them appeared to be perfectly normal. As he stood observing the statue, he noticed that inscribed on the plinth, beneath the concave side of the monument (which Sam believed to be the front), was a short passage of golden words. The piece was apparently called the Jubilee Oracle, sculpted by someone called Alexander in 1980, and the inscription read as follows:

Mankind is capable of an awareness
that is outside the range of everyday life.

The inscription continued to detail how the sculpture was created to communicate with that awareness, but it was that first line which really captured Sam's attention. He considered it no small coincidence that the centre of the disruption, a disruption which had caused an MP to converse with an invisible companion and a tourist to speak in an unearthly tongue and utter Sam's name, was also a monument which was made to communicate with mankind's awareness beyond the normal.

'In essence,' Sam said, looking up from the inscription with widened eyes, 'while we're used to living in this plane of reality, this spot on the Southbank seems to be a focal point of who knows how many different dimensions. Normally, each dimension is sandwiched one on top of the other, the higher dimensions barely perceivable to the lower ones, but here they all flow and mix together like some kind of transdimensional cocktail. And the Oracle statue...' He moved around the bronze monument, keeping the TechnoWand pointed at it at all times while he circled it. 'It seems to be operating like a window or gateway to these dimensions; an Akashic node which opens doorways to realms beyond the real.'

'Think of it, if you will,' James added, 'like a motorway interchange with countless lanes and exits and fly-overs, but they all combine to use the same roundabout.'

'A focal point of freakiness,' Alice said, attempting to sound like she understood both what was going on, and its implications.

'Exactly. It's causing a disturbance in the Akashic field, and the problem is... It's growing. The disturbance is gradually spreading out like ripples across water. The bigger it gets, the weirder things are going to be.'

'Brilliant,' she said drily, 'so what do we do?'

'We reverse the polarity,' James said, staring fixedly at his laptop. 'Reverse the flow of the cross-rip, cause the weirdness bubble to shrink back into itself, and stop the energetic output.'

'I'm not going to pretend I understand that entirely, but it sounds like it might work.'

'One energetic reversal, coming up!' Sam declared, pointing his probe at the Oracle. The crystalline tip began to glow brighter and brighter.

'Wait!' James leapt to his feet, his hand outstretched in a gesture for Sam to stop. 'If we resonate on a frequency even remotely off from the quantum baseline signature of the statue, it could have the opposite effect! Or worse, we get sucked inside-out and upside-down into another dimension.'

'You might try to make sense of the extraordinary through scientific principles,' Sam said with a dismissive wave of the wand, 'but in the old days before quantum physics, Magick was understood as an art of the Will.'

'It's not as simple as just willing the Universe to-' James began to argue, but it was already too late. The hole in the centre of the statue glowed vibrantly, and a bright beam of energy shot out from the heart of it and connected with the probe's crystal. Sam had just enough time to make an "oh no" face before they were engulfed in a flash of light.

The Southbank suddenly found itself three people fewer.

Gaze into the Eye of the Oracle,
Behold the phantasmagorical.

CHAPTER III

The kettle whined a high-pitched whistle, billowing steam from its spout. Sam Hain lifted the kettle off of the stove, pouring the boiling water into his mug with a satisfyingly gentle splashing. The liquid turned a golden brown as it made contact with the teabag, and he added a dash of milk. Reaching for the two slices of bread which had just popped out of the toaster, he slathered them in butter and sat down at the kitchen table. He sipped the tea, releasing the satisfied "ah" sound one traditionally makes when first sipping a decent cup of tea. The toast crunched perfectly as he took a bite. This morning, he thought to himself, was almost perfect. It was missing only one thing...

Lorna emerged from the bedroom, her mousey-blonde hair draping down her shoulders in untamed waves. She was still wearing her nightshirt – or rather, one of Sam's old shirts – which came down to just above her knees, and a pair of inexplicably pink bunny rabbit slippers flopped about on her feet as she walked over to him. She stood behind him, leaning over and hanging her arms loosely around his neck, before planting a delicate kiss on his cheek. Sam smiled to himself. Now this morning was perfect. 'Morning, bunny,' Lorna said softly, her voice croaking with that just-woken-up croak.

'Hello, you,' he replied. He took one of her hands in his, stroking her slender fingers, and tenderly kissed the back of her hand. 'How're you this morning?'

'Couldn't be better, waking up to you,' she said. As she began to pull away, she ran a hand through his hair and ruffled it lovingly, and made her way across to the kitchen counter. The early morning light poured in through the window, bright and crisp, illuminating her perfectly in Sam's eyes. 'What's for breakfast?'

'I didn't expect you up so soon,' he said, between a mouthful of toast, 'otherwise I'd have done you something. Toast?'

Lorna glanced over her shoulder, smiling at him with that radiant smile he remembered so well. Despite the slightly drowsy look on her face, her blue eyes sparkled. 'I know I can be a sleepy-sheepy, but I've got things to do!' Grabbing a couple of slices of bread from the breadbin, she popped them in the toaster and set the dial to 4. 'Besides,' she continued, walking back over to him and resting her head on his shoulder, 'I wouldn't get a chance to see you before you had to go. You're going to be late if you don't hurry up, mister.'

'I don't care,' he said in a whisper, wistfully turning to kiss her forehead, 'it can w-'

A knock came rapping at the door of the flat. It came twice, thrice, and whatever the "-ice" equivalent of four is. Sam groaned in frustration as he stood up to answer it. His feet moved heavily, reluctantly, shuffling towards the door as the knock came again. He unbolted the door and swung it open, to find James Mortimer standing the other side.

'Come on, Sam,' James said, 'we're going to be late.'

Sam simply stared at his friend standing in the doorway, before looking back over his shoulder towards Lorna, who was contently sorting out her own toast and coffee for the morning. 'Not now, please,' he pleaded, 'just let me stay here a little longer.'

James adopted a condescending stare, his hands firmly in his pockets as he tapped his foot impatiently. 'You know how Professor Watt feels about lateness. He'll have us hung, strung and quartered if we're even a minute behind.' He looked over Sam's shoulder and across to Lorna as she reached up into the fridge. 'For God's sake, sis, put some clothes on.'

In a teasing retaliation, Lorna gripped the hem of the nightshirt between her fingers and twirled a little pirouette in the kitchen. 'I am wearing clothes!' She then waggled her toes in the ends of her slippers, so the bunny heads flopped up and down as if nodding affirmatively. 'Bleep blop,' she squeaked, which presumably was slipper-rabbit for "she's right, you know".

James simply rolled his eyes with mock exasperation. 'Come on,' he said, 'we need to get a move on.'

The room was mostly deserted. Tables and chairs arced around the outside of the small room, but only half of them were occupied with students. Nonetheless, Professor Watt stood at the front of the class with his tweed jacket and chalk, scribbling across the blackboard as if he was addressing a packed-out lecture hall.

'So, if we presume that the myriad realities contained within the multiverse are not as separate and distinct as we perceive, say, different galaxies,' Professor Watt lectured, 'but in fact every conceivable reality, every possible dimension, and every universe in all of their forms are, in fact, layered on top of each other like intangible layers of sediment, then transdimensional travel isn't just theoretically possible, but remarkably simple with the right knowledge.'

Several of the students had fallen asleep in their seats, their heads resting on notepads and textbooks as if they were the most comfortable pillows in the world. Sam and James were sat side-by-side, and while James sat attentively looking towards the front of the room, Sam had his brow furrowed as he examined the blackboard. Nothing was written on the board, aside from what appeared to him to be a complex sigil surrounded by alchemical symbols.

'Now,' Professor Watt continued, 'with the right knowledge and a sufficient concentration of Akasha, one would be able to punch a hole in what they consider "reality" and access another world, another dimension. At this point, one would also be able to dwell in a realm outside of the various realities, and tread within that space which permeates all other dimensions, the void space between countless realities, as if it were a corridor leading to limitless doorways. One would, essentially, become a Void Walker, if you will.'

The professor spun on his heels with a flamboyant enthusiasm, his chalk pointing into the room like a precision laser. His eyes seemed to glaze over. 'Who here has any ideas as to how one might be able to create a stable gateway between dimensions, without first securing an anchor on the other side? A portal which would mean the lines between respective realities would become blurred?' The chalk traced around the perimeter of the room, skimming over all of the students – both sleeping and awake – as he hummed thoughtfully, although he seemed not to notice any of the other students present. Instead, the chalk's aim settled on Sam Hain. 'Samuel,' the professor exclaimed, 'perhaps you can give us some insight into accessing and utilising transdimensional energies?'

Sitting somewhat awkwardly in his seat, Sam continued to stare obliquely ahead. He was still focussed on the sigil upon the blackboard, trying to decipher what it could possibly represent. The other symbols orbiting the pattern were placed at each point where the lines of the sigil intersected with the binding circle. It clearly represented something, he mused, but what?

'Samuel? We're waiting.' The professor's voice came again. 'I'm sure the whole class would be interested in hearing your insight.'

'I'm not sure, sir,' Sam said with a dismissive wave of the hand. 'This is presuming the laws of physics would allow such a manipulation of reality?'

'Oh, physics be damned!' Professor Watt said. 'We all

know the laws of reality are not rigidly bound entirely by the current understanding of physics. You of all people would know this, surely?'

'I'm not sure I follow, sir,' Sam lied.

'Come on, Sam,' James said, gently nudging his elbow into his side, 'I know you know this.'

'This doesn't strike you as a little odd?' Sam asked in a conspiratorial whisper, facing James. James stared blankly back at him. 'Professor Watt taught creative writing classes, not courses on the theoretical application of metaphysics.' James shrugged non-committally in response.

Professor Watt glared at Sam, his feet tapping irately on the vinyl floor. The chalk snapped between his fingers. 'Samuel! If you would kindly supply an answer when asked a question, rather than gossip with your friend...'

'I can't,' Sam replied bluntly, his gaze meeting Professor Watt's with an intense and challenging stare.

'I thought you were the brightest student in the room, if not the whole university, Samuel. Am I mistaken? Don't you want to prove why you're our star pupil?' Professor Watt asked, his tone growing progressively more antagonistic, goading Sam's pride. Sam responded by simply shrugging his shoulders.

'This isn't some kind of optional quiz for extra credit, young man,' the professor suddenly began to rail against him. 'This is your assignment, and unless you can supply me with the answers I'm looking for, I'm going to have to assign you detention. Indefinitely.' His eyes turned entirely black, not unlike a pool of oil and very much unlike human eyes.

Sam considered this reaction to be somewhat more extreme than it really warranted, especially from a tutor who would normally be discussing the importance of narrative arcs rather than transdimensional travel. He did not answer. He simply maintained his steady glare towards the professor, who appeared to be close to erupting in fury.

'Answer me! How would you open a stable portal from one dimension to another without a sustainable foothold? How would you punch a hole into reality to make one realm and another indivisible from each other?' The professor's voice sounded like it was coming from somewhere other than the professor himself; a deep and booming voice which vibrated through Sam's mind.

'What even is reality? How can you prove any of this is real?' Sam asked, a smug smirk creeping up his lips. 'Because I have a sneaking suspicion that things are not quite as they seem.'

'Don't talk back to me, boy!' Professor Watt bellowed, flinging the remainder of his chalk at the blackboard. It shattered into a plume of white dust. The sleeping students stayed fast asleep, apparently not even remotely disturbed, and remained flopped lifelessly across their desks like crash-test dummies.

Sam stood up, placing his hat upon his head, and fixed his stare on the thing which claimed to be Professor Watt. 'Listen, we're not going to get anywhere like this. If you really want to probe me for details, you're going to have to try harder than appealing to my ego or intimidating me. This little pantomime is over.'

The thing which wore the illusion of Professor Watt glared through its oil-black eyes for a while, its anger seeping off of it in visible wisps like a heat haze. 'So be it,' it intoned in a voice far deeper and darker than anything remotely human. A black, viscous fluid started to ooze from Professor Watt's mouth and eyes as the illusion began to melt away. The professor's form quickly dripped out of existence, and the rest of the classroom faded away into nothingness, leaving Sam entirely alone in an empty space.

'Thank you,' he said, straightening the lapels of his jacket, 'now if you don't mind, I'm going to go back to my memory of the perfect morning. Until you dream up a new game to play, don't interrupt me before I've finished breakfast.' He sat down at the table as the rest of the kitchen reconstructed itself around him, taking a sip of perfectly brewed tea and a bite of perfectly toasted toast, as Lorna draped her arms lovingly around his neck and planted a delicate kiss on his cheek.

'Morning, bunny.'

Until he could conjure up a way out of this realm of illusions, Sam was more than happy to stay in this memory, and make the moment last eternity.

*The Oracle can an insight give
To a life one once did live.*

Chapter IV

Alice fondly remembered the stories and fairytales her grandmother used to tell her. When she was growing up, she and her family would often holiday with her paternal grandparents in Ireland, staying in their little cottage in the countryside a short distance from Galway. She and her brother and sister would often be out playing in the fields, across the green and rolling hills which seemed to stretch out and over the horizon.

Her grandmother would take her on adventures, trekking across the valleys and through deep and mystical forests which seemed to sing with magic. One of her favourite memories was sitting atop the hill of Cnoc Meadha with a picnic, while her grandmother told her tall tales of the Tuatha Dé. She told her stories of the aos sí, of the friendly faerie folk and of the larking leprechauns. Alice had been enraptured with these stories, listening intently about the magical creatures and fae who blessed the land, who would grant kindly mortals favours, and play tricks and mayhem on those who did not pay them proper respect.

Alice often dreamed of being a faery on those holidays. Dragonfly-like wings would carry her aloft, amongst the flowers and the trees, and she would dance among the leaves with the other fae. Swirling and spiralling in the air, sparkling with magic. She tried to carry on her faery double-life in her waking life too, but this mostly happened on Halloween. School uniforms were not conducive of faery wings.

As time went on, the dreams of the fae were shrugged off in Alice's teenage years. With subsequent holidays to

Ireland, Teenage Alice had felt more drawn to the sullen grey cliff-faces, standing battered and windswept beneath a stormy sky. In her adult life, it seemed as if she had left that part of herself behind, her faery world all but forgotten. Although that did not mean she hadn't still enjoyed the stories her grandmother would continue to tell until she passed away. Nor did it mean she didn't still occasionally feel the call of the faefolk and their mystical kingdom.

It was much to her surprise, then, that Alice now noticed these thoughts and feelings resurfacing after many years. Even more surprising was the fact that she was no longer on the Southbank, and instead she found herself stood in a strange yet somehow familiar world. The smell of fresh, damp earth enriched the air, and tall green trees stretched up to the blue skies above. She was surrounded by vibrantly coloured flowers which sprouted up amidst the rich green grass. Purples, blues, reds and yellows dotted the land. She knew this place, but also knew it was nowhere she had been before.

The sound of gentle fluttering came through the forest. The soft beating of wings grew louder and louder, at first from a single direction, but soon Alice could hear it all around her. It didn't sound like the feathered wings of birds in flight, it was more like a papery fluttering, not unlike what one might expect giant butterflies to sound like. She looked around, glancing into the dense forest and up into the trees to try to see what it was. Shapes darted between the trunks of the trees, too fast for her to get a proper look at them.

'Hello?' Alice called into the forest, and immediately wondered if that had been a wise idea. She didn't feel anything amiss, though – if anything, she felt calm and peaceful in this forest – and she had grown to trust her instincts.

'Hi there!' a voice replied from somewhere above her.

Something dropped down from a branch high in the trees and, with the last minute buzzing of insect-like wings, the figure landed gracefully in front of Alice. He stood tall and proud. Straight and silk-like auburn hair flowed down to his waist, framing an angular face with piercing green eyes, and two pointed ears poked through from beneath his hair. His clothes resembled a simple green tunic, if tunics were made entirely of stitched-together oak leaves. A pair of large dragonfly-like wings folded down behind his back, resembling a multi-coloured cape which shimmered and shifted shades in the light of the sun.

Alice gawped. Her eyes boggled and her mouth hung slightly open.

'Are you okay there?' The man tilted his head quizzically. 'You seem surprised.'

It took a while for Alice to answer as her brain struggled to keep up with what she was seeing. Slowly, she closed her mouth and cleared her throat. 'You're, um... You're a faery?'

'Yes,' said the faery.

'Then yes, I am a little surprised. A lot surprised, actually.'

'Why?' The faery continued to look at her with a kindly, questioning expression. 'It stands to reason that when you enter the Faerie Realm, you'll meet faeries.' He smiled a welcoming smile.

Again, Alice struggled to find the words to say. She felt like she was two steps behind the reality which stood before her. It occurred to her that she wasn't entirely sure of how she ended up in the middle of the forest in the first place; the last thing she remembered was being on the Southbank with Sam and James, but that felt like a distant memory to her now. 'How did I get here?' she eventually asked.

'Through the Fae Doorway, of course,' he jovially

replied.

'Of course...' Alice mused, not seeing any "of course" in the matter whatsoever. 'And how, precisely, did I do that?'

'I imagine you followed the call, didn't you? That's how most cross from the mortal plane into this world. Let's see,' he said as he leaned in closer, as if inspecting Alice intently. His eyes narrowed, his pointed ears twitched. She stood perfectly still as she was subjected to the inspection, not sure if she should be feeling nervous yet or not.

'Yes,' declared the faery, as if reaching some grand conclusion, 'your spirit recognised the call, and helped guide you here. You may not have ended up where you intended to go, but you are precisely where you need to be. Through an artificial gateway, by the seems of it.' He sounded almost judgemental about the fact.

'You mean the statue on the Southbank?'

'Possibly, I'm not too familiar with the layout of your world in that way. Come, let me show you our world.' The faery unfolded his wings, and began to hover a short distance above the ground. 'Follow me!'

He flew directly upwards, darting through the air and reaching far above where Alice was still stood. He lingered a while, high among the branches of the trees. Alice simply stared up at the faery, her mind boggling. This evening was turning out very different from what she had expected. *This has got to be a dream,* she thought, *this isn't real.*

'A dream, perhaps, but real nonetheless,' the faery called to her, sitting on one of the branches with his head peering down at her from between his knees. 'Are you coming or not?'

'How can I?' Alice shouted back up to him. 'I don't have wings!'

'Don't be silly,' replied the faery, 'you've just forgotten how to use them. It's quite easy; just jump and don't land.'

Alice furrowed her brow, wondering what kind of

bizarre dream she had found herself in. She tried to make sense of what had happened to lead her here, but the answers were making themselves exceedingly difficult to pin down. Something on her back twinged, not unlike a pulled muscle but without the pain, and she instinctively reached around to rub the space between her shoulders. This only added to her confusion, as her fingers met with something unexpected; she could feel something on her back, or rather two somethings, long and rigid, yet silky to the touch. The somethings twitched, and she glanced over her shoulder to see what they were. She was startled to see a glimpse of what appeared to be a pair of wings similar to the faery's.

Still trying to wrap her brain around the situation, Alice thought she may as well try to follow the faery's instructions. She jumped, springing herself up from the tips of her toes, and closed her eyes, thinking about not coming back down. Her eyes remained firmly shut for a while and, with trepidation, she peaked out from beneath the lid of one eye. Looking down, her feet were still not back on the ground. She was hovering a good foot above the earth. It didn't make much sense to her, but by this point she was willing to just go with it and worry about what did or did not make sense later.

'See? Easy!' the faery called down to her, and with a beckoning hand he gestured for her to join him. Instinctively, Alice began to fly upwards – slowly, at first, but gathering speed – into the canopy of the trees which had previously seemed so high above her. She refused to look down to see how far she had flown, though. Realising how far below her the ground was, she thought, was a sure-fire way to forget about not landing.

They soared through the trees, weaving among the branches in a graceful flight with an ease which felt as if they were leaves floating in the wind. Alice marvelled at the forest around them, its tall and majestic trees rich and green, bathed in the golden sunlight. Motes of light drifted lazily through the air. The atmosphere was one of pure magic and wonderment, which wasn't all that surprising seeing as she was capable of flying with a faery.

'So, it's Alice, isn't it?' he asked, spinning in the air and flying backwards so he could face her.

'Yes,' said Alice with a slightly confused smile, 'how did you know? And what should I call you, faery-man?'

'Call me Alvin,' replied Alvin.

Alice stifled a giggle. 'Alvin?' she repeated, looking at him with amusement. 'Not like Oberon of the Ancient Forests or something more... Y'know, faery-like?'

'Nope, Alvin. Friend of the Elves,' he said. 'It's a very faery name!'

She wasn't sure what she had been expecting from a faery. She hadn't been expecting to meet a faery in the first place, let alone exchanging pleasantries with one while flying through the treetops. Ahead of them, amongst the upper most branches of the trees, she could see shapes which, at first glance, looked like large mushrooms on the trunk of the tree and out along the branches. Drawing closer, Alice could see that these were not simply mushrooms. They were linked together with wooden bridges and walkways. Along the walkways were buildings, homely wooden huts and mushroom-esque domes, just as she had imagined the fae of folklore would dwell in.

The next thing Alice noticed was that the small buildings seemed to be not quite as small as she first thought, as they grew larger and larger. As did the trees around her. It occurred to her that maybe it was not a matter of them actually growing bigger, or even drawing closer, but perhaps she was growing smaller. She didn't feel as though she was shrinking, though, so she couldn't quite tell which was more accurate.

'Home again, home again, jiggity jig,' sung Alvin as he

fluttered down onto one of the wooden platforms at the end of a branch. 'Welcome to our humble abode.'

Alice looked around herself with a sense of childlike wonder. It reminded her of the dreams she used to have as a child, and that same magical atmosphere she had felt at the Irish sacred places seemed to surround her. There were mushroom-like buildings all around her, with wooden huts and doorways built into the trunk of the tree they had landed on. Despite the strangeness of it all, she felt peculiarly at home in this faerie village.

Across the bridge from the platform they had landed on, Alvin led Alice through the village, cheerily giving her the welcome tour. She took in the sights as he pointed them out to her. Mushrooms with doors and windows towered above them like organic townhouses. The tree itself played host to even more doorways, with little windows carved into its trunk, which Alice assumed must lead to the faery equivalent of an apartment complex. Along the walkways, myriad market stalls offered all manner of fantastical wares. Baked goods, drinks served in acorn shells, jewellery and trinkets, and clothes crafted from moss, leaves and woven from fine silk-like materials, were on offer from many of the stalls and wooden shacks which lined the street. One stall, staffed by an elven lady with long, pointed ears, silken brunette hair, and vibrantly blue eyes which sparkled like a lake in springtime, had a large sign hanging above it which read "Elvi's Jeans", and seemed to sell blue legwear.

It wasn't just faeries who lived in this strange tree-top village. Pixies and gnomes, who looked suspiciously like the ornamental garden variety with pointy red hats and enormous beards, roamed the boardwalks. Some of them rode on the backs of spiders or in insect-drawn carriages, as if they were miniature eight-legged horses. Even smaller creatures, which resembled walking furry conker shells, waddled about the village, making odd burbling and honking sounds. The place was vibrant and alive with such a mix of interesting and outlandish sights, it put Alice in mind of a folklore-ish Camden Market.

Towards the far end of one of the streets, Alice could see another of the faerie buildings ahead. It was a large, squat structure with a wide overhanging roof which resembled a portobello mushroom. Alvin carried on along the path ahead of her, leading up to the base of the mushroom, and opened the circular doorway into its stem. He held the door wide and gestured for her to enter.

'You live inside a giant mushroom?' she asked, stepping over the threshold and into what she presumed to be the entrance hall. She courteously wiped her feet on a rich green mat, which felt not unlike moss.

'In a manner of speaking,' Alvin replied, following her in and closing the door behind them. He indicated towards a twig-like spiral staircase. 'This is just the foyer, our homes are up there.'

Heading upstairs to the level above, Alice found herself standing in a circular living room. Little skylights had been built into the dome-like ceiling above, allowing the golden glow of the sun to light the room. Large oak leaves lay across the floor like rugs, and rustic wooden furniture filled out the room. From sofas and armchairs to dining tables and bookcases, decorated with throw-pillows and cloths of silk-like fabrics, the place resembled something out of *Country Living* magazine. It felt cosy and homely to Alice, despite the clutter of crockery, books and acorns which seemed to cover every surface.

Two pixie-like creatures were preparing something in the kitchenette, and when they noticed Alice and Alvin's arrival they scurried over to them both, carrying a platter of pastries and drinks in little acorn cups. 'Welcome, welcome,' they said in unison, presenting Alice with their offerings. She appreciated the hospitality she had been greeted with, especially as she couldn't help but feel like she was somewhat of an outsider in their world.

'Please, take a seat and make yourself at home,' Alvin said as he took one of the cups himself, 'pardon the clutter; several of us faefolk live here, and there's not mush-room.' He chuckled heartily, and high-fived one of the pixies.

'Alvin,' the other pixie said with a wide smile, 'you're a pretty fun-gi!' She too received a high-five, and the two pixies bowed their heads respectfully before heading off to another room in the house.

Alice wondered where Sam had got to, why she found herself in this faerie realm by herself, and where he had ended up instead. He would have enjoyed the puns.

She took a seat on the sofa which – despite the fact that its frame was crafted from raw wood and had twigs sticking out of it – was surprisingly comfortable. She relaxed herself back into the soft throw-cushions, placing the drink she had been given on the coffee table, and took a bite of a pastry. The icing stuck to her fingers in the way which only the best confectionery does, and it tasted exactly like a cinnamon roll, only the sweetness of it was more natural, less refined. She washed it down with a sip of the drink, which was a refreshingly fruity tea.

Alvin took a seat next to her, crossing one leg over the other, revealing the long and pointed elven boots he was wearing. She hadn't noticed them before, largely because she had been more distracted by his wings. He drank his fruit tea as well, reclining into the soft cushions. 'So,' he said, 'what do you make of our little village?'

'It's... Weird, and wonderful, and magical,' she said, still glancing around the room. She kept noticing new and interesting things, such as large chunks of crystals of every colour and odd ornaments and trinkets on display on the shelves and side-tables. 'I've not really thought about faeries, not since I was a little girl anyway, but everything I've seen reminds me of what I used to imagine it might be like. My grandma used to tell me stories-'

'I know,' Alvin said, nodding kindly, 'atop Cnoc Meadha. She loved telling you those stories. You helped her keep the magic alive.'

Alice stared at him. 'How did you know?' She wasn't really confused, more mystified that he knew about her childhood memories of Cnoc Meadha.

'I was there,' he replied, and seeing the bemused expression on Alice's face he decided to elaborate. 'Where she took you to tell those stories were places of mystical power, where the worlds of Men and Fae are one. Cnoc Meadha, the Isle of Skye, Glastonbury, are but a few of these places. And when people tell stories of fae and myth and folklore, it sings us into your world. Her words, and your belief, sang us to you through the sacred realms; much like now, you have followed another song which has led you here.'

'Don't get me wrong; I love this place, everything I've seen, experienced, but...' Alice paused, trying to find the right words. It was the question which still played at the back of her mind, and she hadn't yet found an answer. 'Why was I brought here?'

'To remember,' Alvin said. He gazed at her with eyes which were the colour of the forest, and seemed to reflect as much wisdom. 'To remember what you had forgotten. To reconnect with that part of you which feels as though you're disconnected. To dream the dreams you have not in so long.'

'Why is it that whenever I ask a question, I feel like the answers I get only make things more vague and confusing?' Alice gave Alvin a wry smirk as she spoke, and took a sip of her fruit tea.

'Because,' Alvin replied, reciprocating the smirk, 'the answers you seek, only you can find! Doesn't mean we don't give you a nudge in the right direction, of course.'

He smiled at her with kind eyes. 'For so many years, you forgot all about this world, discounting it as a childish fantasy and not believing we, or what you felt and believed in your heart, were real. Hopefully now you can begin to remember, and reconnect, with that part of you which has been lost. And what's wrong with a little childish fantasy, anyway? Sometimes that can be more real than you would think.'

Alice thought about his words, remembering the stories she used to love as a child, the dreams of being a faery and the once unshakable belief that they were indeed real. It had been a very long time since she had thought of that mystical world – adult life has a way of making people forget about such things – and even after meeting Sam Hain and getting caught up in his world of ghosts and demons, she still had not considered that maybe faeries and elves were just as real as the monsters. In her mind, the world Sam had opened her eyes to seemed all too dark and foreboding to have room for faeries frolicking through mystical glades and dancing around stone circles.

As she thought of this now, sat inside a house built inside of a mushroom, it seemed obvious to her. Of course the sprites and elements of folklore would exist as well, just outside of the realms of everyday perception. She wondered then if every time she had misplaced her keys or found her purse somewhere she didn't remember leaving it, maybe that was the faefolk causing mischief, trying to get her attention. Alice could almost believe this to be true.

'Thank you, Alvin,' she said, 'I still don't fully understand how I got here, but being shown this world of yours has been a magical experience.' Something caught her eye then. She hadn't really noticed the windows, nor the views out of them. She had been too distracted by the reality of standing in a faery house. But as she gazed out of the window ahead of them, she could see something swirling in the distance. 'What's that?'

She stood up, carefully placing the acorn cup on the coffee table, and made her way towards the window. Peering out, she could see swathes of forest, vibrantly green and bathed in the golden light of the sun. The mushroom had a particularly nice view over the forest. It seemed to stretch all the way to the horizon, treetops for as far as the eye could see. But, just short of the line where earth met sky, she could see a vast wall. It spanned the breadth of the horizon, the parapets sticking up just above the treeline. Beyond it was darkness.

Thick black clouds swirled above the forest beyond the wall. The trees looked gnarled and dead, their branches barren and twisted, perpetually shrouded in darkness, as if in that part of the world it was forever night. Alice stared at the darkness, feeling a sense of fear and dread welling up in her heart.

'That,' Alvin spoke solemnly, joining her by the window, 'is the Nightmare Realm. Our barrier has held back the twisted monstrosities which dwell there for millennia, so that none may disturb our world. We never venture near there. It is a place of evil, and of deception. A place where a soul's worst fears and darkest feelings manifest...'

Foolish eyes should not perceive
A realm designed to deceive.

CHAPTER V

The mist swirled and billowed through the undergrowth, around the gnarled roots and thorns, like ghostly shadows dancing to an unheard song. The twisted trees grew close to one another, barren branches loomed like claws and tangled together, wrapped in sickly-pale vines. They stood tall and imposing, eerie sentinels of the forest, devoid of all colour and life. Somewhere in the distance, something called out with a feral whoop. Nature seemed to conspire to make this place as unwelcoming as possible.

It was a foreboding, nightmarish place, James thought as he tried to push his way forward through the burnt-looking bracken. A thick, off-white stick snapped, cracking and crunching beneath his feet like bone. It made him shudder. The back of his neck prickled, as if he could feel eyes on him, but there was no-one and nothing around. As far as he could tell, at least.

Pushing his way through the branches and bracken, James tentatively stepped through this forbidding forest. He tried to get some kind of bearing, wanting nothing more than to find the quickest way out of this sinister place, but the trees surrounded him for as far as he could see. Every time he turned to face another way, the forest seemed to shift and shape itself to cage him in. Staring up at the sky above, in the vain hope of seeing something beyond the trees, his gaze was met only by a thick canopy of gnarled, bone-like branches. James Mortimer was not a claustrophobic man, but in this place and in this moment, he could feel his chest tightening, his breaths shallowing, his anxiety rising.

Bloody stupid know-it-all Sam, James's thoughts cursed as he walked, *he had to think he knew better! And now I'm trapped in Christ knows what dimension because of him...*

Each step crunched and echoed all around him as he made his way through the forest as best he could. The cold mist lapped at his feet, sending uneasy shivers coursing through his veins. Thorns and bracken wrapped around and clung to his legs like claws, and he was sure a branch had just reached out to grab him. He steeled himself against the lingering sense of dread, which only seemed to grow stronger with each passing moment, and snapped off one of the branches which blocked his path.

This was not, James decided, a good place to come for a walk.

Other than the sound of his footsteps and the rasping of his own breath, the forest was completely and entirely silent. He paused, his ears straining for even the slightest of sounds, but he was met only with oppressive silence. Shapes of oily shadows crept in closer, slinking beneath the tangled thorns before weaving up and around the pale dead trunks of the trees. Darkness closed in around him, and James reached for his phone to use as a light to guide the way. Thumbing through the icons, he tapped the torch, casting a small cone of white light ahead of him. The light cut through the suffocating blackness, but it only served to cast more eerie, unnatural shadows.

Somewhere, in the darkness ahead of him, two slit-like shapes seemed to reflect the light from his torch.

The whooping sound came echoing through the trees again, sounding closer than before. He spun around, and was convinced he saw a shape darting among the tangled branches. Now it wasn't just the sound of his own breath he could hear, but the pounding of his heart.

'I'm not afraid,' he said into the darkness, and was disappointed to find that his voice wavered as he spoke, 'you're not scaring me.'

His words were met with silence.

'Show yourself,' he said, attempting to sound more commanding. Nothing happened. The silence hung in the air, but nothing came. 'What is this place? How do I get out of here?' He knew it was futile to ask, but he felt so hopeless he couldn't think of what else to do.

Behind him, something crunched. The sound of twigs snapping beneath feet. The first sound he had heard, other than the strange whooping noise, which he knew had not come from him. He wheeled around, spinning on his heels, almost stumbling into a nest of dead nettles. The light from his torch illuminated the space in front of him and the trees seemed to have parted, as if to frame the sight which stood before him.

In the middle of the impenetrable inky blackness which lay before him, there was a figure. A figure of a woman. Her eyes were black as the shadows themselves, her hair was lank and unkempt, and her complexion as white as bone. She remained still, staring at him silently, like a ghostly apparition hovering in the darkness.

'Lorna?' James breathed, his voice pitched incredulously.

'What's up, bro-bro?' Lorna replied. In spite of her ghostly, almost wraith-like, appearance, she sounded as bright and lively as she always had been.

'What are you- How ar- What is this?' His words stumbled over each other as his thoughts clamoured and bustled to be spoken. His mind raced. Although he hardly felt at ease, James was relieved to see his sister rather than some unimaginable horror lurking in the shadows. Relieved, but confused.

Lorna did not answer him. She simply hung there, seemingly floating in the void and surrounded by darkness, and smiled sweetly at him. He mustered a half-hearted smile back at her, his brain still playing catch-up with the reality he was presented with. Thoughts raced through his head at such a speed he could barely contemplate one before another crossed his mind. *What is this place? Why is Lorna here? Is this real? Am I dreaming? Am I in a nightmare?* His mind eventually settled on one very important question; a question he dreaded what the answer may be.

'Am I dead?' His voice was twinged with fear, and he could feel his throat closing up as he tried to speak those words. His breaths felt heavy and laboured, and his heart pounded at a sickening rate deep within his chest. His arms went numb.

The ghostly figure of Lorna fixed him with a long, stone-faced stare, before she broke into a grin as she giggled a high pitched, girlish giggle. 'No, silly,' she said, 'you're not dead.' Almost as suddenly as she had broken into a giggle, Lorna's face snapped back to a stony, stoic expression, and her voice became monotone and serious. 'Although you might be if you stay here any longer. Come on, follow me.' The apparition of Lorna turned and slowly drifted away, deeper into the shadows.

'Wait!' James shouted after her, but she did not wait. He lurched forward as he rushed to keep up with her, stumbling through the dense undergrowth and crashing through branches. Again the forest seemed to try and claw at him, tree limbs reaching like gnarled fingers, but James continued to charge onward regardless.

No matter how fast he ran, the ghostly form of his sister always seemed to be far ahead of him. His legs carried him forward, charging through the forest almost unhindered, bounding over tangled thorns and between the twisted trees. The light from his torch bobbed and jumped unhelpfully in front of him, until eventually the torchlight no longer illuminated the dense growth of pale trees; instead, it illuminated nothing. The light simply dissipated into the blackness. The ground seemed clearer, nowhere near as overgrown as the rest of the forest, and the trees seemed to part and give way to a clearing.

The sky hung low, heavy clouds looming over the clearing. Around him, James could make out the shapes of trees surrounding the area, but with more open space and the sight of the sky above, he was not feeling quite as claustrophobic any more. Not that that made being in this place any better. The air felt thick with misery and hatred.

'Lorna!' he called out. She had disappeared, seemingly dissolving into nothingness just before he had reached the clearing. He spun around, desperately searching for any sign of her. 'Lorna!'

James's calls were met by the same eerie whooping sound he had heard before. It echoed through the glade, whistling among the trees. It sounded hollow, empty, not unlike the sound of blowing across the lip of an empty glass bottle. The noise rose in pitch, and a shudder ran down James's spine. Slit-like eyes seemed to glow in the darkness between the trees. He froze.

As it happens, freezing in place was probably the last thing he should have done. Accompanied by another – much closer – howling whoop, James felt something crash into his back, knocking him to the floor. His lungs ached as he struggled to his feet, winded from the impact. Something hot and wet began to radiate out from between his shoulders. A searing, stinging sensation caused him to wince in agony.

A black shape scurried in the periphery of his vision; something tall and lanky, with long, spindly limbs. James whirled around to try and see what it was, almost losing his balance again, but the thing always seemed to be just outside of his vision. He lurched forward, attempting to break into a pained run, away from whatever it was that had attacked him. Without Lorna in sight, James didn't know where to turn, and simply made a dash for the trees ahead of him.

Another unnatural whoop echoed throughout the clearing, but James didn't stop to see what unearthly creature was making such a haunting sound. His primary thought – his only thought – was escape. Where to, he wasn't sure, but anywhere other than near those things. The trees ahead of him twisted and warped as he drew closer, their branches separating to open a pathway, and in the darkness he could see a natural tunnel forming. For such a forbidding looking place, James was surprised the trees were ready to accommodate him. It was suspicious to say the least, but as he saw it, he wasn't presented with many other options. He continued his staggered run into the forest.

The treeline sealed itself behind him, the branches creaking as they wove themselves together and interlocked, forming a solid wall. Something was scratching behind the wall of branches, snarling in frustration. James did not stop running for some time, until exhaustion overcame his body and he slumped to the floor, fighting to catch his breath. Now his legs were no longer running, it was his mind's turn to begin racing. Everything had happened so quickly. So weirdly. He hadn't had time to make sense of it all, and even now, kneeling on the dry and barren earth, he still wasn't sure he could make sense of any of it.

He glanced around through bleary eyes, his vision blurred and blotched, struggling to see farther than a few feet in the pitch black forest. He reached for his phone again, using it to try and illuminate his surroundings. The bone-white trees arched up and over him, and he felt like he was staring out from inside a ribcage. Although the branches weaved together tightly, there were gaps between them, through which James could see a swirling black void above him. This was no normal night sky, and this, he concluded, was no normal world.

Ahead of him, through the thick black of this world which his torch could not quite penetrate, James could see another shape. It seemed distant at first, but it drew closer and closer, slowly but surely making its way towards him. James scrambled to his feet, his body aching and lungs still tight from trying to catch his breath, but he certainly was not going to let whatever it was finish him off without a fight. Or, at the very least, without a flight. The pain in his back from where the thing had struck him burned fiercely.

The shape came closer still, and eventually James was able to see what it was. He breathed an audible sigh of relief, which rattled up from the depths of his lungs and out into the night air. The ghostly pale form of Lorna Mortimer came into view. She stared at him from within darkened sockets, looking to him with pleading eyes which glistened with tears. As if operating under a will other than her own, Lorna lifted her hand to James.

'Help me,' she spoke, her voice quiet and shaking, 'please. Help me.'

James slowly stepped forward, tentatively but almost hypnotically approaching the apparition. He knew everything was weird, everything was off, and everything was – quite frankly – fucked in this world he found himself in. But if his sister needed him, he could not for a second imagine not doing anything and everything he could to help her. He stretched his arm out to her, extending his hand for her to take it.

'It's okay,' he whispered, 'it's okay, sis. I'm here. Don't worry. We'll get through this together.' Something stung in his heart; he wished he had said those words to her years ago, when he still had the chance. 'Just take my hand, Lorna.'

Lorna's hand twitched as she reached forward to grasp his. A pained smile crept up her lips as she stood there, the tips of her fingers gently brushing against James's. 'Pleas-'

A howl and whoop interrupted her, and in a whirlwind motion two black shapes lunged from either side of the tree-tunnel. They were tall, almost human looking things, with lanky legs and spindly arms, their bodies thin and stretched. Their heads were featureless aside from their narrow, glowing red eyes, but when they opened their mouths they revealed rows of impossibly large, serrated teeth. Long, predatory claws clasped at Lorna, ripping the flesh from her bone and tearing her apart in a vicious flurry. She shrieked in agony, a blood-curdling wail which seemed to echo through the trees, as the monsters tore her apart.

The apparition of his sister evaporated before James's eyes, almost mercifully, so he did not have to bear watching as these things savagely tore her to pieces for much longer. Without a moment's thought or hesitation, he wildly flung himself forward in a pained and vengeful rage, swinging his fists at the creatures. Flesh did not meet flesh. Instead, James's fist passed through one of the creatures as if he was punching smoke. The two incorporeal monstrosities snarled, and almost as quickly as they had arrived, they disappeared back in amongst the trees.

To his surprise, James did not scream or shout in agonised frustration, or in sadness or in loss. He felt far beyond that, as if this wicked forest had thrust its dead, icy claws through his chest and ripped out his soul. Collapsing to his knees again, he slumped down on the cold, hard ground where but a few moments ago Lorna had been standing, and he wept. Hot tears stung his eyes and burned his cheeks as he silently sobbed.

'It's still not too late, James Mortimer,' came a voice James felt he should recognise, echoing throughout the trees, 'there's still time. There is still a chance you could save your sister. We can help you.'

Chapter VI

'You know you can't change what happened, right bunny?' Lorna gazed up at Sam, her blue eyes soft and loving. They walked hand-in-hand across the grass of Hyde Park in the light of the evening sun, Lorna's summer dress flowing casually in the light breeze, while Sam pretended he wasn't too warm still wearing his jacket. They stood on the shore of the Serpentine lake, staring across the sparkling blue waters which mingled with the reflection of the orange sunset.

'I know,' Sam replied, 'it doesn't mean I don't wish things could have been... different.'

'You always did the best you could, and I could never have asked for more.' Wrapping both of her arms around Sam like a sloth clinging to a tree, Lorna held onto him tightly. 'Even if you could travel back in time, I don't know if there was anything you could have done better. I'm sorry you had to go through... Well, everything it must have put you through.'

'Don't discount time travel just yet,' Sam said, pulling Lorna even closer to him in an embrace, 'I could keep trying and trying until I get it right!' Judging by Sam's tone of voice alone, anyone would assume he was joking, but Lorna knew there was more truth to it than Sam would like to let on. He kicked a stone, launching it from the lakeside path and into the water, skipping across the surface twice before disappearing. The water rippled with each skip, sending concentric circles out across the lake.

'Don't be silly,' Lorna playfully slapped Sam's chest, 'you know the Universe gets stroppy when you try to influence the natural order of things.'

'I know that too.'

He stood staring out at the lake in solemn silence for a while. Time seemed to stand still in that moment, the sensation of Lorna's arms wrapped around him, her body held against his, the intoxicating scent of her perfume mixed with the summer evening air. They watched the sun as it hung low above the horizon, silhouetting the city's towering buildings against an orange sky. Sam wrapped his arm around Lorna's waist, holding her tighter than was necessary, and delicately kissed the top of her head. 'I've missed this,' he eventually breathed, speaking more to himself than anyone else.

Lorna looked up at him, her eyes glistening. 'I'm always here, Sam. I might not be alive in the traditional sense any more, but I haven't stopped existing. It's just easier for you to be with me in this place.'

'What is "this place"?' Sam asked. He believed he already knew the answer to that question, but he needed to hear it from her.

'You know exactly where you are, you silly goose!' Lorna said. 'You're in a place beyond. That weird statue thingamy-doo-dah opened a doorway to places where things outside of the real are real. In a sense. I don't know quite what to call it. The spirit realm, the Imaginarium, the Mindscape, Dreamy-land, whatever...'

'Like the Void?' Sam added.

'No. Well, sort of, that's kind of like the space between spaces. I don't ever go near that place. It's kind of spooky there, like a shadow of the Imaginarium. Cold and dark and empty. And too many weird things dwell there; I'd rather stay as far away from them as possible. This bit, though, this is nice. And it's lovely you're here with me too.' Stretching out her arm, Lorna slowly waved her hand across the sky in front of them, painting a vibrant rainbow which arched high above the city's skyline. A park bench materialised behind them and, taking Sam's hand, she guided him back to sit there. She rested her head on his chest and sighed contentedly. 'If only you'd come here more often.'

Stroking her hair as they sat beneath the rainbow Lorna had painted, in the glow of the perfect sunset, Sam wished he never had to leave this place. This was different from the breakfast he had shared with her; this was something new, a moment which was not a memory or a dream. But nor was it real, and that played on Sam's mind too much for his liking. 'I can't stay here forever, though,' he eventually said.

'I know,' she said, lightly tracing her fingers across his chest. 'But you can always come back here any time, in the quiet stillness of your mind.' She leaned up to him, and planted a delicate kiss on his lips. Sam closed his eyes, enjoying the sensation of her lips on his, a feeling he had not felt in years. 'The Imaginarium's a funny ol' place. On the one hand, it exists; on the other, it doesn't. It's somewhere in between, really. It's like, everything's there and it is as it is, but it's also what you make of it. It's a place that partly exists in your mind, and partly exists in and of itself. We're in an extension of your own imagination, bunny, and I'm so happy you invited me into it.'

'You're not just a manifestation of my imagination, though, are you?'

'No,' she replied, 'I'm not.'

'You exist independently of my thoughts and memories... You are actually...'

'I am actually me, yes,' Lorna giggled. 'Don't worry, you're no madder than you were before, and I'm not just some kind of fever dream. Like I said, I might not be alive any more, but that doesn't mean I stopped existing.'

Sam held her tighter then. His eyes suddenly felt a lot more watery than usual. He could feel his cheeks beginning to get hotter, and his nose seemed to get bunged up. He sniffed, and blinked his eyes rapidly. 'Bloody hell,' he muttered, as – despite his best efforts to suppress it – he felt a single, burning tear run down his face.

'You daft thing,' she said, delicately brushing the tear from his cheek, and squeezing him tightly. 'Don't be sad!'

'I'm not,' he said, shaking his head, 'well, I am. And happy, too. I don't know. I miss you. I miss being with you; but I am with you. Not really, but sort of, and... Bollocks, emotions are fiddly things, aren't they?'

'I know,' she said sympathetically, resting her head on his chest again. 'Emotions were never really your strong suit, my love. You could fight off a legion of demons, but you could never face your own.'

They stayed there on the bench by the lake, holding each other in a tight embrace, neither one wanting to let go of the other. The park was perfectly peaceful that evening, still and quiet without another person in sight. Which, of course, there wouldn't be; this moment was mostly Sam's creation, a place for he and Lorna to be together, and he would not have wanted anyone there to disturb them, illusionary or otherwise. Time was at a standstill, allowing them both to enjoy the eternal and constant-now. Sam had made sure of that.

However, one thing he had not made sure of, and one thing he had not anticipated in the slightest, was that the trees had started to turn brown. It took him a while to notice, too wrapped up in the moment with Lorna, but as the trees seemed to wither away from his reality, the sky blackened. The sunset and rainbow dissolved into thick, swirling storm clouds, and the lake turned from a pleasant blue to a murky grey.

'Bunny?' Lorna spoke nervously, glancing up at the stormy skies and nudging Sam urgently. 'This isn't right.'

Sam snapped out of his reverie, the moment he had wished could last forever rapidly falling away before his eyes. The trees were barren and dead, the once green leaves now brown and curled on the floor. The bark turned white and the trunks cracked and hollowed. The grass swiftly died out, sweeping across the park as if some plague had befallen the plant life, leaving the ground looking dead and desolate. The storm continued to swirl overhead, Sam's perfect dream rapidly descending into a nightmare.

'No,' he said, 'no, this is not right in the slightest.' He stood up from the bench and looked around at the barren wasteland which had suddenly superseded his world. He focussed his mind, reaching his hands up to the sky and motioning as if to part the blackened clouds. He struggled to break the illusion, only a slither of the once beautiful sunset could be glimpsed through the small hole he had created in the storm, but it was quickly swallowed up by the nightmare. He fought against the darkness which had closed in on them, trying to push back the clouds and restore life to the trees, but his efforts were futile. Somewhere in the distance, he thought he heard something bellow a whooping howl.

Lorna stood by his side, holding onto his hand so tightly he thought she might actually bruise his knuckles, and he gripped her hand back with equal intensity. She too struggled against the seemingly unstoppable nightmare, but to no avail. Try as they might, the storm simply grew stronger and stronger.

'I'm scared,' she whimpered, 'this shouldn't be happening.'

Instinctively, Sam wrapped his arms around Lorna and pulled her into his protective embrace as close as possible, attempting to shield her from whatever may come next. She clung onto him as if she feared being swept away by the gale-force winds. 'I know, sweetheart,' he said with a tone he hoped sounded like a reassuring whisper, 'whatever this is, I won't let it get to you.'

The little colour which remained in the world faded away, the vision before them turning monochrome. Everything began to blur and swirl around them, melting away like a painting which had had water spilled on it. What had once been Hyde Park, and then a desolate Hyde Park, now was distorted beyond recognition, merely an oily shadow of what it had been before. In amongst the swirling chaos, a tear appeared in the fabric of their reality; a portal forcibly breaking its way into their dream. Through it, they could see James stepping forward, emerging from the portal and standing alongside them.

'Lorna?!' James exclaimed in disbelief, before he noticed the maddening chaos which whipped around them like a tempest. No sooner had he felt the hope of seeing his sister again was it taken away from him once more. With an anguished howl, Lorna was ripped away from Sam's arms and towards the portal, swept away by the nightmare's current.

CHAPTER VII

The portal swirled in front of them, the intangible nothingness spiralling around and around at an ever increasing speed. It pulled at them, like the inescapable and unrelenting force of a black hole. Sam and James attempted to hold their ground, digging their feet into the earth and pushing themselves away from the vortex. Neither of them could look away from it, watching helplessly as Lorna was drawn closer and closer towards the event horizon.

'You lost her once before, can either of you bear to lose her again?' a voice echoed in their minds, taunting yet somehow tantalising, as if it were trying to tempt them. 'Does it remind you of the moment you failed to save her? The moment neither of you can forgive yourselves for your own inaction.'

'Sam!' Lorna screamed in terror. 'James!' Her arms reached out, her fingers desperately clawing the air. 'You've got to do something!'

James continued to try and pull himself away from the inexorable draw of the portal, fighting against the force of a vacuum which had drained the world from around them. He held his arm up to his face, attempting to shield himself from the swirling chaos. 'No. No, no, no,' he uttered beneath his breath, 'this can't be happening. This is all an illusion!'

'Illusion or no,' spoke the voice, 'what would you be willing to do to save your sister?'

'We won't play your sick games!' Sam railed at the portal. He too struggled against the singularity, feeling its pull drawing him closer, as he reached his hand out to Lorna. She grasped at the empty nothingness, trying to pull herself back to him, but to no avail.

'So stoic, so... Stubborn,' the voice taunted from the ether. 'Why do you resist?'

Wide-eyed with terror, Lorna lurched backwards towards the portal, yelping as the constant and unstoppable pull of the Void dragged her in. The vision of sheer horror etched upon her face was a sight Sam could not bear to see. He braced himself against the whirling currents of the vortex, desperately trying to reach her.

'If you can't escape this illusion, if you can't turn away, what then?' The voice echoed around them. 'You wanted your time with this girl to last an eternity, so here. Have an eternity.'

With another shriek, Lorna was pulled off of her feet and into the air, falling backwards into the gaping maw of the portal. It twisted and swirled violently as she hurtled towards it, and she was caught, trapped on the brink of the Void, in a never-ending fall into oblivion. She screamed an agonising scream which seemed to echo for eternity. Sam watched in horror as Lorna clung on to the last vestige of the world beyond the cusp of the Void, tears streaming down her face and nothing but terror reflected in her eyes as she screamed in her final moments. 'Bunny! *Please!*'

Lorna's final terrified plea struck Sam like a spear through the heart. He felt himself shatter into a million pieces as she called out to him, reached out to him, in her final yet never-ending moment. He felt the fear and pain and loss he had felt the first time he had lost her. He felt the failure and the remorse, the desperation of wishing he could have done more to save her. More than anything, he felt the determination to not lose her again. 'Oh bollocks to it,' he declared, and without warning he charged and flung himself at the portal, towards Lorna.

He felt his heart break in two for her, seeing her petrified face staring at him from the portal, tears streaking her face and unimaginable horror in her eyes. And he felt his heart become whole again as he caught her in his arms, hovering on the brink of the event horizon. Without a moment's thought, Sam instinctively spun around, pulling Lorna from out of the vortex's grip and putting himself between her and the portal. Before he had had time to realise what was happening, Sam was tumbling into the howling abyss of the Void.

It was impossible to tell precisely what had happened. One moment, Sam had lunged at the portal, pulling Lorna from its clutches and throwing himself in her place. The next, he found himself adrift in what he could only describe as a nightmarish nexus.

Nebulous swirling colours whirled like storm clouds through the otherwise pitch-black space of the Void, bursts of lightning crackling between nebula. The shapes and colours shifted in the darkness, fractal patterns warping as if looking through a kaleidoscope. Grotesque, growth-like planetoids – which resembled gargantuan mould spores – hung unnaturally in space, some drifting lazily through the nebula, while others were linked together by unearthly, organic bridges. They glistened, as if coated in a layer of black, viscous fluid. An ever-present and unending sound of thunder rumbled in the distance.

Sam felt a twisting, nauseating sensation churn in the pit of his stomach. It was as if everything in this dimension was an affront to his being, assaulting each and every one of his senses. It was a place no mortal being should ever be. There was no up, no down, no ground beneath him, and no sense of anything he could begin to make sense of. He floated, lost and thoroughly directionless, in the gravity-less Void.

From within the deep rumbling of thunder, Sam heard something. It sounded like a low and ominous chuckle, masked beneath the dimension's persistent roar, but as Sam tried to focus on it, it grew into a roaring laugh. The

voice which had previously echoed in his mind now shook the space around him as it cackled.

'You are in our domain, Sam Hain,' the voice intoned, and out of the corner of his eye Sam thought he could see something moving. A congeries of tentacles writhing within the clouds of the gaseous nebula. 'The Void. The space between spaces. The shadow of the Imaginarium. We hold dominion over this cosmic chaos, where rules and natural laws cease to exist, and meaning has no meaning. Here, you are nothing but a nuisance to be disposed of.'

'Why the change of heart?' Sam bellowed into the Void. 'I thought you were putting me through this to try and get answers from me. What happened to the stable vortex idea?'

Attempting to manoeuvrer around in space, Sam felt as if he was swimming through a cosmic sea. He reoriented himself, slowly spinning around in zero-gravity, until eventually he could properly face what he thought he had seen in the nebula. In the clouds, he could make out the shape of an immense black mass, shifting and twisting beneath the nebula, like watching the shadow of a school of fish beneath the ocean's waves. He propelled himself forward, swimming closer to the cloud for a better look, to make sense of the senseless world he found himself in. As he drew closer, he could see that it was not just a single being; the shadowy mass seemed to be formed of many unearthly creatures, slithering and writhing in unison.

'You have proven that you will refuse to make yourself useful. We have other means to achieve our ends,' the voice replied plainly. 'Now you are but a mere inconvenience which needs to be removed.'

Sam watched the ever shifting forms swimming through the nebula, regarding them with a mix of both intrigue and horror, when suddenly one of them broke from the school. He could see its form more clearly now, as it moved through the Void as a squid with far too many tentacles would swim through the sea. However, Sam found himself getting a much closer look at the monstrosity than he would have liked, as the squid-like creature swam straight for him at an alarming speed. Without a moment to think, Sam reached for his TechnoWand and aimed it at the creature, firing a stream of energy in its direction. The stream seemed to burn with a violet flame, crackling against the grotesque creature with a shower of sparks. Its tentacles retracted as if cringing in pain, and a piercing screech echoed from its multitude of mouths.

As Sam began to utter an incantation for protective magick, arcing the wand around himself in a large circle, the squid-like being made another dive for him. This time, it succeeded. Its many sickly tentacles flailed violently, encasing Sam within its grip and pulling him in towards its bulbous body. A mess of mouths, lined with knife-like teeth, gnashed and oozed in Sam's face. He struggled against it, kicking out and trying to punch his attacker, but with very little success. The creature's tentacles constricted him, squeezing tighter and tighter.

Shadow of the Imaginarium, Sam thought as he gasped for breath, the tentacles restricting his lungs from breathing in. His chest was tight, and he could feel himself becoming light-headed. Dread sat heavily in his stomach like a boulder. His mind, however, was scrambling for ideas.

Violently jerking and twisting in a bid to break free, Sam was able to completely release one of his arms from the tentacled-grip. With his wand in hand, he projected a powerful burst of magick at the squid-like monster. The energy seared through the creature's limbs, severing a number of the tentacles, and sending a bolt of burning energy directly into the being's central mouth. It shrieked again, as chunks of cosmic calamari were blown out into the Void.

The tentacles loosened their grip of Sam, gradually falling away as he wriggled himself to freedom.

'You're brighter than you seem,' the voice spoke, 'it appears we underestimated you.' It was hard for him to tell, as the voice spoke in such a monotone manner, but Sam thought it sounded almost impressed, and more than a little frustrated. The body of the squid-like entity began to reconstitute itself, its wounds healing over, severed limbs reattaching themselves.

'You said it yourself,' Sam replied, distancing himself from the creature as it reassembled itself, but confident and more than a little bit pleased with the plan he had devised, 'this is the shadow of the Imaginarium. There are no rules here. So I can make my own.' He began to trace a tall rectangular shape in the air in front of him, its outline ablaze in a light blue flame. Something resembling a wooden door began to form between the flames.

'No!' the voice boomed. The squid's tentacles waved wildly as they reattached to the body. 'You can not do this!'

'Just watch me,' Sam said with a smirk, and he stepped through the perfectly normal doorway which hovered in the perfectly abnormal Void.

The kettle whined a high-pitched whistle, billowing steam from its spout. Sam Hain lifted the kettle off of the stove, pouring the boiling water into his mug with a satisfyingly gentle splashing. The liquid turned a brownish-black as it made contact with the coffee granules. Reaching for the two slices of bread which had just popped out of the toaster, he slathered them in peanut butter and sat down at the kitchen table. He sipped the coffee, releasing the satisfied "ah" sound one traditionally makes when first sipping a decent cup of coffee. The toast crunched perfectly as he took a bite. This morning, he thought to himself, was almost perfect. It was missing only one thing...

Lorna emerged from the bedroom, her mousey-blonde hair draping down her shoulders in untamed waves. She was still wearing her nightshirt – or rather, one of Sam's old shirts – which came down to just above her knees, and a pair of inexplicably pink bunny rabbit slippers flopped about on her feet as she walked over to him. She stood behind him, leaning over and hanging her arms loosely around his neck, before planting a delicate kiss on his cheek. Sam smiled to himself. Now this morning was perfect.

'Morning, bunny,' Lorna said softly, her voice croaking with that just-woken-up croak.

'What do you think you're doing?' the voice echoed, emanating from the toaster.

'Hello, you,' he replied. He took one of her hands in his, stroking her slender fingers, and tenderly kissed the back of her hand. 'How're you this morning?'

'You know there is nothing you can do. You are in my domain!' the toaster bellowed.

'Couldn't be better, waking up to you,' she said. As she began to pull away, she ran a hand through his hair and ruffled it lovingly, and made her way across to the kitchen counter. The early morning light poured in through the window, bright and crisp, illuminating her perfectly in Sam's eyes. 'What's for breakfast?'

Sam gestured to the place next to him on the table, where a full English Breakfast fry-up now sat waiting, freshly served and steaming hot. A generous puddle of brown sauce sat on the side of the plate. Lorna grinned broadly, and half-skipped back to the table, sitting herself down on the seat next to Sam before eagerly picking up her knife and fork. Sam placed his hand lovingly on her knee.

'This isn't how this moment occurred!' The voice seemed furious now, shouting from the toaster.

'You're quite right,' Sam said, 'I didn't have peanut butter on my toast that day. But hey: my mind, my rules.'

'You are in my domain!'

'Possibly. Possibly not. That's the beauty of conceptual dimensions; whatever you will to be will be.' He smiled, turning to Lorna, who gave him a knowing wink as she crammed a sizeable forkful of scrambled egg and a chunk of hash brown into her mouth.

'You can not possibly believe this to be a victory,' the toaster spat, sending a plume a breadcrumbs into the air.

'Not in a word, no,' Sam said, and he draped his arm around Lorna's shoulder. 'You created the illusion for me, playing on my thoughts and feelings by trying to rip her away from me again, but you ignored one very simple thing. In reality, I was powerless to prevent what happened then. Moments ago, I thought I was powerless to stop it happening again. But in the Imaginarium, if you know it all to be in the mind, what stops you from changing your mind? You tried to drag us out of my mindscape and into yours; I thought I'd return the favour. I changed my mind about being sucked into the Void, and decided I'd rather have breakfast with my girlfriend. So here we are!'

'Impossible!' the voice bellowed. Two slices of very burnt toast leapt out of the toaster in defiance.

'Oh really? Because last I checked, it's also impossible for a toaster to have an opinion.'

'Y'know, Sam,' Lorna said as calmly as if she was discussing the weather forecast, 'I don't remember us ever having a possessed toaster.'

'You know, I think you're right,' Sam said, casually standing up from his breakfast and running his fingers through Lorna's hair, as he started to make his way towards the toaster. A slice of blackened bread flung itself at him, but other than leaving a few charred crumbs on his jacket it seemed to have little effect. He unplugged the toaster, which made a disgruntled growling sound and emitted a plume of thick black smoke. Picking it up cautiously and, holding it at arm's length, he carried it to the front door.

The door swung open, revealing the swirling chaos of the Void beyond it. Coral-like structures orbited in the deep; nebulae drifted like clouds through the inky black, shifting shapes and changing colours; countless eyes seemed to peer out from the intangible depths; eager, hungry and predatory.

'Time to send you back to whatever twisted corner of the Imaginarium you came from,' Sam addressed the toaster. He dropped it, swinging his right foot in a wide arc and kicking the kitchen appliance into the Void. The dimensional doorway rippled. The toaster vanished. The voice was silenced. Sam dusted his hands together with the satisfaction of a job well-done, slammed the door shut on the howling abyss of the Void, and returned to finish his illusionary breakfast.

'That,' Lorna said, with a broad and approving grin on her face, 'was awesome.'

Sam sipped his coffee with an exaggeratedly nonchalant sip. 'That was nothing,' he said, waving his hand as if brushing off the remark with faux-humility, 'you missed the part when I punched a twelve-foot long space squid while floating in the cosmic chaos of the Void.'

'Well get you, mister interdimensional hero!' She giggled, taking his hand in hers and weaving her fingers between his. 'But really, though, that was awesome. Who'd've thought you could trap the essence of a transdimensional terror in a toaster?'

The door to the flat opened again, and for a brief moment Sam was convinced the squid-like creature was about to emerge. He turned to face the open door, and on the other side of it he could see the Southbank. The setting sun cast an orange glow over the dwindling crowd of people milling about the riverside.

'Well,' he said, gazing out into reality, 'I guess that means its time to go back.' He stood, pulling Lorna up with him, and he kissed her, passionately. He didn't want to leave, but unlike the first time through this memory, he knew it was time. 'I'll see you tonight, beautiful,' Sam said, his lips lingering on hers.

'You know this isn't really real, bunny,' Lorna spoke sadly, 'I've been gone a while. No playing around in the mindscape can change that.'

'I know,' he said, holding her head close to his chest as he stood in the doorway between the kitchen and reality, 'but still... I'll see you tonight.'

'In your dreams,' she replied, playfully slapping his arm.

'Precisely,' Sam said. He held her tight, nuzzling his nose into her hair, and stepped backwards through the open doorway.

CHAPTER VIII

There was a flash of brilliant white light and the sound of applause echoed in the distance. Sam, Alice and James found themselves on the Southbank once again. Each of them felt as if their heads were spinning, their vision blurred and their hearing made everything sound as if they were underwater. A small group of people had gathered by the side of them, staring at the three with awed and confused expressions while they applauded.

As their vision began to clear and they started to get their bearings in reality once more, they turned to face the crowd with an equally perplexed expression. Sam took a low and slightly wobbly bow, exclaiming a show-manly 'thank you! thank you!' to their unexpected spectators. One by one, the audience began to filter away from the trio, mumbling things about smoke, mirrors and optical illusions.

'Dudes, wicked show!' one man remarked as he passed the three of them. 'Amazing those little lights could project that display. It was like watching a star-gate or some shit. But how could you make yourselves disappear and reappear like that?'

Sam stared at the man as his mind played catch-up with the real world. Truth, he thought, was far stranger than fiction, and he tapped his nose with a sly glint in his eye. 'A magician never reveals his secrets,' he said, and the man winked, shook his hand, and continued on his way along the Southbank's walkway. The three of them were left alone, standing around the Oracle.

Like a puppet with his strings cut, Sam's body drooped, his shoulders slouching and back arching forward, as he breathed a long groaning sigh. 'Well that was... Weird, and really quite horrible,' he said. His body ached in ways he could not begin to describe, and his face was drawn and haggard. He would have likened it to a hangover, only with more existential anguish.

'You can say that again,' James said. He too bore the face of a man with emotional trauma, and was looking decidedly more pale than usual. His eyes were bloodshot, and had sunken back in sockets framed by darkened circles and heavy bags. When he blinked, he was sure his eyelids made a scratching sound. He looked as if he had not slept for days. 'That was like... Like an unending nightmare you can't wake up from.'

'What the hell did you two go through?' Alice said, sounding surprised and much more jovial than either of them. 'I had a lovely time in that vision-y thing.' Her hair seemed to shine a radiant gold, her eyes sparkling and her cheeks flushed with a warm and healthy shade of rosy pink. A contented smile rested comfortably on her lips.

Sam stared at the concrete beneath his feet for a moment. 'Unbearably nightmarish visions and fighting off transdimensional terrors, mostly,' he said. 'I think that was a category five dream demon.'

'Oh, were you in a kind of twisted dead forest by any chance?'

Sam shook his head. He wished he could put some of the things he had seen into words, but he struggled enough to make sense of his own perception of them, let alone try to relay it to someone else.

James, however, gave Alice a quizzical look. 'Yes,' he said, 'how did you know?'

'Faeries told me,' Alice replied matter-of-factly, shrugging her shoulders. She then made a face which was caught somewhere between confusion and a little bit of worry. She couldn't quite place her finger on it, but something felt odd, and she glanced over her shoulder. 'Hey, where are my wings?'

Sam and James exchanged questioning glances at each other, before casting their gaze over to the bronze statue which had caused all of this nightmarish weirdness. The Oracle stood on its pedestal, looking just as innocuous and inanimate as it had done when they first arrived. It certainly did not look like it was prone to opening gateways in the mind, transporting people to other worlds, or causing a multi-dimensional leak on the Southbank.

'What are the readings like now?' Sam asked, nodding James in the direction of the laptop. All of the equipment was still set up around the Oracle exactly as they had left it, and when James knelt down in front of his computer he noticed the time on the clock.

'Either the computer's frozen, or we've only been gone for five minutes...' James mused aloud. He knew that his time trapped in the nightmare forest had certainly been longer than five minutes; it felt like the horrors had gone on for much closer to eternity.

'Nope,' Sam said, leaning over James and waggling his finger over the mousepad, causing the cursor to dart erratically around the screen, 'not frozen.' He stood tall, straightening the lapels of his jacket with an air of knowledge and wisdom. 'Time flows differently in parallel dimensions. What may have felt like hours or days for us was mere minutes in our reality.' He didn't know for sure, and it was only a theory, but it sounded right to him. 'Graph's still squiggly though.'

'I noticed,' James replied, eyeing the screen curiously. 'Just don't go trying to meddle with it before I've analysed the readings. Please. We're not getting sucked back into that again.' He looked at the graph, charting the myriad lines which spiralled around and around each other chaotically, and tapped furiously at the keyboard. The graph split into several mini graphs, isolating the dominant patterns. Although the lines still resembled a frantic scribble, there was at least some kind of discernible pattern to the chaos. The readings measured the Akashic energy predominantly flowing counter-clockwise.

Alice had stopped looking for her faery-wings, after remembering that she had not actually had wings (which weren't a part of a Halloween costume) for the vast majority of her life, and peered over James's shoulder at the display on the laptop, intrigued.

'Okay,' he announced with a conclusive tone, 'although the readings are still subjected to the principals of uncertainty, and the quantum trajectories can change from moment to moment, the dominant trend suggests the Akashic energy is more or less circulating in an anti-clockwise current. So, if we reverse the direction of the energetic output, we can invert the weirdness bubble and close down the node.'

'Wait a minute,' Alice interrupted, 'wasn't this thing built for this reason?'

James turned around to face her, raising a curious eyebrow, and Sam furrowed his brow thoughtfully.

'The inscription says humanity is capable of a perception beyond the everyday, right? And the way it's sculpted, it looks like an ancient fae portal. My grandma used to tell me that people who truly believed and were in tune with the fae could look through these things and see into the faerie kingdom. Shutting it down could be like boarding up someone else's windows, or barricading their door.'

'When did you become an expert on faery portals?' Sam asked, surprised and more than a little impressed.

Alice looked down at the time on the laptop. 'About five minutes ago, I think,' she said.

'How about this,' Sam postulated, 'we can't allow this nexus of Akashic energy to keep building up, otherwise the weirdness bubble will just continue to expand and London will be overrun by faeries, goblins, spirits, space-squids and who knows what else lies in the Imaginarium. There are some realms the other side of this Oracle I would rather not think about. Our world and countless others could start to bleed into each other. It'd be an explosion of the extraordinary, but not in a good way. Although, rather than shut it down completely, what if we neutralise it?'

He paced around in circles as he spoke, tossing his transphasic probe from one hand to the other with a satisfying clinking sound. He turned and faced the Oracle, staring down the concave hole in the statue and through the gap in the middle. He could see the setting sun's orange glow reflecting off of it, casting strange curving shapes in the light.

He continued. 'It does seem to have been built for an otherworldly purpose. The structure, the material, it's conducive for magickal means; the inscription suggests a purpose beyond the realm of normality... We can fix the irregular spike in Akasha, reversing the excess energy flow, but other than that the Oracle will remain as it always has done. It won't pose a threat any more, but it will still open doorways in the mind for any who know how to use it.'

He turned to Alice and James, holding the probe at the ready. 'Besides, the Universe gets stroppy if I try to mess with the natural order of things.'

James nodded, slowly and uncertainly at first, but the more he thought about the idea, the more he believed it would work. *After all*, he thought, *this may be the key for bringing Lorna back...*

'That sounds good to me,' Alice said, feeling a relief she did not expect to feel when talking about transdimensional portals or magic statues.

'Agreed,' James added, 'it'll take a little while for me to run the calculations, but it should be possible to lower the output, without closing it up completely.'

'Or,' Sam said, waving the TechnoWand aloft, 'I could simply seal up the cross-rip by reversing the energy flow.'

He pointed the tip of the probe towards the Oracle, and with large, winding gestures, he rotated it in a clockwise direction. In his mind's eye, Sam could see the rift; a tear in space overlaying reality, which emanated from the middle of the sculpture, leading to a nebulous other-reality beyond. Wisps of energy leaked and spiralled out from the portal in the opposite direction, but as he focussed on weaving the stray strands of energy – essentially re-stitching the fabric of reality – the wisps began to change course and follow the direction he was waving the probe. The portal began to shrink, winding back in on itself.

He muttered something beneath his breath, an incantation which seemed to speak directly to the Oracle.

> *'Seal the rift, reverse the flow,*
> *Reveal your insights to those who know.*
> *The Imaginarium opens to the wise,*
> *A sight glimpsed through the Oracle's eyes.'*

The vision of the portal continued to grow smaller and smaller, and for a moment Alice thought she could see the last of the loose strands of energy being tamed back into the Oracle, until all that remained of the statue's interdimensional doorway was a small window, held perfectly in the hole in the very heart of the sculpture. There was a fizzing noise, shortly followed by a crackling sound, and the devices James had set up around the statue's plinth sparked. Wisps of purplish smoke rose up from the devices.

James spun around to study the laptop again, rapidly tapping icons and updating the readings of the statue. The graphs shifted and changed, morphing from the lines which resembled a toddler's scribbles to a more linear-looking waveform. Balance, it appeared, had been restored.

'It worked,' James said, still staring at the readings on the display. 'There's still a channel of extra-dimensional energy running through here, but it's nowhere near as powerful or invasive. It's steady and stable.'

'Job well done then!' Sam said as he pocketed the probe with a flourish. 'The Imaginarium obeys the will of the perceivers, so resetting the Oracle's portal was only a matter of changing the rules. Now, if anyone else comes looking through the Eye of the Oracle, unless they know what it is they wish to see, it'll seem just like any other statue. Anyone who comes looking to access the Imaginarium will unlock their own doorway, and find it in their Dreamscape.'

'So that's that then? Another paranormal problem put to rights,' Alice said cheerily, 'shall we go for a celebratory drink? There's a place a little further along the Southbank that does amazing cocktails.' This was probably, Alice reflected, the first time since she had been involved in one of Sam's cases and was actually feeling okay by the end of it. More than okay; since emerging from her dream in the Oracle, she was in exuberantly high spirits.

Sam and James, on the other hand, were very much not.

'It's a nice idea,' James said sombrely, 'but I'm afraid I'm not really feeling it tonight. Another time, perhaps.' Now that the energy spike he had detected was resolved, he had no desire to stay there any longer than needed. Visions of everything he had experienced in that nightmarish landscape played on his mind, and try as he might to block it out of his thoughts, the image of his sister being torn apart by the shadows of the forest haunted him.

'I would love to,' Sam said, although his voice sounded equally as morose as James's, 'but I am... I am exhausted,' *both emotionally and physically*, he thought. Old emotional wounds, ones he thought he had managed to keep hidden even from himself, had resurfaced, and he needed time to process that. Although, he considered, despite a demon's best efforts to deceive him, to break him, he had been reunited with the love he had once lost. Lorna. Real, actual (albeit non-physical) Lorna. Even though he knew there was no way of changing what had happened all those years ago, or bringing her back into this reality, the Imaginarium had given him the chance to be with her again. And he was sure he could see her again, in the quiet of his mind.

'Actually, you know what,' he said, 'after that, I could probably use a drink.'

'Brilliant!' Alice beamed.

As they walked along the Southbank, among the dwindling crowds in the twilight of the evening, Sam decided to slow his pace. He watched as Alice continued to walk ahead – or rather, bounce ahead; there was an undeniable spring in her step – and he hung back slightly with James. 'How are you doing after... Well, you know?' he asked him, looking to his friend with a sympathetic eye.

'Can't say I really wanted to experience any of that,' James said, his eyes averting Sam's and instead staring out across the Thames. 'It's not something I think anyone can truly move on from, but I thought I was doing okay. Until I had to watch her being ripped away from me again.' He fell silent, lost in the solemnity of his thoughts, until eventually he could face Sam again. 'You?'

Sam puffed out his lips and exhaled exaggeratedly. Now it was his turn not to meet James's eye. 'Me? Yeah, fine, fine... Not sure it was something I wanted to go through either, but...' He trailed off, taking a sudden interest in looking up at the sky. 'There were some good bits, too. For a start, I got to be with her again, no matter how fleeting, and she wasn't just a memory or a product of my imagination. She was actually her, actually Lorna. She may not be living, but it doesn't mean she stopped existing.'

James nodded solemnly, but he offered very few words in reply. 'I know.' He simply managed a half-hearted smile, before turning his gaze to the sky as well. A faded, dusty purple canopy stretched across the city, flecked and dotted with the pinprick lights of distant stars.

That night, James did not sleep. He tossed and turned in his bed, staring up at the ceiling in the impenetrable blackness of the night. His back seared with a burning pain, but when he had gone to treat the wound he had sustained in the foreboding forest, there was no sign of injury. That part, at least, had been an illusion, he thought. However, other visions played over and over again in his mind. Visions of Lorna getting torn apart by the creatures, her fading from his vision, and having to watch, powerless, as she was drawn into the Void. He had no memory of what had happened after Sam threw himself in to save her. His heart ached, but worse than that, it made him angry. Angry that he had been forced to witness losing his sister again and again. Angry he was powerless to stop it. But he remembered what the voice had said, what it had promised him in the dark of the forest. He could fix it all. And neither he, or her, would ever have to go through that pain again.

Alice, on the other hand, had had a much better night. In a bar further along the Southbank, after saying their goodbyes to James, she and Sam talked and laughed over cocktails (she had a cool and refreshing mojito; Sam, rather fittingly, had opted for a Dark 'n' Stormy). At times, Sam had seemed distracted. He had not wanted to talk about whatever was on his mind, though; instead, he was more than happy to tell Alice about how he defeated a space squid dream demon by escaping the Void and intentionally misremembering a possessed toaster. The whole thing sounded terribly weird and confusing, she had said, and excitedly told him of her time with the faeries. Sam could not quite make sense of the physics of how Alice, a five-and-almost-a-half foot tall woman, could fit inside of a portobello mushroom. He appreciated the puns, though.

As she lay in bed that night, Alice felt herself literally

drifting off to sleep. At first she gently floated, like a leaf caught in a soft breeze, but soon she found herself flying. Through the lush green treetops she flew, high above the rich undergrowth below, until she could see the faerie village ahead of her. Small wooden buildings, and houses the shape of mushrooms, loomed into sight, and she could see the faefolk, merrily waving, welcoming her back.

It had gone past midnight before Sam decided to call it a day. He had returned home to his flat in Hampstead to reflect on all he had experienced; after everything he had been through, he needed to be in his own space, his own atmosphere.

His mind was awash with visions of the cold and endless Void, the infinite expanse which seemed to froth with chaotic and unnatural forces. Having had a glimpse of this eldritch dimension, feeling and seeing the reality of its unrealness first-hand, thoughts of the Void now haunted him and clawed at the back of his mind. He feared such a realm could drive a mortal man to insanity. In front of the altar in his flat, surrounded by burning candles and pyramidal crystal prisms, and shrouded in the smoke of burning copal resin, Sam had sat and meditated to still his mind. He drove away the thoughts of that forbidding dimension, banishing it from his mind, and turned his focus on to the positive realms of the Imaginarium. If there was one thing he could be sure of after this evening, it was the power of his own mind.

You can always come back here any time, in the quiet stillness of your mind, Lorna's words whispered softly in his ear, and he smiled.

As he climbed into bed, resting his head on the pillows, in the quiet stillness of the night, Sam found himself by the lakeside in Hyde Park. It was alive with the feeling of springtime; the fresh scent of the air, the bright green of leaves on the trees, and flowers coming into bloom. He sipped from the perfect cup of tea, before sitting on one of the park benches overlooking the lake. The waters glistened a sparkling shade of blue. He gazed wistfully out across the lake and reached across the back of the bench, wrapping his arm around Lorna, pulling her in for a close embrace. He felt her head rest upon his shoulder as they both gazed off into the infinite horizon.

This, he thought, was perfect.

SAM HAIN
OCCULT DETECTIVE

CONVERGENCE

Prologue

Tom Hopkins was looking very pale and more than a little bit shaken when he met with his friends that afternoon. He was a burly looking man, tall and muscular, with shaggy and unkept hair, and sporting a sleeve of tattoos. If asked, anyone would have described him as a blokey sort of bloke, so to see him visibly shaken was unusual. When he had arrived at the Crone and Maiden, looking as white as a sheet and with haunted eyes, his friends had sat him down and brought him a pint to calm his nerves, before asking what had happened.

'Well, you see,' Tom began to recount his experience, gingerly picking up his beer and taking a long, hearty gulp, 'I was on the Central Line on me way 'ere... It was pretty dead, to be honest, not many people on the tube, which was alright. Had me headphones in listening to some tunes, mindin' me own business, when the train came to a screechin' halt and all the lights went out. Couldn't see nothin'.'

The train had been held at a red light on the line, which was not entirely unexpected from the London Underground, and it had stayed there for five minutes in the pitch black of the tunnel. Normally, the driver would announce the reason for the delay and apologise for the wait. On this occasion, however, in the lightless tube in the impenetrable blackness of the underground tunnel, there was no announcement. Only the persistent crackling of static over the tannoy.

'Didn't think much of it, mind, had The Clash blaring in me ears didn't I? So I sat and waited for the train to get a move on. Lights came flickerin' back on, and sat opposite me is this old dear and her grandkid, right? Hadn't seen 'em there before, but figured I hadn't been payin' attention when they got on. Anyway...'

The tube had carried on undisturbed for the remaining two stops, and when the train arrived at Tottenham Court Road, Tom removed his headphones and stood up to alight at the station. 'So I'm stood by the doors waitin' for them to open, and the old bid and her granddaughter come and stand next to me. Must've been the kids birthday or somethin', as she was holdin' a red balloon, and she smiled at me. Sweet as you like! I smiled back at her, and at her grandmother, who didn't seem to take quite as much of a shine to me.' The old woman had narrowed her eyes in a judgemental stare and pulled her granddaughter closer to her. 'Probably thought I was some sort of thug.'

'Anyways, so I turn back to the door waitin' for it to open, and notice something not right...' He trailed off almost intentionally dramatically, and took another gulp of beer. 'It was just me standin' there. In the reflection of the window. No old biddy or sweet little girl or even a red balloon. Just me. So I turn to face them again, the smilin' girl and her judging granny lookin' back at me, then back to the window where their reflection certainly ain't.'

His friends had started to smirk, trying to suppress their amusement while exchanging humoured looks with one another. 'So what,' Carl interrupted at this point, visibly entertained and with a voice laced with sarcasm, 'you reckon you seen a ghost?'

'Oi!' Tom exclaimed. 'Don't you go laughin' at me, it proper wigged me right out, right? And it gets creepier...'

He told them of how the old woman and the little girl had followed him off of the tube, the grandmother shuffling and the granddaughter skipping ahead of her, tailing closely behind him as he walked along the platform. After rounding a corner to head to the exit, Tom had turned around to see if they were still behind him. He could hear the shuffling and the skipping, but neither the woman or the girl were in sight. Confused and unnerved, he had made his way up the escalator to the exit, and he saw them both reflected in the mirrored wall by the side of him. And yet, when he looked to see if they were there behind him, there was no-one in sight.

He had looked back into the mirror, where the little girl was still holding her grandmother's hand, and she was beaming at Tom with a wide smile. Too much of a wide smile. Her lips stretched out further and further across her face, until she was literally grinning from ear to ear. She bore rows of long, knife-like teeth, which seemed far too big to fit inside of her mouth. This was not, he thought, something he had expected to see from a smiling little girl. Nor was it something he felt particularly comfortable about.

'Shit, mate,' Shabhir said when Tom had finished telling his ghost story, and subsequently also finished his pint, 'I thought you'd seen someone get hit by the train or something, not a friggin' ghost!'

'Ooooo, spooky-scary!' Mo chipped in, waving his fingers with the trembling wiggling motion trademarked by campfire storytellers. 'I mean, Christ man, you're probably just spookin' yourself out. There ain't no such thing as ghosts.'

'Nah, you're 'avin' us on, mate,' Carl said, 'probably didn't even happen! Anyway, I'm goin' for a slash then gettin' a drink, who's 'avin' what?'

'If it didn't happen,' Tom said, 'then why's there an old woman and a little girl with a red balloon stood by the bar?'

The group looked over to where Tom was pointing, and sure enough there the old woman and her granddaughter were, standing by the bar, hand in hand. His friends promptly burst out laughing.

'An old lady and her granddaughter in a pub on a Sunday afternoon? Super creepy!' they mocked, and Tom's face turned from pale white to a flushed, embarrassed pink.

What none of them had noticed was that the old woman and the little girl were staring at them. And, in the mirror which stretched across the back wall of the pub, neither the girl or her balloon or her grandmother had a reflection.

Chapter I

Sam Hain had had enough of human beings.

This was true of most days, but this one was proving to be especially challenging. The tube had been packed to capacity with commuters crammed into each carriage like a tin of particularly unhappy sardines. Forlorn and weary faces pressed against the glass, staring out of the doors, squeezed in too tightly, contorting around each other at uncomfortable angles just to fill in any empty space. Sam would have found the sight amusing if it were not for the fact that he was one of the forlorn and weary faces pressed against the glass, staring out of the doors. He had been elbowed in the head one too many times on this journey, and the thought of stepping out at Holborn into the fresh, open air (as fresh as one could consider central London air, anyway) was tantamount to wandering in the gardens of Eden.

This, he thought, was why he avoided travelling at rush hour.

But today was different. Today, something untoward was afoot, and Sam Hain was the only man for the job. It had proven to be a surprisingly busy few weeks for him, and the occasionally slow and often sporadic career of an occult detective had suddenly become a boon of activity. For Sam, this was quite exciting, being presented with new and interesting cases, supernatural sightings and ghostly goings-on, but something was troubling him. As good as it was for him to find himself so busy with the paranormal, the influx of occult occurrences generally meant one thing: bad news.

What, precisely, this bad news was, he hadn't a clue. All he could be sure of was that with so many events in such a short space of time, something must be going on behind the stage curtains. What that something was would have to wait, though, as he found himself alighting at Holborn station and making his way towards the street level, eager to leave the crowds of people behind him.

The street level was not much better than it had been below ground. People milled about the pavement, in and out of coffee shops and jostling through the entrance to the Underground, swarming like ants over a picnic. London commuters have a very particular way of seeming as if they are always in a very important hurry to get somewhere, while not really getting anywhere at all. They would rush and they would dawdle, moving hither and thither, weaving out of the way of each other and into the way of others, occasionally stopping to do that synchronised side-ways dance people do when they bump into each other, accompanied by the chant of 'sorry, so terribly sorry' and politely laughing.

As Sam emerged from the station, he found himself met by such a crowd of people. He tried to make his way up the road, only for people to barge past him, cut across his path or slow to a lackadaisical saunter ahead of him. One man simply came to an abrupt standstill in front of him. Sam suppressed an agitated growl, and ducked into an alcove just off of the pavement to escape the throngs.

Standing on a doorstep which smelled very prominently of stagnant urine, he fished inside of his jacket pocket, retrieving a crumpled cigarette. Sam balanced the cigarette between his lips, flipping his Zippo open and lighting it in one swift motion. Taking a long drag and exhaling a plume of smoke with a satisfied sighing sound, he gazed up at the blue skies. *Fresh air*, he thought, and even in his mind the tone sounded more than a little sarcastic.

He began to weave his way through the hoards of commuters, many of whom blithely marched across the roads regardless of how many oncoming buses there were, and Sam headed towards the location of the latest paranormal problem. The Lethaby Building of Central Saint Martins.

The building itself was a grand and imperious looking place. Old wooden doors set within the facades of Edwardian architecture exuded an air of classical London, and it towered above the streets below. It had a long history in the arts industry, being purpose built in 1908 and housing the Central School of Art and Design; over a hundred years on, the building still played host to the arts as a filming location and for production offices. Sam was not here for any of this, of course, but it was a costumier in one of the production offices who had first encountered the strange problem, and had shared a very blurry picture online of what appeared to be an apparition causing mischief in the props department.

Sam Hain strode up to the wooden door off of Southampton Row, flicking the last of his cigarette away and causing a shower of embers to burst from its still-lit tip as it hit the wall. Hand clasped around the old door handle, he twisted and pushed the door as he stepped forward. The door made a disgruntled rattling sound, and Sam almost walked into it as it failed to open. When the door refused to open one way, Sam tried the other. The door did not wish to be pulled open either. As is natural when a door is decidedly and firmly shut, rather than simply acknowledge that the door will not in fact open, Sam rattled it forcefully, thrusting forward and pulling backward vigorously, but to no avail. He decided to try the next door along, only to find the same problem. And the next one. And the next one.

Sam had walked almost a full circuit around the building when he stumbled on some luck. There was a goods delivery entrance around the back, manned by a single security guard, which led to an open door. He surreptitiously watched the security guard, checking his phone while he stood a short distance from the entrance so as to not seem too conspicuous, and after a while his moment of opportunity arrived. The guard turned around, talking into his radio, and began to pace slowly up towards one of the delivery vans. Seizing the moment, Sam made a dash for the entrance, skirting as close to the far wall as possible, and made his way to the open door. Through the bins and refuse he went, carefully creaking open the old door which led to the lower level.

It was dank and drab inside on the lower ground floor, with worn old floorboards and peeling white walls and the smell of damp lingering faintly in the air; it was a complete contrast to the pompous exterior of the building. Sam followed the winding corridors around the basement, from vacant space to empty office, storage cupboards to dilapidated toilets. Eventually he found a staircase, a wrought iron series of steps which led to the original wooden stairs and back up to the ground level.

As he rounded the top of the stairs, each step creaking as he walked up the old wooden steps, Sam was met with a sight which was a far cry from the basement below. Ornate, lavish Edwardian architecture characterised the entrance lobby he found himself in, and it felt like he had taken a step back in time. Polished marble pillars rose from polished marble floors, reaching up to the arching ceilings above. The doorways and windows were set in wooden frames in the plaster walls, the soft light of day casting white beams and dust motes in the air. Wooden staircases wound their way up the building, leading to the myriad levels above. The place felt opulent, almost regal, in its style. And best of all, Sam thought, there was not a soul in sight.

His feet echoed against the marble floor, the sound clopping through the empty halls. He took in the atmosphere of the space for a moment, enjoying the tranquil stillness, the peace and quiet of this normally inaccessible place. It felt like exactly the kind of place which would have the occasional ghostly visitor. He turned his glance towards the stairway, his eyes following it up and up as it snaked around the inside of the building. Little paper signposts pointed in various different directions; So and So Studios this way, This and That Productions that way, Holding and Fitting the other. None of it meant anything to him, but he figured if he was going to get close to finding this apparition, he was going to have to investigate the different departments of Lethaby Hall.

He wandered the corridors of the first floor, following the signs which pointed him around corners and into several rooms. With his TechnoWand drawn and holding it ahead of him, he carried on his search, peering into any room which didn't have a locked door. He was having very little luck finding anything substantially supernatural – for the most part, all he could find were empty rooms and vacant office spaces – but the steady pulse from his probe's crystal suggested there was something beyond the ordinary present. Sam allowed his feet to guide him, as if following some unspoken direction or innate intuition.

It wasn't until he had reached the third floor of the building that he felt he was getting somewhere with his investigation. The TechnoWand was glowing stronger than on the lower levels, and a stillness hung in the air. It wasn't quite the tranquil stillness of the lobby, it was more of an eerie, cloying nothingness which made the air feel heavy and stagnant. This was also, he learned from a paper sign which was stuck to the wall with BluTac, the main floor for storing costumes and wardrobe for the productions on site. It was logical to infer, he deduced, that if a costumier was to witness an apparition, it was likely to be here.

An old and heavy wooden door creaked loudly on its hinges as Sam slowly pushed it open, slipping through the opening and into the room labelled "The Wardrobe". The floorboards groaned beneath his feet. It was dark inside The Wardrobe, with the only light filtering into the room coming through the windows at the far end, mostly blocked by rail upon rail of costumes. It was like stepping into a labyrinth made entirely of rejected outfits from Liberace's wardrobe. Row upon row of clothes rails filled the room, with little pathways snaking their way between them, all laden with costumes ranging from the historically accurate to the theatrically flamboyant. Sam slowly followed the snaking pathway, past the World War I uniforms and past the Baroque dresses and doublets, through the Medieval rags and through the 1970s bell-bottom jeans. He kept his senses alert, peering over the rails and keeping his ears sharp, paying attention to any sense of a cool breeze, an incongruous scent, or a bitter taste.

The crystal at the tip of Sam's probe glowed, emitting a bright white light which illuminated the path ahead of him and cast tall, eerie shadows across the far wall of The Wardrobe. Shadowy shapes moved and twisted as he made his way forward. He failed to notice the shadow of a suit of armour casually walking towards him.

'Hello?' Sam called out into The Wardrobe. 'Anyone not from this dimension here?' No answer came from the shadows. 'Don't be shy,' he said to nothing in particular, 'I mean you no harm. Unless you mean me harm, of course, but we'll cross that bridge if we come to it.' Something which sounded like metal rubbing against metal broke the silence. The floorboards creaked out of time with Sam's own footsteps. He spun around, pointing the TechnoWand into the shadows, but nothing was there.

The hairs on the back of Sam's neck began to prickle. An involuntary shudder ran down his spine. The faint scent of something rotting reached his nostrils, and a metallic taste cloyed at the back of his mouth. A sensation sunk deep into the pit of his stomach. A smirk crept across his lips as he cast his eyes around the room. 'Here we go then,' he muttered, turning back around and coming face to face with a fully armoured knight. 'Hello there.'

The knight offered no response, the suit of armour standing stoically still and silent.

'So... Friend or foe?'

The knight began to raise its right arm, the armour clinking against itself. Sam stood his ground, until he realised the knight was brandishing a particularly sharp looking sword in its hand. The knight raised its blade high above its head dramatically.

'Foe then,' Sam said with a nod, and immediately leapt back as the sword came swinging down. It clanged against the floor where he had been stood, and the knight began to pace towards him, slowly, purposefully, menacingly. Sam stepped into an en garde stance, raising the TechnoWand like a rapier. The animated suit of armour swung its sword wildly, slashing at Sam and sending rails on either side of them crashing and clattering to the floor. With a few well timed steps back, Sam narrowly avoided the chopping of the blade, and with a wave of the TechnoWand he cast a bolt of energy into the knight's right hand. He had only intended for the shot to disarm his attacker, but Sam was pleasantly surprised to find he took the knight's arm clean off.

A wispy tendril of purplish smoke, like a ghostly arm, hung down from the exposed shoulder. The knight raised its still-armoured left arm, clenching its fist and waving it angrily at Sam.

'I warned you,' Sam said, pointing the probe up to the helmet. Another bolt of energy shot from the crystalline tip, hitting the knight squarely between where its eyes should be, and the helmet was sent flying from atop the suit of armour and into the wall. The purplish smoke rose up from the space where a head should normally be, filtering out of the armour as if the lid keeping it in had been removed. It swirled in the air above him in much the same way storm clouds do, and the remnants of the knight collapsed to the floor noisily. Sam winced at the clattering, and turned his attention to the purplish smoke, which was reassuming a human shape and slipping into a rather fetching frilly Renaissance dress.

'What're you doing now, you pernicious bugger?' Sam asked, firing another bolt in the direction of the haunted dress. It missed, singeing through several of the costumes, while the dress took flight. It danced and twirled in the air, flying in circles around the room. Sam was preparing to take another shot at his now airborne adversary, when the door to The Wardrobe suddenly burst open.

'What the bloody hell is going on in here?' demanded a large man wearing a fluorescent vest which was emblazoned with the word "Security".

'As you can see,' Sam said, not taking his eyes off of the ghostly form in the flying dress, 'you have a Class Three Animating Possessor.'

'What?!' the security guard bellowed. 'You're damaging production property, mate. Do you have any idea how much this stuff costs?'

'Basically, there's a ghost which enjoys playing dress-up. I'm not damaging anyone's property, I'm bloody well saving it.' He fired a quick pot-shot at the dress again, leaving a scorch mark in the ceiling.

'How in God's name is that dress flying?'

'I told you: ghost,' Sam said wearily, 'don't you people ever listen?'

The dress dived at the security guard, its smoke-like arms flailing wildly, swooping over his head as he ducked. It did a little loop-de-loop in the air, before making a lunge for Sam. He ran, throwing himself to the floor just as it glided over him. He could feel its incorporeal fingers reaching to him, clawing at his shoulders as he landed on the wooden floor with a thud. From beneath the rails, he caught a glimpse of a standing mirror on the other side of the room. Crawling back into a staggering run, Sam darted towards the far end of The Wardrobe. The smoke-like being in the dress let out an unearthly shriek.

'Right, I have an idea,' Sam said to himself just as much as the security guard. 'That thing is going to make another pass, and I'm going to be ready for- Duck!' The flying dress took another dive at the security guard, who dutifully followed orders and promptly ducked, yelping a particularly high-pitched yelp. It swirled around again, and came shrieking towards Sam, its arms outstretched and its smoke-like head revealing rows of inhuman, sharp teeth.

At the last second, Sam swung the mirror around and held it up in front of him. The ghostly being did not have time to veer away, and instead flew straight into the mirror. Its incorporeal form disappeared, as if swallowed by the reflective surface, and the dress slumped to the floor. Letting out a sigh of relief, Sam turned the mirror around to make sure it had worked.

A forlorn and weary face was pressed against the glass, staring out of the mirror, as if it was squeezed in too tightly, contorting around itself at an uncomfortable angle. Its smoke-like claws scraped against the surface of the mirror from the other side.

'Good,' he declared with a tone of finality, 'time for you to go. Bye-bye!' Opening one of the windows, Sam hefted the mirror up onto the windowsill, leaning his head out and looking down to the courtyard below. 'Watch out!' he shouted down, and toppled the mirror out of the window.

There were a few seconds of heavy silence, followed by a sudden crashing, shattering sound, and quickly proceeded with a distant cry of 'Jesus Christ that was close!'

'Sorry!' Sam called back out to the courtyard with a casual wave and turned away from the window, only to be confronted by the burly security guard. The ghost had proven to be a bit of a challenge, and it was mostly incorporeal; this man was decidedly much more corporeal.

Sam gulped audibly.

'Right,' said the security guard, his face fixed sternly and his tone as opposite to amused or friendly as one could get, 'explain to me, fully and concisely, what the hell is going on here.'

'Well,' Sam began, his voice wavering in the face of the guard, 'this place has – or rather, had – a ghost haunting it. A class three animating possessor, to be precise, causing a disruption in the local Akashic nexus and – by extension – The Wardrobe. I tangled its quantum essence in a reflective reality and severed its transdimens-'

'Hey!' the guard interrupted. 'I said concisely.'

'I trapped a ghost in a mirror and shattered it so it couldn't climb back out.'

'Right,' the guard said, slowly and uncertainly. His eyes narrowed and fixed Sam with an intense stare, and he sucked air between his teeth. 'You best be on your way, then.' He turned and started making his way back towards the door.

Sam followed a short distance behind him, his face caught somewhere between relief and confusion. 'Wait, you... You're okay with that? That's a good enough explanation?'

'Why wouldn't it be?' the guard asked wearily.

'Well, it's just, normally, people don't believe me when I tell them why I'm in their house, or have intentionally broken a priceless antique, or been surrounded by animal carcasses.'

'Quite frankly, I don't care about your explanations. I saw what that thing was, and I'm not going to lie, it scared the crap out of me. But you still broke in, caused damage to private property, and could've hurt someone by throwing a mirror out of a third-storey window.' The guard stopped by the door to The Wardrobe, opening it and gesturing for Sam to go first. 'But I won't tell anyone any of that, as long as you tell no-one I shrieked when that thing came at me.'

Sam nodded a single and stoic nod. 'Agreed,' he spoke, and stepped through the open door, following the corridor back to the stairway.

'At the foot of the stairs, turn right, follow the hallway to the left, and there'll be a little wooden door. It'll take you right out onto Southampton Road,' the guard offered helpfully. He did not follow Sam out of The Wardrobe; instead, he turned around to start tidying up the mess that had been left in the wake of Sam Hain.

'Thank you,' Sam replied, casting a casual wave over his shoulder, and proceeded to follow the instructions he had been given. He walked down the three flights of stairs, no longer so concerned about how loudly they were creaking, reaching the marble-clad foyer of the building, and heading right down the corridor. He passed by several old and dusty rooms, some filled with worn-looking tables and chairs, which put Sam in mind of a Victorian boarding school. At the very end of the hallway was another, smaller looking foyer, and the little wooden door.

The opening was surprisingly small for something called a door, and seemed to be about half the size of a more traditionally shaped door, but it was a door nonetheless. Hunching over and squinting into the bright light of the world, Sam squeezed his way through the opening and out onto the street. Going from the interior of Central Saint Martin's and out onto the busy streets of Holborn felt like stepping forward through time.

With the satisfaction of another paranormal predicament put to rest, Sam reached into his pocket, pulled out another crumpled cigarette, and began walking. He would follow his feet wherever they would lead him, until he found a nice enough café to sit down in and enjoy a decent cup of coffee.

CHAPTER II

Alice Carroll had had enough of people.

It had been a challenging week at work to say the least. She had put herself forward for an assistant manager role a few weeks beforehand, attended a brief informal interview with the department manager, and had been anticipating the result ever since. It wasn't exactly a position she felt passionately about, but it would mean a pay rise for some of the work she already did, as well as taking on a few extra responsibilities, so she thought it was worthwhile applying for at least. After two weeks of silence from management, Alice had walked herself into HR that Monday morning to ask whether they had come to a decision yet.

The woman behind the desk had nodded and turned around, where Alice's manager, Jan, and the head of recruitment were sat having coffee. 'Have we any news on the assistant manager front?' she asked.

Jan looked up from her coffee. 'I'll let you know as soon as we've made a decision, Alice,' she called from across the office.

The head of recruitment looked up as well, and he too called across to her, 'Jan will let you know as soon as a decision has been made.'

The woman behind the desk turned back to face Alice, smiling sweetly. 'Martin says that Jan will let you know as soon as they've made a decision,' she said helpfully.

'Thank you,' Alice replied with a courteous smile to all involved in this unnecessary relay race of information, and promptly left the room to return to the shop floor. She had shirts to fold.

It wasn't until lunchtime that Jan called Alice back into the office. She sat her down, and spent a few minutes silently sorting out paperwork on her desk before addressing her. Jan's face was serious and solemn, as if she was about to break the news that a close relative had recently passed away, when she told her that she had not been selected for the assistant manager position. She offered no reasoning as to why Alice's application had not been successful, and simply gave her the plain platitudes that it had been a difficult decision and that she regretted having to give her this news, but thanked her for her time and for her application. This, in itself, was not necessarily a bad thing; what had really pissed Alice off, however, was the fact that she had been the only person to apply for the position.

Through the rest of the week, she had to force herself through smiling small-talk with Jan, and had to casually explain she was not taking on the role when her colleagues asked how she got on. In truth, it did not really matter to her; Alice had no desire to climb the retail ladder, and in a way she was relieved she wasn't taking on the extra responsibility, so she could have "off" days when she didn't need to put in any more effort than was absolutely necessary. It was almost relaxing. The bit which bothered her was that, despite being the sole applicant, she had been rejected, and although she tried to tell herself otherwise, she couldn't help but feel that it was a personal rejection.

The days dragged by, the shifts were long and tedious, and sometimes the hours were earlier than she would have preferred (she wasn't a fan of being out of bed before the clock hit double digits). Some days were more tolerable than others, when the few colleagues she counted as friends were working too, or when she had to serve customers who she actually enjoyed helping. Some days were less tolerable, when colleagues she had never really exchanged any words with were working and she had to push through awkward conversation, or when she had to deal with particularly argumentative customers. One monotonous day followed after the other, whittling away eight hour shifts of folding shirts and rearranging hangers, and on the rare occasion actually providing a customer with Alice's unique brand of friendly, informal and helpful service. The one thing which was keeping Alice's spirits high, the one thing she was truly looking forward to at the end of the week, was the fact that she had been asked out on a date.

Several weeks previously, on a particularly injudicious night out with Rachel (two-for-one cocktail pitchers, while good financial sense, tend to lead to nights entirely devoid of sense), Alice had been introduced to a man named Paul. Paul was, for all intents and purposes, the very model of a man; he was tall and handsome, with short but scruffy light brown hair and a well-groomed beard, piercing blue eyes, and a toned physique which showed itself off even from beneath his clothes. And he was interesting. They had got to know each other a little bit over a few drinks that night, and Paul talked briefly of his adventures backpacking across Europe, and of his wide tastes in music and literature. Their conversation melted the rest of the night away, and as they parted ways they had exchanged numbers.

From that day on, they had been in almost constant contact. Ranging from the good morning messages to talking about their days, sharing stories and talking into the small hours of the morning. After getting to know each other better, their late night conversations had grown a little more suggestive and flirtatious, but Paul never took things too far. He had always remained a perfect gentleman, albeit one who wasn't afraid to make his intentions known. Alice had enjoyed his conversation, his company, and the excitement when he would suggest giving her a full-body massage after a stressful day at work, or holding her in his arms while they fell asleep. Even though they had not met since that first night, Alice was starting to like this man, and she felt like her heart leapt every time she received a new message from him. As it turned out, during one night while they talked into the early hours of the next day, she discovered that Paul felt similarly, and he had invited her out for a proper date at the end of the week.

Alice, naturally, had said yes.

By the time that Friday came around, Alice was beginning to feel nervous. An excited kind of nervous, but nervous nonetheless. Work, as much as it had dragged by that day, had been an almost welcome distraction for her; it helped keep her mind from becoming too focussed on the date while also having something to look forward to when her shift was over. She waited impatiently for the evening debrief to come to an end, not really paying attention to anything her manager was saying, and was rather preoccupied with looking at her phone. Paul had sent her a message shortly before her shift had ended.

Looking forward to seeing you soon :), it read.

She rushed up to the locker room as soon as she had clocked out, quickly pulling off her work clothes and slipping into a fitting – but not too revealing – summer dress, kicking off her flat shoes in favour of a pair of modest high heels, and topped up her make-up in the mirror. She sprayed herself with a few squirts of a perfume which smelled mainly of patchouli, and ran a brush through her hair. Slinging her handbag over her shoulder and exhaling a nervous breath, she locked the outfit of Work-Alice behind in her locker, and readied herself as Date-Alice. With the chirpy *beepity-beep* of the staff security door, she stepped outside and began to make her way to meet with Paul.

The sun still shone brightly over London that evening, the skies gradually oranging as the summer's day slowly turned to a warm twilight. People milled about the street, as they left work and made their way home to their families or joined friends in the nearby pubs and bars of Fitzrovia. Glasses chinked and friends laughed as the crowded bars already spilled into the streets, taking up the pavements outside of the pubs. Alice weaved her way through the crowds, threading between groups and squeezing past tourists, paying no attention to the myriads of people around her. It was as if she was in a world of her own.

When Alice arrived at Russell Square, Paul was already stood waiting for her. A smart pair of jeans topped his newly polished shoes, and a fitting shirt with the top two buttons undone was framed neatly in a well-tailored blazer. He beamed a smile in her direction when he saw her approaching and began to walk over to her, opening his arms wide and leaning in to give her a peck on the cheek.

'Hi,' Alice seemed to squeak as she spoke.

'Hello, you,' Paul said in a soft yet sonorous tone, 'good day?'

'It was okay, better now though,' she replied with a smile. 'Although I'm starving now!'

'What a happy coincidence that we're going for dinner, then,' Paul said as he slowly began to lead the way to the restaurant. 'It'd be a disappointingly short meal if you weren't hungry.'

Paul had booked them a table at an upmarket restaurant in the heart of Bloomsbury. The waiter who led them to their table romantically placed a candle between them, and a small vase with a single red rose, and – rather less romantically – a bottle of olive oil. He scurried away after delivering them their menus so they could browse in peace, and scurried back over when Paul gestured to him that they were ready to order.

Alice had been eyeing the prices on the menu warily. A simple selection of bread – not even as a starter, more of an appetiser – seemed unnecessarily expensive, and for the few slices of bread which actually came with the order (albeit nicely presented in a little basket) Alice wondered whether the bread had been baked by saints or if its golden crusts had been infused with actual gold. Neither of these were the case. And nor was it the case that she needed to worry about the cost, as Paul seemed more than happy to order a bottle of wine between them at a price which made Alice see stars. He waved a casually dismissive hand towards her. 'Don't worry about it, I'm paying. Just order whatever you fancy.'

For a brief moment, Alice considered replying "can I order you, then?" but thought better of it for a first date, and instead nibbled on a piece of expensive bread (it tasted like bread) and took a sip of wine (it tasted like sharp, rotten grapes mixed with a sweet black cherry). Returning her attention to the menu, she decided to order the tomato bruschetta for starters, followed by the risotto al funghi (finished with a hint of chilli and truffle oil).

Conversation over dinner had been perfectly pleasant. Paul told Alice about his time backpacking across Europe as part of a travelling indie rock band (investment banking, he explained, was the job he used for financial security), and the bizarre adventures they would end up going on. 'What about yourself?' he asked. 'Have you had any weird or interesting adventures lately?'

Alice thought about this for a moment. She 'hmm'd while her memory cycled through the adventures she had had in the past year. Having a malicious metaphysical entity in her head at Halloween had certainly opened the doorway to a lot more exciting and terrifying adventures in her life. Joining an occult detective in a haunted townhouse in Knightsbridge, investigating a murder and being attacked be a demon reanimating a corpse, rescuing the occult detective from an underground organisation of spooks, and stepping through a gateway into a faerie kingdom... Upon reflection, she considered these were probably not good stories for a first date.

'It's been a while since I've had a proper holiday,' she

replied, fiddling with her napkin. 'I've been at work too much to really have time for adventures like that.' That was a lie, but it was significantly more sane and believable than saying "just the other month I was whisked away to another dimension and was given a tour around a faerie village".

'Oof, I know that feeling well,' Paul said, 'it's easy to get caught up in that trap of always working to keep bringing money in. But what's the point in earning money if you're not going to use it for exciting experiences? You need to allow yourself time for a break, for an adventure, for something new.'

Alice smiled. Very few people ever told her this. She was used to her parents carrying on about having a respectable job and working to save up and buy a house and settle down and all those other sensible grown-up things. They didn't care much for the time she had put into her art degree (although they liked the art she created as a result, they did not see it as a viable career), and thought she would have been better studying business. Too many people, she thought, focussed on the idea of making money without much idea of what to do with it. It was a breath of fresh air to find someone who seemed to have a firm grasp on his life, who was not driven purely by work and money, but by a will to use it to experience more things in life.

'Totally,' she said, nodding her agreement. 'Easier said than done with London rent though, right?'

He laughed, raising his glass. 'I'll drink to that.' He sipped at the wine, placing the glass back down with a delicate clink. 'But it's possible to strike that balance, life isn't all work and no play. Work hard, and play hard!' He winked.

'Work hard, play hard,' she parroted.

Their conversation continued to wind on, taking the myriad twists and turns and tangents as any conversation does. From favourite holiday destinations to favourite films, to favourite bad films and worst holiday experiences. They talked and laughed over dinner, sharing stories and ideas, marvelling at the fact that they must have been at the same Bon Jovi concert a few years ago and probably passed each other at some point. They shared a bite of each other's meals (Alice's risotto al funghi was delicious), and happily ordered dessert when the waiter came around to clear their plates.

'This might seem like an odd question,' Paul began as he picked up a biscotti to go with his after-dinner coffee, 'but... Do you believe in ghosts?'

'Ghosts?'

'Yeah, ghosts.'

'Yeah, I do,' Alice replied, taking a rather large spoonful of her chocolate sundae, almost – but not quite entirely – regretting having such a big mouthful when the ice cream froze the roof of her mouth and stung her teeth.

'Have you ever seen one, or experienced anything supernatural?'

Her brain was still feeling a bit frozen from the ice cream, and images from her adventures with Sam Hain flashed through Alice's mind again. *Christ, where do I begin?* She pondered for a moment. *Nah, it's all too... weird.* 'I mean, yeah, in a sense,' she said, figuring sharing any of her stories of the supernatural at this point might be a bit too much, 'but I think everyone has experienced something they can't quite explain at least once. Have you?'

Paul seemed to hesitate, staring into the void of his pitch-black coffee thoughtfully. 'You're probably going to laugh,' he said, 'but I think my flat might be haunted.'

Alice did not laugh. Instead, she eyed him with curiosity. 'Haunted how?' she asked, taking another mouthful of sundae. 'Apparitions? Voices? Things going bump in the night?'

'Maybe you should come over, and we can see what goes bump in the night,' Paul said with a sly smile and a flirtatious glint in his eye.

'Smooth,' she giggled. 'Maybe.'

'But it's good to see you're just as fascinated by the paranormal as I am,' he continued, 'because that wasn't just a set-up for a cheesy line. Sometimes my lights flicker for no reason; I'll hear someone moving around in another room, but when I go to look there's no-one there; and I'm sure I've seen it once, too. If you wanted to check it out after, share some ghost stories and stuff, you're welcome to stay over?'

'I would,' she replied, not entirely dishonestly, 'but I have to be up early tomorrow, so I won't tonight.' She stared into Paul's blue eyes for a moment, before adding, 'thank you, though.'

'No, no, that's fair,' he said, 'another time perhaps?'

'Oh yes,' Alice said with a smile, 'now I have two reasons to want to come round to yours some time.'

Their conversation carried on long into the night. Other diners came and went, candles burned low, and the last of their dishes had been cleared away some time before Paul signalled he was ready to pay the bill. Alice offered to pay at least a little something towards dinner, but as she reached for her purse and suggested splitting the bill, Paul had dismissed it with a wave of his hand.

'Don't be silly,' he said, as he tapped his PIN into the card machine, 'I've got this.' Alice felt a little guilty that he was paying for the full bill, she thought she should contribute at least something, but Paul had resisted her offer each time she suggested it. In a way, she quite liked the fact that he had treated her to such a nice dinner, but it didn't alleviate her personal sense of owing something. Next time, she thought, she would pay for dinner.

After leaving the restaurant, Paul had walked her back to the underground station. He hugged her goodbye, leaning in and giving her a peck on the cheek. 'This has been a lovely evening, Alice,' he said, moving away from the hug but still holding her gently by the shoulders, 'we'll do this again some time.'

'Definitely,' Alice replied, smiling up at him, 'thank you for a wonderful dinner, and wonderful company.'

'Text me when you're home safely.'

'You too. See you!'

Paul began to walk away while Alice rummaged through her handbag for her Oyster card, and he waved her a final farewell wave over his shoulder. She grinned and waved back to him, before turning to enter Russell Square station.

The tube journey was a short and unexciting one. Alice had changed at King's Cross for the Victoria line train to Highbury and Islington, from which home was only a brief walk, and even though she knew she had no signal on the Underground she still found herself checking her phone habitually. She resigned herself to the drone-like experience of the tube, but couldn't help but smile. Overall, this evening had left her feeling contented.

It was a little after midnight when Alice got home. As soon as she set foot through the door, she kicked off her heels and headed for her bedroom. She could hear Rachel's voice coming from the other room, presumably on the phone to someone, and she decided she would fill her in on the date the following morning. Dropping her handbag on the floor, Alice flung herself onto her bed and pulled out her phone to message Paul.

I'm back home now, she wrote, *thank you again for a lovely evening. I had a really wonderful time. :)*

Alice then sat, and waited. She stared at her phone, watching the symbol go from a spinning loading sign, to a single tick to denote the message had been sent, and then a double tick for delivered. Smiling to herself, she flicked back through their messages, rereading their conversations and replaying the date in her mind. It was a thought she didn't want to entertain too much, but from the way his words brought a smile to her face, and being with him had made the butterflies in her stomach dance an intricate dance, she was starting to think she really liked Paul.

Scrolling back down to the last message, Alice saw that the double ticks of her message had turned blue. The text had been delivered and read. She smiled, and awaited his response. After ten minutes – or rather, what had felt to Alice like a short eternity – had passed, Paul replied. He said that he had had a wonderful time as well, that he really liked her, and that they should go out again some time soon. This made Alice smile. He then sent a second message shortly after the first, saying that he was getting into bed, but was feeling too hot that evening to wear pyjamas. This, too, made Alice smile. She messaged him back, agreeing that they should go on another date soon, and also agreeing that perhaps it was too warm for pyjamas, but maybe still just chilly enough that it would be nice to snuggle up in bed together.

Paul did not reply.

Paul did not reply the following day either. He did not message her good morning as he usually did, nor did he apologise for falling asleep without saying goodnight to her as he did on some nights. When Alice opened her messages in the morning to see if she had somehow missed something, she saw he had been online within the hour. Yet still, he had not messaged her.

She wrestled with herself throughout the day. Maybe he was simply busy, she thought, but no matter how busy he was surely he would have at least a few minutes to send her a quick message. Even a "sorry, busy at the moment, will get back to you properly later" would have sufficed. She toyed with the idea of messaging him again (ranging from the self-deprecating "I wasn't that awful company, was I?!" through to the concerned "is everything okay?" to the sarcastic "guess I don't have to worry about paying for dinner next time."), but she resisted the urge. Nonetheless, she found herself running circles in her mind, about why he had not messaged her back, whether she had done something wrong or if she could have done anything differently. Rachel had, rather helpfully, suggested that perhaps she could have put herself out more, which Alice rejected as awful first date decorum.

Forty-two hours had passed since their first date (not that Alice was keeping count), and Paul had yet to message her. She did not want to seem too desperate by hounding him with texts, but she thought it would be an idea to try and just get in touch with him; casually and breezily. She had sent him a simple good morning on the morning of the second day of silence, asking how he was. The message was sent, and then delivered, and then read. And still, Paul did not reply. He did not reply within the hour, and he did not reply by the evening. He had, it seemed, read her message and simply ignored it.

This, it was fair to say, had left Alice feeling incandescent. A sickening cocktail of dejection, sadness, regret, anger, frustration, confusion, an onset of lingering ennui, and sudden lack of desire for dinner coalesced inside of her. She had gone from several weeks of getting to know this man, beginning to really like him, and it seeming like he felt the same as her, to suddenly feeling as if none of it had even happened just two days after a perfectly lovely date. From suggestive and flirtatious messages, which Alice had found herself enjoying more than she would like to admit, to nothing.

Even though she knew she would not have done anything differently, and that they had both had a good time together (he could have made an excuse to leave early if he wanted, she thought), she still could not help but run over the situation in her mind. Over and over again. *Was I not enough?*, she thought, *was I too much? Did I say too much, or too little? Maybe I should have kissed him. But if that was what he wanted, why didn't he move to kiss me? He was a perfect gentleman, he said he would be on a first date, so he couldn't have been expecting me to push for more... What the hell is wrong?*

As trivial as Alice usually thought such short-term relationship hang-ups could be, and how she tried to tell herself she had been doing just fine a few weeks ago before she even knew he existed, these thoughts still played in her head like a track on repeat. It did not make her feel good. Stood in the kitchen that evening while cooking dinner (or rather, the comfort food Alice wanted for dinner: spaghetti on toast), she had vented to Rachel about it all.

'Men will be men,' Rachel said rather blasé. 'Trust me, sweetie, a lot of them only want one thing, and if they don't think they can get it from you they'll just drop you and move on to the next woman. You either jump into bed with them, or you don't exist.'

'Not all men are like that,' Alice said, 'and I don't think Paul is like that either. Well, I didn't think he was like that, anyway...'

'Maybe if you'd slept with him-'

'On a first date?'

'It can be good! Although sometimes you can wake up with a sore head, an empty bed and no message to be read... It's just what men are like.'

'Sam's not like that,' Alice said, emptying the contents of a tin of alphabetti-spaghetti into a saucepan and turning the dial on the hob to 4.

Rachel paused for a moment. 'No,' she said slowly, as if with much consideration, 'he's not. But he doesn't count.'

'Why not?'

'Well, he's not exactly... Normal. Is he? I mean, I'm not even sure he exists when there's not something weird going on. It's like he just pops up, says something about the supernatural, and then disappears off the face of the Earth again. Can you imagine dating him? It'd be so weird, being with a guy who believes that monsters under the bed are real and that the postman is a werewolf.'

Alice thought about this. She could not remember Sam ever saying anything about a werewolf postman (although the local postman was especially hairy), but she could believe the bit about the monsters under the bed. After all, she had seen the things which lurk in the shadows, the world which exists just beyond the scrim of reality; Sam had shown her these things, so the thought of it did not seem as bizarre to her as it did to Rachel.

'Even so,' Alice said, 'we're not talking about dating Sam. I'm more concerned about why Paul hasn't replied, and why the hell I feel so dejected by that. I didn't know him long, I should just be able to move on.'

'That's all you can do,' Rachel replied, 'just forget about the twat and move on. You're too good for him anyway, babe.'

'You're right,' Alice said, mustering a smile as she placed two slices of bread under the grill, 'thank you. I need to put this shit behind me.'

Rachel nodded with a sympathetic smile. 'I'm here if you need to talk.' She reached for her cup of coffee and turned to leave the kitchen. The sound of the television turning on, and the noise of some kind of soap opera, came from the living room.

The spaghetti bubbled and boiled in the saucepan. Small gelatinous globules of sauce pimpled on the surface and burst almost as quickly as they had appeared. Pasta shapes gently drifted and rolled in the orangey-red sauce, carried along in the lazy current as they boiled. Alice reached for a spoon to give the spaghetti a cursory stir, but as she looked down into the sauce pan, she noticed something odd. Letter-shaped pieces of pasta began to roll to the surface and, while this is not unexpected from a bubbling pan of alphabetti-spaghetti, the letters rose to the surface in a very particular pattern.

The letters wobbled in the boiling, molten sauce, bubbles bursting stickily around them, as Alice stared at them. She felt a sinking feeling drop through the pit of her stomach, her body becoming numb and an unpleasant tingling sensation in her teeth. The letters which bobbed and floated on the surface spelled a sentence. A sentence Alice would much rather not have seen, least of all in what was meant to be her comfort food.

'Not this again,' Alice muttered to herself as she read the foreboding alphabetti-spaghetti. She quickly stirred the sauce, returning the letters beneath the surface and mixing them in with the other pasta shapes. The same letters resurfaced, spelling out the phrase and spacing themselves so as to adhere to proper sentence structure. She stirred again, trying to deny what she had seen, but sure enough the letters found their way back to the top.

'I need Sam,' Alice said aloud, not necessarily to anyone or anything in particular.

'I mean, sure,' Rachel replied, appearing in the kitchen doorway, 'like I said, he's a bit strange, but if that's what you fancy...'

'No, no,' she said, beckoning Rachel over to the cooker and pointing into the saucepan, 'I mean that I need Sam.'

They gazed down into the saucepan together, reading the letters which drifted across the surface of the alphabetti-spaghetti. "Darkness is coming", they read.

CHAPTER III

Darkness encased him. Oily black shadows spun and spiralled and swirled around him, swimming around and around like a school of eels encircling him. Sam stood at the heart of the surging maelstrom, the whirling darkness spiralling upwards like being in the eye of a storm. He reached forward, touching the seemingly impenetrable wall surrounding him. The black veil rippled to the touch, and Sam felt the cold, wet substance ooze along his hand. A viscous, oil-like fluid blackened the tips of his fingers. Forcefully, he plunged his hand deeper into the blackness, and then he thrust his other hand into it, pulling the darkness away like opening a pair of particularly slimy curtains.

Beyond the veil of shadows, Sam could see the gaping depths of the Void. The eerie vaporous nebulae which drifted in oblivion, the darkness which lay beyond, blacker than the night, and the grotesque spherical structures which grew like enormous vile fungi or diseased deep sea coral. Somewhere in the Void, he could see the writhing tentacles of something unearthly, unnatural. He wondered why he was in this place, what had brought him to this forbidding realm, when he noticed a doorway ahead of him. Floating amidst the sickening clouds stood a set of grand double doors, built of strong oaken wood and adorned with iron fittings. The handles were shaped like the heads of lions. He stepped from out of the swirling darkness and into the Void, making his way towards the doors and pulling them open.

On the other side of the doorway, Sam found himself stood in a vast chamber. His feet echoed on the marble floors, each sound bouncing off of the ornately carved walls. Grand and ancient statues stood around him, all seemingly looking down on him, their bodies worn from countless centuries, their faces stoic and stern. Ahead of him, Sam could see five figures standing in a circle around an artefact. He drew closer, straining his eyes in the dark of the chamber to see what it was they were gathered around. The sound of reality tearing apart ripped through the air, and suddenly the vision ahead of him was gone, replaced by a swirling vortex of emptiness and an inescapable aura of dread. From out of the nothingness, a multitude of glowing, pustulous eyes blinked asynchronously at him. With a piercing screech unlike any sound he had heard before, vicious mandibles lunged towards him.

'Sam!'

Sam Hain awoke. He found himself in the much more reassuringly earthly and real surroundings of his flat in Hampstead, laying across the sofa, surrounded by an untidy array of paper and books. He slowly lifted his head from the arm of the sofa, feeling an uncomfortable crick in his neck and a piece of paper clinging quite happily to his left cheek. He peeled the paper away from his face, briefly examining the Solomonic sigil he had drawn on it. It was the Fourth Pentacle of Mercury, a magickal seal which summoned the Intelligences of Mercury to bring understanding of hidden knowledge and wisdom. Whether his dream had been a sign that the sigil was working or not, Sam was not sure.

He kicked his feet around from the sofa and onto the floor, displacing more sheets of paper which were strewn around the room. Drowsily, Sam stood up, and almost immediately regretted it when his vision swayed uncertainly and his head throbbed. Sleep, Sam sometimes thought, was a waste of valuable time; in this case, he was wondering if he could do with more of it. He waited for the feeling to pass before heading to the kitchen to make himself another cup of tea and return to his work.

Walking back into the living room with his tea in hand,

Sam made his way back to the sofa. He kicked a pile of papers out of his path, shoved the books which occupied his sofa onto the floor, and promptly flung himself down into his seat. The tea splashed and sloshed in the mug precariously, but somehow he had managed to not spill any of it. Leaning forwards and putting the mug onto the cluttered coffee table at the heart of the room, he rested his chin in his hands and stared at the wall ahead of him. The fireplace was dusty and cold, clearly not having been lit in a while, and the mantelpiece was adorned with myriad oddities and trinkets which even Sam wasn't sure what all of them were. But this was not his focus. His attention was drawn solely to the part of the wall above this, which no longer resembled a wall at all. Instead, it was a confusing, jumbled and frenetic mind-map.

The entire wall was covered in printed documents, post-it notes and pinned pieces of paper covered in Sam's scribbled handwriting, photographs and maps, all linked with connecting threads of string held in place by push pins. Each string was a different colour, threading through each connected case, every relevant note, and any tangentially linked element. It was Sam's attempt at bringing order to the chaos, but instead it looked like a very confused spider had tried to make several different rainbow-coloured webs in the same place. At the heart of this all was a large map of central London, covered in marker pen crosses, circles, and the all-important push pins from which the connecting threads radiated out.

It did not matter how long Sam stared at the mind-map. The mind-map was impervious to such scrutiny, and stubbornly refused to give him any further insights. If anything, it seemed all the more determined to make no discernible sense whatsoever.

It had only got more complicated these past couple of weeks, with each new and unusual case Sam stumbled upon. They ranged from the mundane, like a spectral apparition on the underground or disembodied noises in a pub's function room, to the more complicated, such as a less-than-human Void Prowler lurking in the shadows of the side streets, or the ghost which had been animating the wares in a costume department. He realised he had not added that last one, and quickly drew another cross on the map near Holborn station. He stood back, folding his arms across his chest and chewing on the pen thoughtfully.

Nothing new. Just one more mark to add to the collection of marks which seemed to congregate around the very centre of the city. There were a few outliers, naturally, however Sam found that the main density seemed to gather around Soho and Bloomsbury. Some of these marks were cases Sam had investigated personally (denoted by black marks and linked by blue string) whereas others were sightings he had seen reported on social media and online occult groups (red marks and red string). Purple string connected the ones which bore similar apparition hallmarks. Yellow string linked those which were simply disembodied voices or sounds, often accompanied by a feeling of eeriness or dread. Green string ran between the cases and occurrences Sam couldn't quite define. He was determined to find what the common connection between these cases was; after all, everything – no matter how tangentially – is connected. There must be some root cause to so many occult occurrences.

He wound the thread of blue string around the push pin he now attached to the map just over Holborn. It formed an isosceles triangle when connected to Saint Pancras Church and Soho Square. Other than that, Sam could not gleam any further insight. He scratched his head and ruffled his hair with frustration, turning around and picking up a book on esoteric London from the coffee table. He thumbed through the pages, but found nothing of importance. No Ley Lines running through or along his string guides, and no areas of particular paranormal importance. He threw the book back down and shrugged inconclusively.

Sitting on the sofa, Sam closed his eyes and focused his mind. If he could not find the answers in the external world, he thought, perhaps looking within would hold some kind of insight. In his mind's eye he saw the map of London, its myriad circles and crosses, the connecting threads and the dense cluster of marks around the centre of the city. The marks began to shift and change place in his vision, slowly drifting around each other much like bacteria in a drop of water. Their movement seemed random at first, simply moving for the sake of moving, until he noticed a pattern forming. The marks began to converge, moving together in clusters and gravitating to one point, a point at the very heart of the map, a point which was exactly-

His phone beeped and buzzed, snapping Sam out of his reverie and disrupting his focus. The marks shot back to their proper places as his eyes opened, staring at a non-shifting map. *Bollocks*, he thought. Reaching for his phone frustratedly, Sam slid the lockscreen with his thumb and opened the message. Seeing it was from Alice, he was not quite as annoyed by the interruption.

What do you make of this?, the message read, and attached was a picture of a saucepan filled with alphabetti-spaghetti. The words "darkness is coming" were spelled out on the surface in little pasta shapes.

Not much, Sam typed his reply, *it's a niche piece of art, quite post-modern. Not personally to my taste, but the Tate might pay a pretty penny for it. -SH*

It's not art, you idiot, Alice fired back almost instantly, *it spelled itself out when I was cooking dinner.*

Your dinner was a saucepan of haunted alphabetti-spaghetti? Something prickled at the back of Sam's mind, an intangible sense of foreboding waved over him. It was stupid for him to be concerned about a few pieces of alphabetti-spaghetti, though, he tried to tell himself.

417

Shut up! I'm not even going to say about coincidences; the Universe isn't so lazy as to spell out a message in my dinner without some reason. What do you think?

You'd be better off with a tin of haunted spaghetti hoops. The most spooky thing that can say is "ooooo". Sam smiled to himself as he pressed send, thinking that was a terribly funny joke. Deflecting his concerns with humour did not help, though. He couldn't help but think of each time those words had come up in the past, and how they never led to anything good. He sent another message. *Joking aside, that's a very strange and unsettling thing for spaghetti to do. It's not something to be overlooked. There's no telling what's behind it. Firstly, do you have any rock salt?*

Stop trying to be funny, that was barely a joke xD, Alice replied. *And I thought so too. Why in my spaghetti? Yes, I have rock salt, what are you thinking?*

Okay, Sam typed, and he thought for a moment. Figuring out what to do with a saucepan of sinister spaghetti was a first for him. *Sprinkle the rock salt over the spaghetti, it will help purify the energy of any negative forces.* He paused again. Words, he considered, held power. Words and thoughts and intents were central to the practice of magick. *Then rearrange the letters so your pastamancy spells something less sinister.*

It took five minutes for Alice to reply, presumably while she tried to find a good anagram. *I've got "Nicknames Sir Dogs". Is that good?*

It almost makes sense, Sam said, *I would say to serve and enjoy, possibly on toast or as a side with chips and fried eggs, but it's better not to risk it. Who knows what force is at work here. Just throw it away.* Sam's thumb hovered over the send button, when a thought occurred to him. *Why don't you come over? I could use your help with something I'm working on, and we'll do dinner. I suppose I should eat something somewhen.*

Done. And that sounds good to me :), Alice replied. *What's the case?*

I'll fill you in when you get here.

Sam placed his phone back on the coffee table, and began to tidy up the sheets of paper which littered the living room. He flipped through them as he piled them up, skimming over each printed document and array of notes to present to Alice when she arrived. At the very least, he considered, making his data vaguely organised enough for someone else to understand (rather than his own unique form of disorganised organisation) may bring new ideas to the fore.

He sipped his tea contemplatively.

CHAPTER IV

When Alice had arrived at the tall red brick house on Constantine Road, Sam's landlady had let her in and pointed her down the stairs to the occult detective's basement flat and "office". The old wooden steps creaked as she made her way down towards the door at the base of them. Above the brass plaque which read "Sam Hain - Occult Detective", a symbol had been crudely etched into the wood of the door which resembled the Eye of Ra within a triangle, within a circle. Reaching out to the door knocker, Alice gave it three cursory raps.

An indistinct noise, which sounded not too dissimilar to a voice, came from the other side. It sounded almost like the voice had said "come in", although it could have easily also been saying "cumin" or "Moomin". On reflection, Alice considered "come in" was the most likely possibility, turned the cold metal handle of the door and pushed it open.

Alice was used to Sam being a particularly disorganised man. In her mind, it was as if he had his own unique system for organisation, one which sometimes even he was not sure of how it worked. She wasn't one to judge; she had her own form of organised mess in her flat. But the sight she saw beyond the door brought this to a whole new level. It was no mere organised mess. It was chaos. It was as if a tempest had whirled through this North London flat, leaving nothing but anarchy and entropy in its wake.

Sam's wall of cases was as muddled as ever, although she noticed the amount of notes, connecting threads and indecipherable scribbles had at least doubled since she had last visited his home. The oaken wooden floors were almost completely hidden by the countless sheets of paper strewn around the room. Books piled high on the arms of the sofa and coffee table. A desktop computer had been rigged up on the coffee table as well, its wires snaking around themselves and all jammed into an extension cable, and an open laptop sat precariously atop a pile of books. A thick smoke filled the room, the scent of frankincense hanging heavily in the air.

'Sam?' Alice called into the room. The one thing that was actually missing from this room was Sam Hain himself. 'Sam?'

A mass of unruly black hair sprung up from behind the sofa, followed in quick succession by a head, shoulders, and chest. Sam spun around to face the doorway, smiling over to Alice and greeting her with a friendly 'hello.' Despite his upbeat demeanour, Alice suspected she could see the signs of weariness in his eyes, darkened bags hanging below his eyelids, and his hair was not in its usual state of misrule; this was the hair of a cartoon character who had just been shocked.

'I hope you like pizza,' Sam said as he waved his hand in the direction of a couple of large pizza boxes, 'I ordered us some when I knew you were on your way.'

'Of course I do! Who doesn't? Thank you, a good pizza is much better than spooky spaghetti on toast,' Alice said, carefully stepping over what appeared to be a short wall made of esoteric encyclopaedias. 'Are you okay? You're looking a bit... Worse for wear.'

'Nah, nah,' Sam said, brushing the comment aside with a wave of his hand, 'I just haven't had a good night's sleep in... I don't know how long, actually.' He stepped over the back of the sofa, tea cup and saucer in hand, and, placing the crockery down on one of the bookshelves, embraced Alice with a hug. He wrapped his arms around her, squeezed tightly for a second, and with a friendly pat on the back released her again. 'Between the memories and visions of the Void, and this case, sleep is an unwelcome interruption.'

'Okay,' she replied, 'don't you think actually getting some rest would do you good? Maybe help you think a bit clearer?'

'Ah, I'll rest when I'm dead,' Sam announced, turning to face the cases which riddled the wall. 'Actually, no, bad choice of words. I'll rest before then, obviously. If I can't sleep, I'll meditate or something.'

'Good. I mean, it looks like you could really use a break-'

'I could really use a break in this case!' Sam sounded frustrated, almost stumbling over his words as he spoke, and gesturing wildly at the wall. 'Something's going on, and whatever it is I don't have a good feeling about it.'

'So tell me, what is going on?' Alice asked. She moved towards the pizza boxes, opening the lid of the top box. Steam rose from the open box, releasing the tantalising, irresistible and mouth-watering aroma of a freshly cooked pizza. The cheese glistened, cooked to that perfect golden shade, and the crust was thick and oozing with a cheesy stuffing. She gleefully took a slice.

'Well,' Sam began, lowering his voice to a conspiratorial tone, 'something, somewhere, is going on. That's a pretty certain fact, as the Universe is constantly in motion and thus there must always be something going on in some form or another. But this, this is a very particular something in a very particular somewhere with very particular goings on...'

'Well that clears that up.'

'I can't quite place my finger on precisely what it is, but there's been a sudden surge of supernatural situations springing up across the city. There was the apparition of a woman wandering around St Pancras Church, the creature stalking the side-alleys of Soho, the haunting in Central Saint Martin's, numerous other spectral sightings. Each of them, in their own right, are fairly unimportant. But combined...' Sam trailed off as he approached the map pinned to his wall. He waved his hand across the mass of little crosses he had marked on the map. 'More and more of the extraordinary has been happening lately, and they seem to be mainly around the centre of London. Individually, this wouldn't matter, but so many of them, so close together in such a short space of time, there's something bigger going on.'

'Do you have any ideas?' Alice sat herself down on the sofa, moving a pile of crumpled papers to the side and crossing her legs comfortably. She placed the pizza box on the table in front of her, and took another bite. The melted cheese dangled from the slice like string. She delicately wiped the grease from the corner of her lips. 'You having any of this or not?'

'None at all.' Sam spoke flatly. He wandered back towards Alice and joined her on the sofa. His body seemed to flop as he sat down, his shoulders slumping forwards as he slouched into the cushiony seat. He exhaled a long, exasperated sigh. 'Ideas, that is. But I'll have some of the pizza,' he clarified, reaching to take a slice. The triangular slice drooped unhelpfully as he tried to take a bite.

'I can't make much sense of it,' he spoke through a mouthful. 'From the cases I've investigated to the ones I've simply heard about, I have tried to find some kind of pattern connecting them, some kind of rhyme or reason behind it. But look,' he waved his hand at the wall again, its mess of pen marks and lines of thread, 'I can't see any discernible pattern there. Maybe you're right, maybe I do need a rest to come back to it with fresh eyes. But also, I was hoping you might be able to provide some new, keen insight.'

Alice smiled at him. 'You're the detective, what do you think I'll see that you can't?' She turned to face the wall, squinting at it with scrutinising eyes, before returning her attention to Sam. 'All I can see is a load of squiggles, notes and string.'

'Alice,' Sam began, his eyes fixed upon the wall, 'have you ever wondered where I'd be without you? On our adventures, your help, your insight and support, has been absolutely invaluable to me.' He cleared his throat loudly. 'Now, do you have any thoughts?'

'Only that you're not very comfortable with paying compliments to people,' she replied, shooting him a quick, good-humoured smirk. 'but other than that...' A silence came over the room as Alice paused. She chewed on another slice of pizza contemplatively. She thought of the adventures that she and Sam had been on, the world just beyond the real that he had shown her, the lights that guide them, the things which lurk in the shadows, and the bizarre experiences they had shared. There was one thing which stuck out in her mind, and when she had noticed that it was there, it stubbornly refused to be ignored.

'Darkness,' she eventually said, staring at the map. 'Darkness is coming... This might be a silly question, but is my alphabetti-spaghetti connected?'

'Purely circumstantial,' Sam said, 'I doubt the spaghetti has any bearing on the Wardrobe Mistress or the Prowler of Poland Street.' Sam Hain often thought of his life in titles.

'You said to me when we first met, that Halloween night, that this "darkness is coming" thing was important, right? And don't you believe that everything is connected?'

Sam shifted in his seat. 'That does sound like something I would say,' he mused, stroking his chin thoughtfully. 'What are you thinking?'

'Well,' Alice said, leaning forwards and resting her head on her hands, 'if there's no such thing as coincidence, and everything's connected, then the fact that every case I've joined you on has involved the phrase–' she paused to make air quotes '–"darkness is coming", and it spells itself out in my spaghetti at the same time as you're charting this web of weirdness–'

'Web of Weirdness. I like it.'

'That's got to mean something, right?'

'Right,' Sam said slowly, a look on his face which suggested he was either on the cusp of a grand epiphany or had forgotten to turn the cooker off. 'Right,' he repeated. Standing up, he dropped a half eaten slice of pizza back into the box, and slowly approached the map on the wall. His eyes darted across the city's layout. 'Right,' he said for a third time.

Taking one of the threads of string from the board, Sam unravelled one of his nonsensical patterns and began to loop it around five push pins he had stuck into the map. 'Point the first: Islington, All Hallows' Eve, the night when our two paths converged, and that thing first uttered those words.' He secured the string to the top-most push pin which marked Highbury and Islington station. He then pulled the string down and to the left.

'Secondly, our night in Knightsbridge; the spirit of Louise Haversham gave you the warning that darkness is coming, and we closed a Void portal which inexplicably opened in that family's attic.' Tying the string around the push pin in Knightsbridge, Sam pulled the thread taut. He twanged the string, and it reverberated pleasingly. With the loose end of the thread, he now pulled it up and right.

'Point C,' he announced, 'the Grimditch Butcher, the demon summoned by the reckless use of blood magick speaks of the coming darkness.' He tied the string to the Grimditch push pin, looping it around and carrying on towards the left, crossing the thread which ran from Islington to Knightsbridge, and attaching it to the pin on Regent's Park. 'Can't forget the Regents, their experimentation with Voidwalkers, and when you mounted a daring rescue to get me out of their facility. Cypher mentioned he had seen what was coming, that darkness from beyond the Void...'

Sam dragged the thread to the lower right of the map,

down to London's Southbank. 'And then our gateway to the Imaginarium, the Eye of the Oracle. Whatever possessed the tourist knew that phrase would grab my attention, but in doing so it led me to L-' Sam cut himself short, and focussed on circling the thread around the pin. 'Now this might not look like much right now, but! As you rightly said, Alice, your alphabetti-spaghetti is connected, because...' Sam drew the last remaining stretch of thread back up to the pin on Highbury and Islington, tying it to the first knot he had made. 'Because, it completes the pattern.'

Stepping back, Sam admired his handiwork. Why it had not occurred to him before, he was not sure, but Alice's words had triggered a series of thoughts to run through his mind. Suddenly, it all became clear.

'Well that's... Something,' Alice said, standing up to join Sam by the map. She stared at it, intrigued and more than a little mystified. 'That's a little bit too precise to be just a random coincidence, isn't it?'

'The Universe is rarely so lazy,' Sam muttered, holding his chin in his hand as he contemplated the map.

When the threads connecting each of the cases he and Alice had been on together were drawn in order, linking each case which bore the foreboding message that darkness is coming, the pattern formed an almost perfect pentagram. Each of the five cases marked the tips of the five-pointed star which stretched across central London. Contained within the pentagonal shape, at the heart of the star, were the districts of Covent Garden, Soho and Bloomsbury. The densest cluster of crosses marking the recent paranormal phenomenon lay perfectly within this shape.

'What does it mean?' Alice asked.

Sam remained silent for a moment. He stared at the pattern. He stared at the crossing threads which formed the pentagram, at the marks of each unexplained event he had seen or heard about which sat at its centre, at the myriad notes and ideas he had scrawled about each one. He had tried to draw connections between them all, to find an answer, to make sense of them. And now the solution was staring him in the face. It had been in front of him the whole time.

'I have no idea,' he breathed, 'but I suspect nothing good.'

CHAPTER V

In the dimly lit basement flat of Constantine Road, Sam Hain set himself to work. Candles flickered and licked at the shadows with their orange tongues. Thick white smoke filled the air, cloying and sickly sweet, billowing from a cast iron cauldron which had been placed on the coffee table. The paper and books he had been digging through had been cleared away, or at least as clear as Sam was capable of making things. The occult detective sat upon the sofa, legs crossed in the lotus position, his eyes shut and looking for all the world to be in a peaceful state of meditation.

This was, of course, not exactly as it seemed. Despite his outward appearance of Zen serenity, Sam's mind was whirling like a pinwheel in a hurricane. His thoughts raced and stumbled over each other as he tried to make sense of the evidence which had been presented to him. The cases and series of events which had led to this moment were not the important thing; what was important was what linked them all together. The pentagram over the map of London burned with bright green fire in his mind's eye. Other lights shone like tiny etheric diodes across the map, blips where he would have marked off each instance of the recent events. The closer to the centre of the pentagram they were, the more tightly they were packed together, until they seemed to coalesce into one large, glowing mass.

Focus. Sam felt a whispering voice graze over his ear. It was a woman's voice, but it wasn't Alice's. *Concentrate. You're close.* It did not come from anywhere outside of himself. Instead, it seemed to be murmuring from somewhere inside his mind.

Lorna? Sam asked the voice in his mind. He wasn't entirely sure, but the voice certainly felt like the presence of Lorna's spirit.

Hiya! The reply came, somewhat more jubilantly than it had been whispering.

How're things?

Pretty good. It's nice when you meditate like this, I can speak with you more clear- Hey! What did I say about focus? The vision of the map, the pentacle, and the glowing points had faded from Sam's mind, and the spirit of Lorna Mortimer found herself in a mental projection of Sam's living room. *Don't get me wrong*, she spoke, *I'd love to stay and chat with you, bunny, but I'm trying to help you put a stop to this. Your mind has been stuck in a rut for a while, and now that the pieces are coming together a lot of things are about to make a good deal of sense.*

Sam stood up from the imaginary sofa in the imaginary living room of his mind. *All right, fine*, he said to Lorna, who stood by the fireplace, leaning against the mantelpiece in a short and summery playsuit. With a flick of his wrist, Sam brought the map from off of the wall to hover in the middle of the room. The pentagram reignited in green fire. He glanced around his mind's projected representation of his flat. *Do you at least like what I've done with the place?* Somehow, Sam's living room in his mind was in even more of a state of untidy chaos than the physical one.

Yes, very "you", sweetie, Lorna said with a humoured tone. *Now, focus.*

Sam focussed. The pieces began to come together again. The pentagram burned vibrantly, and the tiny beacons of light blinked back to life across the map one by one. He tried to keep his mind trained on the vision of the map which levitated before him, concentrating on the lights which glowed brighter and brighter, coming together in a dense cluster at the heart of the green burning star, seemingly gathering around one spot. In one place. Like a focal point. A focal point at the very core of the pattern, in the middle of the city.

'The British Museum!' Sam declared triumphantly, snapping himself out of his meditation with a jolt.

'Huh? Really?' Alice said somewhat sleepily. She had dozed off, reclining lazily in the armchair after finishing dinner and while waiting for Sam to complete his attempt at location scrying. 'I, uh, I pretty much finished that whole pizza without you, while you were all Zen and stuff. I'm feeling disgustingly full. Just having a quick food-coma nap.' She patted her stomach contentedly. The pizza was precisely what she had needed; it was far more satisfying, filling and comforting than alphabetti-spaghetti on toast.

'No time for napping,' he said, standing up and wobbling uneasily when he realised his legs had fallen asleep. His legs and feet tingled uncomfortably as the nerves came back to life. 'If this is as problematic as I think it is, then we haven't got a moment to lose.' *Thank you*, he thought to Lorna, having not had a chance to say it before he startled himself out of the meditation, *thank you for your help, my love.*

'And what do you think it is?' Alice pried as she pulled herself up out of the armchair.

'I'm still not entirely sure, but we can't let it continue a moment more,' he said. He darted from one corner to another, first throwing his long overcoat on in a whirlwind motion. As it billowed out, the waft of air it created sent some of the more well-organised notes flying through the room. Secondly, he grabbed his hat from on top of one of the bookshelves, firmly placing it upon his head. He briefly adjusted the position of the brim so it was at a more rakish angle. 'More and more supernatural events have been cropping up, seemingly becoming more prominent with each passing day. The densest cluster of events lay in the heart of the "darkness" cases, and at the core of all of this, is the British Museum. There must be a connection. And the longer we leave it, the more whatever it is will make itself evident; but given the strength of these events, I don't think we can let it get to that point.' Brushing past the mantelpiece, Sam grabbed the Void crystal he had found in the house in Knightsbridge and thrust it into his pocket.

'What are you doing with the Void thingy?'

'I don't know, it just feels important,' Sam replied plainly. He then picked up a small, ornate-looking notebook and his transphasic energy probe – which Alice refused to call anything other than a TechnoWand – and pocketed those too. 'Let's go.'

The evening was colder than one might expect of an early-summer's day. A cool wind blew down Hampstead high street, and the blue skies and orange sun were gradually being overtaken by thick grey clouds. Something, Sam thought, must be afoot.

On the walk to the Underground station, he had sent James a message to meet with them both on the way. He had promised to fill him in on what he knew so far, and that he would appreciate any help his friend could give him. Of course, James had agreed, and suggested they meet at Leicester Square where their paths would cross. This was the route they were now travelling on.

The tube was surprisingly not too crowded heading into central from Hampstead; at this time of the evening, most people were heading out of the city centre and back home, rather than the other way around. Sam appreciated this. It meant that they didn't have to fight through the crowds or stand by the doors, crammed in like sardines. They could take a seat and relax until they reached their stop. At least, that was what he had hoped. However, relaxation and peace was something which rarely found its way into Sam's life. Least of all when he expected it. This situation was no different.

They had just passed Euston station, only a few short

stops from Leicester Square, when Sam noticed something was not quite right. The lights on the underground train flickered, sending the carriage into darkness, bursting back into light, and then fading to black again. This was not entirely unusual for the London Underground. What was unusual, and certainly not part of Transport for London's normal service, was that in the brief darkness of the flickering lights, something had appeared. Two somethings, to be precise. Seated opposite Sam and Alice, where previously there had been no-one, was an old woman and a little girl with a red balloon. He did not remember them getting on at any station – although he couldn't say that he had been paying particular attention to the comings and goings of other passengers – and they could not have made it to those seats in the brief moments of darkness. But these facts were not the strangest things. Neither of them, Sam noted when he looked up at them, had a reflection.

He nudged Alice, and attempted to nod subtly in the direction of the two. She looked at him, over to the two of them, and then back to him. She wrinkled her brow with confusion.

'No reflection,' he whispered as discreetly as possible.

Alice looked over again, and her brow unwrinkled as her eyes widened. Her head snapped back to face Sam. 'Ghosts?' she mouthed. 'Vampires?'

Sam shook his head slowly, shrugging his shoulders. 'Too early in the day for vampires,' he replied in a low and hushed tone. The lights flickered once again, and it was then that Sam realised he had something more to worry about. It was now no longer just their lack of reflection which bothered him; as the lights dipped and flickered, sending the carriage into a moment of darkness, the shape of the woman and the girl became something else. Something he could not quite determine in the shadows. Something hulking, something unnatural, and something which most definitely was not either an old woman or a little girl. Merely glimpsing its silhouette in the darkness of the carriage had sent a shiver down Sam's spine.

The lights came back up, and it was as if nothing had happened. The little girl smiled at him, and waved her balloon around as if showing off the fact that she had a red balloon. Sam didn't think that was much of an accolade to boast about, but then again this was just a little girl... At least, whatever it was appeared to be a little girl. Possibly a little girl ghost, he thought, attempting to deny whatever it was he had just seen in the shadows. But he could not get the image of the thing which wore the image of a little girl, and of an old woman, out of his mind. He forced a smile back across the carriage to her, trying to ignore his thoughts. The old woman scowled at him, and he averted her steely gaze. Out of the corner of his eye, he thought he could see the woman tapping rhythmically on her knee, and he was sure her hands were covered in grey, reflective scales instead of skin.

'The next station is: Goodge Street,' the automated announcement cheerily spoke. 'Doors will open on the left hand side.'

The old woman and little girl stood up. Or rather, the thing which looked like an old woman and a little girl transitioned from a sitting position to standing without much motion in between. Sam made no effort to hide the fact he was watching them with great interest. Sparks flashed outside of the tube's window as it rounded a corner. Neither the girl or the old woman seemed to be affected by the motion of the carriage, not swaying or losing their balance with any of the jolts or turns. They glided gracefully along the carriage, drifting past the windows without the courtesy to cast a reflection in any of them, and stood by the doors of the train. It slowed to a gradual halt as they pulled in at Goodge Street station.

'Alice,' Sam said, leaning in towards her, 'you carry on

down to meet James, and I'll find you both at the museum. I need to follow that little girl and the old woman.'

Before Alice had a chance to reply, Sam had leapt out of his seat and started to make his way along the carriage. Halfway, he quickly darted back towards her. 'That sounded really weird, but you know what I mean.' With that, he hurried back through the train to the doors. People started to filter onto the carriage, and he had to push his way through as they barged their way onboard. He jumped out of the door, narrowly avoiding having the tail-end of his coat caught in the doors as they slid closed, and began to follow the shape of the anomalous travellers.

Alice carried on with the rest of the journey uninterrupted. Why Sam had needed to jump off and follow the two ghosts, she didn't really know. Nor was she sure why he didn't want her to go with him. But she was only a couple of stops away from Leicester Square, where she would meet James Mortimer before heading back to rendezvous with Sam at the museum. Presuming he was done with whatever quest he had decided to embark on by then. She sat back, plugged her headphones into her phone, and intended to relax for the remainder of the journey.

Sam made his way through the winding, packed-out corridors of the underground station. He weaved through the throngs of people as they came and went, trying to catch up with the things – or thing – which looked like an old woman and a little girl with a red balloon. Above the heads of the crowd, the balloon bobbed merrily a short distance ahead of him. Sam followed it, like a predator stalking its prey.

He didn't quite know what he was planning to do. It wasn't as if he could corner them in the middle of a crowded tube station; most people probably would not take too kindly to a man harassing an old woman and her granddaughter, and they certainly would not believe his reasoning. Besides, he had a policy about not causing a commotion in plain sight of the general public, especially not when it could put others in danger. He would have to be discreet. He would have to be cunning. He would have to be-

The red balloon disappeared from sight, turning a corner and down another corridor. The stream of commuters carried on their way, either flowing down to the platforms or heading towards the lifts and stairs up to the surface. The old woman and the little girl with the red balloon took neither of these routes. They had turned down one of the least busy corridors, and as Sam rounded the corner he saw the balloon being dragged through a doorway. A large metal door closed behind the balloon, with a sign which said, in big, officious letters: "No Entry – Authorised Personnel Only". *This*, he thought, *is perfect. Neatly tucked away, out of sight from the general public.*

Approaching the door, Sam disregarded the sign. As far as he was concerned, he was authorised personnel; very few Transport for London employees would know how to deal with the supernatural, after all. He turned the handle and pulled the metal door open. Despite being quite heavy, it opened with surprising ease. It was as if they were asking for people to trespass. Casting a quick, cautionary glance over his shoulder, he slipped inside the open doorway, closing it behind him.

It was dark inside the place of no entry. The simple incandescent bulbs which hung from the ceiling cast very little light into the dim space, a stark contrast to the fluorescents of the underground's corridors. This passageway was far less aesthetically appealing than the other areas of the station, and all things considered that's not very appealing at all. It is no coincidence that very few people would consider the London Underground "scenic".

There was no sign of the old woman or the little girl in the dimly lit passageway, but somewhere in the distance he could hear the faint sound of a child singing.

'*Mary, Mary, quite contrary, how does your garden grow...*' The little girl's voice sang from somewhere in the bowels of the underground station, the sound slowly lilting through the air. It made the hairs on the back of Sam's neck prickle. He knew he had to venture deeper.

The corridor stretched on for longer than he thought it would. He walked the length of it, his boots clopping against the bare concrete floor. It was marred with stains of paint and water damage, and scratches and chunks of it appeared to have been chipped away. It melded seamlessly into the equally barren wall and ceiling, a square tunnel of concrete which seemed to run on for longer than the station's platforms. Old and rusted pipes jutted out into the corridor (unsurprisingly in the areas where water damage was most prominent) and the occasional fuse box was fastened to the wall. Every ten yards or so, another lightbulb hung from the ceiling, dusty and alone, casting an orange-yellow circle of light onto the floor.

Maintenance tunnels, Sam thought, were really quite boring.

And still the voice sung, at times echoing all around him, and at others it faintly called to him from far away. He proceeded along the tunnel, moving slowly and cautiously, keeping his eyes and ears open for whatever this thing was.

As he approached the end of the corridor, Sam saw a set of concrete stairs spiralling down, deeper into the underground network. He followed them, walking on the wider edge of each step as he wound his way to the lower level. He jumped the final two steps, and was unsurprised to find at the base of the stairwell was another concrete corridor. It was not as long as the one above, it was only a few meters, but at the end of it was another metal door. It seemed older than the one he had entered, with equally old warning signs and an exclamation point inside of a yellow triangle nailed to the door. He had not come this far just to allow a few unfriendly signs to stop him now – they were only advisory, anyway, he told himself – and he pushed the door open.

On the other side of the door, Sam found himself standing on a tube platform. It was long and curved, the other end of the platform somewhere just around the bend, but it did not look like it had been used in a very long time. Soot had built up on the walls, blackening the tile work, and the thick, dry smell of dust clung to his nostrils. And it was dark, almost entirely devoid of light. But only almost. From somewhere a little out of sight, a wide beam of light cast itself upon the soot covered walls, faintly illuminating the rest of the platform. Dust motes drifted and danced in the beam.

But something else moved in the light too.

Sam stood and watched as two shadows appeared on the wall in the wide yellow glow of the spotlight. One seemed to be slightly hunched, shuffling as it moved. Linked to it by the hand was a smaller shadow, more upright, and holding a tether with an upside-down teardrop shape floating at the end of it. He watched the two shadows intently, observing them. He was undecided whether he should make his presence known, but it quickly became clear that that would not be necessary.

Like shadow puppets being played out on the wall, the two figures began to shift. They twisted and turned around themselves, transforming into something else, something unrecognisable, in front of his eyes. The figures of the old woman and the little girl seemed to fuse into one. The balloon drooped as if it had suddenly lost half of its helium. The shapes which had once appeared so innocent on the surface became a singular, monstrous form. And then it spoke.

'Why do you follow us, mortal?' The voice was deep and

437

booming, and not at all the voice of either an old woman or a little girl.

'Curiosity,' Sam announced to the unearthly shadow on the wall.

There was a low, guttural 'hmm' from the shadows. 'Then you either do not value your existence, or you lack the awareness to understand what we are.'

'Neither, really,' he said blithely, slowly making his way along the platform, creeping closer to the source of the shadow. 'I think I have some awareness of what you are.'

'You are foolish, then,' the thing bellowed.

Sam could now see the light was being cast from out of a passageway halfway along the platform, presumably leading to the main, but disused, stairwell for this abandoned platform. 'You wouldn't be the first to say that,' he said, 'so enlighten me. What, precisely, are you?'

The thing which was at one time an old woman and a little girl with a red balloon heaved a groaning growl of a sound, its entire body hulking in the shadow it cast upon the wall. 'We are that which dwells in darkness, the forgotten shadows which swim in your nightmares, the ones which lurk deep within the Void itself.' A rasping breath came gasping from the creature. 'Mortals know us well, yet our truth is unknowable.'

'I don't know, you're explaining it pretty well, seeing as you're talking to just a *mere mortal*,' Sam said, reaching for his energy probe. Pulling it from out of his coat's breast pocket, he quickly polished the crystal tip with his thumb. He grasped the metal hilt of the TechnoWand, feeling its energy pulsing through it. The shadow projected in the spotlight shifted and writhed, as if turning to face him. The drooping shape which had once resembled a balloon bobbed and swayed in front of something which Sam thought looked like a distinctly unpleasant mouth. He edged along the platform, getting closer to the creature.

'Yet you do not flee. You are indeed a foolish one.' The shadow leapt from the beam of the spotlight, like a pouncing animal, but instead of some hulking monstrosity leaping out onto the station's platform, the old woman and the little girl with the red balloon appeared. They stared at Sam, their eyes as black as oil.

'Clever costume,' Sam said as he stared back at them. He took a hesitant step back, making sure there was a good amount of space between him and them. It. He thought of the thing in plural when it looked like the two people.

As the creature spoke, the mouths of the woman and the girl moved in unison. 'We mask ourselves among your kind as we hunt, hidden in plain sight. The hunted do not fear the hunter when they can not distinguish between predator and prey.' The little girl smiled sweetly, but her smile bared jagged and pointed teeth in a mouth far too large for any human. 'There are so many in your world whose absence will not be noted; those whose presence will not be missed. They wander lost, and alone, in the quiet darkness of the night. They rest in the damp and deserted alleys on nests of cardboard. They welcome us, a friendly sight when in need, shortly before they meet their end.' The two figures stepped forward, their feet moving in perfect synchronicity. The balloon bounced playfully in the air. 'So too will your end go unnoticed.'

'I wouldn't count on either of those statements being true,' he retorted, raising the TechnoWand and waving it in a spiral in front of him. He gave it a flick as he reached the centre of the spiral, sending a burst of white energy streaming into the two people. They staggered backwards, hissing through inhuman mouths.

The old woman and the little girl shuddered. They shook uncontrollably, convulsing and twisting, their limbs bending and snapping at unnatural angles. The sound of bones crunching echoed along the empty platform. Their appearance began to melt, slipping from reality like water off of an oily surface, giving way to something else. The red balloon drooped, its rubbery surface shifting into a bulbous sack which glowed in the darkness; its tether became a wiry tendril which sprouted from the girl. She opened her mouth wide, baring countless serrated teeth as her jaw grew larger and larger, folding the little girl over herself as she was turned inside out. Her entire body transformed into one large, grotesque fish-like face with a vast and gaping maw.

The sickening, unfolding, twisting transformation spread across the two figures. The old woman bent over double, melding into the fish-like head as the two morphed and fused together as one. A large and hulking body, covered in shimmering black scales, seemed to grow from the fish-like head, replacing its original form with something far more unsettling than a scowling old woman. Legs became scaly, lizard-like limbs with clawed feet. A pair of pustulous eyes, each one formed from what had been the heads of the little girl and the old woman, blinked from either side of the monstrous entity's head. Its gaping maw stretched larger and wider than a mouth had any right to be, as if the creature was more cavernous jaws and knife-like teeth than anything else. Small writhing tendrils, like feelers, sprouted along the body, waggling in the air as the thing finished its transformation. To Sam, it seemed to resemble a very misshapen anglerfish on four reptilian legs.

The hideous creature shook itself, in much the same way a dog shakes itself after getting wet, as if it were adjusting to its sudden transformation. It hissed, revealing a long, snakelike tongue from behind its rows of steak-knife teeth. It leaped at him, launching itself from its backwards-jointed legs at an alarming speed. Sam had just enough time to throw himself out of its way, narrowly avoiding its unnaturally large head and clawed feet. He collided with the tiled wall of the platform, heavily and ungracefully. Regaining his balance, he started to retreat back along the platform, staggering as he ran.

From somewhere behind him, he heard the creature snarl and hiss, and the sound of claws clicking against the platform. It drew closer and closer, much quicker than he would have liked, and before he had the time to think, something heavy smashed into the back of him. Sam was thrown to the floor, and he could feel the thing soaring over him. He pushed himself back onto his feet. His chest felt heavy and bruised, winded from the impact. Looking up, he saw the monstrosity by the doorway he had entered, cutting off his escape route. It turned and faced him, a black viscous fluid oozing from its maw, dripping stickily on the floor.

Sam raised the TechnoWand once more, firing a bolt of purple energy towards the creature. The bolt sizzled as it cut through the air, seemingly ablaze with violet fire, and it hit the entity squarely between its bulbous fish eyes. It reeled, taking a staggered step backwards, and the energy dispersed as it rippled along the oily scales. It shook itself again.

Spinning on his heels, Sam began to run again. Normally, he thought, that kind of magick would at least incapacitate a creature; it could dissipate a low level entity entirely, but this thing seemed to completely diffuse the effect through its scales. It could still feel pain, though, and it was not entirely immune to attack.

He could hear it, the thump of its feet, punctuated by the clack of its claws, as it galumphed after him. It was getting closer. The sound of its feet on the platform became more rhythmic, less asynchronous, and Sam suspected it was preparing to leap at him once more. He turned to look over his shoulder as he ran, and saw the creature propel itself into the air, lunging towards him. Without a moment's hesitation, Sam fired another bolt of energy at the creature. It struck the monster's underside, and although its scales dissipated the energy, the force from the blast sent it sprawling backwards, hitting the floor somewhere a few yards behind him with a wet thud.

Sam did not stop to see what had happened. He simply kept running. The doorway the monster had emerged from came up on his left, and he immediately ran through it, almost tripping over the construction light in the process. Laying next to the light was an orange fluorescent jacket with the letters "TFL" printed on it, a toolbox stained with something which looked suspiciously like blood, and a severed hand clutching the handle of the portable battery powering the light. *One of the creature's victims*, Sam thought as he ran past the remains, grateful that the dead man's light provided just enough visibility for him to see where he was going. Up ahead, he could see a set of stairs, presumably leading back to the level above.

The creature had got itself back on its feet and was once again in hot pursuit. It charged around the corner in a blind rage, sliding across the floor and slamming into the tile-clad wall of the passageway. Tiles shattered and broke away from the impact. It shrieked aggressively, lurching towards Sam. Its mouth gaped open, its razor sharp teeth glinting, salivating viscous black drool.

Sam fired another shot, and another. The two purple bolts struck the vile monstrosity, one sparking against the creature's scaly hide harmlessly, the other hitting it in the jaw. It wailed an agonising wail and seemed to recoil in pain. *There's a weak spot, then*, Sam thought as he turned and began to run up the stairs. He took two steps at a time, desperately hoping to put as much ground between himself and the creature as possible.

Thankfully, the thing which had once been an old woman and a little girl with a red balloon, but now more closely resembled an anglerfish with legs and too big a mouth, was not particularly good at climbing stairs. At first, it tried to leap after Sam, but failed to land its feet on the steps, and slid back down. Then it tried running up the stairs, but as its legs flailed asynchronously it only managed a few steps before tripping over itself. Eventually, it elected to slowly walk up, carefully placing each clawed foot upon a step before the next one. It may have looked unwieldy and cumbersome, but the creature was slowly and surely climbing the stairs.

Rounding the corner at the top of the first flight of stairs, Sam started to make his way up the next flight. It was darker now that the light from below was out of sight; the only thing keeping the stairwell from complete blackness was the slight reflection of the light bouncing off of the tiles lining the first set of stairs. Sam could just about make out the steps in front of him, still taking them two at a time, but somewhat more gingerly. His eyes were trying to adapt to the dark, but his vision wasn't perfect. In his rush, he stepped on the hem of his coat and tripped forwards. He scrambled back to his feet, partly crawling his way up the steps as he did so, knowing the thing – while being admittedly slow – was not too far behind him. He staggered over the top steps and was about to start running down the corridor ahead of him, when he noticed something.

It was not a corridor at all. Sam found himself stood at the top of the steps and only a few yards away from a wall with a set of double doors. "Maintenance Access Only", read a sign on the doors, "Keep Out". Today had already been a day for disregarding signs, and Sam saw no reason to start following instructions from inanimate objects now. He jogged towards the door, uncomfortably aware that the creature was now at the base of the second flight of stairs, and was relieved to find that the padlock which held the chain across the door was not locked. In the very faint light, Sam could just about make out the shape of a bloody hand-print smeared across the door; presumably another victim of this thing, and the unfortunate soul who never got around to locking the door properly.

Discarding the padlock and chain on the ground with a

loud clang, Sam pushed the bar on the double doors. He threw them open, stepping out onto a small platform. It was a square space, not much wider than the corridor he had come from, and set a short distance back from one of the disused tube tunnels. The screeching sound of tube trains elsewhere on the network echoed through the tunnel, and a faint white light helped partly illuminate the area. There wasn't much to look at, only the soot covered tunnel and the small platform with a maintenance panel and a cabinet of tools, but Sam appreciated he was not completely lost in the dark. His eyes seemed to be adjusting better in the low light; he felt like he could see somewhat better than before.

There was a hideous, bubbling snarl from behind him, and he wheeled around to see the monster. It was shrouded in the darkness of the corridor beyond the doors, but the bulbous sack which hung above its anglerfish-like head glowed and illuminated the wet, scaly and vicious face of the creature. It stalked towards him, its eyes glimmering in the dim light. Sam raised the probe, and fired at it again. The creature shook the energy bolt off as if it were nothing, and broke into a lop-sided run. He had nowhere to go; either chance his luck here on the platform, or jump down onto the tracks and hope he wasn't trapped.

He chose the former.

Leaping wildly into the air and gnashing its monstrous jaw ferociously, the creature launched itself at its prey. Instinctively, Sam dropped to the floor, laying as flat as possible across the concrete. He could feel his feet dangling off of the edge of the platform, and prayed the beast would not land directly on him. He felt the rush of the air and a foul stench he could only liken to stagnant water and gone-off fish as it propelled itself over him. There was an unpleasant thud some distance away, as the thing landed on the tracks by the side of the platform.

Not wasting a single second, Sam began to pull himself forward, kicking his feet as he struggled back up, and lurched towards the doors as he broke into a run before he was even fully standing. He could not fight this thing and win – not right now, at least – and he knew his best bet was to escape. He knew he could not allow it to continue dwelling in the shadows of an abandoned tube line, though, especially not when it was preying on the homeless and maintenance workers. As soon as he was through the doors, he would seal them shut behind him, buying him enough time to escape and then return to either destroy this thing or send it back to the Void once he had discovered a spell potent enough.

He looked over his shoulder to see the thing standing on its hind legs, mouth agape and roaring a blood curdling, bellowing roar. He was about to pull the doors shut when something unusual happened (as if everything leading to this point were not unusual enough). The light in the tunnel seemed to grow brighter. The noise of the trains on the rails grew louder. A warm wind blew. The creature's roar seemed to meld with the honking sound of a train's horn. In the blink of an eye and with a rather loud and sickening wet thud, the thing which resembled an anglerfish with lizard-like legs was quickly replaced by a speeding Northern Line train heading for Morden via Charring Cross.

Oily black blood and viscera erupted from the impact, and the screeching of the train's brakes pierced Sam's ears. Sparks flew up from the track. A little red light blinked on the maintenance panel. Sam breathed a half-hearted sigh of relief. He closed the double doors to the platform behind him, wrapping the chain around it, reattached the padlock, and slowly began his walk back through the station. In a way, it was relaxing knowing he was no longer in mortal peril; on the other, it was going to take him a while to wind down from the adrenaline now surging through him.

In the final, split second before the train had hit the creature, Sam was sure he had seen it return to the form of the old woman and the little girl with the red balloon.

He preferred not to think about that.

In Leicester Square, Alice was having to fight a battle of her own. First of all, the droves of rush hour commuters were making the idea of personal space feel like a far-flung fantasy. They swarmed the platforms and escalators, weaving in and around each other, and finding a magical way to dally and dither right in Alice's way. Generally speaking, she wasn't an impatient woman, but this was really starting to put that to the test, and she could feel her patience wearing thin.

Secondly, when she got to the ticket barriers, she jumped from one queue to another while the other travellers slowly filtered through the gates. Tickets and cards were rejected, barriers steadfastly refused to open for some but were more than happy to part for others, and Alice just wanted to get out of the claustrophobic atmosphere as soon as possible. When she got to the barrier, she touched her Oyster card to the reader. It beeped merrily, and the little gate threw itself open before her, only to immediately snap shut on her as she was part way through. She tried to push herself forward, but the gate would not budge, so she had to wiggle herself free while walking backwards as bystanders stood and tutted as if she were to blame for the issue.

Thirdly, trying the gate for a second time, her Oyster was declined because the system considered that she had already touched out. This pushed Alice's patience that little bit further. Especially when she explained this to a particularly unsympathetic guard, who treated her as if she were the single greatest inconvenience to walk into his life.

Lastly, her Oyster card had taken itself overdrawn, and top-up points were either conveniently out of order or were distinctly unhappy with accepting her cash. Instead, she found herself reluctantly queueing up for the card payment machine. *Whatever*, she thought, dejected.

After what had felt like eternity, but was in fact no longer than ten minutes, Alice emerged on the streets of London. She sighed, taking in a few deep breaths of the city air, before heading to meet James at the café around the corner.

CHAPTER VI

Bounding up the steps of the Grecian temple style portico at the main entrance of the British Museum, Sam pushed his way through the crowds of people. They milled around the doors, slowly filtering out of the building. An automated announcement came over the tannoy, signalling that the exhibits would be closing in ten minutes. He casually brushed off one of the guard's warnings that the museum was due to shut for the day, weaving his way against the flow of the people leaving, and made his way through the vast doors.

He had been waiting outside of the museum for ten minutes, and had text Alice to find out where she and James were, but received no response. He assumed they must have been on the tube. He would have waited for them a little while longer were it not for the fact that the museum was closing soon. He had to get in before they locked him out. As he stepped through the grand doors into the entrance hall of the museum, he sent them both a quick message saying that he was inside, asking them to join him there as soon as they could. If he had to, he thought, he would just have to get to the bottom of this one on his own.

Inside, people still slowly meandered around the exhibits, glancing at statues and reading plaques as they made their way towards the exit. Museum staff tried to gently usher the public out for the night, but it didn't seem to be speeding up proceedings. Thankfully, many of them were too distracted with trying to move tourist groups that they failed to notice the man in the hat and overcoat striding into the museum, towards the centre. Towards the Great Court.

The Great Court was empty when Sam arrived. It was a

vast, circular space, with a high glass ceiling which curved in towards the middle and met at the top of a tall cylindrical building. Two grand flights of stairs curved around and up the side of the cylinder, which was once the museum's Reading Room, but it was now closed to the public. The place was desolate and cavernous without anyone else around, and even though it had been but a few moments since Sam had last passed any visitors or staff, it felt as if the museum was abandoned. He walked slowly, conscious of even the slightest sound his footsteps would make. Even the lightest tread seemed to echo throughout the chamber.

'Museum's closed, pal,' a voice came echoing from somewhere in the Great Court.

Sam wheeled around, expecting to see a guard standing in the doorway behind him, but there was no one in sight. His head turned this way and that, trying to find the source of the voice, but he was entirely alone in the empty room. He knew better than to believe that he could have imagined it and, reaching into his pocket, Sam grasped the handle of the TechnoWand. He tried to tell himself he was ready for anything, but he knew that was not exactly true. Instead, he hoped that the anything simply wouldn't happen.

'Didn't you hear me? You're not supposed to be here,' the voice came again, 'unless – and I highly doubt it – you're here to make a deal?'

'No deals here,' Sam shouted back into the air, making his way slowly towards the staircases. He could see a sign posted at the bottom of each one. "Facility Closed for Private Exhibit: Regents of the Golden Ages", the signs read. For a cabal such as the Regents, they really had a knack for naming even their secret things something obvious. Scanning the room, Sam's eyes peered scrutinously at every corner, every shadow, every doorway. Nothing. 'Just doing my job,' he said, peering over his shoulder again.

'As am I,' replied the voice. It no longer echoed, and sounded much closer than it had before. When Sam faced directly ahead again, he found himself face to face with a man.

At first, Sam assumed this was just another security guard, and then he noticed the man was not wearing an ID. Nor was his jacket marked with the British Museum branding. Instead, the man in front of him wore an impeccably tailored black suit: slim line trousers atop a pair of shining black brogues, a slim fitting jacket with narrow steeped lapels and a perfectly white shirt with a thin black silk tie. He was a tall man with a gaunt face and a stone-like expression, piercing grey eyes set beneath a furrowed brow and slicked back hair. On the notch of his lapel he wore a golden pin the shape of an Ancient Egyptian Was Sceptre (there was a similar, significantly older looking one in the Rameses exhibit a few halls away). Sam recognised the man, but the recognition only made the situation worse.

'Agent Smith,' he spoke slowly, lowering his voice to a discontented tone and thrusting his hands into his pockets. Sam tried to stand tall, but somehow Agent Smith always remained a few inches taller. 'What an unpleasant surprise. Where's Agent Jones?'

'Reconstituting. After that brouhaha at the Hub, his essence needed time to repair,' Smith replied. 'And I wish I could say the same for you, but your being here is hardly a surprise. You really don't know when to stop, do you?'

'Thank you, I pride myself on not giving up.'

'You shouldn't. It leads you to being bound in the back of a limousine and then left in a Regents' cell for not listening to reason. You really should learn to listen to the advice of those infinitely your better, otherwise,' the agent shuffled his feet with mock-awkwardness, 'you end up in situations like this.' In a single swift motion, Smith reached into his jacket and pulled out his gun, aiming it at Sam. Lightning coursed through the barrel, crackling impatiently.

In a reciprocating and in no way as swift motion, Sam fumbled with the TechnoWand in his pocket, catching the crystal tip on the lining, tugging it free and aiming it at Smith. 'Looks like we've reached an impasse.' Sam straightened his shoulders and faced Smith side-on, holding the TechnoWand at arm's length and striking a dramatic pose, his free hand clenched into a fist by his side.

'What do you think you're going to do with that? Will me out of existence?' Smith raised a quizzical, mocking eyebrow. 'I survived our last encounter; the same can not be said for your friend and the others who could not escape. You know my essence is not as fragile as you beings of flesh and blood. My kind are constructs, thoughts given form. For as long as people believe in the Men in Black, the shadowy agents who conduct the clandestine will of secret societies, we exist. For as long as these cabbalistic organisations exist, and the Regents see us fit for purpose as they always have and always will, we exist. There is little you can do to stop-'

'Don't bet on it,' Sam said as he swung himself around, bringing up his clenched fist and using the momentum to strike the gun. The lightning in the barrel of the gun ceased crackling as it flew from Smith's hand, clattering to the floor and skimming several feet away from the agent. Without a moment's hesitation and absolutely no forethought, Sam seized the opportunity of the disarmed agent, spun on his heels and ran. 'And don't waste time monologuing,' he shouted over his shoulder as he ran back towards the main exhibits, 'it's too cliché!'

Smith growled as he knelt down to pick up the discarded gun. He turned a dial on the side of the gun's chamber, causing the electrical current to build up. The weapon made a high pitched whine. A small diode turned green. Standing upright again, Smith narrowed his eyes towards the fleeing form of Sam Hain. He raised his right arm, gun in hand. 'You can't stop us, Sam Hain!'

An arc of electrical energy tore through the air. It crackled viciously as it cut its jagged path, bursting from the muzzle like a bolt of lightning. Sam narrowly avoided the bolt, ducking behind one of the statues on display in the Great Court. The beam buzzed past him harmlessly, although it left a sizeable scorch mark when it impacted the white wall.

Sheltering behind the statue, Sam fumbled with his TechnoWand. It would be no match for Smith's Arc Gun (as Sam now dubbed it), but at the very least he could project and amplify a magickal protection field. Whether that would be enough, he was not sure, but it was better than nothing. He felt the cold, smooth surface of the Void crystal in his pocket, and an idea began to form in his mind. Another hissing crackle cut the silence, followed by the very solid sound of shattering stone. The statue of a horseman atop the plinth Sam was sheltered behind suddenly found himself without a head. Now, evidently, was not the time to try and figure it out; instead, Sam started running again. He kept his head low, his body hunched, and his legs incessantly carrying him forwards.

He paid no heed to the other bolts of electricity which soared around him, his only focus was on reaching a place of relative safety; somewhere more defensible. The one thing he was acutely aware of, however, was the fact that the sound of feet running seemed to be following him. It wasn't the echo of his own feet pounding the floor, and it wasn't Smith; well, maybe it was Smith, but it certainly wasn't *just* Smith. The sound of multiple pairs of feet chased after him, and Sam was relatively certain in the knowledge that each pair of feet was likely attached to another agent of the Men in Black.

He wasn't too sure which thought was worse; being pursued by multiple pairs of disembodied feet, or by a team of agents. Neither was particularly reassuring.

Weaving around the corner of a doorway, Sam charged through the next room. He had no plan, and certainly no idea where he was heading, but he would have to worry about that later. Right now, not being shot was very high on his agenda. As he sprinted through the next doorway, he slammed it shut behind him, pulling a bookcase down in front of it, in a desperate bid to slow down his pursuers. He didn't spend much time taking in his surroundings, but at a brief glance he was either in the throw cushion, travel mug and stationery exhibit, or he was in the gift shop. The distinction was somewhat unimportant, but Sam was willing to hazard a guess and say the latter. He threw a rack of postcards over and scattered some throw cushions to try and put at least some kind of obstacle between him and his assailants.

'Go around. Spread out, cover the area. Make sure every nook, every cranny, is searched. Do not underestimate the enemy.' A muffled voice was shouting from somewhere behind the closed door. The faint sound of marching feet echoed.

Enemy?, Sam thought. A part of him was a little proud of that. They rated him as such a legitimate threat that they would actually refer to him as "the enemy" instead of "a nuisance" or "that idiot". On the other hand, of course, it only really meant bad things for him, and that quickly overshadowed the unintentional "enemy" compliment. At least, he considered, they were going to have to take a longer route around. That bought him some time. He carried on running towards the other door at the far end of the gift shop.

Sam barrelled around the corner just outside of the door, when he ran into something. The something was soft yet firm, warm, and staggered backwards much like he did. It also let out a yelp of surprise. Regaining his balance, Sam saw that the something was Alice. Standing a few feet behind her was James, looking perplexed.

'Bloody hell, you scared me,' Sam panted, grabbing Alice by the arm and pulling her around the corner into the gift shop and gesturing for James to follow. 'And sorry. Very nice running into you both, though.'

'Yeah, you too,' Alice said, 'although maybe not so forcefully next time. What the hell are you do- What did you do to the gift shop?!'

'Long story short, I had a bit of a run in with the Men in Black. This was meant to slow them down.'

'And did it?'

'Well, they haven't come through the door yet.' He nodded in the direction of the hastily barricaded door, and then turned to his old friend. 'James, good to see you.'

'It'd be nice if we saw each other over a casual drink for a change, instead of getting caught up in conspiracies,' James replied.

'Bit late to suggest that now. The Regents have set up some kind of private function in the Reading Room, and have their well-dressed goons keeping the place secur- Hang on, how did you get in? The place is closed.'

'Side entrance,' James said casually, 'showed an ID to the guard by the staff entrance, and he let us in the back way.'

'See, you're much more into these conspiracy adventures than you'd like to let on,' Sam said with a grin. Alice fiddled with one of the buttons on her denim jacket. 'Anyway, I doubt they're here for a special private exhibit, so we need to find out what, why, and how to stop whatever it may be. We're going to have to get moving before the Spooks show up again.'

As if on cue, the Spooks showed up again. The sound of footsteps on marble floors drew closer and closer. Alice's eyes widened. 'You couldn't have said that a few minutes sooner?' she hissed.

'Well, I didn't know! Right, find something to hide behind. James, did you bring the Arc Gun?'

'The Arc Gun?'

'You know, the gun that fires an arc of lightning.'

'Is that what we're calling it?' James sounded incredulous. He reached beneath his jacket. 'Yes, got it right here,' he said, unholstering the weapon from his waistband and gripping the hilt.

'Good, I have a feeling we're going to need it,' Sam said, and he motioned for them to move away from the doorway.

Alice scurried over to the gift shop's checkout. It was a long, curved desk, almost semi-circular, sleek with its thick opaque glass surface and brushed steel, and when she rounded the corner she was relieved to see the space beneath the tabletop was empty. She crawled into a small cubby hole between two cupboards under the table. It felt reassuringly like a good hiding spot; tucked away from any immediate danger, and she would be just out of sight from all but a few specific angles.

It was then that Sam and James rounded the corner of the desk, and crouched down behind it too. James flattened his back against one of the cupboards, clasping the Arc Gun in both hands and inspecting the gun's chamber as if he was suddenly a firearms expert. He nodded over to Sam. Sam too squatted behind the desk, clutching the TechnoWand in one hand and producing a smooth stone from within the pocket of his coat. The Void crystal. He placed the crystal on the floor and began to trace a pattern above it with his probe. Twisting awkwardly, Sam reached into a different pocket with his spare hand, pulling out the ornate notebook. He unfastened the catch which held the book shut, and flipped through the pages.

The footsteps sounded louder and clearer than before.

'Guard we three from harmful power, protect us in this needful hour,' Sam began to mutter, reciting the words from the notebook.

'Why do I let you two drag me into these situations?' Alice hissed from the cubby hole. James simply held his finger to his lips. Sam was either ignoring her, or focussed more on his incantation. She believed it to be the latter.

'Shield us from those who would hurt or maim; with hammer and lightning, sword and flame.'

Voices could be heard in the distance. Muffled at first, but as the sound of well-polished brogues clopping on marble floors became crisp and clear, so too did the voices. 'In here,' said one of the monotone voices.

Cautiously leaning towards the edge of the desk, James peeked his head around the corner. At first, he counted three legs walking through the door to the gift shop, which didn't make much sense, so he teased himself a little further out to get a better look. Two pairs of legs, followed by a third and a fourth, walked through the door. Four Men in Black slowly set foot in the gift shop, their Arc Guns armed and ready. One of them looked towards the desk, and then snapped his head down, staring directly at James. 'There!' the agent shouted, aiming his gun and firing.

A bolt of energy zipped through the air, scorching the ground beside where James's head had been. He ducked back quickly, shifting his position and blindly firing a quick returning shot over the top of the desk. He glanced over to Sam. The Void crystal was glowing.

'No harm shall pass this barricade, may our adversaries be dissuade.' The crystal's glow pulsed for a moment, and then emitted a sudden wave of energy. The wave emanated outwards in a sphere, instantaneously spreading out until it was encompassing Sam, Alice and James like a bubble.

James popped up from behind the desk, aiming the Arc Gun at the group of agents. He fired a stream of lightning-like energy towards them. The faint, hazy surface of Sam's magickal shield seemed to shimmer and ripple as the beam passed the surface of the projected bubble. The beam coursed through the air, missing the agents by a hair's breadth, and made short work of a display of mugs which read "My Friend Went To The British Museum And All I Got Was This Lousy Old Relic".

The agents shot back. Another stream of crackling electrical energy surged towards the desk. This time, however, it did not scorch any surface or destroy any property and, much to James's relief, it did not cause any harm. The beam impacted the bubble surrounding the trio, fizzing and spitting and hissing as the two energies made contact, turquoise and cyan sparks bursting from the metaphysical shield a short distance from James's face. He breathed a sigh of relief, and pretended not to hear Sam murmur 'thank the gods that worked.'

Sam poked his head above the desk and, with a motion as if cracking a whip, he swung the TechnoWand around himself and brought it to an abrupt stop in front of him, pointing directly at one of the agents. A bolt of purple energy erupted from the probe's crystalline tip, hitting the agent squarely in the chest. He began to dissolve, a burning hole of violet fire spreading outwards as his energy was dispersed. Progressively, his human features began to melt away, and in the final moments the agent was entirely faceless, looking like nothing more than a mannequin in a suit before he completely disappeared into the ether.

The remaining three agents returned fire. In synchronicity, three bolts of lightning burst from their Arc Guns, hitting the metaphysical shield with the same violent hissing, crackling energy. They held their fingers firmly on the triggers, maintaining an unrelenting stream surging against the protective barrier. From behind the magickal shield, James took aim and shot again, this time taking one of the Men in Black out too.

The agents' weapons were beginning to have an effect. Even though their offence had been reduced, the continued streams of energy from their Arc Guns was starting to weather Sam's barrier. The energy bubble surrounding the three of them seemed to fizzle and flicker before their eyes as it began to lose power. Sam took cover behind the desk again, tracing the shape of a pentagram over the surface of the Void crystal. He muttered something which sounded like another incantation beneath his breath. James too ducked down, just as the energy dome above them dissolved into nothingness. Two streams of electrical energy hissed overhead, carving a burning path of destruction across a bookshelf dedicated to the history of canals.

'Why the hell do I keep getting dragged into this insanity?!' Alice yelped, covering her head with her hands.

'Bollocks!' Sam exclaimed, and although his voice sounded frustrated it came from a place of desperation and fear. 'Bollocks bollocks bollocks!' The Void crystal lay at his feet, as dead and dull as a chunk of flint. 'Okay, James, we'll take our chances with a quick pot-shot. You take the one on the left, I'll take the one on the right.'

James nodded his agreement, readying himself to swiftly stand, fire, and duck down again. A sudden bolt of energy burst against the surface of the desk, sending a stack of gift cards flying into the air and raining down on the three of them.

'On the count of three,' Sam said, holding three fingers up. He began to shake his hand as if playing a game of Rock Paper Scissors, retracting the first finger at the end of the motion. Then the second, and then the third. Holding his hand in a fist, he gave a sharp nod to James, and in unison they both stood up and fired. James's shot hit its mark, instantly dissolving the agent on impact. Sam missed his target, instead hitting a throw cushion with the embroidered message "Tomb Sweet Tomb" which promptly burst into a cloud of feathers. They both recoiled, retreating back behind the cover of the desk almost as quickly as they had emerged.

There was one final shot fired by the last remaining agent, shortly followed by the sound of shoes on marble, running, growing fainter and fainter. The surviving Man in Black had decided not to meet the same fate as his colleagues, and instead chose to retreat. As the sound of the running agent faded into silence, Sam, Alice and James slowly crawled out from their cover behind the desk. The gift shop was left, rather unsurprisingly, in tatters. Miscellaneous memorabilia, mugs and cushions and keychains and postcards and novelty erasers, lay strewn about the room. Burn marks from the Arc Guns ran along the walls and floor, charring the tabletops and bookshelves. Some books still smouldered from where the lightning gunfire had scorched them.

Sam puffed out his cheeks and slowly, loudly, exhaled. 'Someone's going to be thrilled they have to tidy all of this up tomorrow morning,' he said, surveying the damage, 'this is going to be good fun to try and explain away rationally.'

Dusting off the chalky remains of what was once an "I <3 Hieroglyphics" mug from his jacket, James nodded to the security camera in the corner of the room. 'The Regents would never risk any of what happened here reaching the public. They'll erase the security footage, run a tidy up operation and do a bit of house-keeping, in a very literal way.' Raising his arm, he took aim and shot the security camera. A chunk of melted plastic fell to the floor, smoke rising from the charred remains. 'It's better if there's no footage at all, of course.'

'Can we please not fire those things without warning?' Alice asked. She wasn't really asking, more making a firm request, even demanding, in a tone caught somewhere between the nervousness of someone who had just been fearing for their life, and the severity of a scolding mother. 'It's bad enough getting caught up in this-this... This!' She waved her arms around the room. 'Do you know how many gunfights I wanted to be in? None! And how many have I been in now? Two. Two!'

'And you've survived both,' Sam said, completely missing the point. 'You know I'd do anything I could to prevent you coming to any harm, right? We're already over my ideal amount of shoot-outs, but unfortunately I don't think we have much of a say in the matter at the moment, and that one probably wasn't our last.' He strode purposefully past both Alice and James, making his way towards the door. He poked his head cautiously around the corners of the doorway, turning to face this way and that like a startled meerkat. Motioning with his hand, Sam beckoned them both towards him. 'Looks like we're clear for the moment. We should get moving before anything else happens.' He paused and waited, as if expecting something else to happen; Sam was almost used to saying things and then the things happening, as if the Universe had a sense of irony and dramatic timing. Much to his relief, nothing happened.

The three of them stepped cautiously through the door, out of the gift shop and into the hallway beyond. Sam and James faced back-to-back, the TechnoWand and Arc Gun held at the ready, covering their path. Alice hung back slightly, following a few steps behind them. Sam had asked her to allow them to move a little bit ahead, so they knew the route was clear and, in the case that it wasn't, Alice would not be in the main line of fire. In a way, this reassured her, but it was not enough to alleviate the anxiety of the situation. She had picked up a replica of a ceremonial dagger from the gift shop, and although she had no idea what she would do with it (if it was even robust enough to use in self-defence), simply holding it in her hand made her feel a little bit more secure.

Rounding a corner, they found themselves in a long, lavish gallery. The room stretched out before them, seemingly running the entire length of the museum. Its walls were adorned with glass-fronted bookcases filled with old, yellowing tomes, and display cabinets housing worn pieces of parchment, fragments of scripture and miscellaneous ornate items lined the causeway. Plinths proudly displaying marble busts and statues, vases and fonts, stood at intervals throughout the room. A sign by an ornate baroque display piece served as an introduction to the Renaissance exhibit.

Sam, Alice and James had reached Enlightenment.

Their footsteps echoed throughout the vast room as they walked. Sam and James continued to move slowly and purposefully, their eyes barely blinking and their heads gradually panning around. They took great care and attention in casing the room, anticipating an ambush. But an ambush never came. The Age of Enlightenment exhibit was as quiet and empty as a museum should be at that hour, and there was no sign of any secret agents or clandestine cults.

'A bit quiet, don't you think?' James murmured to the other two, barely turning his head to face them.

'That's what they'd want us to think,' Sam mused. His eyes darted corner to corner, statue to statue, scanning the shadows. Still there was nothing. 'Don't let the peace lull you into a false security.'

'Wouldn't dream of it.'

'Normally being in a museum this quiet and empty would be boring me to sleep,' Alice said with a hushed tone, 'but I think this silence is making me more on edge than the guns.'

They continued to tread their way carefully through the room. Occasionally, Sam would cast a cursory glance over the displays as they moved past them, looking over some very aged books and ornaments. He paused momentarily to read a piece of weathered parchment paper encased within one of the glass cabinets. The paper was frayed and crumbling at the edges, stained by the passage of time.

What force and strength can not get through, I with a gentle touch can do, and many in the streets would stand, were I not as a friend in hand.

Sam stopped to mull this over, but when his brain failed to yield any immediate answers he decided to worry about it later. It was not so much a matter of him being interested in the piece, but more the fact that his mind kept desperately trying to find a distraction from having to eye each and every corner and shadow with the utmost suspicion and scrutiny. He glanced up from the parchment, facing towards an open doorway. The door led out from the side of the Age of Enlightenment, and through the doorway the open space and white marble of the Great Court could be seen.

'The Great Court is through there,' Sam said, nodding his head in the direction of the door, 'the Regents are somewhere in the structure in the middle of the Court.' He broke away from the other two, weaving his way between two cabinets and leading them towards the door. 'And as much as it goes without saying: whatever it is they're doing in there, they don't want us getting in the way. I say, we go and get in the way.'

He peered through the open doorway, gazing out into the Great Court beyond. It was just as empty, as desolate, as abandoned as it had looked when he first walked in. There was no sign of the Regents, of their Men in Black, or of Agent Smith waiting to gloat and monologue. It was simply an empty space, with nothing save a couple of statues and an information desk. In the middle of it all the Reading Room stood tall, and at its very top Sam was sure he could see lights flickering. He could just see the base of the stairs from his position. He thought of making a run for it; he could probably reach the stairs in a matter of seconds, and be in the building confronting the Regents within mere minutes. He glanced over his shoulder towards James.

'I'm going to need you to cover me,' he said, gesturing into the Great Court using hand-signs he had seen in action dramas on television. 'It's deserted out there, but that makes me all the more wary.' He crouched down, pressed against the wall, and James followed suit, taking a similar position on the opposite side of the doorway. 'If I make a run for the stairs, you provide covering fire from this position and keep the agents off my back.'

James saluted, half-sarcastically, and unholstered the Arc Gun. 'I'm not seeing any signs of activity out there. The coast is clear. Move on the count of three?'

'Precisely what they want us to think... I'm ready.'

James had just begun to shape his mouth to say 'one', one finger partly outstretched, when he was interrupted. A deafening scream echoed through the room, piercing the silence. In unison, Sam and James leapt to their feet and whirled around in time to see Alice being carried away by an agent. He carried her over his shoulder with surprising ease, as if she weighed no more than a small bag of flour, and in spite of her kicking, flailing and driving a replica ceremonial dagger between his shoulder blades, the agent seemed unperturbed and unhindered.

'Alice!' Sam exclaimed, and immediately began to give chase. He motioned for James to put down the weapon when he saw him lifting the Arc Gun up to fire at the agent. The last thing he wanted to do was risk Alice being shot by a stray blast. They charged through the exhibit, closing the gap between them and the agent. Alice continued to try to break free of the agent's grip, attempting to strike him however she could, but her efforts seemed no more than a mere annoyance to the agent, as if she were no more of a problem to him than a bee buzzing around on a summer's day.

'Let go of me, you-' she grunted, her voice somewhere between fear and anger, '-you arsehole! Put me down!' She was able to grab the replica knife from between his shoulder blades – it was sharper than she had given it credit for – and pulled it back out, only to drive it into his back again. The agent showed no sign of pain, made no noise or motion in response, and from what Alice could see she was sure he did not even bleed.

At the end of the room, the agent darted through the doorway and immediately disappeared around the corner. Alice's sounds of protest grew fainter as they disappeared out of sight. Still running only a short distance behind, Sam and James pursued them. They barrelled through the doorway the agent had run through, but as soon as they turned to follow in the same direction, they hit an obstacle. A glass-fronted bookcase stood in their way.

The bookcase was one of many which lined the walls of the long room, which seemed to span the length of the museum. The cases displayed a vast amount of books, yellowed with age and dating back several hundred years. Display cabinets filled out the rest of the gallery, containing worn pieces of parchment and ornaments, and plinths proudly displayed busts and statues. A sign by an ornate baroque display piece served as an introduction to the Renaissance exhibit.

They paid little attention to the bookcase which inexplicably stood in their way, and instead carried on sprinting towards the door at the far end of the room. Running through the exhibit at full pelt, their feet pounding the marble floor, they charged through the next door, but as soon as they went to turn the corner, they hit an obstacle. A glass-fronted bookcase stood in their way.

The bookcase was one of many which lined the walls of the long room, which seemed to span the length of the museum. The cases displayed a vast amount of books, yellowed with age and...

'Hang on,' said Sam, waving his finger in the air as the realisation dawned on him, 'we're back where we started.'

A sign by an ornate baroque display piece served as an introduction to the Renaissance exhibit.

'I thought it looked familiar,' James agreed, 'but this is...' He paused, looking between the door they had just entered, and the door at the far end of the room. 'Didn't we just run out of that one over there? And didn't we... Didn't we come in this door earlier?'

'Yes, it's like we've looped around somehow. Maybe, if we go back through this door...' Sam turned around and exited through the door he had entered, and entered through the door he had exited.

Waving down the length of the room, back to the door he had just left through, Sam shouted over to James. 'Yeah, no, definitely a loop of some kind!' He then turned around, exiting through the doorway, and entering back into the room through the door on the other side.

'This is new.'

Chapter VII

'Have you noticed that if you look through the door at just the right angle, you can see us on the far end of the room?' James pointed out as he gazed through the doorway they had both entered and exited more times than they would care to count.

'Yes, yes I have,' Sam replied. Even though he was standing only a few feet away from James, his voice sounded distant. His reply was muttered, a murmur beneath his breath, as he focussed. Sam was crouched just inside of the threshold of the door, tracing the tip of the transphasic energy probe around its frame. The wand-like device hummed a persistent and low hum. The crystal pulsed with a faint shade of turquoise.

He slowly unfolded himself, his crouch gradually lifting up into a standing position, following the outline of the doorway with the TechnoWand. He had to stretch up to reach the top beam. It continued to pulse and hum, and in almost perfect harmony Sam made a 'hmm' sound.

'What is it?'

'Well, it's just as I suspected,' Sam announced, examining the TechnoWand before placing it back in his coat pocket, 'we're caught in a loop.'

'You needed a TechnoWand to tell you that?'

'It's nice to confirm these things properly. At least we know for certain this is some kind of metaphysical trap and not just us making the wrong turnings.'

James nodded slowly, thinking more about the loop itself than Sam's revelation. He stared through the doorway again, looking straight down the gallery they were standing at the opposite end of. As he thought about the loop, an idea started to form in his mind. *What if*, he considered, *what if this is a quantum loop. If every atom in the Universe is connected at the quantum level, and these particular atoms have been bound to the atoms on the other side of the room...* He was not sure if the theory bore any form of validity, or how that changed their situation, but it was an idea at least. *That, or a disappointingly short-distance wormhole.*

'What if,' James spoke as the idea began to coalesce, 'this pocket of the Universe has been stitched together at the quantum level? This doorway, inextricably bound to that doorway.'

'Okay,' the occult detective mused, holding his chin in his hand. He tapped his foot, looking through the door ahead, into the gallery stretching out before them, and then over his shoulder to see the same gallery stretching out behind them. 'Are you suggesting we try to disentangle the atoms? Because I don't know about you, but I didn't really pack anything for messing with the fabric of the Universe.'

'No, easier than that. We could step between the atoms.'

'We need to talk about the definition of "easier".'

'I know it sounds stupid, but if we could step between the atoms we'd be outside of the loop and back into the rest of the museum.'

'And how do you propose we do that? Shrink ourselves to the subatomic level?'

'To bring magick and science together for a moment; matter is merely energy condensed to a slow vibration, right? So if we can raise our energetic vibrations...'

'We could operate at a frequency just beyond the physical, and step between the atoms,' Sam finished, his eyes widening at the idea. 'That's bloody genius!'

'How would we manage it, though?'

Sam tapped his nose knowledgeably. 'Magick and science unified,' he said, 'if our will affects magick in the Universe around us, and thoughts become things, we need to believe we can step between atoms.' Closing his eyes, Sam began to take several deep breaths. His chest rose and fell, inhaling and exhaling to a slow rhythm. 'In a state,' he said on one inhale, 'of complete relaxation,' he exhaled, 'we can forget' - inhale - 'reality's illusions' - exhale - 'and transcend them.'

Following his lead, James began to take several deep breaths too. With his eyes closed, feeling his body rise and fall with each breath, he allowed his mind to go blank. His thoughts floated around in the ether of his imagination, a realm detached from normal reality, as he felt himself drifting into an almost meditative state. In his mind's eye, he saw the world not in its composite state, but the atoms which formed it. He could see the corridor beyond the atoms which bound them in the loop.

'Step between the atoms.'

Wiggling his fingers, rotating his neck and shoulders to relax the muscles, and starting to jog on the spot, James readied himself. With one last deep inhalation, he ran forwards. Sprinting towards the door, he imagined his body passing through the atoms as if they were no more of an obstacle than a curtain of beads. He was now the other side, and slowly he opened his eyes. He was still in the Age of Enlightenment.

He had not escaped the loop.

Sam followed suit shortly after, standing beside James in the same room they had hoped to escape. 'Well, that didn't work,' he said.

'It was a stupid idea,' James spoke flatly, 'the science behind it was unfounded at best. But it was worth a shot, at least.'

From behind them, they could hear the sound of someone applauding. Not an approving or congratulatory applause, more of a sarcastic slow clap. They turned to face the source of the sound. Standing in the doorway, a smug smile on his chiselled face, was Agent Smith. He ceased his sarcastic clapping.

'Good effort, but not good enough,' he intoned, 'it wouldn't be much of a trap if we made it that easy for you, now, would it?'

'What have you done with Alice, you- you- you-' Sam bellowed, but he struggled to think of a good insult to punctuate his outrage with. Nothing sprang to mind, so he settled for 'bastard.'

'What have *I* done?' Smith held his hand to his chest in mock offense. 'Why, I have done nothing to your little protégé. My masters, on the other hand, may have some ideas for her...' His mouth twisted into an even smugger grin, which Sam didn't think could be possible, and he was overwhelmed by the sudden urge to punch him.

So he did.

Sam's fist arced through the air, landing a fast and firm right hook to Smith's bottom jaw. There was the thud of fist meeting face, the crack of knuckles meeting jawbone, and the agent's head was knocked sideways by the blow. His jaw hung at an awkward angle. As the pain from the punch ran through his fingers, Sam shook his hand out. It was worth it for that moment of satisfaction. Smith held his jaw, and with a distinctly unpleasant sound like the crunching of bones, he moved it back into place. He spat, an oily black globule of spittle marring the white marble floor.

'You're not going to make many friends treating people like that, you know,' Smith said. His eyes narrowed as he stared down at Sam.

'I don't make a habit of it,' he retorted, gently massaging his knuckles, 'I reserve that special greeting only for people who really deserve it.'

'I'm sure the Regents are going to be so disappointed you couldn't stop by to say hello before tonight's grand finale. It's going to be quite the show, I hear.'

'I do so hate to miss it,' Sam said, staring back at Smith, his eyes unwavering and fixed solely on the agent. Despite his sarcastic tone of voice, the expression on his face showed nothing but his resolve. He was not in the mood for playing the agent's mind games. 'What is the answer to this little game of yours?'

'When one does not know what it is, then it is something; but when one knows what it is, then it is nothing.' Agent Smith nodded a single, almost courteous, nod, and stepped between the atoms as he turned to walk out of the gallery.

'Bloody conceptual entities, able to just *do that*,' James said, 'they have it so damned easy.'

'It's a riddle,' Sam spoke, oblivious to the fact his friend had been speaking.

'Hmm?'

'What Smith just said. It's a riddle.'

'Yeah, I know that, but what does it mean?'

'No, no,' Sam said, pressing two fingers to his forehead and rubbing them in a clockwise direction, 'as in, the answer is "a riddle".'

'Oh, right,' James replied, not entirely understanding Sam's point. 'I've never been much good at riddles, so that was lost on me. Why is that important?'

Sam did not bother to give him a full reply. Not immediately, at least. Instead, he simply said 'because,' and proceeded to march down the length of the gallery, weaving his way through the statues and glass cabinets. Agent Smith's parting sentence had sparked something in Sam's mind, and he had to satisfy his curiosity. Stopping at one of the cabinets, he stared into the display. 'Because of this,' he finished as James joined him, pointing to a piece of old parchment paper.

'What force and strength can not get through,' James read aloud, 'I with a gentle touch can do, and many in the streets would stand, were I not as a friend in hand.' He paused and ruminated on the sentence, staring upwards at the high ceiling above them as if the answer may be up there somehow. Unsurprisingly, it was not. 'What are you thinking, Sam?'

'I'm thinking,' the occult detective replied, spinning around with a swish of his coat, 'that this might be the key.' He too then paused for a moment, before snapping his fingers as the answer came to him. 'Oh! A key. I just got that.'

'What?'

'The riddle. It's a key. Both figuratively and literally.' He began to peer inside the cabinet, leaning so close to the glass casing that his breath created misty patches of condensation. Inside was the scrap of parchment with the cursive riddle, a fragment of pottery – which the label detailed had been found by a 19th Century archaeologist in Jerusalem – and an aged silver ring which bore the red cross insignia of the Knights Templar. Nothing which resembled a key, though. 'We're going to have to look around for it.'

Moving to one of the other cabinets, James looked over the artefacts it contained. 'And how do we know what we're looking for?' His eyes cast over a collection of antiquities, of old flint arrow heads which dated back hundreds of thousands of years, and an inscription about the birth of archaeology.

'Scholars in the Age of Enlightenment studied ancient religions in an attempt to dispel the mistrust of rituals and magick at the time,' Sam said as he surveyed another of the displays, 'and unearthed many relics of bygone religions. It wouldn't surprise me if we were to find an ancient, yet magickal, key within one of these cabinets.' As he said this, he found he was looking at a collection of 18th Century coins which depicted the likenesses of several kings and queens he didn't know. *But not this cabinet.*

He passed the Rosetta Stone, which stood upon a pedestal, encased in glass, and he took a moment to marvel at the slab of granodiorite. In some ways, Sam wished the key was somehow connected to the Stone, not least because of its place in understanding Ancient Egyptian history, but also because it seemed like just the kind of thing which would be connected to the Regents and whatever magick they were weaving. For a brief moment, he wondered if he could read hieroglyphics whether it would grant any insight.

While Sam was busy ogling the Rosetta Stone, James was slowly moving along a row of cabinets, inspecting their contents. Old books and ancient parchment, figurines and idols, fragments of pottery and utensils, coins and jewellery, all from varying eras and regions. Then something caught his eye. A large, perfectly preserved, golden key, glistening behind the glass. It sat upon a cushion of purple velvet, almost presenting itself to him. Cautiously, James traced his fingers around the edges of the cabinet, feeling for the gap between the panes of glass, finding the hinges of the opening. It was firmly locked. 'What about a very conspicuous looking golden key?' he called over to Sam, who immediately jogged over to join him.

'Looks like it could very well be the thing,' he said. The butt of the key bore a symbol, an ancient occult sigil. It was a circular shape, with the inside space divided into four quadrants across the diameter. Each quarter contained two characters, and the outer circle was inscribed with a versicle in Hebrew.

'According to this,' James said, examining the information panel beside the key, 'this was found in the ruins of the Temple of Solomon. The translation of the versicle reads: *Lift up your heads, O ye gates, and be ye lift up ye everlasting doors, and the King of Glory shall come in.* Sounds like we're on to something.'

'Definitely,' Sam nodded affirmatively, 'looks like the Fifth Pentacle of Mercury, to me.' He produced a marker pen from the inside of his coat and, removing the cap and moving past James, Sam proceeded to draw on the front of the cabinet. The thick back ink marked the surface as he quickly drew a circle, with eight spokes radiating out from its centre. At the end of each spoke, Sam drew a collection of different symbols. The pen squeaked as it moved back and forth across the glass.

'Sam. Are you seriously scribbling over a cabinet in a museum?' James asked.

'Yes,' he replied, 'not just scribbling, though. The First Pentacle of Jupiter.' He stopped for a moment, resting the marker pen on the top of the cabinet while he consulted his notebook, checking his work. With a satisfied nod, Sam closed the book and proceeded to write Hebrew lettering around the outer rim of the circle. 'I invoke the Spirits of Jupiter, among whom Parasiel is the Lord and Master of Treasures, and teacheth how to become possessor of places wherein they are.'

Sam tapped the tip of the TechnoWand against the glass in the middle of the sigil where the eight spokes converged. The door to the cabinet obediently opened. Sam reached for the key, delicately removing it from its velvet cushion and holding it up triumphantly. He grinned at James broadly. 'What would you rather, force entry and possibly smash a glass cabinet, setting off alarms, or leave a little felt-tip drawing?'

'Fair point.'

They made their way to the far end of the gallery again; to the doors which should normally lead to another room, but which instead only served to take them back around to the other side of the room in a fashion which defied all known laws of physics. Standing on the threshold, Sam and James stared ahead into the gallery which was behind them. At the very far end of the room, they could see themselves staring out of that same door.

'I hate this loop,' Sam said, 'let's break the bloody pattern.'

'Well, no time like the present.' James reached for the doors, pulling them shut. The doors behind them at the far end of the room simultaneously began to shut too, apparently also bound by the same inextricable and inexplicable rules of the loop the two of them were caught in. The hinges creaked, and the latch clicked. The doors were firmly shut. 'Now, let's try that key...'

Sam pushed the key into the hole beneath the door's handle. Slowly, he began to turn the key in the lock. It rotated with perfect ease, as if there were no lock at all, and as the key had been turned a full 360°, there was a gentle yet satisfying click. With a nod of the head, as if confirming to himself that the key had indeed turned the lock, Sam pulled it back out and pocketed it. He turned to James. 'Moment of truth.'

Together, they pushed the doors open again. Beyond the doorway, there was no gallery. There was no Age of Enlightenment exhibit, no statues or ornaments, no rows of bookcases displaying ageing books or glass cabinets filled with antiquities. More importantly, there was no sign of either of them stood on the opposite end of the room they were about to walk into. It was, for all intents and purposes, a perfectly and reassuringly mundane room, with a stairway and toilet facilities. Neither of them could remember the last time they were so pleased to see something so underwhelming.

'Thank god that's over.' James breathed a sigh of relief.

'Yeah, it's enough to drive one loopy,' Sam said with a humoured smile creeping up his lips. James didn't seem to be as amused by his pun as he was. 'Now, let's go and rescue Alice, and find out what the bloody hell the Regents are up to.'

CHAPTER VIII

Walking through the corridors of the empty museum, in the quiet dead of night, Sam and James could not help but feel that something, somewhere, was wrong. Given that they had been caught in a shoot-out with secret agents, and then trapped in a quantum looping room, this was hardly surprising. But what in particular felt wrong was that, after everything else, the atmosphere seemed all too peaceful. All too *normal*. They did not encounter any more of the Regents' Men in Black, nor did they have any run-ins with anything paranormal or transdimensional. There was not even anything as inconvenient as a night security guard. The British Museum seemed to be entirely deserted.

Their feet echoed with each step they took, walking through darkened rooms and exhibits without even the slightest disturbance. If anything, Sam thought, the quiet emptiness was even eerier than the supernatural secret agents. He almost wished for some of the exhibits to come to life, so the tense anticipation of expecting something to happen wouldn't keep hanging over him. Of course, the exhibits did not come to life.

As they rounded the corner into another exhibit – cheerily called "Living and Dying" – they were greeted by the sight of a large, particularly contemplative looking, statue of a head reminiscent of the monuments of Easter Island. The head stared directly at them, its stony brow furrowed and its lips pouted, as if it was judging their presence. They paid very little heed to the judgemental head, though, as just over the angular shape of its shoulder they could see it. The large, white, column-like building which stood at the centre of the Great Court. The Reading Room. The location the Regents had chosen for their own nefarious purposes.

Standing at the door to the Great Court, James suddenly thrust his arm out, holding his hand against Sam's chest and gently pushing him back. 'Wait,' he breathed, his eyes darting around the room as he craned his neck to look through into the large empty space beyond the doorway. 'Doesn't this feel too... Too *empty*?'

Sam nodded his agreement. 'After everything else, yes. It's eerily empty. It's exactly as a museum would be after it's closed, which is far too normal for my liking.'

'Precisely.' He scoured the space ahead of them, peering intently at every doorway, every corner and recess, in case any agents were laying in wait for them. It appeared that the Great Court was empty. Nonetheless, James tightened his hold around the grip of the Arc Gun, priming the weapon. He nodded his head in the direction of the Reading Room. 'Come on,' he said, 'it's clear. Let's move.'

They dashed their way across the Great Court, moving quickly and partly crouching down as they darted from the doorway to the Court's Shop immediately ahead of them. The shop cut into the base at the back of the Reading Room. It mostly comprised of the standard fare of any gift shop, with books and stationery and ornaments. Taking cover inside, Sam and James knelt down behind one of the displays, waiting to see if there were any shouts or gunfire or any sign of action at all from the agents. Nothing. The place remained as inactive as it had done since escaping the Age of Enlightenment loop.

'Okay,' Sam said, 'the stairs up to the Reading Room are just the other side of here. We're going to need to skirt around the outside of the column to reach them.'

'I think we're in the clear, but if you begin to make a move, I'll cover your approach,' James replied.

They began to move. Standing up from behind the display and hastily moving out of the shop, they started to creep around the base of the column, working their way towards the stairs. Sam took the lead, TechnoWand in hand as he scurried forward, keeping as close to the wall as possible; James followed a short distance behind, Arc Gun raised and ready to engage in case they were not quite as alone as they thought. They tucked into the bookshop which cut into the side of the Reading Room's structure, using it as extra cover in the event someone was watching their approach. But still there was no sign of the agents. There were no sounds of marching feet, no bolts of lightning, no men in well-tailored suits mobilising to stop them.

'Is it just me,' James hissed forwards to Sam as they approached the bottom of the stairs, 'but is it somehow *more* spooky without those Spooks?'

'You're not wrong. Spooklessly spooky,' he said.

Rounding the base of the stairs, they began to make their way up the steps towards the upper level. The concrete steps wound around and up the central column of the Great Court, and were more numerous than they would at first appear. The gentle incline of the stairs led Sam and James from the bottom at the southern side, up and around until they were on the next floor on the northern side. They had taken the stairs slowly, keeping an eye on the front and watching their backs, still staying low.

As they reached the top of the stairs, directly ahead of them was a restaurant. At first glance it looked like a particularly nice restaurant – even if it was closed at this hour – with pleasant seating and an open kitchen, and positioned on the balcony outside of the Reading Room, giving diners a view of the Great Court below. The chairs were stacked neatly on the tables, and everything was closed down for the night. But amidst the forest of stacked tables and chairs, somewhere in the shadowed darkness of the restaurant after hours, was a flickering orange light, as if from a candle's flame. And voices. Muffled, hushed, indistinguishable voices. Sam and James dropped as low to the ground as possible, moving slowly and quietly, creeping closer to the restaurant and to the voices.

'All is proceeding as planned,' said one of the voices, which sounded distinctly reminiscent of Agent Smith, 'it shan't be long now.'

'Mmph, hrm mmff hrrmm,' said the other, which didn't really sound much like words, but more like muffled words being spoken through a gag.

'Yes, I agree,' replied the voice of Agent Smith, 'how about a toast? To the infinite potentials of the Void.' There was a chink of glasses, shortly followed by more muffled attempts at words. 'Of course, you can't drink it just yet. Not like that, at least.'

Sam and James exchanged concerned glances to one another. They remained crouched behind the outer-most table of the restaurant, tucked away out of sight. Peering over the tabletop, Sam could see two figures sat at a table, silhouetted by the orange glow of a candle. A small vase of delicate flowers sat beside the candle, and two glasses of a red-brown liquor (Sam presumed it to be sherry) which glowed amber in the candlelight sat in front of each figure. In the low flickering light, he could faintly make out the likeness of Agent Smith, but he could not see the face of the other figure. He ducked back down behind the table, nodding to James.

'You know,' Agent Smith's voice came from the middle of the restaurant, 'you're not as clever or as sneaky as you think you are.'

Both Sam and James froze. 'Us?' they mouthed to each other, raising eyebrows and making sceptical expressions to one another. Smith could just as easily be talking with his wordless guest. In fact, they both thought, secure in the knowledge that they had been particularly sneaky on their approach of the restaurant, it was very unlikely he could be addressing them.

'I am addressing you two,' said the voice of Agent Smith,

followed by the sound of a delicate sip of sherry, 'and yes, before you start mouthing to each other incredulously, I know you're there. Now stop hiding, you're embarrassing yourselves.'

The two of them stood up to see Agent Smith sitting at the table, swilling the glass of sherry in his hand, and staring at them. His face was neither kind or malicious. If anything, he seemed entirely unsurprised by their presence, and he simply gestured for them to join him and the other silhouetted figure at the table.

Instinctively, James raised the Arc Gun. The chamber pulsed with energy, electrical discharges crackled from the muzzle, and his finger began to slowly squeeze the trigger.

'Don't even think about it,' Smith said, dismissively waving a hand in James's direction. Two red, laser-like dots traced their way up Sam and James. They could not spot where the dots were coming from, but neither of them was willing to gamble that these unseen agents were armed only with laser pointers. 'If you try anything – either of you – it all ends. Pulling that trigger would be the very last thing you do. And it would be a waste. In case you have forgotten, Mister Mortimer, even if you were so lucky as to shoot me, it wouldn't be long until my essence wove its way back into the Regents' nurturing bosom. Now, come, relinquish your weapons.'

James lowered his gun, and solemnly walked towards the table. Following behind him at an even more sombre pace, Sam clutched the TechnoWand tightly in the palm of his hand. He glared at Smith. Neither of them said anything.

'Leave your little toys on the table, boys. My colleague and I shall take very good care of them for you.' Agent Smith grinned a sardonic grin. 'You remember Agent Jones?'

The silhouetted figure rose from its seat, folding its arms and slowly turning to face them. Agent Jones was a short and stocky man, but that was as far as this particular Agent

Jones could be likened to the one Sam had met before in the back of the Regents' limo. This Agent Jones bore one very striking trait which set him apart. Agent Jones had no face.

His head bore the shape one would expect of a head; the cheekbones were raised, the chin a prominent jut below the face (or lack thereof), indents for the eye sockets set beneath the firm ridge of a brow, and a slight elevation where noses normally go. However, none of the key features were present. The sunken indents were left eyeless, the forehead not even marked with eyebrows (in fact, Agent Jones had no hair at all), no evidence of a nose or a mouth, and instead of ears he simply had a small hole either side of his perfectly bald head. In many ways, he resembled a mannequin made of flesh.

'He's not quite the man he was when last you met,' Smith said, still with that grin plastered across his face, 'you might not have recognised him. But he never forgets a face. Except his own, of course. He's not fully reconstituted himself yet, but he didn't want to miss out on the occasion.'

'Hrm hmphhrrmph,' said Agent Jones. The shape of his chin moved up and down, the skin which seamlessly covered where a mouth should be stretched like putty as he tried to speak.

Neither Sam or James knew how to process, let alone react, to the faceless man stood before them. His meat-mannequin head tilted itself towards them, and Sam suspected that if he had eyebrows, Jones would be raising an enquiring glance. The faceless agent held out his hands – which seemed to have figured out the usual routine of four fingers and a thumb, with joints and knuckles and fingernails – requesting their weapons. James obliged, taking a laborious and defeated step forwards, placing the Arc Gun in Agent Jones's outstretched hand.

'Now your turn, Samuel,' Smith intoned, inclining his

head as he stared at the occult detective. Sam stared back. His jaw tightened, and his teeth ground against each other.

'Sam,' James gave him a nudge, motioning towards the faceless agent.

Reluctantly, Sam too stepped forward, and dropped the transphasic energy probe into Agent Jones's hand. It didn't sit right with him, handing over his most trusty tool to the enemy. He barely ever parted with it, and now he found himself voluntarily relinquishing it. He tried to tell himself it wasn't voluntary, that if he did not comply then things would be undeniably worse, but it didn't help.

'Hmmph hm,' Agent Jones said, securing the Arc Gun in an empty gun holster on his belt, and secreting the TechnoWand inside his jacket pocket.

'That wasn't so hard now, was it?' Smith spoke with a hollow cheeriness, spreading his arms wide as if welcoming the two of them. He finished the remainder of his sherry in a single, large gulp. 'Come with us. There are some people who are very eager to meet you. They just wanted to make sure we took the... *necessary* precautions before this little meet and greet.'

'Don't fool yourself,' Sam spoke. His voice was low and tinged with a pent up rage. 'My transphasic probe is no weapon, it is just a tool. A tool which works as an extension of my own will. I am no more disarmed without it than a rifle is without a scope.'

'Shh,' James hissed to him, 'don't try to rile them now.'

Sam's statement was, in a manner of speaking, true. Being without the TechnoWand did not render him powerless by any means. However, without it, not only as a tool to aid his focus but also as a vessel to channel his magickal energies, there was no telling how potent or how accurate his magick would be. And for Sam, it was more than a tool; since he had first crafted it several years ago, it had become an extension of himself

It was then, as they were led on a slow walk not unlike a funeral march towards the entrance of the Reading Room, that Sam noticed something. A weight inside his breast pocket, a dense shape which caused his coat to sway unevenly with each step. And it was not his phone, or his notebook. It was something which, despite his better judgement, felt like hope.

The doors to the Reading Room were swung open as Agent Smith marched up to them, revealing the inner chamber beyond the threshold. The doors led into a large circular room, its walls lined with countless bookcases stacked three storeys high, held beneath a high domed ceiling. The ornate architecture of the Reading Room, in its blue and cream with trimmings of gold, seemed all the more grand in the dim light of the lamps and candles which cast their low orange glow into the space. Beyond the windows, the sky had turned an inky black, dotted with the faint pinpricks of starlight.

Rows of study desks radiated out from the centre of the room, all directing in towards the heart of the chamber, where a circular formation of resource desks were arranged. Lamps and candles flickered at the ends of each row of desks. It felt like stepping back into the 19th Century.

Agent Smith led them down between a row of desks, down to the centre of the chamber. Sam could make out the shapes of other figures in the room, silhouettes like wraith-like apparitions standing in the shadows, watching from the darkness. And in the middle of the room, five robed figures stood in a circle, facing each other. From his position, Sam could not quite see them fully, but he suspected they had positioned themselves as the five points on a pentagram. As much as he could appreciate the aesthetics of the Reading Room, Sam did not like it one bit; something about the atmosphere and the cloak-and-dagger cultist air made the hairs on his neck stand on end.

Approaching the five robed figures, their faces shrouded by hoods which hung low over their eyes, Agent Smith took a knee. Kneeling before the figures, who did not deem it important to turn to acknowledge his presence, he spoke reverently. 'Most venerable ones,' he said, and it occurred to Sam that this was the first time he had ever heard this agent talk *up* to anyone, 'those who shine their guiding light unto us from the shadows.' The Regents still did not acknowledge the agent's presence. 'I bring you the man you seek, the one who has impeded your great work. And another, the one responsible for the Regent's Park Icarus Hub being compromised.'

In unison, the five robed figures slowly turned. At first they nodded to Agent Smith, who then stood back up and moved to the side of the gathering. Then they stared at Sam and James, and although their faces were still shrouded in the shadows of their hoods, the two of them could feel their eyes on them. Silence hung heavily in the air.

'Hello,' Sam said faux-cheerily into the austere silence, 'you must be the Regents I've been hearing so much about.' The robed Regents did not answer. They simply maintained their stare. In return, Sam Hain fixed them with an equally unwavering and challenging glare.

One by one, the robed figures removed their hoods. Firstly, a particularly stern-faced woman in the latter half of her middle-age, her mouth persistently downturned into a dour expression as if she was in a constant state of regret for biting into a lemon. A man approaching his sixties with an equally austere expression, his more-salt-than-pepper hair slicked back, and narrow rectangular glasses perched upon a beak-like nose. Another man, at least half the age of the previous one, with a traditionally handsome, chiselled-features face, a well-groomed beard, and piercing blue eyes, beneath a head of short but scruffy light brown hair. Sam did not recognise any of these people; nor did he expect to.

The remaining two, however, he did recognise, although it took him a short time to realise who and why. Another man removed his hood, revealing a soft, round face with almost perfectly black hair which had been combed to the side. As he squinted, he began to recognise the features of someone he had seen in the case files from Grimditch. Ryan Nicholls. *I knew those alibis were too convenient to be true*, he thought. The final hood was lifted, revealing the ginger beard and green eyes and perpetually grumpy face of...

'Lloyd Turner!' Sam exclaimed. 'When I was digging around your house in Knightsbridge, you kept denying anything supernatural was going on. Did you have a change of heart, or was that all just deep-cover?'

'Mister Hain,' Lloyd Turner said unmovingly, 'trust you to find yourself sticking your nose where it does not belong. Again.'

'I think the older guy is that defamed politician, Timothy Carmichael,' James whispered to Sam.

'Hmm, quite the gathering,' he muttered back to his friend, 'what about the woman and that guy?' He pointed to the stern-faced woman and the handsome man.

'No idea.'

'Bring in the girl,' the woman declared, clapping her hands together. Two agents peeled away from the shadows and disappeared out of sight. They returned almost instantly, holding the figure of a woman by the arms. Her head was covered by a sack, but a telltale wisp of blonde hair fell from beneath it. She put up little resistance, but she made no effort to walk with them either, instead allowing them to drag her as she let her legs trail limply behind them.

'Stand up,' one of the agents instructed as they dragged

her into position alongside Sam and James.

The woman did so, but not without thrusting her elbows left and right to shrug the agents' grip off of her. They pulled the sack from off of her head, and Alice shook her hair out. She squinted into the darkness, moaned something which sounded like a string of particularly unpleasant expletives, and then looked up. Her eyes immediately lit up, changing from a morose and distant glaze to suddenly showing a glimmer of hope.

'Sam!' she exclaimed, her voice making no effort to hide either her happiness or her relief. 'James! Thank God you're he- Hang on.' Alice cut herself short when the figures of the Regents caught her attention. She stared at the five of them, all facing towards her, and as her eyes focussed through the dim haze of candlelight she could make out their faces. Two in particular. She stared at them, transfixed by the handsome man and the stern-faced woman whom neither Sam or James could identify. The light drained from Alice's eyes, her face expressing a mix of confusion and horror. 'P-P-Paul? J-Jan?! What the fu-'

'Hey Alice,' Paul said with a nonchalant tone, 'sorry we had to get you this way. It would have been easier if you had just been willing to play along. We could've had some fun with each other, too...' He shot her a cheeky wink, which beforehand would have made her feel a little weak at the knees, but now only served to stir a nauseating sensation in her stomach.

'You didn't think I believed all of your sick days were genuine, did you?' Jan straightened her robes officiously. 'I know all about your little double life, missy.'

'Of course,' Sam mused aloud as the pieces began to slot into place in his mind. 'You've been operating from the shadows, but hidden in plain sight. Following your agenda as you see fit. It all adds up now. It's all connected. Every piece of it. Each time a case has been linked to the oncoming darkness, one of you has been associated with it in some form.' He then looked to Paul, who seemed to be perpetually emanating come-to-bed eyes, and scowled. 'Except for you, I don't know what part you played, and I'm not sure I want to know.' Shuffling closer to Alice, Sam moved so that he was standing by her side and said, 'are you doing okay?' He received a sharp and painful *thwack* to the shoulder by the butt of one of the agent's Arc Guns for that.

'Well, aside from fearing for my life in a shoot-out, being suddenly kidnapped by one of these Spooks, having a bag put over my head, and then discovering that my manager and a guy I went on a date with are actually supervillains... Yeah, I'm doing okay.' Alice's voice sounded as if she was anything but okay, and she too received a *thwack* from the butt of the gun for daring to answer. 'Ow!'

'Supervillains? Supervillains?!' Jan began to cackle, which did nothing to dispel such accusations. 'Don't be so naive. We may work in the shadows, but that doesn't mean we *are* the shadows.'

'Since time immemorial,' Tim Carmichael began, 'the Regents have been the custodians of mankind. The guiding light, shining wisdom for the benefit of humanity. Always hidden in the shadows, behind the figureheads of power, while we plot the course of history. Shaping the world as it was meant to be.'

Sam could not suppress the urge to scoff at these words. 'Coming from a politician who has never affected any change and has consistently failed to deliver on his promises, I find that hard to believe. Must be difficult to "shine your wisdom" since having to step down, too, I imagine.' *Thwack!*

'That's politics,' Tim replied dryly. 'The Regents have helped to nudge society one way or another. Through politics, through social zeitgeists, through technology. All for the benefit of the people.'

'People don't know what they want.' It was Ryan

Nicholls turn to speak. 'They want to feel safe, they want to feel secure, but they also want to feel as if they have the freedom to choose their place in the world. They don't see the paradox in those wishes; unlimited freedom breeds chaos and anarchy. To be truly safe, one must be willing to give up their liberties. They make up conspiracies to explain away anything which goes wrong in the world; nothing terrible could ever happen without someone masterminding it, right? Even the most awful of catastrophes needs to have a human face behind it, to help people not feel so powerless in the face of terror. Our knowledge and guidance guarantees the world takes the turns it needs to take, all the while the people have the illusion of freedom while we ensure a safe and secure course for society.'

'Safe and secure. Naturally,' Sam rebuked. 'And I presume it's for this "safe and secure society" that you're responsible for the fact that the darkness is coming?'

The five Regents laughed, a condescending and almost pitiful laugh. 'You think *we* are behind that?' Lloyd Turner's beard bristled and seemed to glow a deeper shade of red in the candlelight. 'No, we are not responsible for the coming darkness. We strive to harness it, for the good of mankind. Our agents should have already made that clear to you by now. And as the energies converge on this place, we will make our link to the Void and tap into the powers beyond our reality.'

James shook his head, partly out of disagreement but mostly in frustration. 'And you say we're naive. That sounds incredibly unwise. Have you not been paying attention to everything that's been going on?'

'The creatures your experiments and studies have allowed to bleed through into this world,' Sam added, 'the rifts in reality which could have done god knows what, the entities which have actively harmed and ended human lives. I just fought some kind of horror from the deep on the Underground which had been feeding on the homeless and the lost! Another maligned monstrosity, brought into this world by your actions.'

'Necessary work breeds necessary risks,' Ryan shrugged. 'Just like Grimditch. Some lives may have been lost, but it was all to further the greater good. Had you not come in and meddled with our work.'

'Regardless of what you say or do,' Jan said, 'there is nothing that can be done to stop it. We've been preparing for this moment for a while, now. The Convergence has begun. No doubt you've been seeing its effects recently; those ghostly apparitions, unusual disturbances, even things like the creature you described.'

'Think of them as the flotsam and jetsam of the Void. Errant and unwanted elements washed up on the shores of our reality from the Akashic waves. They're unavoidable side effects, carried along by the currents. Especially for a tidal wave such as this.' Ryan turned back to face the middle of the circle, and one by one the other Regents followed suit.

As the five Regents stood in the pentagram formation, facing inwards towards each other, something began to happen. A crackle of electricity sparked in the air. The lamps and candles on the desks began to shake. The old books in the Reading Room's many bookcases rattled against their glass doors. The floor began to tremor, as if in the midst of an earthquake. Instinctively, Sam reached out and grabbed Alice's arm, preparing for the worst. The heavy shape in his breast pocket seemed to vibrate and tremble.

'This is it,' Agent Smith spoke, turning to face the three of them, 'this is the moment. The moment their work reaches its climax, the moment these five will attain transcendence. They wanted you to bear witness to their triumph, so that you may know all you could have had before your essences are swallowed by the infinite abyss of

the Void.'

'What?!' Sam bellowed. It was hard to tell if he shouted out of outraged incredulity, or so his voice could be heard over the increasingly loud rumble which shook the room.

'Did no one mention this to you? Oh, what a shame. You are – for all of your *interruptions* – our guests of honour. Presented to the Void as an offering; helping to ingratiate the beings which dwell within, and removing the thorn in our collective sides too.'

'You are all making a very, *very* terrible mistake,' Sam hissed. He took a step forward as he was about to make a lunge for the Regents, but Smith held up a cautionary hand. Two agents raised their weapons.

'What did I say to you before? Don't try it.'

A bolt of lightning shot up from the floor in between the five Regents. It made a deafening cracking sound as it zigzagged its way from floor to ceiling, electricity sparking and licking off of the main bolt. The Regents began to chant then, their voices droning in an eerie harmony. A thick black shadow began to rise like smoke from the floor, spiralling around the column of lightning and encasing it, like a storm cloud had been contained within the very middle of the room. It swirled and spiralled, swimming around the current of energy.

Jan was the first to go.

The oily black shadow sprouted a thick tendril which wrapped itself around her, starting around the ankles and slowly winding its way upwards, enveloping her. Jan threw her head back and opened her mouth wide as if she were screaming in agony, but no noise came. Instead, something darker and more tangible than a shadow billowed from her lips, streams of blackness pouring from her eyes. The darkness gathered above her, and when the last of its black essence had passed from her body, Jan slumped to the floor. Lifeless.

Alice steadied herself against Sam as she watched her now former manager fall to the floor. He tightened his grip on her, in an attempt to be of some kind of reassurance, but he wasn't sure there was anything which could be remotely reassuring now. Alice's mouth hung open, but she was in too much shock to utter a sound.

A wraith-like shadow hung above Jan's crumpled body. It hovered in the air, resembling the silhouette of a torso in tattered rags, with long, spindly, almost skeletal arms and a featureless head as black as the night. The wraith bore no legs, its shadowy form simply trailing away in a smoke-like tail. It shrieked and took flight. The thing swam through the air above the heads of the remaining Regents, before disappearing up and through the domed ceiling, passing through the building as if it was not there at all.

'This is not going to go the way you think it will,' Sam said to Smith, his voice low and possibly the most serious he had ever sounded. 'These efforts to harness the oncoming darkness, to draw power from the Void... They're opening themselves as conduits for whatever sinister forces are at work, and they will be used and discarded without a second thought if we allow this to continue.'

Agent Smith shrugged apathetically. 'The Regents' will shall be done.'

'Seriously?! Are you *that* indentured that you can't see this is going to go horribly? No ounce of free will to act against their wishes even to *save* them?'

'Oh, sod this,' James announced. Without a moment's warning, he charged forward, throwing Agent Smith to the side as he ran, full pelt, towards the spiralling column of shadow and lightning. Two agents moved to step in his path, but James knocked them down as if he were a rugby player running the length of a pitch with the ball. He had no idea what he was going to do; maybe if he tackled the remaining Regents, broke their pattern, interrupted their chanting, it would have some effect.

When he was within a short distance of them, another tendril unravelled itself from the column. It snaked around in the air, writhing and twisting its smoky form, electricity crackling from its ethereal limb. It lashed out. The tendril struck James squarely in the chest and sent him flying backwards, crashing into one of the desks.

'James!' Sam and Alice shouted in unison, but as they prepared to move to his side two more tendrils waved at them in a way Sam could only describe as admonishing them.

Tim was the next one to be taken.

The former politician collapsed to the ground with a thud, another wraith tearing its way from out of his body. This one resembled a vulture, hovering over the corpse of the man who had been its vessel. It beat its shadowy wings, and with a trilling, cawing, screeching sound, the form of the vulture flew up and through the ceiling in much the same manner as Jan's wraith.

The remaining three Regents stayed standing in their positions, seemingly unaware of the fate of their colleagues. Or, if they were, they simply did not care.

Reaching into his breast pocket, Sam could feel the cold, smooth surface of the Void crystal. An idea had been forming in his mind and, given the circumstances, he knew he had to try it. He pulled the crystal out, holding it in both hands and tracing his thumbs over its smooth surface. It seemed duller than it had before, presumably drained from its use projecting an energy shield, but still in the grooves of its sigil markings it glowed with a purple hue. Holding the crystal close to his lips, Sam whispered an incantation into it.

'Hey, Smith!' he shouted over to the agent. 'Remember what I said earlier, about not being disarmed even without my TechnoWand? Well, watch this!'

Agent Smith tilted his head curiously as Sam wound his arm back. He spun it around like a cricket bowler, and at the apex of his swing he released the Void crystal. It soared through the air, straight towards the column of lightning, passing through the swirling smoke which surrounded it.

Holding his arms out in front of him, his hands a couple of feet apart, Sam began to squeeze the air. His fingers gnarled, his teeth ground together, and his arms shook as if under great strain. He fixed his stare at the anomaly which had opened up between the Regents, and with his hands Sam began to condense it. At first, nothing seemed to happen. It looked as if Sam was trying to crush an invisible can, while the swirling energy several yards ahead of him remained unaffected. But after a moment, something began to happen. The column of smoke and lightning no longer connected floor and ceiling. It seemed to be receding, shrinking down into the middle.

Sam groaned and grunted as he exerted his will upon the anomaly. He envisioned himself squeezing it down into the Void crystal, and while he envisioned it, it began to happen. Tendrils lashed out from the smoke and the lightning, writhing as if they were in pain. An unholy howl bellowed from the heart of the room, a cry of agonised frustration from something unseen. Sam continued to press the anomaly, his hands gradually coming closer and closer together as he fought against the forces which tried to push against him.

Neither the Regents or the agents in the room seemed to pay him any heed. Their eyes had turned a solid black, and were all staring, transfixed, at the anomaly.

His vision began to blur. Dark shapes floated across his eyeline, like blind spots forming in front of his eyes. He blinked rapidly, trying to dispel them, but it had little effect. Staggering backwards as a wave of energy pushed against him, he felt a hand reach out and hold his arm. He turned, and in his dotted and blurred vision, he could see Alice.

'Now let's send this bloody thing back to the shadows. Let's show them not to mess with Sam and Alice,' she said to him with a smile; a reassuring but pained smile. Sam smiled back, giving her a silent nod.

Alice now also stretched out her arms, gnarling her fingers and beginning to push against the anomaly from the Void. At first, she was surprised to feel genuine resistance struggling against her hands and arms, as if the Void was fighting back. Together, she and Sam fought to contain the chaotic anomaly, their hands slowly closing the gap between them while the cascading lightning and swirling clouds of darkness gradually shrank. The anomaly was condensing down, further and further, until eventually it was no longer a cascading column of energy.

With their hands now almost pressed together, Sam and Alice could see their efforts were working. The anomaly had shrunk down into a ball of lightning, crackling and sparking viciously, encircling the levitating Void crystal at its heart. With a final push, their straining groans turning into primal shouts, the two of them squeezed the last of the anomaly into the crystal. It sparked a few impotent sparks, jagged currents of electricity lashed out, and it fizzled its final death throes.

As the last jolt of electrical energy was condensed into the crystal, a shockwave erupted from its centre. It burst forth in the blink of an eye, knocking the three standing Regents, Sam and Alice off of their feet and onto the floor. The agents seemed to dissolve and melt away from existence as the shockwave passed through them, disintegrating their essence in its wake.

Everything turned black.

CHAPTER IX

Alice awoke on the hard, carpeted floor of the Reading Room. Shifting and stirring as she came to, slowly moving to sit upright as a dull ache throbbed throughout her body, she looked around. It was much darker inside the chamber, the candles and lamps having been blown out in the shockwave, and it was still night outside. She had been out for an indeterminable amount of time, but at least dawn still had not broken. Stars glinted peacefully in the black heavens above.

She rubbed her eyes habitually as she struggled to her feet. Every muscle and joint ached as if she had been doing a very intensive workout, and she let out an involuntary groan as she stretched her neck. A reciprocating groan called out from under one of the desks, and Sam Hain crawled out from beneath the table. He ran his hand through his hair, only to pause and widen his eyes as he realised his hat was no longer safely perched on his head. Feeling around the floor, like a short-sighted man looking for his glasses, Sam reached out to find his hat. No luck.

What he did find was a pair of feet wearing Doc Marten boots, which he quickly found were attached to a pair of legs which were, by extension, attached to an Alice.

'Hello,' she said, dropping the black fedora onto Sam's head. He couldn't work out if he was more relieved to see her safe, or to have his hat back. Probably the two, equally, he thought.

'Hello,' he moaned back as he heaved himself onto his feet, 'you okay?'

Alice nodded and gave an uncertain 'yeah.' She peered into the black space around them, trying to see through the impenetrable dark of the night. 'I mean, everything hurts, but things seem alright. Right?' She hesitated for a moment. 'The fact it's dark in here is just because it's night, right? This isn't the darkness that... came, is it?'

No candles burned in the room any more, and no lamps cast their light into the chamber. And certainly no columns of lightning served to illuminate it. The only source of light they had came from the stars and the moon above, their faint glow gleaming in through the windows. The small amount of light which was cast by the moon created thin, silvery slithers along the floor and long, eerie shadows crept around the patches of light.

'No,' Sam said, glancing around the room, 'no this isn't *the* darkness, we're fine.'

In the pale moonlight, the occult detective looked around the Reading Room. The bookcases and study desks were undisturbed. A few papers had been blown from their places on tabletops, and now had strewn themselves about the room. Other than that, the room appeared entirely normal. There was no sign of damage from either the anomaly or from the shockwave. There were no agents standing on the sidelines, or faceless Spooks laying on the ground. The Regents were nowhere to be seen, neither those who were still standing in the last moments Sam could remember, or the bodies of those who had crumpled to the floor.

Sam pulled his phone from out of his trouser pocket, and with a flick of his finger he turned the torch on. It cast its white light into the room and, moving it like a search light, Sam began to illuminate the many shadows which the moonlight had not dispersed. The beam traced its way along the floor, until it settled over something large and crumpled on the ground. A body. The only body in the room other than Sam and Alice. He darted over to it, kneeling down and giving it a very firm shake.

'James!' Sam shouted, jostling the body of his friend as

497

he tried to wake him. There was no response. The body still lay there, motionless. Alice came and knelt by the side of him too, as Sam tried to shake him awake again. 'James?'

The body of James Mortimer suddenly heaved, taking a rasping breath in and immediately started coughing, as if breathing had surprised the lungs. 'Lorna!' he exclaimed, once the coughing had subsided, and he sat bolt upright.

'No: Alice,' said Alice, helpfully. She turned to Sam and said in a hushed, but not so subtle, tone, 'do you think he has a concussion? He mentioned before that I reminded him of his sister, but...' Sam didn't reply, he simply nodded with a kind smile.

'No, yes, sorry. I was... I was somewhere else,' James wheezed, 'what happened?'

'Well,' Alice began, 'we managed to stop that portal thingy. I'm not really sure exactly what happened after that, but the point is that portal's closed and the Regents don't seem to be about any more.'

'You wouldn't know anything had happened here at all,' Sam added, standing back up. He extended his hands down to help Alice and James back onto their feet, pulling them up as they stood. 'No trace of anything at all. Well, except for one thing...'

Sam made his way towards the centre of the room, to the very spot the column of lightning had first sprung forth. The carpet and ceiling were not even charred from the incredible amount of electricity which must have been surging through that spot. But what there was, in the middle of the floor, was a smooth, crystalline stone. The sigil carved into its surface seemed to glow, and the whole crystal pulsed with a vibrant shade of purple. Veins of turquoise lightning darted just beneath its surface, and at its very heart a black cloud swirled like oil in water.

'Hey-hey,' he said with a triumphant tone, 'would you

look at that? We actually managed to squeeze that bloody thing into the Void crystal.' He wrapped his arm around Alice, pulling her close and planting a jubilant kiss on the top of her head. 'Couldn't have done it without you. Either of you.' He hastily added the last part, turning to James, but not offering him the same embrace and kiss. He proffered a friendly fist-bump instead.

'So, that's that then,' James breathed, staring at the swirling storm inside the Void crystal, 'interdimensional crisis averted.'

'For the moment,' Sam sighed as he placed the crystal safely into his coat pocket. He did not feel particularly comfortable carrying that condensed tempest of an anomaly in his pocket, but it was the safest option for the time being. *I'm going to need to securely seal this thing away soon*, he thought, and wondered if he could possibly invest in a magickally sealed vault. 'I doubt that's the last incursion from beyond the Void we'll ever see. If there's one thing I know about the dark beings which try to claw their way out of the abyss and into our world, it's that they're persistent bastards. And I'm willing to bet this isn't the last we've heard of the Regents, either.'

'What did happen to them?' James enquired. 'If we all survived the blast, then they must have too, surely?'

'I don't know, it's hard to say,' Sam said, casually kicking a pair of narrow, rectangular dark-tinted glasses under the nearest desk. 'Their Men in Black seemed to evaporate in the blast wave, at least. As for the Regents themselves...' He looked back to the spot where the five had been standing for the ritual. There was no trace of them. 'I'd be more concerned about whatever those twisted monstrosities were. They traded the lives of their own for something much, much worse.' He gazed wistfully out of one of the Reading Room's windows, out into the black night sky and glistening pinprick lights of the distant stars. 'This fight is far from over.'

Alice moved to stand by the occult detective's side, placing a supportive hand on his arm. 'Maybe,' she spoke softly, 'but we won this round. We stopped the anomaly and closed the portal before it was too late. And when we're next needed to put things to rights, we'll do it again.'

'Yeah,' Sam said distantly, still staring off into space, 'you're right.' He slowly turned and began to walk back towards the doors of the Reading Room. His coat swished and swayed behind him as he strode towards the exit. 'Come on, we want to be long gone by the time the museum's morning staff turn up.'

Scurrying to catch up with Sam's stride, Alice began to follow suit. James did not follow them both immediately. Instead, he crouched down and reached beneath the desk, fishing in the shadows for the glasses Sam had kicked away moments before. His fingers gingerly rested on the slim frame of Agent Smith's narrow, tinted glasses, and something about them compelled James to pick them up. He held them up to his eyes briefly, balancing them on the bridge of his nose. They were a perfect fit. Gently folding the arms of the glasses inwards, he delicately placed them in the breast pocket of his suit jacket. He glimpsed an Arc Gun in the shadows too and, knowing it was bound to come in handy again, he grabbed it and secured it in the waistband of his trousers. He stood up and started to follow Sam and Alice out of the room.

They were almost at the door when Alice noticed something gleaming on one of the desks, reflecting a slither of moonlight from the shadows. She darted off to the side, heading towards the desk to investigate what it was. As she drew closer, she could begin to make out the shape of it. It was a short metallic thing, gleaming and chrome-like, probably no more than ten inches long and about an inch in diameter. At its tip was a pointed quartz crystal, and at the opposite end was a polished black stone. She picked it up and turned it over in her hand.

'Sam,' she called over to the figure in the greatcoat and fedora hat, silhouetted against the doorway, 'are you forgetting something?' She held up the TechnoWand, waggling it between her fingers playfully.

'Oh, you absolute *blessing*, you!' Sam exclaimed, jogging over to her with a jubilant spring in his step. 'I thought I'd lost that when Smith and Jones dematerialised; I was worried I'd have to try and craft another transphasic energy probe. Thank you.' He took the TechnoWand from her outstretched hand, hugging the magickal device in his palm, and tucked it neatly inside his overcoat. With a flourishing twirl more lively than he had seemed before, Sam marched back to the exit of the Reading Room and flung the doors open. Striding over the threshold, he led them out of the chamber.

Their journeys home were relatively and thankfully uneventful. As the main doors of the British Museum were securely locked, James had taken the lead to guide them out through the access corridors which were left open for the overnight staff. Behind a desk near the exit, a security guard dozed peacefully. The three of them did not wake him as they quietly tip-toed out of the back door, leading them out onto Montague Place, on the opposite side of the museum than Sam had entered.

The night air was crisp and refreshing, the streets of London pleasantly deserted and quiet at this early hour of the morning. The faint twinkling of stars could still be seen beyond the orange glow of the street-lamps. It was still too early for the London Underground to be running, though, so the three of them resigned themselves to taking the night buses home. They walked through Russell Square, meandering up the empty roads to Euston Station, where myriad buses served to ferry the late night travellers out on their journeys to anywhere in the city.

Heading out west to Ealing, James's bus had arrived

first. He bid the other two a fond farewell, and wished them safe trips home, before boarding the 390 for the first leg of his journey. Sam and Alice waved to him as the bus pulled away from the station, leaving them standing by the bus stop alone.

'I, uh, I was going to ask,' Alice began to speak, somewhat sheepishly, 'would you mind if I crashed at yours for tonight? It's just, y'know, with everything, the Men in Black abducting me, and seeing my manager and a guy I was kind of sort of dating opening a portal to another dimension...' She paused and thought about what she had just said. For a moment, she marvelled at the fact she hadn't had a breakdown by now. 'I mean, you come across as this bumbling idiot who doesn't always know what's going on and-'

'Thank you,' Sam interjected with a mock sarcastic tone.

'You know what I mean! No matter what, against impossible odds, you seem to sort things out in the end. And I know you always try to make sure I'm safe. Even when we do end up in a firefight with supernatural agents or face an anomaly which could bring about Armageddon.' She stopped to look up at the live timetable. The N5 bus which would take them to Hampstead was a few minutes away. 'Plus, I'd rather not travel back on my own. I often find I get some drunk or a right weirdo sitting next to me, and the night bus always smells like wee.'

Sam smiled at her kindly. 'And what makes sitting next to this weirdo any better?'

'You're the nice kind of weirdo,' she replied, as if it was an obvious fact, 'I mean, like, you're not *normal*, not by a long shot. But you're not like the night bus variety of weird; you're not going to be muttering to yourself, or having a heated argument with someone who's not there, or start chewing your toenails, or forget that personal space is a thing.'

'Are these really the people you've had next to you on

night buses?'

'Oh yeah,' Alice said in a voice which seemed to suggest even the mere memory of her late night encounters still pained her.

'Of course you can stay over,' Sam said, 'it's not a problem. I've got a spare room you can use.'

'Thank you.'

'Any time.'

The N5 bus emerged from around the corner, slowly pulling up to the bus stop outside of Euston Station. Sam flagged it down with a wave of his hand, and was pleasantly surprised to see that the bottom deck was entirely empty.

In the basement flat on Constantine Road, by the soft and comforting glow of the bedside lamp, Alice climbed into bed. Sam's spare room was a basic affair, with just enough space for a bed and a bedside table, but it was cosy and warm. And, Alice thought, it was far better than walking alone through the streets of Islington back to her flat, as she would have been by that point had she not come back to Sam's for the night.

Sam had brought her a mug of hot chocolate just before heading for bed, and they hugged as they bid each other goodnight. He jokingly warned her about the monsters which lived under the bed, but, knowing Sam, Alice was not entirely sure he was just joking. She placed the hot chocolate on the table by the side of the bed, propping up the pillows against the headboard, and slipped in beneath the sheet. Sam had left a comic book by the side of the bed, too, for her to read and unwind after the events of the day, which she picked up and began to flick through the pages.

The comic told the story of a girl, lost and alone in an enchanted forest, as she journeyed through a world of magick and mystery, guided along by the whimsical, esoteric and other-worldly characters who dwell in those mythical woods. Sipping the sweet and creamy hot chocolate, Alice smiled to herself. Although she was sure nothing could comfort her after the events of that night, this certainly came close. She flipped the page of the comic. The girl in the book was receiving cryptic wisdom from a magician and a high priestess. Alice was enjoying the story, but her eyes were growing heavier with each passing moment. Before she knew it, she had drifted off into a restful sleep.

On the other side of the flat, in the dark of the room illuminated only by a series of candles arranged upon an altar, Sam Hain opened the lid of a small wooden box. Its surface was carved with myriad patterns and symbols, occult sigils and signs, a large pentacle on its lid. He delicately placed the Void crystal inside the box, the stone still glowing with veins of lightning among the swirling vortex of clouds within. It was vibrant enough to cast its eerie shades of purple and blue into the room. Closing the lid of the box, Sam held it carefully in one hand, while with the other he waved the TechnoWand around it in circular patterns. A bright blue aura traced the path of the wand's crystal, weaving around the box like ethereal chains, sealing it shut. He placed the box at the back of a cabinet beside the altar, arranging a small pile of books in front of it, hiding it away.

Sitting cross legged in front of the altar, in the dim glow of the candlelight, Sam closed his eyes and began to breathe slow, deep breaths. In, and out. He stilled his mind, quietening his conscious thoughts and allowing himself to wander in the astral planes as he slipped into a meditative state. A headache he hadn't noticed was there until now started to fade, feeling like a pressure being lifted from his brain. In his mind's eye, Sam was adrift in the cosmos, swimming among the stars and the nebula and the spaces in between. The spirit of Lorna took his hand as they swam together in the ether.

I'm always by your side, bunny, Lorna's voice echoed in Sam's mind. *Even if you do not feel it, even when you do not know it, I am always here with you. And I'm proud of you.* Sam smiled to her, both in the projection of his mind, and as his lips involuntarily curved into a warm smile as he sat there before the altar. And together, they soared through the astral planes of the Imaginarium.

Meanwhile, some seven miles west, James Mortimer was not having quite as restful a night. He lay in his bed, tossing and turning in the dark, drifting in and out of sleep. His back ached, his neck was stiff, and his head pounded. He had taken a couple of ibuprofen tablets before bed in the hope it would alleviate the aches and pains, but they didn't seem to have much effect.

Whenever he closed his eyes, he could see it. The chaotic stream of lightning coursing from the floor to the ceiling of the Reading Room. The smoke-like screen of darkness which encircled it. The entities which had spawned from the mouths of those Regents who had given themselves to the Void, their bodies falling lifeless to the floor. The black tendrils which had sprouted from the darkness, writhing like malicious tentacles, and which had struck him as he made a run for the portal. He knew little of what had happened since that moment, but whenever he cast his mind back he could feel something tightening in his chest, something wrapping itself around his heart and clawing at his mind.

He awoke in a cold sweat, and while his eyes still adjusted to the darkness of the room, he was sure he could see shadowy figures standing around him. Flicking the bedside light on, the shadows immediately dispersed, leaving him alone in his room.

His head continued to throb.

EPILOGUE

The past week had been a particularly run-of-the-mill and mundane one for Alice. After the events at the British Museum, she had taken a few days to de-stress, mainly choosing to spend her days in the comfort of her pyjamas and watching reruns of old comedy series. But she had to return to work eventually, and she was not looking forward to it.

When she walked into the department store on Oxford Street on her first day back in work after the incident, she was relieved and not entirely surprised to see that Jan was absent. Jan seemed to always be as much a part of the store as the clothes they stocked and the fixtures on the wall, and Alice often had a hard time imagining her living a normal, human life. As it turned out, of course, Jan did not live a normal, human life. It was an unusual feeling, setting foot on the shop floor and not being berated about the time by the stern-faced woman in the ill-fitting polyester shirt. On reflection, Alice considered it would be significantly weirder if she had been there, seeing as she had watched Jan's body fall lifeless to the floor of the Reading Room.

The image still haunted her whenever she thought about it too much. She tried not to.

One of the section coordinators had taken on the managerial role for the time being, at least for the duration of Jan's "long term leave of absence". Alice wondered how long term that leave of absence could feasibly cover before people started asking questions.

The days were whittled away with serving customers, fetching stock from the stockroom, and fixing the displays. It was all quite tedious and wholly unremarkable. Many people carried on about their days as if nothing was any different. For many, it really was no different. They had no idea of the truth, of the events of that night or of Jan's whereabouts. As far as everyone else was concerned, everything was entirely and perfectly normal.

It was the normalcy which bothered Alice the most. The more she experienced with Sam, the more it became a jarring juxtaposition, living one life in the fantastical and supernatural reality of magick, and another in the rather humdrum reality of work and taxes. In a way, she found it relaxing to escape into the "real" world, folding shirts and talking about the weather. But it is hard to witness the opening of a chaotic portal which claimed the life of one's former manager and could have unleashed untold horrors. It's not the kind of thing one can just move on from and carry on as if everything is normal.

That Thursday evening, after another particularly dull and dreary day at work, Alice was preparing to settle down for a quiet evening. She had got into her pyjamas almost as soon as she had got home, brewed a cup of tea, and sat down in front of the television. No sooner had she turned the TV on was there a knock at the door.

The knock was rhythmic. Recognisable.

She got up and opened the door, to find Sam Hain standing there.

'No time to explain,' he said without as much as a "hello" or "is now a good time?".

'The ghost of a Victorian theatre director has manifested at the Vaudeville and won't rest until his alleged masterpiece has been performed to a full house. Are you in?'

'I'm in,' said Alice.

About the Author

Bron James is an author of science fiction, fantasy and magical realism. He was born with a silver pen in his mouth and has been making up stories for as long as he can remember. His professional début work of fiction, the first instalment of the *Sam Hain* series of novellas, was released in October 2013 to celebrate *All Hallows' Read*.

Born and raised in the south of England, Bron presently resides in London where he lives with his cat, more spiders than he can count, and a ghostly presence which likes to hide his keys. He spends his time writing stories, drinking tea, and dreaming improbable dreams.

www.bronjames.co.uk

A Krampus Carol

A one-off Sam Hain Christmas Special short story

It's the most wonderful time of the year, and Sam Hain is looking forward to enjoying a quiet and relaxing Yuletide season. However, only a few days before Christmas, a teenage boy comes to seek Sam's help to save his family from an ancient supernatural evil…

IF YOU DO NOT FROM THIS LESSON LEARN
FOR YOUR MISBEHAVIOUR YOU MUST BURN
YOU HAVE ONE DAY TO SET THINGS RIGHT
PRAY I NEED NOT RETURN THIS NIGHT

Available on Amazon Kindle

Far Beneath the Distant Stars

I urge whoever receives this to take note of my experiences, of the fate that befell the Endeavour and all who served aboard her, and to take heed so that the same doesn't happen again. May no-one else be forced to suffer the same fate. Do not return to Lyrae 438b.

The Endeavour Expedition was to be a journey of discovery, carrying a crew of researchers to a world 500 light-years away. It promised to be a mission that would pave the way for the future of extrasolar colonisation. However, when members of the expedition start going missing, the crew of the Endeavour discover that something beyond their darkest nightmares lies just beneath the surface of this remote, forbidding planet...

A cosmic horror sci-fi novella set 150 years into the future, *Far Beneath the Distant Stars* catalogues the mission of the starship Endeavour through the logs of an exogeologist as he witnesses the fate of the expedition unfold before him.

Available on Amazon Kindle

Printed in Great Britain
by Amazon